HISTORICAL

Your romantic escape to the past.

The Kiss That
Made Her Countess
Laura Martin

A Cinderella To
Redeem The Earl
Ann Lethbridge

MILLS & BOON

THE KISS THAT MADE HER COUNTESS
© 2024 by Laura Martin
Philippine Copyright 2024
Australian Copyright 2024
New Zealand Copyright 2024

First Published 2024
First Australian Paperback Edition 2024
ISBN 978 1 038 91080 6

A CINDERELLA TO REDEEM THE EARL
© 2024 by Michéle Ann Young
Philippine Copyright 2024
Australian Copyright 2024
New Zealand Copyright 2024

First Published 2024
First Australian Paperback Edition 2024
ISBN 978 1 038 91080 6

MIX
Paper | Supporting
responsible forestry
FSC® C001695

Published by
Harlequin Mills & Boon
An imprint of Harlequin Enterprises (Australia) Pty Limited
(ABN 47 001 180 918), a subsidiary of HarperCollins
Publishers Australia Pty Limited
(ABN 36 009 913 517)
Level 19, 201 Elizabeth Street
SYDNEY NSW 2000 AUSTRALIA

Cover art used by arrangement with Harlequin Books S.A.. All rights reserved.

Printed and bound in Australia by McPherson's Printing Group

The Kiss That Made Her Countess

Laura Martin

MILLS & BOON

Laura Martin writes historical romances with an adventurous undercurrent. When not writing, she spends her time working as a doctor in Cambridgeshire, where she lives with her husband. In her spare moments, Laura loves to lose herself in a book and has been known to read from cover to cover in a single day when the story is particularly gripping. She also loves to travel—especially to visit historical sites and far-flung shores.

Visit the Author Profile page
at millsandboon.com.au for more titles.

Author Note

When my lovely editor asked if I would like to write a book that would be a part of A Season of Celebration, celebrating seventy-five years of Harlequin, I was thrilled. Ten years ago, my first book was published, and it has been a wonderful decade writing for a line of books I had read and admired for a long time before ever putting pen to paper. I have huge respect for the other Harlequin Historical authors and am always excited to see what books are published alongside my own each month.

The Kiss That Made Her Countess starts at a Midsummer Eve ball. I wanted to invoke some of the mystery and magic of Midsummer to create a spectacle that would sweep Alice and Simon along, something so special that they would forget the rules they should follow and the expectations of Society. I hope you enjoy their story and experience some of that Midsummer magic for yourselves.

DEDICATION

**To my boys,
everything is so much more fun with you**

Chapter One

Northumberland, Midsummer's Eve, 1816

Not for the first time that evening Alice felt ridiculous. She glanced down at the borrowed dress, the hem splattered with mud, and the delicate shoes. If they ever made it to Lady Salisbury's ball she would trail dirt all over the ballroom floor.

'Come, Alice. We can't stop now,' Lydia called over her shoulder before vaulting over a wooden fence. Alice followed a little more slowly, wondering how she had been dragged into this madcap plan. 'We're almost there. I swear I can hear the music.'

With as much grace and elegance as she could muster, Alice climbed over the fence, closing her eyes in horror as the material of her dress snagged on a protruding nail. There was the sickening sound of ripping fabric as she lost her balance and the dress was tugged free.

'Lydia, wait,' Alice shouted, looking up to see her friend plunging head first through a hedge. She had no choice but to follow, grimacing as she spotted the ripped area near the hem of her dress. Hopefully she would be able to mend it and clean it before her cousin even noticed the dress was missing.

She paused before the hedge, wondering how Lydia had made her way through the dense foliage, and then a hand shot out and gripped her wrist. Lydia was giggling as Alice emerged, an expression of surprise on her face, and soon Alice was laughing too.

'Just think, in a few minutes we will be whirling across the ballroom in the arms of the most handsome bachelors in all of Northumberland,' Lydia said as she gripped Alice's hand. 'Maybe there will be a dashing duke or an eligible earl to sweep you off your feet.'

For a moment Alice closed her eyes and contemplated the possibilities. It was highly unlikely she would meet anyone at the ball that could save her from the impending match that made her heart sink every time she thought of her future.

'My last night of freedom,' she murmured.

Lydia scoffed. 'You make it sound as if you are on your way to the gallows.'

'That is exactly what it feels like.'

'Surely he is not that bad.'

Alice screwed up her face and gave a little shudder. 'I am well aware I have lived a sheltered life so have not come across the scoundrels and the criminals of this country, but Cousin Cecil is by far the worst person I have ever met.'

'Perhaps your parents will not make you marry him.'

'I doubt they will save me from that fate.' Tomorrow Alice's second cousin, Cecil Billington, was coming to stay for a week with the single purpose of finalising an agreement of marriage between him and Alice. As yet

he had not proposed, but Alice was aware of the negotiations going on in the background with her father. She
hadn't dared enquire as to the specifics; even just the
idea of Cecil made her feel sick.

'Then, tonight will have to make up for the next forty
years of putting up with Cecil.'

Lydia grabbed her by the hand and began pulling
her over the grass again. The house was in view now,
the terrace at the back lit up with dozens of lamps positioned at equal intervals along the stone balustrade.
Music drifted out from the open doors, and there was
the swell of voices as those escaping the heat of the ballroom strolled along the terrace.

'Someone will see us,' Alice said, feeling suddenly
exposed. There was only about thirty feet separating
them and the house now, but it was all open lawn, and
by the time they reached the steps leading up to the terrace it would be a miracle if they made it even halfway
unobserved.

'Then, let us act like we belong. We more than look
the part. If we stroll serenely arm-in-arm, I wager no one
will pay us any attention. We are just two invited guests
having a wonderful time at the Midsummer's Eve ball.'

Alice considered for a moment and then nodded. 'You
are right. If we try to creep in, it will be obvious immediately. The only way we have half a chance is by pretending we are meant to be here.'

Instantly she straightened her back and lifted her chin,
trying to mimic the poise and confidence of Lady Salisbury, the hostess of the sumptuous masked ball. Sometimes Alice would catch a glimpse of the viscountess
stepping out of her carriage or taking a stroll through the

extensive grounds of Salisbury Hall. She looked regal in her posture and elegant in her movements, and Alice tried to copy how she held herself and how she walked.

'Wait,' Lydia called and slipped a mask into Alice's hand. It was delicate in design, only meant to fit over the upper part of the wearer's face. White in colour, it had an intricate silver pattern painted onto it, a collection of swirls and dots that glimmered in the moonlight. Alice put it on, securing the mask with the silver ribbon tied into a bow at the back of her head. She looked over to Lydia to see her friend had a similar mask now obscuring the top half of her face.

Lydia slipped her arm through Alice's, and together they strolled slowly across the lawn. Despite her urge to run, Alice knew this ruse would work best if they moved at a sedate pace. No one blinked as they ascended the stairs onto the terrace, and Alice heard her friend suppress a little squeal of excitement as they reached the doors to the ballroom.

Neither girl had ever been to a ball like this before. On occasion they would attend the dances at the local Assembly Rooms, but even those were few and far between. Once Alice had begged her parents to allow her and her sister to stay with some friends in Newcastle to enjoy the delights of the social calendar there, but worried about their daughters' reputations, her parents had refused.

'This is magical,' Alice whispered, pausing on the threshold to take everything in. The room was large and richly decorated. The walls were covered in the finest cream wallpaper. At set intervals there were large, gold-framed mirrors, positioned to reflect the guests on the dance floor and make the ballroom seem as if it were even bigger than it was. From the ceiling hung two magnificent chandeliers, each with at least a hundred candles burning bright and illuminating the room. In between the mirrors on the walls there were yet more candles, flickering and reflecting off the glass and making the whole ballroom shimmer and shine.

The assembled guests added to the vision of opulence, the men in finely tailored tailcoats with silk cravats and the women in beautiful dresses of silk and satin. The theme of this masked ball was the Midsummer celebrations, and many of the guests had dressed with a nod to this in mind. Some women had freshly picked flowers woven into their hair or pinned to their dresses as they normally would a brooch.

'I have never seen anything like this,' Lydia said, her mouth open in awe.

'Thank you,' Alice said, squeezing her friend's hand. 'For making me come tonight. You're right. I deserve one last night of happiness before a lifetime of being married to vile Cousin Cecil.'

Lydia leaned in close and held Alice's eye. 'Enjoy it to the utmost. Dance with every man that asks, sip sparkling wine like it is water, admire all the marvellous women in their beautiful dresses.'

'I will.'

For a moment Alice felt a little overwhelmed. This was not her world, not where she belonged, and she was aware she didn't know how to talk to these people. It felt as though someone might come and pluck her out of the crowd and announce *Alice James, you do not belong here*.

A young gentleman, no older than Alice and Lydia, approached, swallowing nervously. He smiled at them both, showing a line of crooked teeth, and then directed his focus on Lydia.

'I know we have not been introduced, but may I have the pleasure of the next dance?'

Alice watched as her friend blushed under her mask. Lydia was bold and confident on the outside, but sometimes she would stutter and stammer amongst people she did not know.

'I would be delighted,' Lydia said, giving Alice a backwards glance as her partner led her off to the edge of the dance floor to wait for the next dance to be called.

Suddenly alone Alice felt very exposed, and she shrank back, aghast when she brushed against a large pot filled with a leafy plant with brightly coloured flowers. It wobbled on its table, threatening to crash to the ground. She lunged, trying to steady it, and as her hands reached around the ceramic she had an awful vision of the container crashing to the floor and the whole ballroom turning to her in the silence that followed, realising she shouldn't be there.

'Steady,' a deep voice said right in her ear, making her jump and almost sending the pot flying again. An arm brushed past her waist, reaching quickly to stop the plant from toppling.

For a long moment Alice did not move, only turning when she was certain there was going to be no terrible accident with the plant in front of her. When she did finally turn she inhaled sharply. Standing right behind her, just the right distance away so as not to attract any disapproving stares, was the most handsome man she had ever laid eyes on. He wasn't wearing a mask, and Alice reasoned there was no point. Everyone in the room would know who he was just by looking at his eyes. They were blue, but not the same pale blue of her own eyes but bright and vibrant, piercing in their intensity. He had that attractive combination of blue eyes and dark hair that was uncommon in itself but that, added to the perfect proportions of the rest of his facial features, meant he was easily the most desirable man in the room.

'Thank you,' she said, her heart still pounding in her chest from the worry that she was about to cause a scene with the crashing décor. 'That could have been a disaster.'

Simon smiled blandly at the pretty young woman in front of him and turned to leave, not wanting to get caught up in conversation with someone he should probably know. There were hundreds of young ladies in Northumberland he'd been introduced to, and he could never remember their names. It was one of the tribulations of being an earl: everyone knew you, everyone recognised you, and most expected you to remember them.

His brother had been good at that sort of thing, remembering every face and name, making connections between members of the same families. When out on the estate or visiting the local village Robert would stop and talk to almost everyone he met, enquiring after the health of various ailing relatives or newborn babies. Robert had been loved by their tenants and staff in a way that was impossible to follow, especially when Simon had trouble remembering even a fraction of the names of the people he encountered in the local area.

As he turned he spotted his sister-in-law entering the ballroom. He had a lot of time and respect for Maria, the dowager countess, but right now he did not want to see her. Recently she had been urging him to marry and settle down, which was the furthest thing from what he had planned for his life. Tonight no doubt she would have a list of eligible young ladies lined up for him to dance with, all perfectly nice and decent young ladies, but there was no point in him seeking a connection with anyone, not now, not ever.

Not wanting to get caught by Maria and her list of accomplished young ladies, he hastily turned back to the woman in front of him.

'I don't think we've been introduced,' he said.

'Miss Alice James,' she said, bobbing into a little curtsy. She looked up at him expectantly, and he realised she was waiting for him to introduce himself.

'Lord Westcroft,' he said, seeing her eyes widen. Unless she was a consummate actress it would seem she hadn't known who he was. He didn't like to view himself as conceited, but generally most people *did* recognise him when he entered a room. It was one of the disadvantages of being an earl.

'A pleasure to meet you, my Lord.'

'The dancing is about to begin, Miss James. I wonder if I might have the pleasure of this dance?'

'You want to dance with me?' She sounded incredulous, and he had to suppress a smile at her honest reaction.

'If that is agreeable to you?'

She nodded, and he held out his arm to her, escorting

her to the dance floor just as the musicians played the first note of the music for a country dance.

He had been dancing all his life, and over the years been to hundreds of balls and danced countless dances. Before his brother had died he had quite enjoyed socialising, but everything had lost its shine after Robert's death. Miss James stood opposite him and beamed, looking around her in delight. She was young, but not so young that this could be her first ball, and he wondered if she approached everything with such irrepressible happiness.

The dance was fast-paced, and as it was their turn to progress down the line of other dancers, Miss James looked up at him and smiled with such unbridled joy that for a moment he froze. Thankfully he recovered before she noticed, and they continued the dance without him missing a step, but as they took their place at the end of the line he found he could not take his eyes off her. Even with her mask on he could see she was pretty. She had thick auburn hair that was pinned back in the current fashion, but a few strands had slipped loose and curled around her neck. Her eyes were a pale blue that shimmered in the candlelight, but the part of her he felt himself drawn to was her lips. She smiled all the time, her expression varying between a closed-lip, small smile of contentment to a wider smile of pleasure at various points throughout the dance. When she got a step wrong, she didn't flush with embarrassment as many young ladies would, but instead giggled at her own mistake. Simon realised he hadn't met anyone in a long time who was completely and utterly living in the moment and, in that moment, happy.

As the music finished he bowed to his partner and then surprised himself by offering her his arm.

'Shall we get some air, Miss James?'

She looked up at him, cheeks flushed from the exertion, and nodded.

'That would be most welcome.'

Simon saw his sister-in-law's eyes on him as he escorted Miss James from the dance floor to the edge of the ballroom, stopping to pick up two glasses of punch on the way. The ballroom was hot now, with the press of bodies, and it was a relief to step outside into the cool air.

'I think Midsummer might be my new favourite time of year,' Miss James said as they chose a spot by the stone balustrade. She leaned on it, looking out at the garden and the night sky beyond.

'What has it displaced?' Simon asked.

'I do love Christmas. There is something rather magical about crackling wood on the fire whilst it snows outside and you are all snug inside. But I will never forget this wonderful Midsummer night.'

'Forgive me, Miss James, but have we met before?'

'No.'

'You seem very certain.'

She smiled at him. There was no guile in her expression, and he realised that she had no expectation from him. Most young women he was introduced to looked at him as something to be conquered. Their ultimate aim was to impress him so they might have a chance at becoming his countess. It was tiresome and meant he had started to avoid situations where he was likely to be pushed into small talk with unmarried young women. Miss James had no calculating aspect to her; she was not trying to impress him. It was refreshing to talk to someone and realise they wanted nothing from you.

'I think I would remember, my Lord.'

'You are from Northumberland?'

'Yes, my family live only a few miles away.'

'Then, our paths must have crossed at a ball or a dinner party, surely.'

He saw her eyes widen and a look of panic on her face. He wondered for a moment if she might try to flee, but instead she fiddled with her glass and then took a great gulp of punch.

'I have a little confession,' she said, leaning in closer so only he could hear her words. 'This is my first ball.'

'Your first?'

'Yes.'

He looked at her closer, wondering if he had been wrong in assessing her age. He'd placed her at around twenty or twenty-one. Young still, but certainly old enough to have been out in society for a good few years. It was hard to tell with the mask covering her eyes, but he did not think he had got his estimation wrong.

'I have been to dances,' she said quickly. 'Just not to any balls like this.'

'How can that be, Miss James?'

She bit her lip and flicked him a nervous glance.

'If I tell you, you might have me escorted out.'

It was his turn to smile.

'I doubt it, Miss James. Unless you tell me you sneaked in with the sole purpose to sabotage Lady Salisbury's ball or steal her silverware.'

Miss James pressed her lips together and then leaned in even closer, her shoulders almost touching his.

'You are half-right,' she said, her voice low so only he could hear.

'You plan to steal Lady Salisbury's silverware.'

She flicked him an amused glance. 'No, I am no criminal, but I did sneak in.' As soon as she said the words, she clapped her hands over her mouth in horror. 'I can't believe I just told you that. It was the one thing I was meant to keep secret tonight, and it is the first thing I tell you.'

Simon felt a swell of mirth rise up inside him, and he realised for the first time in a long time he was having fun. Fun had seemed a foreign concept these last few years. In a short space of time he had lost his brother, inherited a title he had never wanted and been forced to confront the issue of his own mortality. He'd been forced into making monumental decisions over the last few weeks, everything serious and fraught with emotion.

'You sneaked in?'

She nodded, eyes wide with horror.

'Are you going to tell anyone?'

'I am not sure yet,' he said, suppressing a smile of his own.

'Lydia is going to be furious,' Miss James murmured.

'There are two of you?'

She closed her eyes and shook her head. 'I need to stop talking.'

'Please don't, Miss James. This is the most fun I've had for months.'

'Now you're mocking me.'

'Not at all.'

'You're an earl. This cannot be the most fun you've had. Your life must be full of luxury and entertainment.'

'I find it is mainly full of accounts and responsibilities,' he said. 'That is unfair and very... I am well aware of the privileged life I lead. It is full of luxury and extravagance, as you say, but not fun.'

'That is sad,' Alice said, and she touched him on the hand. It was a fleeting contact, but it made his skin tingle, and he looked up quickly. There was no guile in her eyes, and he realised the furthest thing from her mind was seduction—whether because she had a young man she fancied herself in love with or because their backgrounds were so far apart she knew there could never be anything between them.

'It is sad,' he said quietly. 'So tonight I charge you with lifting this grumpy man's spirits.'

'And in exchange you will not expose my deception.'

'We have a deal. Tell me, Miss James, how did you manage to sneak in without one of the dozens of footmen seeing you?'

She motioned out at the garden beyond the terrace. Only the terrace was lit, the grass and the formal garden beyond in darkness.

'We crept through the garden.'

He glanced down and laughed. 'I can see there was a little mud.'

'I was terrified when we arrived that I might have foliage in my hair. We had to squeeze through a hedge to get into the right part of the garden.'

'That is commitment to your cause. What made you so keen to come here tonight?'

She sighed and looked out into the darkness.

'I doubt you know the feeling of helplessness, of not being in control of your own future,' she said with a hint of melancholy. She was wrong in her assumption, but now was not the time to correct her. 'Soon I will not be able to choose anything more thrilling than what curtains to hang or what to serve for dinner.'

'You are to be married.'

The expression on her face told him she was not happy about the prospect.

She straightened and turned to face him. 'I am to marry my second cousin, vile Cecil.'

'Vile Cecil?'

'It is an apt description of him.'

'I already feel sorry for you. What makes him so vile?'

Miss James exhaled, puffing out her cheeks in a way that made him smile. He didn't know her exact background, but by the way she spoke and held herself he would guess she was from a family of the minor gentry. Perhaps a landowner father or even a vicar. She knew how to conduct herself but hadn't been subject to the scrutiny many of the women of the *ton* had to endure, so the odd shrug of the shoulders or theatrical sigh hadn't been trained out of her.

'Where to start? Imagine you are a young lady,' she said, and he adopted his most serious expression.

'I am imagining.'

'Good. You are introduced to a distant relative about fifteen years older than you,' she said and held up a finger. 'The age gap is not an issue you must understand. I am aware women are of higher value to society when they are young and beautiful and men when they are older and richer.'

'I did not think you would be such a cynic, Miss James.' Simon was surprised to find he was enjoying himself immensely. There was something freeing talking to this woman who was a total stranger and had no expectations of him at all.

'Is it cynical to observe the truth?' She pushed on. 'This distant relative is unfortunate-looking, with a lazy eye, yellowed teeth and rapidly thinning hair that he arranges in a way he hopes will hide the fact he hasn't much left. But you have been raised to appreciate no one can help how they look so you push aside all thoughts of their physical appearance.'

Simon pressed his lips together. Miss James had an amusing way of telling a story, and he urged her to continue. 'I am channelling those very thoughts,' he said.

'Good. Then he reaches out and with a sweaty palm lays a hand on your shoulder. A fleeting touch you could forgive, but the hand lingers far too long, and all the while his eyes do not move from your chest.'

'He is not sounding very enticing.'

'Then throughout the evening he makes his horrible opinions known on everything from how the poor should be punished for the awful situations they find themselves in to slavery to how it is God's plan for the lower levels of society to be decimated by illness that spreads more when people live in close conditions.'

'I am beginning to see why he is vile.'

'And he does all this whilst trying to squeeze your knee under the table.'

'Your parents are happy for you to marry him?'

Miss James sighed. 'Last year my sister...' She bit her lip again, drawing his gaze for a moment. 'I probably shouldn't tell you this.' Then she shrugged and continued. 'Yet our paths are never going to cross again.'

'What if I add in the extra layer of security by swearing I will never breathe a word of this to anyone.'

'You are a man of your word?'

'I never break an oath.'

'Last year my sister was caught up in a bit of a scandal. Rumours of late-night liaisons with a married gentleman. For a month she and I were forbidden to leave the house, and my parents thought we might even have to leave Bamburgh and move elsewhere. Thankfully a friend of my father's stepped in and proposed marriage to my sister to save her and the rest of our family from scandal.'

'Did it work?'

'Yes, although there are still a few people who cross the street to avoid my mother and me if we are out shopping. My sister is happy as mistress of her own home, living down in Devon, and she has a baby on the way. All things for a short while we thought she might never have.'

'This has pushed your parents to make an unwise match for you?'

'I think they are panicked. They are aware the taint of scandal can linger for a long time, and they keep reminding me I am already one and twenty. There are no local unmarried young men of the right social class so they decided they would arrange the only match that was assured.'

'Could you not refuse?'

Miss James laughed, but there was no bitterness in her tone, just pure amusement.

'We live in very different worlds, my Lord. I have no money of my own, no income, no way of supporting myself. I cannot even boast of a very good education so I doubt anyone would employ me as a governess. My value comes in marrying someone who can support me and any future children and remove that burden from my parents.'

'Vile Cecil is wealthy?'

'Moderately so. Enough to satisfy my parents. He is eager to be married and comes tomorrow to stay to discuss our engagement.'

'He has not asked you yet?'

'No, but that part is a mere formality.' She closed her eyes. 'So you see, this is my one last chance to dance at a ball with whoever I choose, to get a little tipsy with punch and to take ill-advised strolls along the terrace with mysterious gentlemen.'

'Then, we must ensure you have the best night of your life.'

Chapter Two

Alice felt a little giddy with recklessness. She should never have spoken of the things she had told Lord Westcroft, but it had been liberating to talk so freely. She could be confident that after tonight her path would never cross with the earl's again. In a few weeks she would be Mrs Cecil Billington, living a life of misery in some rural part of Suffolk where she knew no one except her odious husband.

'I think we need more punch,' Lord Westcroft said, bowing to her and disappearing inside before she could object. She had only drunk alcohol a few times before, small sips of wine with dinner, and she didn't know what was in the punch, but she was already feeling the wonderful warmth spreading out from her stomach around her body.

He returned with two more glasses and handed her one. As he walked back to her Alice was aware of all the curious stares they received from the other guests. No doubt everyone knew who Lord Westcroft was, and they would probably be wondering who he was spending all this time with. Alice tried to shrink into herself, feeling suddenly self-conscious.

'A toast, to one final night of freedom before you are condemned to a life with vile Cecil.'

Alice smiled, raising her glass and then putting it to her lips. She had never met an earl before, but she had not expected one to be like Lord Westcroft. He was surprisingly easy to talk to and had a laid-back manner that reminded her more of the young lads in the village than what she pictured an aristocrat would be like.

'How about you?' she said after she had drained half her glass. 'I've told you my deepest secrets. It is only fair I hear one of yours.'

For a moment she wondered if she had gone too far as his expression darkened, but after a second he placed his glass on the balustrade and leaned forward, looking out into the darkness of the garden.

'Shall I tell you something I have told no one else yet?' There was a sudden serious note in his voice.

Alice nodded, feeling her pulse quicken.

'I have never danced a waltz in the open air before.' He grinned at her and then held out his hand.

'I thought you were going to confess something serious,' she said, unable to stop herself from grinning at him in relief.

'You are keeping me waiting, Miss James. May I have this dance?'

'Everyone will stare at us.'

'That is true.'

'I am trying not to draw attention to myself.'

'It is far too late to be worried about that. Everyone is staring already.'

'How do you stand all the interest in you?'

'You grow accustomed to it.'

He held out his hand, and Alice took it despite the sensible part of her cautioning against it.

Inside, the first few notes of the waltz had started, and there were a dozen couples on the dance floor, twirling and stepping in time to the music.

She felt a thrill of pleasure as Lord Westcroft placed a hand in the small of her back and, exerting a gentle pressure, began to guide her into her first spin. He was an excellent dancer; he made it look effortless, and once Alice had got her confidence she was able to lift her eyes to meet his and just enjoy the dance knowing he would not let her slip.

For a few minutes she forgot there were other people at the ball: it was just her and Lord Westcroft, dancing under the stars. Every time they spun she felt her body sway a little closer to his, and once or twice his legs brushed hers. As the music swelled and then faded, she felt suddenly bereft and had to chide herself for the romantic thoughts that were trying to push to the fore in her mind.

'Thank you for the dance, Miss James,' Lord Westcroft said, bowing to her, his lips hovering over her hand.

She thought he might leave her then. They had spent well over half an hour together, dancing and talking and sipping punch in the moonlight, and it was not advisable for a gentleman to spend too much time with any one young lady or rumours would begin to circulate. The sensible thing for Lord Westcroft to do would be to bid her farewell and go dance with another young lady.

For a moment she saw him contemplate doing just that. He glanced over his shoulder, looking at the ballroom with an expression of trepidation. Then he turned back to her with a smile.

'Would you like to go for a stroll?'

'A stroll?'

'Only along the terrace and back. Perhaps a few dozen times. I find myself reluctant to let you go just yet, Miss James. I have this fear you will disappear as soon as I look away for an instant.'

'You wouldn't prefer to go and dance with someone else?'

'No,' he said simply.

'Then, I would enjoy a stroll very much.'

He offered her his arm, and she slipped her hand through and rested it in the crook of his elbow. They had only taken a few steps when they were cut off by a statuesque woman in a beautiful green and gold dress. Even with her mask on, Alice recognised Lady Salisbury. There was an expression of concerned curiosity on her face as she positioned herself directly in their path.

'Lord Westcroft, I hope you are enjoying the ball.'

'I am, thank you, Lady Salisbury.'

The viscountess turned to Alice, and Alice felt something shrivel inside her. There was coldness in the older woman's expression that hadn't been there when she had been looking at Lord Westcroft.

'I do not think we have been introduced, Miss...' Lady Salisbury said with a smile that did not reach her eyes.

Alice felt her mouth go instantly dry and her tongue stick to the roof.

'You must forgive me,' Lord Westcroft said before Alice could summon any words. 'I have a little confession to make.'

'Oh?' Lady Salisbury said, not taking her eyes off Alice.

'This is Miss James, a distant relative on my mother's side. She has been staying with my mother these past few weeks. When my mother heard I was attending your ball, she requested I ask you if Miss James could come as my guest, but I completely forgot. When Miss James appeared at my door in my mother's carriage tonight, I panicked and pretended you had agreed to her coming. I have to admit I hoped no one would notice and no word would get back to my mother about my oversight.'

Lady Salisbury looked from Lord Westcroft to Alice and back again for a moment and then broke out into a smile.

'Lord Westcroft, you should have just brought Miss James to me when you arrived. You know I can never deny you anything. He is charming, is he not, Miss James?'

'He is,' Alice agreed.

'I beg your forgiveness,' Lord Westcroft said and then leaned in closer to Lady Salisbury and spoke in a conspiratorial manner. 'And I beg you do not tell my mother of my error.'

'My lips are sealed, Lord Westcroft.'

'Now, Miss James, we cannot have the earl monopolising your time and attention at the ball tonight. I am sure there are many other gentlemen you wish to have the chance to dance with.'

'I have been selfish,' Lord Westcroft said, smiling indulgently at Alice as a distant relative might. 'I promise, once we have finished our stroll, to deliver Miss James to the ballroom where she can enjoy the attentions of all the gentlemen here tonight, clamouring to fill her dance-card.'

Lady Salisbury inclined her head and took her leave, glancing over her shoulder at them before she reentered the ballroom. Alice waited until she was sure the older woman was out of earshot to exhale loudly.

'I cannot breathe,' she said, trying to suck in large gasps of air.

'Be calm, Miss James. Lady Salisbury's suspicions are averted for now.'

'I thought she was going to rip my mask from my face and declare me an intruder, then command her footmen to escort me off her property.'

'I would not put it past her. She does not have the most forgiving of natures.'

'I need to leave,' Alice said desperately.

'That is the last thing you should do.'

She looked up at him, incredulous. He was remarkably calm, but she supposed if his lie was found out, it wouldn't really affect him. Lady Salisbury would forgive the earl, it would be Alice who would be thrown out in disgrace.

'Right now Lady Salisbury is watching you closely. If she sees you scurrying away she will know you were not meant to be here.'

'What do you suggest, then?'

'We stroll along the terrace as we had planned, and then you return to the ballroom and dance with a few different gentlemen before slipping away unnoticed.'

'I do not know if my nerves can stand it.'

He leaned in a little closer, his breath tickling her ear as he spoke. 'I'll be with you.'

* * *

Simon knew he was acting recklessly, but he could not find it in himself to care. No one knew who Miss James was or where she came from, so he did not have to worry as much as he normally would when spending time with a young lady. If he were honest, this evening was the first time he'd enjoyed himself quite so much in a long time, and it was because of Miss James.

In two weeks he would have left England, never to return, so for once he did not have to worry if he were upsetting anyone. There was no requirement for him to nod politely whilst an elderly acquaintance regaled him with a tiresome tale or an eager social climber thrust her daughter in his direction. Tonight he could do whatever he wanted safe in the knowledge that he would never see most of these people ever again. All he had to do was ensure he did not ruin Miss James in the process.

He watched her as they strolled along the terrace, reaching the end in less than a minute despite walking sedately. As they walked, some of the tension seeped from her shoulders, and before they turned back to head in the other direction she was smiling again.

'This is by far the most reckless thing I have ever done,' she said, leaning in so no one else could hear her words. 'I expect you do wild things all the time.'

'Once…' he said, almost wistfully. A few years ago his life had been charmed, although he hadn't been aware of it at the time. He'd lost his father when he was just twelve years old, and for a long time the grief had affected him, but five years ago things had been good. He had been surrounded by people who loved him—his mother, his older brother, his sister-in-law and his lovely nieces—and he'd had the freedom to do whatever he chose. As the second son, the title and the responsibility were never meant to be his. Robert was fair and loving and had ensured Simon had a home of his own and enough income to live a comfortable life. He'd relished his freedom then, the ability to go off at a moment's notice, to follow his desires on a whim.

They reached the end of the terrace again and turned, Simon glancing into the ballroom. Lady Salisbury was still watching them as she spoke to an elderly couple. Her eyes were narrowed slightly, and Simon realised she was still suspicious of his companion.

'Perhaps we should get you out of here,' he murmured, glancing at the steps that led to the garden.

'Surely Lady Salisbury would notice. I can feel her eyes on me.'

'You're right,' he said, feeling a little disappointed. There was something appealing about slipping into the darkened gardens in the company of Miss James. 'Let us go into the ballroom.'

'I feel so sick I might be sick over the shoes of whatever gentleman I am meant to dance with.'

'Don't do that,' he said with a smile. 'That is a sure way to get yourself noticed.'

He led her inside, his eyes dancing over the groups of people before resting on the person he was looking for.

'Forrester, good to see you,' he said, clapping a man of around his age on the back.

'Northumberland,' Forrester said with a grin. He leaned in closer, giving Miss James an appraising look. 'How do you manage to always end up with the most beautiful woman in the room on your arm?'

'Forrester, meet Miss James. Miss James, this is a good friend of mine from my schooldays, Mr Nicholas Forrester.'

Forrester bent over Alice's hand, giving her his most charming smile.

'We need a favour,' Simon said quickly. 'Will you dance the next dance with Miss James? Keep her away from Lady Salisbury. If our hostess asks who she is, tell her she's a distant relative of my mother's.'

'Is that the truth?'

'No.'

Forrester looked intrigued. 'You haven't smuggled one of your mistresses into this society affair, have you, Northumberland?'

Next to him he saw Miss James blush, and he quickly shook his head. 'No, Miss James is completely respectable. Will you dance with her as a favour?'

'No favour needed. Would you do me the honour, Miss James?'

She inclined her head, and Simon watched as Forrester lead her to the dance floor. They had a few minutes before the next dance was called, and he realised he felt a spark of jealousy as Forrester bent his head close to Miss James's to discuss something over the hum of conversation in the room.

He should move on, find some débutante to talk to, so if Lady Salisbury glanced in his direction she would see nothing suspicious, only an unmarried gentleman talking to a woman with a sizeable dowry. Simon cast his eyes around the room, but after a few seconds he found he was drawn back to where Miss James stood with Forrester. They were both smiling now, and he felt a prickle of unease. He hoped she hadn't told Forrester of her true identity.

With his eyes locked on the couple, he watched as they took their places for a quadrille. Miss James danced well for someone who had only been to a few dances at the local Assembly Rooms. Her steps were graceful, and her body swayed in time to the music. His eyes glided over her body, taking in the curve of her hips and her slender, pinched-in waist. For the first time in a long time he felt a surge of desire.

Shaking his head ruefully he forced himself to focus on something else. Desire had no place in his life now, but he would not punish himself for merely appreciating a beautiful woman.

'You're prowling,' Maria said as she approached, her voice low and filled with mirth.

'Prowling? You make me sound like an animal.'

'You *look* like an animal. Perhaps a wolf or a grumpy bear.'

'Just what every man wishes to be compared to,' he murmured.

'If you do not wish to be called a grumpy bear, perhaps do not frown so. Balls are meant to be fun.'

He plastered an exaggerated smile on his face and watched as Maria recoiled.

'For the love of everything that is holy, please stop,' she said. 'How old are you?'

'Thirty-two.'

'Then, why must you act as if you were five?'

'Only for you, my dearest sister.'

Maria was only a few years older than him. She had married his older brother, Robert, when she was nineteen and Robert twenty-three. Simon had been thirteen at the time and reeling from his father's sudden death. Maria had seen a boy struggling with the world and given him the kindness that no one else in his family could at that moment, grieving as they all were, and Simon would never forget it. Over the years their relationship had grown and changed with each new stage of life, but now he was blessed with a sister-in-law who he loved as if she were his own flesh and blood.

'She is pretty,' Maria said, motioning to where Miss James twirled on the dance floor.

'Mmm...' Simon responded. Maria didn't know of his plans to leave England yet. He hadn't told her of the passage he had booked to Europe or his expectation he would never be back. His sister-in-law had suffered so much over the last few years, he knew his departure would devastate her. He would tell her: he wasn't so much of a brute as to leave without saying goodbye, but he didn't want there to be too much time between his revelation and his departure. If anyone could get him to change his mind, it would be Maria.

'Do you know her from somewhere?'

'No,' Simon said, and then glanced over his shoulder. 'But if Lady Salisbury asks, she's a distant relative of my mother's.'

Maria raised an eyebrow. 'What are you doing, Simon?' Then her face lit up with pure joy. 'Are you courting her?'

'Good Lord, no,' he said, pulling Maria to one side, looking round to check no one else had heard her words. He was considered a highly eligible bachelor, with his title, wealth and single status despite being into his thirties. *Everyone* was waiting for him to declare he was finally ready to start looking for a wife. He didn't need any flames being added to that fire.

'Then, who is she?'

'A pleasant young woman I met about an hour ago.'

'Why are you watching her so closely?'

'I'm not,' he said, realising his eyes were on her again. With an effort he looked away and focussed on his sister-in-law.

'Whatever you are doing, be careful,' Maria cautioned him. She flitted between the role of a protective older sister and an excitable friend. There were many people he was going to miss when he left, and Maria was close to the top of that list.

The music swelled and the dance finished, and Simon watched as Forrester bowed to Miss James. They lingered for a moment, talking quietly, before Forrester escorted Miss James to the edge of the dance floor.

'Excuse me,' Simon said, hoping Maria did not follow him, moving quickly to scoop Miss James up before anyone else could. Lady Salisbury was on the other side of the room now and seemed to momentarily have lost interest in the young woman. It would be a good opportunity to sneak Miss James back out the way she had come.

'Thank you for the dance, Miss James,' Forrester said as Simon approached. 'I think Northumberland would run me through with a sword if I asked you to dance again, but I do hope you have an enjoyable evening.'

Once Forrester had left, Simon leaned in as close as he dared and said quietly, 'Lady Salisbury is otherwise occupied. I wonder if it would be best to sneak you out of here now.'

Chapter Three

With her heart hammering in her chest Alice tried to act nonchalant as she followed Lord Westcroft from the ballroom. She looked all around for Lydia but could not see her anywhere and wondered if Lady Salisbury had recognised her as an interloper as well. It was more likely Lydia had realised Lady Salisbury was watching her and slipped away herself. Her friend was highly excitable but astute and observant. Hopefully she was halfway back to the village by now.

'We stand here, pretending to talk, until no one is looking, then we quickly walk down the steps into the darkness of the garden.'

'What if someone sees us?'

'They won't.'

'Would it be safer for me to go by myself?'

She saw him grimace and then shake his head. 'We do not know if anyone is roaming the gardens. There could be all sorts of dangers out there.'

'You make it sound as though wild animals prowl through the flower beds.'

'The truth is much more dangerous. There are unscrupulous people in this world.'

Before Alice could protest any further, he grabbed her by the hand and pulled her down the steps into the shadows of one of the alcoves set below the terrace. They were completely hidden here, out of view from anyone on the terrace above or the ballroom beyond. Someone would have to come all the way down the stairs for them to be seen.

'We'll wait here for a moment and then make a run for it across the lawn,' Lord Westcroft said. His expression was serious, but Alice had a suspicion that he was enjoying himself. They stood quietly for a few minutes, Alice's hand tucked into Lord Westcroft's, and then he nodded to her, and together they set off across the lawn. All the time they were running, Alice felt exposed and was certain there would be a shout from the terrace, perhaps the pattering of feet as people descended the steps into the garden to identify them. Only once they were secreted behind a hedge did she allow herself to breathe normally.

She glanced back towards the house and was relieved to see no one was paying any particular attention to the garden. Hopefully they had made it across unnoticed. Lord Westcroft was also looking back, but after a moment his eyes lowered to meet hers.

Alice felt a spark of attraction between them. She knew much of it was from the excitement of the last few minutes, but she had the irrepressible urge to reach up and trail her fingers over Lord Westcroft's face. She was horrified to find her hand halfway up to his cheek and felt a wave of mortification as he caught it in his own.

'We should get you home, Miss James,' he murmured, holding onto her hand and making no move to leave.

She nodded, her eyes fixed on his.

Alice was never normally reckless. Never before tonight had she sneaked into anyplace she shouldn't be. She obeyed her parents' rules and conducted herself in a manner that was expected of an unmarried young woman. Yet she didn't pull away. She didn't turn her head or break eye contact.

Despite the worry of the last half an hour it had been a magical evening. For a few hours she had been able to pretend she was someone else, swept away in the glamour and opulence of the masquerade ball. For a time she had been able to forget the impending engagement she was about to be pushed into and dance and laugh as if she were free to do whatever she pleased.

Lord Westcroft's thumb caressed the back of her hand, and then before she could stop herself, she pushed up on her tiptoes and kissed him. It was a momentary brush of her lips against his, but as they came together something primal tightened deep inside her, and she realised she wanted so much more.

'Miss James,' he murmured as she pulled away, desire burning bright in his eyes. She thought he might reprimand her. All evening he had been a perfect gentleman, despite the attraction that crackled between them. For a long moment he did nothing, his body so close she could feel the heat of him, and then he gripped her around the waist and kissed her again.

This kiss was deep and passionate and made Alice forget where she was. His lips were soft against hers, and she could taste the sweetness of the punch they had both had. His scent was something entirely different, and she had to fight the urge to bury herself in his neck.

Alice felt her body sink into his, and in that moment all she could think about were his lips on hers. There were no thoughts of consequences, no thoughts of being sensible or respectable. It was just Lord Westcroft and his kiss.

They both stiffened and pulled apart at exactly the same moment. Somewhere to her left, coming from the direction of the house, was a rustling noise. For an instant Alice wondered if it could be an animal, and then the sound came again and she knew for certain it was another person. Whether it was a couple who had slipped into the gardens for some privacy, or one of the servants patrolling to ensure no one was sneaking in after Lady Salisbury's suspicions had been roused, it didn't matter. Someone else was there in the gardens, and if they were caught there would be a horrific scandal.

Alice felt a cold shudder run through her. It would be a repeat of what had happened with her sister, only worse. At least Margaret had a gentleman who had been happy to marry her and save her from the scandal. She doubted even vile Cecil would take her if she got caught kissing the earl in the garden whilst attending a party she had not been invited to.

'I have to go,' she said, pulling away sharply.

'Wait,' Lord Westcroft whispered, catching her hand. 'It might not be safe.'

'I have to go,' she repeated.

This time she wrenched her hand from his and set off at a run across the gardens. She had an advantage, following the route she had crept through with Lydia only a few hours earlier. She weaved around flower beds, squeezed through hedges and pushed herself over fences.

At first she fancied she heard footsteps behind her and thought Lord Westcroft was following her, but somewhere after she had squeezed through the second hedge she lost him.

Only once she was on the road that led back to the village did she slow, her chest heaving, to catch her breath. She desperately hoped Lydia had found her way home already and wasn't trapped somewhere by Lady Salisbury and her suspicions.

Despite the fear of being found out and the frantic dash back through the gardens, Alice could not find it in herself to regret the evening. She had been more reckless than she ever had before, or ever would be again, but for a few hours she had felt alive.

Chapter Four

Simon groaned as he rested his head in his hands, leaning forward onto the desk. He rubbed his temples, trying to alleviate the pounding. Headaches were part of his daily life now, horrible, pulsating episodes of pain that stopped him whatever he was doing and forced him to seek out the relief of a darkened room. For the last year he had been unable to deny that they were happening more frequently and getting worse.

Today however, his headache was a little different. It was the heavy fog caused by drinking too much alcohol, and it was completely self-inflicted.

There was a knock on the door, and he quickly straightened as his butler entered.

'The dowager countess is here, my Lord.'

'Show her in,' he said, hoping he didn't look too terrible.

Maria breezed in, stopping to regard him and shake her head like a fussy mother hen. 'You look terrible, Simon.'

'You look lovely.'

She tutted at his glib reply and sank down into a chair

across from him. 'I have never seen you drink as much as you did last night.'

After Miss James had fled through the gardens, he had followed her, only to lose her a few minutes later. For someone running in highly impractical satin shoes, she had moved fast. He was unsure if they had been spotted and had returned to the ball half expecting someone to come up and make some lewd remarks. As the evening had worn on without anyone saying anything, his relief had led him to the card room, and he had spent far too long playing cards and drinking whisky, trying to forget how good it had been to lose himself for a few minutes in Miss James's kiss.

'We have something very serious to discuss, Simon,' Maria said, her expression grave. For a moment he wondered if she had worked out he was suffering from the headaches. Maria was astute, and if anyone was going to uncover his secret it would be his sister-in-law. 'Last night, in the gardens, someone saw you.'

It took a moment for the words to sink in, and he cleared his throat.

'Who saw what?'

'I had a visit this morning from Miss Elizabeth Cheevers and her mother. It was unannounced and horribly awkward. It would seem they were in the village to shop for some material for a new dress, and when they stopped at the haberdasher's they overheard something disturbing.'

Simon sat a little straighter, his stomach sinking.

'Go on.'

'You were seen in the garden last night, kissing a young woman. By the description, it sounds like Miss

James, but they did not have a name to attach to the rumours as yet.'

Simon felt the world tilt and judder around him for a second, and he had to grip the arms of his chair to steady himself.

'This is bad, Simon,' Maria said, biting her lip. 'It is the talk of the village already, which means by tomorrow the whole county will likely know.'

'They will not know who Miss James is. She kept her mask on the whole time.'

'There are people out there who will make it their whole purpose in life to identify the young woman you were seen kissing. They will think it their moral duty.'

Simon stood and paced to the door and back, trying to order his thoughts. It would be easier if his head weren't pounding so much. For him the consequences were minimal. At worst he would get some snide remarks and a few people avoiding him when he went out and about, but he was an earl and there was only a limited number of people who would dare be rude to him. Added to that, with his plans to leave England in a few weeks, it would hardly affect him.

Miss James was another matter entirely. There was a small hope that she would not be identified. As she was not an invited guest, she would not be the first person to be suspected, but with her distinctive red hair and pretty blue eyes he doubted she would stay hidden for long. He cursed his own stupidity of giving Lady Salisbury her real name, but last night in the moment of their hostess's questioning he had not thought her name would matter.

He closed his eyes. This was the last thing he needed

right now. His plans to leave England could not be disrupted.

'Do not be so selfish,' he muttered to himself, then turned to Maria. 'Please excuse me. I have to try to put this right.'

'You're going to see her?'

'I have to.'

'People will be watching what you do and where you go.'

'I can be discreet.'

'I do not doubt it, but please be careful. I did not speak to Miss James for long, but she seemed a sweet young woman.'

Simon inclined his head and then strode from the room. There was no time to waste. He needed to get to Miss James before the gossip started circling.

Alice sat demurely, her hands folded in her lap and a serene expression fixed on her face, all the while trying not to burst into tears. Across the room her mother sat beaming at her and their new guest. Cecil Billington had been placed beside her on the sofa and had gradually inched closer until his knees were almost touching hers.

'I think you would like Ensley, Miss James,' Cecil said, smiling at her with his mouth full of crooked, yellow teeth. He reached out and boldly stroked the back of her hand as he spoke, and Alice had to use all her self-control to stop herself from pulling away abruptly.

'It is a pleasant village?'

'On the whole, yes. There are plenty of like-minded people to socialise with and a few decent shops. There are more poor people than I would like, but I am working with the other local landlords to raise the rents so we only get a certain class of people in the village. You cannot eliminate the lower classes entirely—we need somewhere for our servants and the people who provide the essential services for the village to live—but I have proposed a system to limit the numbers.'

'Where will the people go who do not make the cut?' Alice asked coldly.

Cecil shrugged. 'That is not my concern. You understand the idea is to make the village a more agreeable place. A place where children can skip freely down the streets and women can walk without fear in the evenings.'

'I thought you said it was a pleasant place already,' Alice said and tried to ignore the warning look she received from her mother.

'Let us not talk of Ensley,' Cecil said, shifting ever closer. 'I am very much looking forward to my stay here, Miss James. I hope you will allow me to accompany you on your daily business.'

'Alice would like that very much,' Mrs James said quickly.

Alice smiled sweetly. 'Today I am going to take a basket of food to Mrs Willow and her children. Mr Willow died last year of consumption, and I understand two of the children have been unwell.'

Alice's mother inhaled loudly and as Alice glanced over gave her a stern look. Cecil looked appalled as she had known he would and shifted uncomfortably.

'Surely you cannot mean to visit a family where there is illness, Miss James? You have to think of yourself.'

'I promised Mrs Willow I would go. She struggles with six children now she is all by herself.'

Cecil curled his lip and flexed his fingers where they rested on her hand.

'Even in the summer months we must be vigilant against disease,' he said.

'Perhaps you could postpone the visit for a few days, Alice,' Mrs James said firmly. 'I am sure Mr Billington would appreciate your time being spent to show him a little of the village and the surrounding area. It is a glorious day. You might even take a stroll on the beach.'

'A promise is a promise, Mother,' Alice said quickly. 'I am sure Mr Billington would not want me to brush off my commitments so readily. It is not an attractive quality in a woman to be unreliable.'

She was saved from further argument by the door opening and their maid slipping into the room. They were not a grand household. Her father's income could only provide enough for one maid and a young lad who helped both inside the house and in the garden. Milly helped Alice's mother in the kitchen and did some of the housework duties around the house, but Alice was expected to do her fair share. All of which had increased significantly since her sister had left home.

'There is a gentleman to see Miss James,' Milly said, turning over a small card in her fingers. She looked in awe of the little piece of embossed card.

'A gentleman?' Mrs James said, standing and casting an apologetic look at Cecil.

'Yes, ma'am,' Milly lowered her voice. 'He says he's the Earl of Northumberland.'

Mrs James's eyes widened, and she took a step forward before turning to Alice.

'Alice James, if this is one of your friends being silly, I will not be impressed.'

In any other circumstance Alice would have had to suppress a smile. It *was* the sort of thing Lydia would do, press an unsuspecting male friend or relative into giving Milly a card with a false name upon it. However, today Alice knew it was no trick.

She felt her mouth go dry and her pulse quicken. There was no good reason for him to be here. Last night had been magical, but Alice was well aware it had been an interlude in her otherwise normal life, nothing more. Lord Westcroft had no place in her small drawing room in their modest home in Bamburgh, just as she had no place in the lofty halls of his grand country house.

'Shall I show him in?' Milly asked, her hand hovering on the door-handle.

'Yes, you had better,' Mrs James said, glancing at Alice again. 'Do you know him?'

Before Alice could answer the door opened again, and Lord Westcroft stepped into the room. He looked out of place in the drab drawing room, and Alice suddenly felt self-conscious. In the cold light of day he would see her dress was made of inferior material, her hands dry and reddened by the manual labour she had to undertake. Normally these things did not bother her, but in front of him she felt a fraud, an imposter. Last night she had soared with all the wealthy ladies, the candlelight allowing her to pass as one of them. It would be painfully clear today she did not fit with the women he was accustomed to.

As he entered the room Alice thought back to the perfect kiss they had shared in the garden before she had fled through the night. It had been magical, everything a young woman could dream of for her first kiss. She found her eyes flicking to his lips now and had to force herself to look away, to focus on the floor as she bobbed into an unsteady little curtsy.

'It is an honour to have you in our home, my Lord,' Mrs James said, bustling over and pausing in front of the earl.

'I am sorry to call unannounced. I hope you can forgive me for dropping in like this.'

'You know an earl?' Cecil muttered out of the corner of his mouth, spittle gathering in the corners in a little frothy bubble.

'A little,' Alice said warily. Lord Westcroft had seemed a sensible man last night and had been aware of the damage that could be done to her reputation by the wrong association. She knew he would not be here if it weren't important. She thought of the rustle in the bushes the night before as they had shared their kiss, the feeling that someone had spotted them, that eyes were watching them, and she shuddered.

'Miss James,' Lord Westcroft said, turning to her with a dazzling smile, 'it is delightful to see you again.'

'And you, my Lord,' Alice said, trying to read his expression.

'And this must be your dear cousin you were telling me about,' Lord Westcroft said, directing his gaze onto Cecil. Alice caught the mischief in the earl's eye and pressed her lips together giving a miniscule shake of her head.

'Billington, Cecil Billington, at your service, my Lord,' Cecil said, stretching out a hand to shake Lord Westcroft's.

'Forgive me, my Lord. I was not aware you were acquainted with my daughter.'

'Our acquaintance has not been a lengthy one,' Lord Westcroft said, allowing Mrs James to usher him into the room. The room was not large, and alongside a low table there was only the armchair Mrs James had been sitting in and the long sofa where Alice and Cecil were. Lord Westcroft seemed unperturbed and took a place next to Alice on the other side.

As they sat his leg brushed hers, and she glanced up at him. For a moment it seemed like they were the only two people in the room; everyone else had faded into the background. Then Cecil cleared his throat, and Alice was pulled right back to reality, sandwiched between the man who could ruin her future and the man she desperately wished she did not have to spend a lifetime tied to.

For one heady moment she wondered if Lord Westcroft had decided to come and rescue her, to declare himself in love after their one evening spent together. Then she looked at his serious expression and knew that wasn't the case.

'Miss James and I met through the course of some of her charitable works,' Lord Westcroft said smoothly. Alice nodded a little too eagerly at the lie and had to tell herself to calm down. Her mother would think it suspicious she had not mentioned meeting a man of his status, although she was hardly going to contradict the earl to his face.

Alice had told Lord Westcroft the evening before of her scheme to pair some of the wealthier families in the village with some of the poorer ones, to provide support over the harsher winters, little parcels of firewood or baskets of food. By joining families one on one, she hoped the wealthier ones would start to feel a little responsibility to their less fortunate counterparts. It would make it harder to distance themselves from the tribulations and struggles of the people they could help.

'I am very keen to get involved with your endeavours, Miss James. I wondered if you might be able to spare me some time to discuss things this morning.'

Alice searched his face, trying to work out what had prompted this visit, but his expression was impassive, a bland smile that was meant to alleviate the concerns of the other people in the room.

'Miss James and I were planning on going for a walk over the dunes,' Cecil said, leaning forward to insert himself into the conversation. 'I understand Miss James's friend is going to make herself available to chaperon.'

'Excellent,' Lord Westcroft said. 'I apologise, Mr Billington, for interrupting your plans like this, but I will not forget your generosity in giving up your time with Miss James for me.'

Cecil opened his mouth and closed it again a few times. It was clear he had meant to accompany Lord Westcroft and Alice on the walk, inserting himself into whatever business they were about to discuss, but Lord Westcroft had quickly outmanoeuvred him.

'Perhaps we should go now, Miss James. I have an appointment this afternoon I wish to keep.'

'Lydia is planning on meeting you?' Mrs James said quickly. Lord Westcroft might be an earl, but the rules of polite society still applied. Even though no one would ever think he could be interested in the likes of Alice, they still had to safeguard her reputation.

'Yes, Mama. She is going to meet us on the beach in twenty minutes.'

'Wonderful,' Lord Westcroft said, rising to his feet. 'It was a pleasure to meet you, Mrs James, and you, Mr Billington.' He bowed to the older woman and shook Cecil's outstretched hand, surreptitiously wiping his hand on his jacket after doing so. Then before anyone could think of any objections, he offered Alice his arm, and quickly they left the room together.

'Let me get my bonnet,' Alice said, running upstairs to fetch it and tie it securely under her chin. It was a glorious day out, but the wind was strong, whipping off the sea with a ferocity that was not common for this time of year. Her skin was so pale it only took a few minutes in the sunlight to turn pink and then burn, but with the wind it was even worse, and she didn't doubt she would have red cheeks later despite her precautions.

They left the house quickly, and Alice was pleased to find they were, so far, unobserved. Her home was on the outskirts of Bamburgh village, at the bottom past the castle that stood proud on the rocky hill. It meant the beach was in easy reach, and they would not have to walk along the high street to get there.

For a few minutes they walked in silence, both looking around all the time to see if they were being watched. Only when they got to the edge of the dunes did Alice feel herself relax.

Waiting as she had promised was Lydia, her eyes alight with intrigue and excitement. As she saw Alice approach on Lord Westcroft's arm she frowned, standing a little straighter.

'This cannot be vile Cecil,' Lydia said quietly as they

approached, clapping her hands over her mouth as soon as the words were out in a bid to claw them back in. Her eyes narrowed, and she shook her head. 'I recognise you.' Five seconds passed and then ten, and then realisation dawned on her.

'Lydia, please,' Alice said quickly. 'Do not make a fuss.'

'This is Lord Westcroft, Earl of Northumberland,' she said, jabbing a finger in his direction. 'The most eligible bachelor in all of England. Last seen at Lady Salisbury's ball last night with a mystery woman in blue.' Lydia turned to her. 'I saw you dancing with him. Although, I didn't know who he was at the time. You're the mystery woman people are talking about.'

Alice felt her heart sink. She had hoped Lord Westcroft was here for some other reason, but deep down she supposed she had known that it was as a consequence of their actions the night before.

'Everyone is saying he was spotted kissing some unknown guest at Lady Salisbury's ball in the gardens.'

Lord Westcroft groaned.

'We were seen?' Alice asked, turning to him.

'It would appear so. I understand gossip and speculation is rampaging through the county.'

Alice felt the world around her tilt, and she clutched a little tighter at Lord Westcroft's arm.

'That is why I thought it imperative to come this morning.'

'Do people know it was me?'

'Not yet,' Lord Westcroft said, stopping and waiting until Alice looked up at him, 'but I think it is inevitable.'

Chapter Five

Alice felt her legs almost give way underneath her, and she was glad of Lord Westcroft's arm supporting her own.

'Perhaps we could take a walk along the beach, Miss James,' Lord Westcroft said, his voice calm. 'We have much to talk about.'

'Everyone will know,' Alice said, shaking her head. She felt sick and hot and as if her whole life were about to implode around her.

'Please, Miss James. I implore you to remain calm,' Lord Westcroft said, his voice silky smooth, and Alice felt some of the panic recede. Perhaps he had a plan, some way of diverting suspicion from her.

In front of her Lydia stood, eyes wide, hardly able to believe what was happening.

'You should do what Lord Westcroft asks, Alice,' Lydia said, motioning for them to go ahead of her across the sand dunes. 'I am sure you have much to discuss.'

Thankfully the wind had kept most people away from the beach, and there were only a few couples in the far distance strolling along the damp sand. Alice picked a path through the dune and onto the beach itself, having to hitch up her skirt as she traversed the soft sand. The climb up the dunes was strenuous even though they were not high along this part of the coast, but the sand was powdery soft, and if you didn't put your feet in exactly the right place you slipped down again. Once at the top she paused for a second to catch her breath and check Lord Westcroft was following her, thinking he might find the unfamiliar terrain difficult, but he was directly behind her, traversing the dunes like a steady-footed mountain goat.

She slipped and slid down the other side, stopping at the bottom to wait for Lord Westcroft and Lydia.

'I'll walk behind,' Lydia said, giving Alice's arm a reassuring squeeze. 'Close enough to count as a chaperon but far enough to give you some privacy.'

'Thank you,' Alice said. She knew how lucky she was to have Lydia as a friend. Not only was the young woman full of spirit and the joys of life, she was loyal and kind too. One of her greatest fears about leaving Bamburgh and starting her life anew, apart from the horror of being married to vile Cousin Cecil, was leaving Lydia behind. She desperately wanted to know how Lydia had fared at the ball the evening before but pushed her questions to the back of her mind. There would be plenty of time for her to catch up with her friend later.

'Come, Miss James. Our time together is short, and we have much to discuss.'

Lord Westcroft led her across the sand. They walked just below the high-tide mark, the sand still damp under their feet. The beach was beautifully clean, the sea clear, with hardly any seaweed deposited on the sand. Alice adjusted her bonnet as they walked, pulling it down a little lower to protect her from the sun.

'My sister-in-law came to see me earlier this morning,' Lord Westcroft said, wasting no time now they were alone. 'She tells me last night we were seen in the garden.' He paused and glanced at her before returning his gaze to the horizon. 'Kissing.'

'Someone actually saw us kiss?' Alice asked, horrified. It would have been ruinous to be merely seen sneaking off into the gardens unchaperoned with the earl, but if someone had seen them kiss, it was impossible to argue there was some innocent explanation for their presence in the garden.

'They did,' Lord Westcroft said. He was looking straight ahead, his posture stiff, and Alice realised he must have come straight to seek her out after he had been informed they had been seen. She felt a swell of gratitude for this man who had shown her kindness the night before and for a short while had made her dream of something other than the future that she was destined for. He could have brushed away the gossip; it would hardly have touched him. A few people might whisper behind their hands when they saw him, but being subject to such gossip would hardly affect his life at all. There were no consequences for men of his social status, not like there were for women of hers. Yet he had still hurried to her, seeking to reach her before the gossips identified her as the mystery woman and ruined her life.

'There is a chance no one will find out who you are,' Lord Westcroft said, glancing at her and grimacing. 'Although, you do have quite distinctive hair. I doubt there is anyone else in all of Northumberland with hair the same shade as yours. Now I think of it I am sure it is why Lady Salisbury was so suspicious at the ball.'

'So the likelihood I remain unidentified is small,' Alice said quietly. She could see her whole life crashing down around her. The devastation it would cause her parents, the end of her life as she knew it. Even Cousin Cecil would declare her too damaged for marriage. She wondered if her sister might take her in: surely the scandal wouldn't reach all the way to Devon. It would be a horrible existence, though, always wondering if someone might know someone who had told them of her infamy.

'Yes. I think you have to prepare yourself for the very real possibility that you will be identified. Of course, there is no proof. You could decide to bluster the whole affair out, especially if you can get your parents on your side. If they swear you did not leave home last night, then I am sure no one will come out and call them liars directly.'

Alice considered the suggestion. 'You mean let people gossip and speculate but deny everything and hope with time things settle down.'

'It might work, and it would mean you could continue your normal life.' He stopped walking for a moment, turning to her and running a hand through his hair. 'I haven't even said I'm sorry, Miss James,' he said and gave her a sad smile. 'I am, from the bottom of my heart. I'm sorry. I shouldn't have kissed you. I have been playing society's game for long enough. I should have been more careful.' He shook his head. 'I pride myself on being a practical person, yet I let myself get carried away.'

'It was not all your fault,' Alice said. 'I kissed you first.'

'I think we were both caught up in the magic of the moment,' he said, his eyes flicking to her lips for a fraction of a second. Alice felt a bolt of anticipation run through her, and she wondered if he felt it too, for he turned away abruptly, offering her his arm again.

For a minute neither of them spoke, and Alice got the sense Lord Westcroft was building up to something. She looked out to sea, trying to imagine her life with the shadow of this kiss hanging over it. She realised, despite what was to come, she couldn't bring herself to regret the evening entirely. She wished she had been more careful, that no one had seen their moment of intimacy in the garden, but she could not wish she had never gone. It had been the first time she had abandoned caution and allowed herself to enjoy the moment, and it had been wonderful from start to finish.

'Vile Cecil arrived as planned I see,' Lord Westcroft said, surprising Alice with his change of direction.

'Yes. I understand he stayed over in Belford last night so he could ride the last few miles this morning. I thought I might have a few more hours before he descended upon us, but it was not to be.'

'Has he proposed yet?'

Alice shook her head. 'No.' She bit her lip and felt her heart sink. 'You think I should press him to before any of the rumours reach him.'

'No,' Lord Westcroft said quickly. 'I would not wish that on anyone, not unless that is what you want.' He paused and then looked at her intently again. 'I just want you to realise what options you have. All is not lost. There is the possibility to live a normal life.'

Alice felt a sudden spark of anger. It felt as though he

were doing his very best to come up with a solution that did not involve him. If he were any sort of gentleman, he would at least mention the idea of marrying her. Alice was not so naïve to think an earl would ever actually end up with a young woman like her, but it would be courteous to at least pretend he would consider it.

She was about to say something to that effect when he stopped walking and waited for her to turn to face him.

'There is another possibility, Miss James,' he said quietly, 'but I need you to really listen as I tell you what I can offer you and what I cannot.'

Alice felt her pulse quicken, and she suddenly wished there was somewhere to sit down, but the only place was the damp sand, and she didn't want to have to explain a wet, sandy dress to her mother.

'In two weeks I leave England,' he said, his expression completely serious with a hint of sadness. 'I plan to travel to the Continent and find somewhere quiet to make my home for the next few months. I have been preparing for this trip for a long time, and I cannot postpone it. There are factors outside my control to consider.'

Alice remained silent, waiting for him to tell her more. It was clear he was not suggesting she accompany him.

'When I leave the country, I do not envisage ever coming back,' he said slowly, his words quiet but clear, and he regarded her intently as if needing to see she understood the gravity of what he was saying. 'Are you aware of my family's history at all?'

She shook her head.

'I was never meant to be earl. My father died when he should still have had a good number of years of life left. He was youthful and healthy, yet one day he just dropped down dead.' Lord Westcroft looked away for a moment, and Alice saw the glint of tears in his eyes. 'For the six months before he died he suffered from debilitating headaches, terrible daily pains that worsened week by week. Then one day he called out in pain, his face a picture of agony, and a few seconds later he collapsed on the floor, dead.'

Alice closed her eyes for a second, wanting to reach out and take Lord Westcroft's hand. He looked devastated, and she realised he must have witnessed his father's death.

'My brother, Robert, became the earl. He was ten years older than me, and for a while he looked out for me like a father. You met my sister-in-law last night. They married just after the mourning period for my father was complete and had three beautiful daughters. There was no reason to think they wouldn't have more children, that they wouldn't have a son who would inherit. I settled into my role as younger brother to the earl.'

Behind them Lydia had stopped too, just out of earshot, and Alice was pleased to see the beach remained almost empty. Horrible as his revelations so far had been, she felt like Lord Westcroft had worse to tell her.

'Then five years ago Robert started to get headaches. Every day he would wake up, and they would be worse than the last.'

Alice's hand went to her mouth. She knew Lord Westcroft's brother was dead, and she could now see where this story was headed. It was terrible.

'One day he dropped dead. He had been out for a ride with his wife and had just dismounted and then collapsed with no warning. The doctor said he was dead before he hit the ground.'

Reaching out Alice laid a hand on Lord Westcroft's arm. To lose one close relative in such a way was horrific, but two would be completely devastating.

He looked at her with haunted eyes and then spoke ever so quietly. 'A year ago I began experiencing headaches. Mild at first, and not every day, but over the last six months they have built in intensity. Every day they build and build until I am forced to lie down in a darkened room.'

'You think...' She couldn't bring herself to say the words.

'I have consulted doctors. They tell me there is nothing to be done and no way of telling when I might be struck down.'

Alice shook her head, unable to comprehend what living with such knowledge would do to you. Every moment he must live in fear of it being his last.

'I am sorry, my Lord. That is no way to live,' Alice said quietly.

'I have made my peace with it, but I have decided I do not want someone I love to witness my death. My mother has suffered enough, my sister-in-law too,' he said grimacing. 'And if I were to die in front of one of my nieces...' He shook his head. 'It is an intolerable thought.'

'This is why you are leaving the country?'

'Yes. I am going to find somewhere peaceful to rent a house, employ someone to cook and clean, pay them well for their services and inform them one day they might walk in to find me dead on the floor.'

Alice shook her head. 'Surely it would be better to

be amongst the people that love you, to spend however long you have with your family.'

Lord Westcroft spoke softly, but there was a steely determination in his voice that Alice realised was born from adversity. 'Every night when I go to sleep, when my thoughts are drifting and I no longer have conscious control of them, I see my father in the moment of his death. I relive the feelings of grief and devastation and shock over and over. I will not inflict that on anyone I love.'

He fell silent, and Alice pressed her lips together. He had lived with this burden for years and had had to face the question of his own mortality for a long time as well. It was not for her to question everything he had been through and the decisions he was making now as a consequence.

'I am sorry for everything you have been through,' Alice said, waiting until he looked at her and then holding his eye. 'It is more than any person should have to bear.'

'I have accepted this as my lot in life. I have had more than thirty years of living in comfort with a family who love me and a very privileged position in society. There are many who have much less than me.' He reached out and took her hand. It was an intimate gesture as Alice felt her heart quicken in her chest. 'I do not normally burden people with the whole story, but I think it is important for you to understand it all, to know exactly what it is I can offer you and what I cannot.'

The wind whipped around them as they stood together on the beach, blowing Alice's skirt against Lord Westcroft's legs, but he hardly seemed to notice.

'We find ourselves chased by scandal, Miss James,

and I think it inevitable your name will be associated with the kiss we shared, even if no one can prove it was you in that garden. I can offer you marriage, a protection of sorts, but it will not be the sort of marriage you expected for yourself.' He paused, checking she was following his words. 'If it is what you choose, I will marry you. It will save you from scandal, and once you become countess no one will care how we were a little careless. You will have my name and title as protection.'

Alice felt her head swim. Even from their short acquaintance she had known Lord Westcroft was an honourable man, but she had not expected this offer from him.

'I would obtain a special licence, and we would marry within the next few weeks. Then I would continue with my plan to leave the country.'

Alice's eyes flicked up to meet his, and she realised the importance of what he was saying and why he had told her exactly what had happened to his father and brother.

'You would be free to use whichever of my houses you wished, and I would ensure there was a good amount of money available for you. You would have a comfortable life, Miss James, but it would be a life spent on your own, at least at first.'

She opened her mouth to speak, but he pushed on quickly.

'Hear the last of my proposition,' he urged her. 'After we are married, you will not see me again. We will not consummate our union, and you will never bear me children. You will live as my wife in name until I die, and then you will be my widow.'

Alice took a step back, unable to take it all in. It was a generous proposition in so many ways, but she wasn't so naïve to think it the perfect solution to her problems. She would become a countess, an elevation in social status most women could only dream of, but Lord Westcroft had made it clear it would not be a normal marriage where their union would be celebrated. Alice tried to imagine her life if she did decide to marry Lord Westcroft. She would be mistress of her own home, finally in control of her own life, but it would be a lonely existence.

'There are some terms that I would ask you to abide by, if you did decide to accept my offer,' Lord Westcroft said slowly. She could see he wasn't sure if he had lost her to her racing thoughts.

'What terms?' It was best to know everything now, to have all the facts in her possession so she could make the best decision.

'I would ask you not to take a lover whilst I was alive.' He pressed his lips together and looked over her shoulder into the distance. 'It would complicate the matter of inheritance if you were to get pregnant.' She nodded, understanding his reasoning, and he quickly continued. 'I would leave you a generous settlement in my will. Enough to allow you to live as a wealthy widow for the rest of your life if you so desired, or to provide a generous dowry to take to your next marriage.'

His offer was kind, his tone calm but firm, and Alice realised he had thought about this a lot on his way to see her. What he was prepared to offer and what he wasn't. It showed how sure he was in his decisions and how convinced he was that he would likely go the same way as his father and his brother soon.

He fell silent and looked at her with those bright blue eyes, and she felt a pang of sadness that there was no desire in them now. What he was proposing was purely an arrangement made to safeguard her reputation and fulfil his obligation. He owed her nothing, but chivalry demanded he take responsibility for his part in tarnishing her reputation.

Alice turned away, desperately trying to weigh up what he was offering her. If she accepted his proposition she would be a countess, mistress of her own home and finally in charge of her own life. Yet she would live alone, with no prospect of love until Lord Westcroft died abroad and released her from the marriage.

She wanted children, a home filled with love, and this would give her none of that, but it would likely mean postponing that part of her life, not forgoing it.

The alternative was Cecil, if he would have her. After this scandal her parents would be more keen than ever to marry her off quickly and quietly, and she would be stuck with Cecil and his pawing hands and horrible views on society for the rest of her life.

'I could come with you,' she offered, turning back quickly. 'If you would prefer someone to look after you.'

'No,' he said sharply and then made an effort to soften his tone. 'I need to be alone. I can offer you my name and my protection, but no more, Miss James, not under any circumstance.'

'I understand,' she said. She would not build this into a fantasy of something that could never be. The decision had to be made on what he was offering, weighing that up with the alternative.

'I do not wish to rush you in your decision, but if we

are going to do this, it has to be quick for a couple of reasons. The first, as I said, I plan to be on a boat leaving London in two weeks, and the second is that rumours will spread fast. If we announce our engagement it will stop any malicious gossip in its tracks. You will be protected by your new title, but that only works if we pre-empt the majority of the speculation.'

'Your offer is very generous, Lord Westcroft,' Alice said, raising her eyes to meet his. 'I do not want you to feel obligated to do this. I never set out to trap you. I never thought this would be the culmination of last night.'

He smiled grimly. 'I know, Miss James. Perhaps we were both a little naïve thinking we could get away with such a deception. Please do not concern yourself with worrying that I might think you did this on purpose. I pride myself on being a good judge of character, and I like yours. If we had met in other circumstances, perhaps we would even have been friends.' He took her hand in his, and Alice inhaled sharply at the contact. 'I would not propose to a woman who I thought would bring my family's name into disrepute. I cannot make this decision for you, but please do not think I am insincere in what I am offering.'

Alice closed her eyes and let the two possible lives wash over her. The first was marriage to Cecil, a man she despised. The second was less conventional, perhaps a little lonely, but contained the chance of happiness along the way. She knew she had to be brave and reach out and grab what was being offered.

'Thank you, Lord Westcroft. I accept.'

Chapter Six

~~~~~~~~~~~~

Simon adjusted his cravat and looked in the mirror. On the outside he looked composed and together, but inside he was less certain about what he was about to do. It was his wedding day, a day he had thought might never happen, yet here he was twelve days after proposing to Miss James, ready to get married.

It had been an odd couple of weeks. He had paused his preparations for leaving England, instead spending all his time preparing for his coming nuptials. Obtaining the special licence that allowed them to marry in haste had taken much time and a small fortune. Simon had called on friends throughout the country to exert their considerable influence and get one issued so quickly. It was a relief to know he would not have to change his plans after the wedding.

There was a knock on his door, and he glanced at the clock. There was still fifteen minutes until the ceremony, but he expected the vicar was already downstairs, preparing for the hurried nuptials.

'Come in,' he called, turning to face the door.

The door opened, and Sylvia, his youngest niece, slipped inside. She was six years old, a confident, happy child who managed to hold the whole family in her thrall despite her young age. She had only been one when her father died, and it saddened Simon that she would have no recollection of him at all.

'Good afternoon, little minx.'

She skipped into the room and threw herself down on the bed dramatically.

'Do you have to get married, Uncle?' she asked, clutching her doll to her chest. 'I don't want you to.'

'I have to get married,' Simon said, stopping what he was doing and coming to sit beside her. 'I would not be a very good person if I did not.'

'I wouldn't tell anyone you had been bad.'

'You might not tell anyone, but I would know.'

'What is she like? I probably won't like her.'

'Nonsense, Sylvia. I think you will like her very much.' He hid a grimace. He at least hoped so. Miss James seemed decent and kind, but he barely knew her. In the course of the last twelve days since he'd proposed, he had spent at most an hour in her company, the very minimum he could get away with. The truth was he didn't want to get to know Miss James. He didn't want to know her hopes and fears, her likes and dislikes. It would make leaving harder. This way Miss James remained a stranger, even if they would be married in an hour.

'Is she very pretty, like a princess?'

Simon considered. 'Yes, she is, although not as pretty as you, of course.'

Sylvia giggled and rolled her eyes. 'You have to say that. You're my uncle. Will you come and live with us, now you are to be married?' At present his sister-in-law and nieces lived in one of the many houses that made up the Westcroft estate. It was modest in size, plenty big enough for the growing children, but small enough to feel homely. Simon had offered Westcroft Hall to Maria and her children, insisting they need not move out of the home they had shared when Robert was alive, but his sister-in-law had refused, saying she could not bear to wake up in the bed she had shared with Robert every day, knowing she would never see his smile or feel his arms around her again. It meant Simon reluctantly had moved into Westcroft Hall, feeling as though he were stealing more of his brother's life from him.

'No, little minx,' he said with a sad smile. Of all the things he would miss about England, his nieces were at the top of the list. He loved the time he spent with them, the fun and laughter they brought to his life. They were one of the main reasons he had decided to go too. It was much better he fade from their memory, dead in a distant land, than they witness him expiring in front of them. That sort of thing scarred a person for life.

'I wish you would. I like it most of all when you are there, and I suppose I would learn to like Miss James.'

'Things will change these next few weeks, Sylvia,' he said, his tone serious. He hadn't told anyone of his plans yet, only Miss James who had been sworn to secrecy. Tomorrow he would bid farewell to his mother, his sister-in-law and his nieces before starting his journey south.

'I don't want things to change,' Sylvia said, her voice quiet, and he wondered if she had sensed something big was about to happen, something more than this sudden marriage to Miss James.

'I know it can be hard when things change, but you

must remember that you are surrounded by people who love you.'

Sylvia looked at him with her big eyes and nodded sadly, perhaps sensing there was more than what Simon was saying, more that would unsettle her.

'Sylvia, stop bothering your uncle,' Maria said as she bustled into the room. 'He has a wedding to prepare for.'

'I'm not bothering him. He likes my company,' Sylvia said, smiling cheekily at her mother.

'Go and find your sisters, Sylvia. I need to speak to your uncle in private.'

Sylvia pulled a face but slipped off the bed and left the room. Maria poked her head out the door after a few seconds to check she wasn't listening outside.

'Everything is ready downstairs,' she said, looking at him with concern. Everyone had been treating him like he had gone a little mad the last couple of weeks. The marriage they could understand, even if it was not ideal. He had been caught compromising the reputation of a young lady. Anyone who knew him would understand that he could not let the young woman in question suffer the consequences of their indiscretion alone, but it was the speed of the wedding that was a shock to his family. After delicate enquiries—which he quickly suppressed—as to whether Miss James was expecting a child, his friends and family had started to give him concerned looks all the time. He knew he could fix things by telling them of his plans, but he couldn't bear the burden it would place on them, knowing he too could follow in the path of his father and brother and expire any day.

'Are you sure you want to go through with this?' Maria asked, hovering near the door. 'There would be no shame in a longer engagement. It would allow you to get to know Miss James a little more. Surely that can only be a good thing.'

'Everything is arranged, Maria. The vicar is downstairs. This marriage needs to happen. What is the sense in delaying things?'

Maria bit her lip and stepped closer, laying a hand on his arm. 'If you told me you loved her, that you could not bear to spend a single moment apart from her, then I could understand the rush, but I do not think that is the case. You speak of Miss James with respect but not love.' She studied his face, and Simon felt as though she were looking into his soul. 'There is something more, isn't there?'

He swallowed, knowing if anyone was able to work out that he had been suffering with his headaches it would be Maria. She had watched her husband go through much the same, and he was worried she could see the same patterns emerging in him.

'Let us just enjoy the day,' he said, giving her a smile that he knew didn't reach his eyes.

Maria sighed but nodded, turning to leave.

'I wish you every happiness, Simon,' she said softly at the door. 'I know you think you do not deserve it, but you do.'

He stalled for a few more minutes before heading downstairs, a heavy weight in his stomach. Even though he didn't plan on sticking around to be part of this marriage he was entering into, it was still another person he was taking responsibility for. With one final check in the mirror, he tried to ignore the dark circles under his eyes and walked from his room.

* * *

Alice shifted nervously, wishing her mother would stop fussing and leave her alone. Her parents were understandably delighted by the turn of events; their daughter marrying an earl was beyond their wildest dreams.

It hadn't been all pleasant when she had first told them: they had been furious that she had allowed her reputation to be compromised, and only a visit from Lord Westcroft to assure Mr and Mrs James his intentions were now honourable could quieten their fears Alice would end up deserted and ruined.

Mrs James stepped back and admired her handiwork, tutted and then reached out to fiddle with Alice's hair again. They had been given one of the many bedrooms in Westcroft Hall for her to get ready in, and now Alice stood in the new dress that had been delivered a few days earlier, a gift from Lord Westcroft for their wedding day.

There was a soft knock on the door, and a moment later it opened and the dowager countess, Lord Westcroft's sister-in-law, entered the room.

'Mrs James, I think everything is almost ready downstairs. Perhaps you would like to take a seat with your husband.'

Mrs James flushed and curtsied clumsily, gave Alice a final look-over and then left the room.

The dowager countess smiled at Alice, her expression warm.

'How are you, my dear?'

'I feel as though I have a hundred frogs jumping inside my stomach,' Alice said and then flushed. It was probably too honest an answer.

'I remember my wedding day. I felt much the same. It

was a small affair in the local church, yet I felt as though the whole world was watching me.' She paused and then stepped closer. 'I know this has been thrust upon you both, but Lord Westcroft is a good man. He will do his duty by you and so much more.'

Alice looked away. Lord Westcroft's family were not aware of the nature of their impending marriage. They thought Alice and Lord Westcroft would live together as man and wife, not go their separate ways after the wedding, never to see one another again.

'You are kind, Lady Westcroft.'

She waved a hand. 'You must call me Maria. After today there will be three Lady Westcrofts. Simon's mother, me and now you. Let everyone else tie themselves up in knots working out who they are talking about, but we will be family and can be much more familiar.'

Alice felt the tears prick her eyes. These last few weeks she had felt bereft and uncertain in her decision. Her parents had been focussed on her elevation in status and what that meant for them. Lord Westcroft had been notably absent, sending her notes to update her on the progress of their impending wedding but only spending at most an hour with her in the last few weeks. It was comforting to have a friendly face, someone to make her think she might be welcomed into this family even if Lord Westcroft was not around to help her find her place.

'You will call me Alice?'

'I would be delighted to, Alice. Now, I do not know where you and Simon are planning on setting up your main residence, but whilst you are here in Northumberland we will take tea together at least once a week and go for long walks about the estate. I know how apprehensive you can feel, marrying into such a wealthy and influential family, and if there is anything I can do to help ease your path, you must tell me.'

'That is very kind, Maria.'

She smiled with a mischievous twinkle in her eye. 'Although, of course, I would not dream of interrupting you during the honeymoon period. Simon did not say if you were going away, but I expect he will at least take you on a tour of the residences he owns around the country.'

Alice dropped her gaze. Maria was a perceptive woman, and Alice sensed her future sister-in-law could tell there was something out of the ordinary about this marriage.

After a moment Maria let out an almost imperceptible sigh and then shrugged. 'I think it is time, Alice. Shall we make our way to the drawing room?'

Alice nodded and followed Maria out of the room, her eyes flitting over the dozens of portraits that lined the upstairs hallway. The house was old, with oak panelling in the main parts, with various wings and rooms added on at different points. It meant it had a haphazard charm and a mishmash of different styles throughout. They were in the oldest part here, built in Tudor times with sloping floorboards and walls that leaned first inward then outward. The walk felt as though it took for ever, even though it must have been less than thirty seconds between Alice leaving her room to getting downstairs.

They paused outside the drawing room, with Maria giving her one last squeeze of the hand before she slipped inside. For a moment Alice was left alone. She wondered if she was making a huge mistake. Lord Westcroft was a good man—she could tell that from the little time they had spent together—but she was not going to see him after they had sorted the practicalities of the next few days. She would be a countess, but a lonely one.

Alice squared her shoulders. She had chosen this path, and now she would follow it. The alternative had been worse, and now she had to find a way to make the life she had opted for bearable.

She ran her hands over the gold silk of the wedding dress, swallowing hard as she pushed open the door of the drawing room to see her future husband standing inside.

Chapter Seven

Ten months later

The house was quiet and dark as he approached, and he wondered if all the staff were in bed. It was late, much later than he had planned to arrive, but his ship had been delayed, and he had spent some time wandering the streets, trying to clear his head after the long and stormy voyage.

The last four days it had rained incessantly, a foreboding welcome back to England after nearly a year's absence. He had taken a boat from Italy, a journey that should have taken a little over two weeks, but because of the weather it had been much longer, and at one point he'd thought the captain was going to declare the trip a lost cause and turn around to seek shelter in one of the French ports.

Finally he had arrived home, uncertain how he felt to be back in London after his self-imposed exile.

He looked up at his townhouse and felt a wave of familiarity wash over him. His father had bought this house when Simon was a young boy, and he could remember visiting it for the first time, enthralled by all the sights and smells of London. His father had taken him by the hand and led him up the steps to the front door, then given him a tour of the house room by room, finishing up in the nursery at the very top. He'd pointed out the view over the square, the rooftops of London beyond, and Simon could remember feeling happy.

He'd spent much time there over the years, first with his parents when they travelled to London for the season, then when he was a young man Robert had given him free use of the house whenever he was in London. Since becoming the earl, Simon had been here even more, with his responsibilities often meaning he had to spend months at a time in London rather than in the wilds of Northumberland.

Before his departure to the Continent he had spent a long time ensuring there was enough supervision and funds to run all of his households without his oversight. He had not wanted to burden his mother or sister-in-law with the day-to-day questions that arose from owning a number of properties and employing the staff needed to keep everything running smoothly, so he had made sure there were senior household servants in each house he owned who were happy to take responsibility without the oversight of a master or mistress. He also employed a land steward and his assistant to collect rents and sort any queries from tenants and make decisions on the wider estate business.

Miss Stick was his trusted housekeeper of the London townhouse. Employed by the family for decades, she was a stiff and proper woman in her fifties with a good head for household accounts and just the right mix of authoritarian discipline and warmth to mean servants under her command were fiercely loyal and hardworking. No doubt, at half past midnight Miss Stick and the small complement of servants in the house were long asleep.

He had not sent word he was returning to England. Throughout his journey back he kept telling himself he would write to his mother, to Maria, to his steward to alert them of his plans to return to the country, but he never had. If he searched his soul he knew it was because he had wanted the chance to change his mind, even up until the boat docked and his feet touched English soil.

'Home,' he murmured as he touched the railing outside his house for the first time in many months. It was a strange feeling: for so long he had thought he would never see home again, convinced he would go to die in some foreign country surrounded by strangers. It was surreal to be back, and for much of the last few weeks he had felt as though he were floating through a dream.

He contemplated knocking at the door and decided against it, instead slipping round the side of the house and going through the gate into the small back garden. There were stairs here that led to the kitchen at basement level, and unless things had changed drastically he knew where Miss Stick hid the spare key.

A smile formed on his lips as he reached up to the lip above the door, his fingers closing around the cool metal of the key to the back door. He put it in the lock, turned it and slipped into the house.

Tomorrow it would be a surprise for the housekeeper to find him returned, but tonight at least the servants could sleep. There would be one bedroom at least kept ready for guests, for he was not the only person to use the house. Maria would often make the trip to London to visit friends and family, and less often his mother would too. He knew they weren't here now, though, for he had received a letter from his mother just before he had left Italy telling him that Maria and the children had just returned from London for the summer and that she was pleased to have them back in Northumberland.

Quickly he secured the door behind him and made his way through the kitchen and upstairs to the main part of the house. In the darkness everything looked the same as it always had, and he felt a sense of familiarity and comfort wash over him.

Upstairs he paused outside the bedroom door. There was a chance that his bedroom was not made up ready for someone to sleep in, but if that were the case he could check the others and choose one where the sheets were fresh to lie down on for the night.

He opened the door, surprised to find the room fresh and cool, a slight breeze blowing in through the open window. It was only open a crack, just enough to air the room and keep it at decent temperature despite the humidity outside. It was unlike Miss Stick to allow a window to stay open all night. She would normally cite the crime rate in this part of the city, figures Simon would not be able to refute but which seemed much higher than he would have imagined.

The curtains in the room billowed slightly with the breeze, and it took his eyes a moment to adjust to the darkness of the room. Outside, the moon was obscured by the heavy clouds that still threatened rain despite the days of downpours, and it was hard to see anything beyond the outline of the furniture. He took a few steps towards the large bed and felt the covers, relieved to find bed-sheets under his fingers. Quietly he closed the door and began to undress. His luggage would follow, and he was too weary to go digging through drawers to find any nightclothes so instead he stripped naked to the waist, throwing his clothes onto the chair that sat in the corner of the room, then gripped the bed-sheets and climbed into bed.

As soon as his body slipped between the sheets he knew something was wrong. There was a warmth there that shouldn't have been, the sort of warmth that can only come from a body. Tentatively he reached out, and his hand brushed against warm skin. For a moment he lingered, too shocked to move, and then he felt the person in his bed rolling over. Quickly he scrambled back, but it was too late. A hand shot out and grabbed hold of his wrist, and in the darkness he saw two wide eyes shining in an otherwise pitch-black room.

The woman screamed. It was the loudest sound he had ever heard, a scream filled with terror. He could not imagine anything more petrifying than finding someone else climbing into bed with you at night when you thought you were safe and alone in your room, so he did not blame her, but the sound pierced through him and made it impossible to reassure her.

From somewhere above he heard clattering as servants leaped out of their beds and rushed towards the stairs that would lead them here.

'I mean you no harm,' he said as calmly as he could muster. 'I am sorry.'

His words took a moment to penetrate the noise, but after a few seconds the screaming stopped and was replaced by a quiet whimpering.

'Miss James, is that you?'

'Yes,' she replied after a moment, scrambling to pull the bed-sheets up around her.

'My sincerest apologies. I did not know you would be in London.'

'No,' she murmured, 'I don't suppose you did.' There was a pause as she tried to compose herself, and then she said with more authority, 'It is not Miss James anymore, my Lord. You may have forgotten our marriage, but by law I am still Lady Westcroft.'

Her voice was cool, almost cold, and if the servants hadn't arrived at that very moment he thought she might go on to say more.

'My apologies, Lady Westcroft,' he said quietly.

'What is happening?' Miss Stick said as she rushed into the room, dressing gown billowing around her, cotton mob cap on her head. 'Lord Westcroft?'

Another servant, a maid he did not recognise, came rushing in behind Miss Stick followed by a young footman. The maid was holding a candle, and finally there was light in the room.

He surveyed the scene, a sinking feeling in his stomach. This was not how he had hoped his homecoming would unfold. He'd wanted to slip in, largely unobserved, and make quiet enquiries to bring himself up to date with the world he had left behind before everyone found out he was home. Instead probably every house on the square would know of his midnight return by the morning, no matter how firmly he pressed his servants on the need for discretion.

Simon breathed deeply and then adopted his most commanding tone.

'I am sorry to have disturbed you all. I thought to return without waking the whole household but was not aware Lady Westcroft was in residence.' Momentarily his eyes met his wife's, and then she looked away. 'Please return to your beds and go back to sleep.'

The maid and the footman turned immediately, but Miss Stick called out to stop them.

'The candle, Mary. You cannot expect Lord and Lady Westcroft to be left in the dark.'

The maid blushed and quickly placed the candle on the mantelpiece before curtsying and hurrying from the room.

Miss Stick waited until they had left and lowered her voice.

'The green room is also made up, my Lord, should you need it,' Miss Stick spoke with the practised discretion of a valued servant, making no assumptions, just letting him know the options available.

'Thank you, Miss Stick.'

'Do you need anything, my Lord? My Lady?'

'No, thank you,' he said, watching as the housekeeper turned to his wife. He was amazed to see her normally stern expression soften a little as Lady Westcroft smiled at her.

'No, thank you, Miss Stick. You have been wonderful as usual.'

The housekeeper's lips twitched, and he was surprised to realise she was almost smiling. Then she left the room, closing the door softly behind her.

For a long moment there was nothing but silence between them. The woman in front of him was a stranger, and he could see how invasive it was to have him climb half-naked into her bed. Yet he felt a flicker of irritation along with the regret at not checking the room was empty.

'It is late, Lord Westcroft,' she said, quietly but firmly. She was dressed in a cotton nightgown, and although it was not made of the most substantial material, it had a high neck and long sleeves that covered her modesty, yet she wrapped her arms about her in a way that made him realise she felt uncomfortable. He glanced down at his bare chest and hastily reached for his shirt, discarded on the chair.

'I will leave you to sleep, Lady Westcroft,' he said, gathering the rest of his clothes. 'My apologies again.' It felt strange to be leaving his bedroom, yet he would not think of throwing her out in the middle of the night. Instead he made a hasty retreat, closing the door on the stranger who was his wife.

Chapter Eight

A lice clasped her hands together to stop them from shaking as she paused outside the door to the dining room. Breakfast was normally one of her favourite times of the day. She loved taking her time over the first meal of the day, savouring her toast and eggs whilst she sipped on a steaming cup of delicious coffee. Miss Stick always ensured there was a newspaper ready and available for her to read, alternating between the more serious publications, which ensured she was informed about political and worldly matters, and the gossip sheets that meant she was never behind when it came to the intrigue of the *ton*. Since moving to London eight months previously, she had followed the same routine. Coffee, breakfast and half an hour with the newspaper before she was ready to face the day. It had been peaceful, but now her peace was shattered.

Straightening her back and lifting her chin, she pushed open the door and walked into the room, clenching her jaw as she saw Lord Westcroft was sitting in her favourite seat. It was the one at the head of the table, traditionally the master of the house's spot, but Alice had lived this past year with no husband and no master, and when she had decided to move her breakfast spot to the head of the table, there had been no one to object. That place was set in front of the large window and caught the best of the morning light.

Telling herself not to be so petty she forced a smile onto her face as Lord Westcroft looked up. He was holding her newspaper, the pages slightly crumpled in his hands.

'Good morning, Lady Westcroft. I hope you managed to sleep again after I disturbed you last night. My apologies again.'

'I did, thank you,' she lied. For hours she had lain in bed wondering what this sudden, unexpected return meant for her. Lord Westcroft hadn't deceived her when he had offered her marriage. He had been clear that he would not be there by her side as her husband, but she had not expected his departure to be so sudden, or so complete. One day after their wedding, he had left. Alice had known he had made plans to sail to the Continent but she had assumed he would escort her to her new home first, perhaps introduce her to the servants, be there as she got to know his mother and sister-in-law. A week, perhaps two—it wouldn't have needed long, but instead he had left without doing any of that. He had also made it clear his journey was one way and that she should not expect him back.

She took a seat at the dining table, looking up when Miss Stick came into the room, a frown on her face when she saw Lord Westcroft sitting in Alice's accustomed place, reading her newspaper. Alice felt a rush of warmth for the housekeeper. She had been terrified of her when she had first arrived in London and almost made the decision to flee back to Northumberland, but slowly she had won the housekeeper round, making an ally out of the older woman.

'Good morning, Lady Westcroft. I will tell Cook to make you a fresh cup of coffee and get started on your eggs. Is there anything else you need this morning?'

'No, thank you, Miss Stick. Join me in the drawing room after breakfast, and we can discuss the meals for the week.'

Miss Stick inclined her head and left the room. Alice felt her husband's eyes on her and turned to him.

'If you would be so kind as to inform me of your plans, Lord Westcroft, insofar as planning the meals and social calendar for the week goes, I would appreciate it.'

He looked at her as if she had grown a second head.

'Social calendar?' he murmured.

She held up a hand and counted off on her fingers, 'I have a number of events planned this week. Afternoon tea with the London Ladies' Benevolent Society, dinner parties with the Hampshires and the Dunns, and a fund-raising event at the end of the week. It would be helpful to know if you will be here or not.'

'You live here?' he asked, puzzlement on his face.

'Yes,' she said, slowly.

'In London?'

'Yes.'

'In this house?'

'Where would you prefer I live, my Lord?'

He rallied, and she silently chided herself for her frosty tone, but the situation was impossible. She had made a life for herself here. It had been far from easy, and it had taken months to build the social circle she had now, but it had been worth it. Now that Lord West-croft was back, his purpose as yet undeclared, she felt as though he might suddenly pull it all away from her.

'I thought you were in Northumberland.'

'I spent a few months in Northumberland after we married, then I moved to London.'

'No one said, in their letters.'

Alice looked away, glad when the maid bustled in with a plate of eggs and toast and a steaming pot of coffee.

She hadn't written to Lord Westcroft: there had hardly seemed a point. Her husband was a stranger, a man she had spent very little time with before they were married and even less after. She knew his mother had written detailed letters telling him about the family and the estate, and so had Maria, but she had asked both not to include her in their letters. They had complied, seeing her discomfort of her new position and wanting to do anything to help her feel accepted and settled.

Lord Westcroft waited until they were alone again and then fixed her with an unwavering stare. 'I know it must be a shock, my turning up like this with no warning.'

'It is,' Alice said, buttering her toast a little more vigorously than she normally would. 'But it is your home. I do not know why I am surprised.'

'Perhaps because I told you I was leaving and never coming back,' he said gently.

Alice put down her knife. She could feel the tension in every muscle of her body. For twenty-one years she had not been in control of her own life. She had lived by her parents' rules, tied to the fate they determined for her, and then suddenly she had been granted her freedom. Lord Westcroft had given her a great gift, she knew that, and her coolness towards him now was only because she feared she might lose that freedom. She exhaled slowly, suppressing the uncertainty and the fear, and turned to her husband.

'How are you?' she said, studying him properly. 'It is good to see you looking so well.'

Simon felt the weight of her scrutiny. Her eyes took their time as she looked over his face and body. He knew what she would see, something entirely unexpected: a man who had gone away to die looking healthier and stronger than ever before.

'I am well,' he said quietly. 'At least, I think I am.'

'You think...?'

He sighed heavily and glanced out the window to where the sunshine was reflecting off the puddles that lay on the street. It had been a difficult truth to come to terms with, almost as difficult as thinking he was dying.

'I told you of my father and brother, their headaches, their sudden deaths,' he said, hoping he would not have to go through the painful history again.

'Yes, I remember, and your mother told me a little more after we were married, after you left.'

'Yes, she suffered terribly. First her husband, then her eldest son. Both struck down in their prime when they had young families to care for.'

'When you left you were getting awful headaches,' Lady Westcroft prompted gently. 'It was the reason you were so keen to leave so quickly.'

'I'd been having them for some time on a daily basis. I'd consulted two reputable doctors, and after listening to the story of my father and brother they both told me the same thing.' He paused, remembering the first time a doctor had looked him in the eye and told him he was going to die. 'They told me in all likelihood I would be dead before the year was out.'

'They couldn't have known that,' she murmured, shaking her head.

'They spoke of a malformation of the vessels in the brain, a condition that runs in families. Apparently it has been seen in cadavers when they have undergone dissection for medical training. Evidence of a catastrophic bleed in the brain and a story of headaches before death.'

She looked away, her fork pushing the egg around on her plate before she laid it down and picked up her cup of coffee, cradling it with both hands.

'They told you that was what would happen to you?'

'Yes.'

'That's terrible.'

'At the time I felt like it only confirmed my suspicions.'

She took a sip of coffee and then looked over at him. 'Yet you're still here and look as healthy as a man in his prime.'

'When I left I was having daily headaches, but over the next few months they gradually dwindled.'

He had been unable to believe it at first, thinking it was perhaps just a short reprieve, but as he had travelled farther from England, his headaches had become fewer. He'd settled in a remote part of Italy, high in the Tuscan hills. It was beautiful there, and for the first time in a long time he had felt at peace.

'When I had been in Italy for two months I sought the advice of an eminent physician in Florence. I explained my symptoms and what had happened to my father and my brother. He told me it was not yet my time to die.'

Lady Westcroft's eyes widened, and she had a look of incredulity on her face. 'Did he explain the headaches?'

Simon shifted uncomfortably. 'He said they were likely caused by the huge amount of stress I was under, imagining myself dying.' For some reason it felt uncomfortable to admit it, that he had brought the headaches on himself. 'He told me it was self-perpetuating. The first time I got a headache I thought it must be the start of the same condition they had died from. The stress of that thought meant I woke every day with a headache that would not relent.'

'It is easy to see how that could happen,' Lady Westcroft said. Now she had lost her frostiness towards him, she seemed more like the reasonable young woman he had proposed to. He watched her as she sipped her coffee. He was ashamed to admit he had not thought much about her this past year. His guilt had been over leaving his mother and sister-in-law behind, along with his young nieces. They had been the reason he had returned, not the wife he had almost forgotten about.

It was only a year ago he had left, a little less, yet he realised Lady Westcroft *had* changed. Not physically, at least not at first glance, but there was something about her manner, a poise and confidence that she hadn't had before. When they had married she had seemed overwhelmed by the wealth and status of the family she was marrying into, yet now she sat in this dining room confident in her role as mistress of the house. He even thought he'd seen her eyeing his chair at the head of the table when she'd entered.

'I am truly glad you are not dying, Lord Westcroft,' she said softly.

'Thank you. So am I.' He paused, deciding to be entirely candid with her. 'The doctor in Italy said there was a good possibility I had the same condition as my father and brother, that he could not guarantee I would not be plagued by the headaches that were the harbinger of a sudden death, but he urged me to resume my life and said it might happen in a year or in forty years.'

'So here you are,' Lady Westcroft said.

'Here I am.'

She glanced at the clock on the mantelpiece and put down her cup of coffee. Her breakfast lay barely touched on her plate.

'I am sure you are still finalising your plans, my Lord,' she said, standing and dropping into a formal little curtsy. 'When you have decided what you will be doing and where you will be staying, please let me know. Now I must leave you. I have an engagement I forgot about.'

Before he had a chance to answer, she turned and hurried out the room. He had the sense she was escaping him, running away from having to interact with him anymore. Leaning back in his chair he laced his fingers together in front of his chest. At least he had begun the conversation between them. Throughout his voyage home he had avoided thinking too much of his accidental wife. In his mind she was living quietly in one of his properties in Northumberland, taking long country walks and occupying herself with needlework or watercolours. He'd thought he would have time before he told her the circumstances of their marriage had changed, that she was no longer wife to an absent husband. He'd imagined arranging a time to meet as they discussed how their lives would continue now he was home. With a groan he remembered instead how he had climbed into bed with her after a year of no contact whatsoever. Never would he be able to rid himself of the terrified look on her face or the awful scream as she saw him in the darkness.

He sighed. It was a lot for her to take in, yet all he wanted was to reassure her. In the main her life need not change. There was no requirement for them to live as husband and wife, even if he were in the country. She could stay at one property, he another. Lady Westcroft was a sensible woman; he may have only known her for a short time, but he had been able to tell that from their acquaintance before their marriage. She was sensible, and he was sure with a little time she would see their arrangement could continue without too much disruption.

For a second he thought back to the kiss they had shared in the garden of Lady Salisbury's party on Midsummer's Eve the year before. It had been a magical moment, and for a few minutes he had allowed himself to imagine a different future.

Quickly he shook his head. It wasn't to be. He had decided long ago he was never going to marry or have children. He had broken his first vow when his hand had been forced after meeting the now Lady Westcroft that fateful Midsummer's Eve, but that didn't mean he had to change his whole life's philosophy.

Chapter Nine

Alice looked round the room in satisfaction. There was a low hum of chatter and everyone was smiling and seeming to have a good time. The London Ladies' Benevolent Society had been established long before she had arrived in London, but she had found them a lacklustre group of four elderly women of the upper-middle class who had good intentions but not much idea as to how to implement them. In the last six months, since she had taken the helm of the society, it had gone from strength to strength. They now had regular monthly meetings, the location of which rotated between the homes of the more influential members, and held fundraising activities every couple of months too. Alice was well aware that initially many of the ladies had only agreed to be part of it so they could get the measure of her, the mysterious new countess that no one knew anything about, but she hoped that now they saw the benefits of a well-run society that could help them focus their philanthropic efforts.

She took a sip of tea and tried to focus on what Lady Kennington was saying as she rapped earnestly on the arm of the sofa with her fan.

'It just is not good enough. These poor orphans are dressed in rags, given gruel to eat and not even taught their letters or numbers, then society acts surprised when they go on to be the next generation of beggars and criminals. There needs to be better provision for them.'

'There is not endless money, though, Lady Kennington,' Mrs Taylor said. She was a wealthy widow who donated both her time and money generously. Alice was pleased at how she had chipped away at the hierarchical structure these last few months. She'd wanted all members to feel they had a voice, an opinion, whether they be duchess or doctor's wife.

'No, there is not. Yet I wonder whether the conditions the poor orphans find themselves in isn't at least a little deliberate. There is a large proportion of society who think people should stay within their own social status. We have all seen how the self-made man is snubbed at society events, even when he is the wealthiest in the room.'

'Do you have a solution, Lady Kennington?' Alice asked. A few months ago she would have worried that there was an unspoken agenda when there was talk of people staying within their own social class, but she had learned it was best to act oblivious to people's opinions. If they never saw you react, they soon got bored and started talking about someone else.

'St Benedict's Home for Orphaned Children,' Lady Kennington announced with a triumphant smile. 'A small orphanage near the slums of St Giles. I think they have beds for twelve girls and twelve boys. At the moment it is in the poorest part of the city, and the children are lucky to reach their fourteenth birthday, when they are thrown back out on the streets.'

'I think I know the one you mean,' Alice said, thinking of the dilapidated building that looked as though it would collapse with the slightest gust of wind.

'We cannot intervene everywhere, but I propose we invest some of our funds there. Make a difference for those twenty-four children and use them as a study to present to Parliament to show the benefits to all society if we look after the poorest amongst us.'

Alice felt a shiver run through her at the idea. More than anything she wanted to make a difference for children. It had been hard coming to terms over the last year with the fact that she would not have children of her own, at least not anytime soon. She had begun to build a relationship with her beautiful nieces, the three children her sister-in-law had gracefully helped her bond with, and she had also recently returned from a short trip to see her own sister and little nephew. She could surround herself with children to love even if she could have none of her own yet, but she also wanted to make a difference to some of the orphaned and destitute children of London. The unwavering support of someone as influential as Lady Kennington would mean projects like St Benedict's Orphanage were much more likely to become success stories.

She was surprised when the door opened and Lord Westcroft walked into the room. He in turn looked stunned by two dozen women crowded into his drawing room, and Alice saw him stiffen and then glance over his shoulder, but it was too late. He had been spotted.

'Lord Westcroft,' Lady Kennington called, beaming at

him. 'You have returned from your travels.' She turned to Alice and said admonishingly, 'You should have told us, my dear. This is exciting news.'

No one else noticed the fraction of a second's hesitation before Lord Westcroft smiled indulgingly and stepped into the room as if he had always planned to spare a few minutes of his time with the ladies. He moved between groups of people smoothly, greeting old acquaintances and bowing to new ones, and Alice watched in wonder as he left each group beaming with pleasure at the small snippet of attention he bestowed upon them. He went round the room before approaching Alice and her little group, greeting Lady Kennington and speaking warmly to Mrs Taylor.

'This is quite the gathering, Lady Westcroft,' he said, looking around.

'Hard to believe six months ago the London Ladies' Benevolent Society was four elderly women and a small pot of donations,' Lady Kennington said, patting Alice on the hand. 'Lady Westcroft has done a marvellous job at getting everyone so interested and invested in the society.'

Lord Westcroft smiled politely and then turned to Alice. 'I hate to take you away from your gathering, but there are one or two things we need to discuss quickly. Shall we step outside?'

Lady Kennington chuckled under her breath and leaned into Mrs Taylor. 'I remember that first blush of love. Only back a day and already he's finding excuses to pull his wife aside.'

Alice didn't respond but stood, smoothing her skirt, and followed Lord Westcroft from the room.

The London house was a good size for a townhouse, but it wasn't large compared to Lord Westcroft's other residences. Downstairs there was the drawing room, the dining room, another small, cosier reception room and Lord Westcroft's study. The study was the only room in the house she had never made herself at home in. It had felt too personal somehow, even though until yesterday she had been under the impression Lord Westcroft was never going to return.

He led her into the study now, closing the door quietly behind him.

'There are a lot of women in our drawing room,' he said.

'I think I mentioned the meeting of the London Ladies' Benevolent Society.'

'I expected something…different.' He leaned against the edge of the desk, his posture relaxed, and the expression on his face one of curiosity rather than annoyance. She had been well aware that he would be surprised by the invasion of his home by twenty-four benevolently minded women and hadn't known how he would take it. She was pleasantly surprised to find he wasn't angry or ordering everyone out, merely curious. 'You came to London less than a year ago for the first time ever?'

'Yes.'

'You knew no one?'

She shook her head.

'Yet here you are, with some of the wealthiest women in England taking tea in our drawing room.'

'You left, my Lord,' Alice said, holding up a hand to stall the interruption she knew was coming. 'I am not placing any blame. You told me exactly what would happen once we were married, but I do not think I had truly understood. I was alone, completely alone. Independent, wealthy, no longer obliged to do what my parents wanted of me. Yet I was lost.'

He shifted, and for a moment Alice thought he might reach out and take her hand. She chided herself at the surge of anticipation she felt at the idea, especially when he merely crossed one leg over the other and rested his hand back on the edge of the desk.

'I could either sit in one of your houses in Northumberland, waiting for you to die so my life could start again, or I could choose to build something for myself now. The first option was just too depressing so I chose the second.'

There was silence for a moment, and she glanced up at his face, relieved to see he was smiling, albeit sadly. 'I left you with quite the dilemma. Please do not misconstrue my intentions in speaking with you now. I am impressed, not annoyed. I think it is a miracle you have managed to get society to accept you so readily, let alone chair a benevolent charity.'

'You do not mind the twenty-four women sitting in your drawing room?'

He grimaced and then shrugged. 'It is not what I would have chosen for my first day back in London, but I acknowledge I did not give you any notice of my return so it would be unreasonable for you to keep the house quiet and not have social plans.' Lord Westcroft paused, looking at her intently before continuing. 'I am keen to discuss our situation and how we will manage things going forward, though.'

Alice felt a bubble of nerves deep inside. She wondered if he would expect her to remove herself to the countryside. So far since returning, he had been polite but distant. She was fast realising that she was still an afterthought in his life. Whatever his reasons for coming back to England, she was not one of them. Alice tried not to be hurt by the realisation she was once again close to the bottom of his list of priorities. She prided herself on being a rational woman and knew Lord Westcroft had given her so much when he married her to protect her reputation, so it felt ungrateful to want him to think more of her, yet it hurt when she felt like a problem to be solved.

She turned away, needing a moment to compose herself. When she turned back it was with steely determination. This might be Lord Westcroft's house, but she had worked hard this last year to find her footing in London, and she wasn't going to scurry back to Northumberland just because it made his life a little more convenient and allowed him to forget he had a wife. If he found it too uncomfortable to be here with her, then he could leave, but she was not going to quietly give up everything she had built for herself these last few months.

'I shall look at my calendar, my Lord,' she said, ensuring her tone was polite and courteous. 'Now, if you will excuse me, I must return to my guests.'

She didn't wait for his response, turning and leaving the study quickly and closing the door behind her. As she walked back through the hall she realised her hands were shaking, and she paused for a moment before re-entering the drawing room, fixing her face into a warm and happy expression that she didn't quite feel.

'Good Lord, Westcroft, you leave the country to die and come back looking healthier than the rest of us put together,' William Wetherby said as he clapped Simon on the back. Wetherby was an old friend, their friendship forged in the difficult days when they had both been sent away to school. Wetherby had been a scrawny lad from a once-wealthy family that had fallen on hard times. He'd had his place at Eton paid for by a generous aunt but had been mercilessly teased about his old clothes and lack of funds to spend in the local town.

Now Wetherby had grown into a giant of a man, broad across the chest with a thick dark beard and a muscular build. He was no longer poor either, having spent the last decade building up a thriving importing business.

Simon smiled, a little surprised at how pleased he felt to see his old friend. When he had left England he had thought it would be the last time he saw anyone he knew. At the time, he had told himself he'd made his peace with that, but now he realised that wasn't the case.

'It is good to see you, Wetherby,' Simon said, accepting the embrace his old friend pulled him into. Wetherby had always been effusive, and the years hadn't changed him in that respect.

There were a few other men gathered nearby who greeted him and shook his hand. London society was made up of a relatively small number of people, and even the men he did not know well he was acquainted with. After a minute Wetherby guided Simon to a corner table and motioned for a couple of drinks to be brought over.

In his youth Simon had not enjoyed the atmosphere in the exclusive gentlemen's club that his father and brother had attended and his membership was expected, but as he had grown older he had come to appreciate the quiet, luxurious atmosphere the club afforded. It was a place to escape many of the demands made on his time, and when he needed it to, it allowed him to spend an hour or so alone with his thoughts.

'I find myself fearful to enquire after your health,' Wetherby said as they sat facing each other.

Not many people knew of the terrible headaches Simon had suffered before he left England, nor the fear he had harboured that the headaches were a sign he would soon die, but he had taken Wetherby into his confidence when he sought his help with obtaining the special licence for his marriage almost a year earlier. Wetherby had worked tirelessly, calling in favours from various friends and acquaintances, to make sure Simon could marry before he left England.

'The headaches have all but gone. A doctor in Florence tells me it is not my time to leave this earth just yet.'

'That is a relief.' Wetherby eyed him cautiously. 'So you are back for good?'

For a long moment Simon didn't answer. It was a question he had put off thinking about throughout his trip home. When it became apparent his headaches were abating, he had been left unsure what to do. The doctor in Florence had been clear he wasn't giving Simon the reassurance that he wouldn't one day succumb to the same condition that had killed his father and brother, just the likelihood that it wouldn't be yet. For a few months after this news, Simon had stalled, trying to enjoy the solitude in his remote Tuscan villa, but all the while, home had been calling.

He had wanted to see his mother and sister-in-law, to receive the bear hugs he loved so much from his nieces and see how they had grown. He felt a deep unease at abandoning his responsibilities and the need to remove the burden he had placed on so many when he had left. More than all of that, to his surprise, was this burning desire to be home. Italy was beautiful and peaceful, but he felt the pull of the familiar.

Yet now he was back, he needed to decide what the future would look like. The likelihood that one day he would die suddenly and violently hadn't changed, it was merely the time frame that had been altered in his mind. He still didn't want anyone he loved to witness his death, and that would mean keeping his distance, yet his heart called for the opposite.

He shifted uncomfortably in his chair. Then there was the question of his wife. He pushed the thought aside. Lady Westcroft made an already complicated situation even more difficult to untangle.

'At least for a while. I will head to Northumberland soon. I wanted to reacclimatise myself to life in England before heading back home, but I should see the family soon.'

'I expect you wanted to see your wife too,' Wetherby said, his eyes flicking up to examine Simon's expression.

'In truth I did not realise she was in London.'

'She has been here for quite a time now. Lady Westcroft has made a significant impression on London society.'

Simon raised an eyebrow. It was clear what his friend said was true: his wife had a busy social calendar and chaired a benevolent society despite arriving in London a mere eight months earlier with no friends and no connections.

'You have met her?'

'Of course. I invited her to share my box at the opera just last week,' Wetherby said as he leaned forward. 'She is your countess, Westcroft, although I hasten to give her credit for the impression she has made. People gave her a chance because you married her, but she has grasped hold of that chance and charmed everyone at every opportunity.'

'It does seem as though she has been busy.' He thought back to the wide-eyed, uncertain girl he had met at the masquerade ball. No one could deny the change in his wife since then, and perhaps it was to be expected. He had left her to fend for herself, and she had thrived. He was pleased for her—the last thing he wanted was for her to be unhappy—but he felt a little uncomfortable too, although if he was asked to articulate why, he would have found it difficult.

'You will take her back to Northumberland with you?'

'I will ask, but I get the impression Lady Westcroft has a full social calendar these next few weeks.'

Wetherby laughed. 'I expect she does. Her company is very much in demand.'

Simon felt a flicker of guilt. There was a lot to feel guilty about with respect to his wife. He'd married her and then abandoned her, and even though he had been completely honest with her before their marriage, he had known that she wouldn't have quite understood the realities of the change in her circumstance. Now he had this horrible feeling that he had trapped her. The deal he had promised her was a short marriage to save her reputation, followed by the freedom of widowhood. She would be wealthy enough to make her own decisions and, after a short period of mourning, could either cultivate a life as a wealthy widow or start to look for a second husband, someone she could share a full and proper marriage with.

He swallowed hard, covering the movement by raising his glass to his lips. He had the sense that he had stolen her life away from her and as yet she wasn't quite aware of it. If he lived for another forty years she would be trapped in this union, never experiencing a love match, never getting to have children of her own. It was not what he had promised her.

He took another gulp of his drink before setting the glass down on the table. Somehow they would find a way through this mess, but he had an overwhelming feeling that he had deceived Lady Westcroft. Never had he pressed her to marry him, only laid it out as an option, but he wasn't sure she would have accepted if she had known it would mean being tied to him for an indeterminate amount of time, unable to move on with a life of her own.

'How are you, Wetherby?' Simon asked, wanting to change the subject, needing the distraction of talking about something else for a while.

'I am well, thank you. I leave in a few weeks for a trip to Africa. I hear the earth is littered with diamonds in places, and I want to see for myself whether this is true.'

Simon grinned. His friend had always had difficulty staying in one place for too long, and every few years would announce a new voyage. Wetherby had shaken off the bad luck that had made him an easy victim during their schooldays and seemed to find success in each of his ventures. Even if the ground wasn't littered with diamonds, no doubt there would be some opportunity his friend would spot and bend to his advantage.

'I must leave you,' Wetherby said, standing and clapping him on the shoulder. 'We should talk properly, perhaps when you are back from Northumberland, but today I have a prior engagement with an architect.' He leaned in closer. 'The chap is a genius, and I'm trying to persuade him to take time away from his other projects to build me a nice little house in the Sussex countryside.'

'I wish you luck,' Simon said, rising and shaking Wetherby's hand.

He was left alone with his thoughts, wondering how to make things right with Lady Westcroft, but aware that short of dying there was no way of delivering the life he had promised her.

Chapter Ten

Simon had risen early, keen to busy himself with some of the many things he had neglected in the time he had been away. He had spent much of the morning going over correspondence that had been kept for him whilst he was in Italy and then around lunchtime had met with his solicitor to discuss some minor legal issues that needed his input. Although he had not consciously sought to avoid Lady Westcroft, he was aware that he had organised his morning so their paths were unlikely to cross.

Now that he was walking home he had a sinking feeling in his stomach. It wasn't that he disliked his wife—far from it. Despite hardly knowing her he felt certain she was good and kind, a sweet young woman who had thrived in difficult circumstances. In a way, that made what he was doing to her even worse. His return had once again thrown her life into turmoil.

Simon slowed as he approached the Serpentine. He had decided to take the longer route through the park back to his townhouse, enjoying the warmth of the early-summer afternoon and also feeling a need to delay his return when he might have to sit and have a serious discussion with his wife about their futures.

As he paused to look at the water, a group of about a dozen ladies seated on the grass a little way from its edge caught his eye. They were finely dressed and as he looked closer he realised he recognised one or two, his eyes sweeping over the group until they settled on the pretty, petite form of his wife. She was dressed in dark blue, a colour that served to accentuate the red in her hair and the beautiful porcelain paleness of her skin. She looked relaxed, leaning back on her hands as she turned her head to talk to the woman next to her.

None of the ladies had spotted him, and so for a moment he just watched Lady Westcroft. She was mesmerising. It was undeniable she was pretty, but that quality became enchanting when she smiled. The smile was natural and easy on her lips, and Simon felt himself drawn to her as he had been on the night of the masquerade ball. He wanted to stride over and pull her into his arms, tracing the softness of her face with his fingers, making it so her smile was directed at only him.

It was an unsettling feeling, and quickly he tried to dampen it. The last thing he needed now was to feel attraction towards his wife. He needed a clear head in the negotiations that were to come about their future, and feeling desire for the woman whose life he was ruining would not help.

As he watched, two young children ran up to the group, talking excitedly to the woman who sat beside Lady Westcroft. The boy had a model boat in his hand and was gesticulating at the Serpentine. Their mother laughed indulgently, but it was Lady Westcroft who stood and took the boy's hand, allowing him to lead her down to the water. She crouched down in between the little boy and girl, listening intently to what they said and then helped them set the boat on the water. On the first attempt it wobbled and nearly capsized, and he found himself smiling as Lady Westcroft threw her head back and laughed alongside the children. The second attempt was more successful, and they stayed watching the boat as it bobbed along in the water.

Simon felt a pang of sadness, both for himself and his wife. He could see by this simple interaction how good Lady Westcroft was with children. Despite not spending the time to get to know her hopes and dreams for the future, he could remember her talking of the idea of children fondly and this being the main concern when weighing up whether she should accept his proposal for the marriage to save her reputation.

At the time, the offer he had made called for her to postpone her desire for a family, but now, with the question of his mortality very much unclear, it might be that Lady Westcroft would never have children of her own.

Simon was about to turn away when his wife glanced up, looking directly at him. For a moment she did not move and then she stood, inclining her head in an invitation for him to join her.

With a sinking heart he walked over slowly. In all this mess he could not deny his own disappointment, even though he felt guilty for even considering trying to live a normal life. Once, long before he had lost his brother, he had assumed he would marry and have a family of his own. Now he knew that would never happen, and even though he'd had years to get used to the idea, sometimes he yearned for a normal life. Then he felt guilty for being so selfish when he was lucky to be alive while his brother was not.

'Lord Westcroft, I did not expect to see you here in the park,' Lady Westcroft said. She spoke warmly although addressed him formally. He was once again impressed at how much she had learned these last few months in London. Not only had she gained the support of the most influential in society, she had quickly refined her country manners that might make her stand out as different.

'I had an appointment with my solicitor and thought I would take the scenic route home. It is a beautiful afternoon.'

'It is indeed. We were meant to meet at Mrs Lattimer's for tea, but no one could resist when she suggested an outing to the park instead.' Lady Westcroft motioned behind her to the woman she had been sitting next to.

Simon looked round, nodding in greeting to the ladies he was acquainted with. They were watching him with open curiosity, no doubt keen to see how he interacted with the wife he had left behind after a single day of marriage.

'I do not want to disturb you.'

She looked up at him with a half-smile on her face. When he had left ten months earlier, she had seemed young and innocent; now there was an air of experience in her poised demeanour, and Simon knew he was responsible for forcing her to grow up.

'It is good to see you, my Lord. I have hardly set eyes on you since you returned to England.'

Simon attempted to smile but struggled to produce more than a twitch of his lips, surprised again at how forgiving his wife seemed. He'd abandoned her in a world she did not know, and now he was threatening to rock the life she had made for herself again.

'Shall we take a little stroll? I am sure Sebastian and Lilith will not mind.' With natural ease Lady Westcroft crouched down and swept the model boat from the water, handing it back to Sebastian. 'We do not want it to sail out into the middle of the lake. I do not relish the idea of wading out to fetch it.'

Sebastian giggled and then wrapped his chubby arms around her neck. Simon watched as his wife's face flushed with joy. Lady Westcroft waited until the two children were safely back in the care of their nanny before she turned her attention back to Simon.

'They are sweet children,' she said with a smile as she followed his gaze before lowering her voice. 'Sometimes I find myself envious of their nanny. I am sure behind closed doors they are sometimes a terror, but you would not believe it when you see them in public.'

'Have you had a pleasant day?'

'Yes, thank you. I spent some time going through the household accounts with Miss Stick this morning. A mere formality, as she is the most organised of house-keepers I have ever met, but I like to learn how to do these things, and she is a good teacher. Then this after-noon has been spent in the sunshine with friends.'

'It does sound a nice way to spend an afternoon,' Simon murmured.

She looked at him curiously. 'I do have a good life, my Lord. I am aware how lucky I am.'

So much hung unsaid between them, and Simon knew they would have to address it soon, but he didn't want to do that here with everyone watching them. What he had to say would be better received in private where Lady Westcroft would have the freedom to react without having to think of who was watching.

They walked a little farther along the path, arm-in-arm. Half her face was in shadow from the bonnet that was tied firmly under her chin, and it made it difficult to work out what she might be thinking.

Simon wished for a moment that this was their life, an easy happiness where all they had to worry about was which social invitations to accept and which to refuse. Quickly he pushed the thought away. The idea of a conventional marriage to Lady Westcroft was tempting as he walked beside her. She was kind and sensible and pleasant to be around. He couldn't deny the flicker of desire he felt every time she looked at him with those blue eyes or the way something clenched deep inside him when she smiled. Yet it was a temptation he could never give in to. It would be unfair, with his future so uncertain. It would be better to offer her a deal where they both led separate but contented lives, only occasionally meeting.

As if sensing his thoughts, she turned to face him again, her eyes rising to meet his. 'You seem troubled, my Lord.'

He cleared his throat but couldn't find the words.

'Is something amiss?'

'I watched you for a moment with those children. You were very good with them.'

'I like children.'

'I know.'

She held his gaze, something defiant in her eyes as if pushing him to confront the big issue that stood between them.

'Would you like children, Lady Westcroft?' The question came out much more directly than he meant it to, but with her standing so close he felt as if his thoughts were all scrambled.

It took her a moment to reply, and when she did her tone was much more formal. 'I understand the limits of our marriage, Lord Westcroft, and I am not a naïve girl any more. I understand a marriage has to be consummated for there to be children.' Her cheeks flushed as she spoke, and he felt like a cad.

'Forgive me, I did not meant to cause you pain. I...' He was unsure how to put into words the turmoil he felt inside. It was impossible to know how to tell Lady Westcroft that because of his mistake in making the assumption that he was dying, he had stolen from her the future he had promised.

She turned away, but before she did, he saw the tears glistening in her eyes.

'I must return to my friends, my Lord,' she said, already beginning to move away. 'Perhaps I shall see you at home later this evening.'

He inclined his head, watching her as she walked back to the group of ladies a little distance away. As he turned to leave he felt a wave of guilt almost consume him. He needed space and time, some way to come up with a plan where no one suffered too much. Here in London, he felt as though everything was pressing in, threatening to crush him.

It was growing dark outside when Alice sat down to see to her mound of correspondence. She had a letter from each of her nieces to reply to, each of different lengths dependent on their ages, and one from Maria as well. She wondered if her sister-in-law knew of Lord Westcroft's return and realised she shouldn't be the one to tell her. No doubt her husband would contact his family soon, if he hadn't already. Gossip travelled at an unbelievable pace, and he had been seen by half the wealthy women in London that afternoon when he had stumbled upon Alice and her friends in Hyde Park. It might be hundreds of miles to the Westcroft estate in Northumberland, but the news of his return would be up there before the month was out.

She enjoyed the ritual of letter-writing and took her time selecting her pen and positioning the paper, ensuring she had good candlelight so as not to strain her eyes.

As she was about to put pen to paper she paused, hearing footsteps in the hallway outside and then a knock on the door. She turned to see Miss Stick entering, holding something in her hand.

'Lord Westcroft asked me to give this to you, my Lady,' Miss Stick said. The older woman was always polite and formal, but Alice had gone to great efforts to get to know the housekeeper in recent months. She could see something was wrong and took the letter in trepidation.

She was puzzled to see her husband's seal on the back and glanced up at Miss Stick briefly.

'I am sorry, my Lady. He left about an hour ago.'

With a sinking feeling she opened the note and let her eyes skim over the words. It was brief, only a couple of sentences, explaining he needed to go and see his family, to tell them he was back before the gossip reached them. There was no indication of when he might come back to London, just an apology for leaving so soon.

For a second she slumped, feeling rejected once again, then forced herself to rally.

'Lord Westcroft has gone,' she said to Miss Stick. 'There is no word as to when he will return. I expect he will stay in Northumberland for some time.'

Miss Stick's expression softened slightly, and then she nodded and held Alice's eye. 'There will be no change to your plans then, my Lady? Everything will continue as normal?'

'Everything will continue as normal,' Alice confirmed.

Once she was alone Alice allowed her control to slip and slumped in her chair. He hadn't even bothered to say goodbye. She could justify his behaviour all she liked, but that was hard to bear. She understood he would have been keen to return to his family, to be the one to tell them he was back in the country so they weren't surprised by the information from someone else, yet it would only have taken a few minutes to bid her farewell.

She thought back to their conversation that afternoon and knew it had likely played a part in why he was so quick to rush away. They were two strangers thrown together by a foolish kiss almost a year earlier. Now he had returned, it would be difficult to unpick the tangled strands of their lives and find a way to live comfortably with one another, whether that meant together or apart. She could see he was struggling with that, but it didn't mean his leaving so abruptly was painless.

Alice looked at the note again. It was short, only a couple of sentences, informing her he was leaving immediately to travel north and see his family.

'There's nothing wrong with that,' she murmured, trying to convince herself. She took a deep breath and pressed her hands down on the little writing desk, refusing to let this latest development throw her off course.

Loudly she exhaled and stood, pacing back and forth across the room. She had known before they married that she would not have a conventional union. But he had told her that her life would be one way, and now it had completely changed. Of course she was pleased he was not going to die alone, far away from family, but she would like a little acknowledgement that his return affected her as well as him.

With an effort she paused by the window, setting her shoulders and lifting her chin. This was a good lesson to learn. Her husband might be back, but he was not ever going to see her as anything more than the woman he married to save her from ruin. She could not expect affection from or companionship with him, instead she would have to continue as she had been, building a life she was content in, even if she were alone.

Chapter Eleven

⟡

The house was quiet as he approached on horseback, each window in darkness despite it being only a little past nine o'clock. This time he had made sure he sent word of his return to London from Northumberland, allowing both his wife and the servants to prepare for his arrival. He wondered if Lady Westcroft had moved from the master bedroom or if she would expect him to sleep elsewhere now she had claimed it as her own this past year. In truth he did not really mind; he'd woken up in many different bedrooms over his lifetime, and another change would not unsettle him. What it did do was highlight one of the many issues they would have to sort out now he had returned to London.

The door opened quickly, and Frank Smith, the young footman, hurried out to hold the reins of his horse to lead it to the back of the house where there was a small stable. Both Simon's father and brother had been keen horsemen, as was he, and his father had added a stable large enough for three horses on the patch of land behind the house. It meant the garden was smaller than it could be, but the horses did not have to be stabled elsewhere whilst he was in residence.

Inside the house was quiet, but Miss Stick came to greet him in the hall and take his hat and gloves.

'Where is Lady Westcroft?' He had spent the journey mentally cataloguing all the issues they needed to discuss now he was back in England, from where they would both live to how they should handle enquiries into their personal lives.

'At the Livingstone ball tonight, my Lord. I doubt she will be back until the early hours of the morning. She tells me it is one of the biggest events of the year, even if half of London has left for their country residences already.'

He frowned. He hadn't considered the possibility his wife would not be at home. He had to admit he had not thought of Lady Westcroft much this past year, but when he had, he'd never thought she would be out enjoying the balls and dinner parties of a London season. Of course he did not begrudge her a little fun, but he was keen to discuss their plans for the future, and after spending the best part of a week on the road to get back to London, he did not want to delay any longer. He'd been a mess when he had left London so abruptly a few weeks earlier, and he regretted fleeing without properly taking his leave of his wife. He wanted to apologise and to begin to discuss the future that they inevitably shared.

'The Livingstone ball?'

'Yes, my Lord. They live just off Grosvenor Square, I believe.'

He checked the time and then nodded decisively. He would go to the ball. Although he had not responded to any invitation, he would not be turned away, and if Lady

Westcroft was there already there would be some expectation that he be in attendance too.

'I need to freshen up and change, then I will go to the ball at the Livingstones' house.'

'Very good, my Lord. We do not have anyone employed as your valet at the moment, but I will send young Smith up with everything you need just as soon as he hands over your horse to the stable-boy.

'Thank you.'

'You're in the green bedroom,' Miss Stick said, watching him carefully. Many men would refuse to let their wives have the master bedroom, but Simon merely nodded his head and made his way up the stairs.

Ninety minutes later he was standing on the threshold of Mr and Mrs Livingstone's house, wondering if he had made a terrible mistake. Mr Livingstone was obscenely wealthy, having made his money in importing luxury fabrics. It was said even Queen Charlotte waited excitedly for Mr Livingstone's shipments to arrive at the docks and would get first refusal on anything new and exotic. The house was illuminated by hundreds of candles, and even from the doorstep he could hear the loud hum of conversation over the music. If he stepped into the ballroom he would be seen by half the *ton* within seconds, and news of his second return to London would spread quickly.

After a moment he pushed aside the doubts, telling himself he had to return to society at some point. Over the next few months he would need to step up and ensure everything for his tenants was running smoothly and see if there was any work that needed doing to his properties, but he would also have to take up his role as earl again in more public ways. In October he would be expected to return to Parliament, and there were always obligations throughout the social season.

The door opened, and he was welcomed into the house. Thankfully the ball was well underway with a dozen couples dancing in the middle of the ballroom whilst everyone else watched from the sides, talking in little huddles.

'Lord Westcroft, we were not expecting you,' Mrs Livingstone said, hurrying over as soon as she spotted him. 'How delightful to have you back in society after your year of travels.'

'It is wonderful to see you again, Mrs Livingstone.' He craned his neck a little, trying to see if he could spot his wife amongst the guests that lined the ballroom.

'You are looking for Lady Westcroft, no doubt,' Mrs Livingstone said with an indulgent smile. 'She is—'

'On the dance floor,' he murmured before she could finish.

For a moment it felt as though time slowed as his eyes followed Lady Westcroft around the ballroom. She stepped gracefully, with none of the hesitation he had felt from her when they had first danced together at the Midsummer's Eve ball. She looked beautiful in a dress of dark green, the material shimmering as she moved, and the skirt swished around her ankles. It complemented her pale skin and red hair to perfection, and Simon could not take his eyes off her.

She smiled then, and he felt a stab of disappointment that it wasn't at him, watching as she dropped her head back and laughed at something her dance partner had said.

He bowed absently to Mrs Livingstone and made his

way through the crowd of people, murmuring greetings as he went. He could not tear his eyes away from his wife, and as the music swelled and then quietened, he was standing at the front of the small crowd at the edge of the dance floor.

At first she did not notice him standing there, but as she turned to face him and her eyes met his, he saw a shadow cross her face. It was momentary, and if he hadn't been watching her so intently he would have missed it, but he felt a sadness that he could be the one to ruin her evening when she otherwise looked as though she were having a wonderful time.

'You're back, my Lord,' she said, excusing herself from her companion.

'I'm back.'

It wouldn't be a complete shock this time. He had ensured he had written before leaving Northumberland and sent the message by fast rider so she would not be taken by surprise at his arrival, but the good conditions on the roads meant he had made fast progress and was in London a couple of days before he was expected.

'Are you well?'

'Yes, thank you. And you?'

She inclined her head, and for the first time he felt regret at how formal their interaction was. It was entirely his fault, he knew that. He'd married a complete stranger and then disappeared for a year. Of course their conversation was going to be stilted and awkward: they barely knew one another.

'How are Maria and the girls? And your mother?' she asked, warmth flaring in her eyes.

'They are well. The girls have grown and changed a

lot in a year, but they are happy and healthy and have progressed well with their schooling.'

'Are they still terrorising that poor governess?'

'Miss Pickles? Yes, she threatened to leave, and Maria had me intervene to ask her to stay. She doesn't think she'll last more than another month.'

Lady Westcroft smiled indulgently, and he marvelled at how she had managed to build a relationship with his family despite not knowing them at all when he had married her. His sister-in-law spoke of his wife so warmly you would have thought they had been best friends their entire lives, and his mother had chided him for not making Lady Westcroft's life easier this past year. It had forced him to acknowledge the guilt he felt at leaving her so soon after their marriage and not even thinking to write to her throughout the year.

'The girls are well-behaved when they are on their own, but when they are all together, they lose the ability to control that naughty streak,' Lady Westcroft said, her voice filled with love. 'Maria spoke of separating them for their lessons if the governess could not cope with all three of them at once. It will be a shame, but perhaps it is the best solution.'

'They put a frog on the poor woman's dinner plate, slipped it in amongst her vegetables when she wasn't looking. Apparently it hopped onto her fork and looked at her.'

'Was that the event that pushed her towards threatening to leave?'

'One of many, I think,' Simon said. He felt himself begin to relax and was reminded again of how reasonable Lady Westcroft was. It boded well for their marriage of convenience, and he hoped they would be able to come to some arrangement about how to live that would suit both of them.

The music started again, the musicians returned from their short break, refreshments in hand, and Simon recognised a waltz, the music they had danced to on the terrace of the Midsummer's Eve ball almost a year ago.

Without thinking he held out his hand. 'Would you care to dance?'

For a second he saw a flicker of hesitation in her eyes, and then she nodded.

'It would be my pleasure.'

Simon felt the eyes of the room on them as they took their place on the dance floor.

'Why does it feel like everyone is watching us?' Lady Westcroft said, leaning in close to whisper in his ear.

'They are. We haven't been seen in public together before, and no one can work out the truth of our marriage. I am sure they are fascinated by it and want to see if they can pick up any clues as to whether we despise each other or can't keep our hands from one another.'

She smiled then, with a hint of sadness. 'Whereas the truth is much more mundane.'

He placed a hand in the small of her back and adjusted his stance so he was holding her close. It would be a positioning that would be frowned upon at any other time, but they were still considered newly-weds, and there was a certain indulgence for reckless behaviour. As the waltz began he remembered the magic of their first dance together and how she had laughed as she missed a step. He got a sense she was on edge now, but not because she thought she would forget the steps. It was incredible how much she had learned in a year, not least how to fit in at these society events.

'You're grinning,' she whispered.

'I'm remembering our first waltz.'

This made her smile too. 'It was a magical evening.'

'An evening that changed our lives.'

As he twirled her she looked up at him, her face now serious. 'I do appreciate what you did for me. Often I think of what my life would be like married to Cecil.'

'Vile Cousin Cecil,' he said, shaking his head. 'Do you know I had almost forgotten about him.'

'He was outraged when he heard I was going to marry you. He came to my parents' house, stood outside and called me all number of horrible names.'

'I did not realise.'

'My mother counselled me not to tell you. She did not want anything to cause any discord. I think until we were actually standing in front of the vicar she was worried you might change your mind, and she would have two disgraced daughters.' She paused and gave a little shrug of her shoulders even whilst they were dancing. 'I hear from my mother that Cecil is still searching for a wife.'

'I pity the young woman who accepts him.'

'So do I.'

They danced in silence for a minute, and Simon wondered if his wife had taken dance lessons in the time he had been away. She stepped with such confidence now, with the ease of someone who was certain they would not forget the steps. He did not want to insult her by implying she had once not been so graceful and intuitive in her movements, but he was intrigued.

'Please do not take this the wrong way, Lady West-

croft, but you dance beautifully now...' He trailed off
as she laughed.

'You mean compared to when we last twirled around
a ballroom?'

'I very much enjoyed our dances at the masquerade
ball.'

She looked up at him, her expression suddenly serious. 'Your sister-in-law was ever so kind to me after you
left. I was like a ship adrift, unsure of what was expected
of me or even how to act. She took me in, cocooned me
in love, gave me a safe space to grow and discover myself and then urged me to fly once I was ready.'

'Maria is a good woman.'

'The very best,' Lady Westcroft said, strong emotion
in her voice. 'When I said I would like to come to London, to look at doing some charitable work and step into
society, she ensured I would not make a fool of myself.
She taught me how to address people and how to walk
into a room with confidence, and we spent many hours
twirling round the drawing room, practising dancing,
trying not to trip over one of the girls.'

Simon felt a stab of guilt. He should have been the one
who guided his new wife through her début in London
society; instead, he hadn't even considered it might be
somewhere she would want to be.

'I can just imagine it,' he said and to his relief found
she was smiling.

'It has been quite the strangest year of my life,' she
said quietly, 'but I have learned so much and met so
many interesting people.'

'I am glad. Tell me, Lady Westcroft, how did you
manage to get these people to accept you?'

'With my rough edges and crude country manners?'

He quickly started to deny that was what he meant and then saw the sparkle of amusement in her eyes.

'You are different to what the ladies of the *ton* are used to.'

'You are not wrong. Did you know when I came to London I got a summons from the palace? The Queen Charlotte herself wanted to cast her eye over me and see what sort of woman you had chosen to be your countess.'

'That cannot have been easy.'

'I almost turned tail and ran all the way back to Northumberland to hide in my childhood bedroom.'

'Yet you stayed. You faced the queen and claimed your place in society.'

'I think her approval helped me greatly. Once she had declared me a darling of the *ton*, everyone wanted to get to know the surprise countess.' She gave a little shake of her head as if remembering the day she had been called to the palace. 'That is not to say that I was confident when I was led down the long corridors to meet the queen. My knees actually knocked together whilst I waited outside to be summoned into her presence.'

'She is a formidable lady,' Simon murmured. 'I am impressed, Lady Westcroft.'

His wife pulled a face and leaned in closer, allowing him to catch a hint of an alluring scent, a mixture of lavender and something else he couldn't quite put his finger on.

'I know there is a great expectation that we address one another formally, but at least in private might you call me Alice? There are three Lady Westcrofts in your family at present, and it gets a little tedious for ever trying to work out who everyone is referring to.'

'Alice,' he said, pleased to be rid of the formality. 'And you should call me Simon.'

'Thank you.'

The music swelled and died away, and they came to a stop in the middle of the dance floor. He bowed and she curtsied, and for a long moment he stared into her eyes. There was something mesmerising about the blue of her eyes, and the spell was only broken when she looked away. He had been going to suggest they take a little refreshment together, perhaps step out of the ballroom into one of the quieter areas so they could spend a little bit of the evening talking, but Alice touched his arm fleetingly and then excused herself, murmuring something about a full dance-card. She disappeared into the press of people around the perimeter of the ballroom before he could protest, leaving him standing alone.

Alice was pleased with the fast pace of the next three dances. It meant she was out of breath towards the end, but also none of her partners expected more than minor snippets of conversation in between the bursts of vigorous footwork. Her partners were all pleasant gentlemen who she had danced with before, mainly husbands of the women she knew socially or through the London Ladies' Benevolent Society.

Out of the corner of her eye she could see her husband prowling around the room. It had been quite a surprise, his turning up this evening. She had expected him back in London in the next few days but had thought they would meet behind closed doors at the townhouse, not at the Livingstones' ball in front of everyone.

After they had shared a waltz, Alice had been eager to get away, hoping that if she kept herself busy and unavailable, her husband might decide to go home or, at the very least, retire to the card tables. Instead he'd watched her constantly, brushing away the attempts by other guests at engaging him in conversation. It was unnerving, and she was sure people were beginning to notice.

She wondered if she could slip away. A carriage waited somewhere outside to take her home once the evening had concluded, but the way Simon was watching her, he would follow her out and suggest they share the carriage home. He was eager to talk, to discuss their future, she could tell by the nervous energy about him, but she needed a little time to compose herself first.

He caught her eye for a second, and she felt a spark travel through her before she quickly looked away. *This* was the problem. Simon had returned to London eager to work out how they would live their lives married but very much separate. It was what she wanted too, to continue to build the success of her charitable work, to find her place in society and enjoy her life in a way she had never been allowed to before this past year. Yet when he stepped close to her, when he looked at her with those brilliant blue eyes, all she could think of was kissing him. It was as if she were swept back to the Midsummer's Eve ball all over again and they were recklessly running through the garden hand in hand. Whenever he came close she felt her heart hammer in her chest, and she got an overwhelming urge to kiss him.

It was highly inconvenient for many reasons, not least because he clearly didn't think of her as anything more than a relative he was responsible for, someone a little troublesome who had been foisted upon him.

She broke eye contact, quickly looking away and trying to work out if there was a way to escape without him seeing her. She hesitated for just a moment too long, and as she stepped away from the dance floor her husband was at her side.

'I do not think there is any more dancing for a while,' he said.

'That is a shame,' she murmured and caught his raised eyebrow. She had to remind herself her husband was an intelligent man and probably had worked out she was trying to avoid him.

'Perhaps we can find somewhere quieter to talk, even if just for a few minutes.'

Alice sighed and then nodded. 'I am fatigued. Unless you wish to stay, shall we share a carriage home?'

He looked relieved, and Alice realised with surprise that he wasn't used to society events. Although he hadn't written to her over the last year, he had sent a couple of short notes to Maria and his mother, and they had shared a little of what his life had been like. From what she could gather he had lived quietly, opting for a villa in a rural location with his closest neighbours some miles away. He had not looked to socialise in his new community, and although his journey back to England would have involved travelling by ship with others, he would not have encountered a situation like this for a long time. Even if he had been attending balls and social gatherings since early adulthood, it would still be quite an adjustment for him to make from his recent experiences.

She felt a little guilty for avoiding him for so long. There were many things he could have done better in their relationship, but wanting to discuss the practicalities of their arrangement now wasn't one of them.

'Should we say goodnight to Mr and Mrs Livingstone?' Alice said as he led her rapidly towards the door.

Simon leaned in, and Alice felt herself shiver as his breath tickled her ear. 'They will not mind if we slip away. They will tell themselves it is only to be expected when two newly-weds are reunited after time apart.'

He placed a hand on the small of her back to guide her, and Alice had to suppress a little groan of frustration. He seemed entirely unaffected by her: it was as if to him the kiss on Midsummer's Eve had never happened.

It took a few minutes to find their carriage amongst the dozens standing outside. Theirs was tucked down a side street, and the driver was sitting on top enjoying the evening air as they approached.

Alice remained silent once they had climbed inside, and Simon instructed the driver to take them home.

It was dark in the carriage as they sat across from one another. Alice could only see the contours of her husband's face and the glint of his eyes in the moonlight, but nothing to help her anticipate how the conversation would begin.

'You looked happy tonight,' Simon said after a minute. 'It was lovely to see.'

His words were not what she expected, and it took her a moment to compose herself enough to answer. 'I am happy,' she said eventually.

'Are you? I worried quite a lot before we married that you were choosing an option that would not give you the life you wanted. You were stuck between a marriage to Cecil and a life that was not the future you had once imagined.'

She was touched that he had considered her feelings in such depth when he'd had so much else to occupy his mind. She chose her words carefully now, not wanting to give him the wrong impression.

'This isn't the life I imagined or the life I hoped for when I was a young girl, yet these last few months I have been content. I cannot lie to you and say I do not sometimes wish for children, for a husband who loves me and a house filled with family, but I am slowly learning there are other ways to seek contentment in life.'

'You are refreshing, Alice,' Simon said, his voice low and serious, a note of wonder about it. 'You always speak your mind even if it makes you vulnerable.'

'I do not think there is any point in lying about one's feelings. If I told you I was blissfully happy and never thought of a different life, then it might influence what we decide on for our future. It is important you know how I really feel. This past year I have not had anyone to hide behind. I've had to assert my own views, to make decisions and bear the consequences.'

'I am sorry you have been so alone.'

'It has not been entirely a bad thing,' she said quietly. 'I have learned a lot about myself and how much more capable I am than I ever realised.'

'I suppose you never had the chance to step out into the world alone before. Young gentlemen often have that taste of independence when they leave home to attend university or go to seek their fortune through work or the military. Yet young women stay under their father's control until they marry.'

'I will always be grateful for the past year. It has shown me I can achieve so much more than I ever thought.'

They fell silent for a moment, and Alice glanced out of the window to see they were already slowing to a stop in front of the townhouse. Their conversation hadn't delved very deep, and she knew soon they would have to sit down across a table from one another and decide what their lives would look like.

Simon helped her from the carriage, and they walked arm-in-arm up the steps to the front door. She felt torn, simultaneously wanting to rip herself away from Simon so he wouldn't have a chance to hurt her and strike up a conversation so he would have to linger.

In the end she bid him goodnight in the hallway and hurried upstairs, feeling her heart pound in her chest as Simon called after her.

'Tomorrow we should talk properly,' Simon said, his voice quiet but clear. She nodded, hoping she would sleep well before the negotiation for her future began.

Chapter Twelve

'Your note was a little cryptic,' Alice said as she strolled into the park, parasol in hand to shield her from the warmth of the sun.

He had been up early, unable to settle. Throughout the night he had been plagued by indecision and by thoughts of his wife that were not helpful in assisting him to come to a sensible conclusion about how he wanted their future to look. He'd risen early and, when there had been no sign of Alice at an early breakfast, had decided to leave her a note to meet him in Hyde Park, dressed in her riding habit.

When he had first arrived in the park it had been quiet, with only a few other early-risers out for a brisk morning walk or for a ride. On his trip back to Northumberland he had picked up his beautiful horse, Socrates, and this morning had enjoyed a long ride without the pressures of travelling on the dusty roads. Before Alice's arrival he had also hired a horse for her to ride. There was something about having the breeze on your face and the thought of freedom to gallop off towards the horizon that helped to clear the mind. It would also ensure their conversation didn't become too heated or

intense. Alice was an immensely pragmatic woman—
he had seen that in how she had reacted to impossible
situations this past year—but they were talking about
her entire future.

He saw her eye with uncertainty the horses he was
holding by the reins.

'You wish for us to ride?'

'I find I do my best thinking on horseback.' He paused
as she regarded the horses with trepidation, realising he
did not even know if his wife could ride. 'You have ridden before?'

She nodded slowly. 'Twice. Both unmitigated disas-
ters.' For a long moment she would not meet his eye,
and then she sighed. 'But I suppose I could try again.'

'What went wrong before?'

'Do you remember my friend Lydia?'

'The young lady you sneaked into the Midsummer's
Eve ball with?'

'Yes. When we were younger she persuaded me to
ride her father's horse with her. We thought it would
be easy, but as soon as we were seated the horse got
spooked and reared up, and Lydia tumbled to the ground.
The horse took off along the high street, and I could do
nothing but close my eyes, cling onto its neck and hope
I did not die.'

'How old were you?'

'Eight or nine. The horse ran for three miles before
it calmed.'

'You managed to stay on its back?'

'Somehow I did.'

'That is impressive.'

'I thought I would die if I fell. We got into so much

trouble I wasn't allowed to see Lydia for a month, and my father took a cane to my hands, whipping them so badly they bled.' She turned over her hands and looked down at them. Simon had the urge to reach out and run his fingers over the skin of her palms but stopped himself just in time.

'What about the second time?'

'That was a little less dramatic, and less illicit. My sister had a suitor in the days before—' She glanced up at him quickly.

Alice had told him of her sister's near disgrace, the weeks of turmoil as the whole family thought there was no way to save Margaret's reputation. Then a surprise proposal had materialised, followed by a quick marriage.

'Before her marriage,' he finished diplomatically.

'Yes. They would go walking over the fields, and I used to have to accompany them to chaperon. One day he brought his horse and suggested I ride. I was nervous, but Margaret was keen as it would give her a little more privacy with this man she thought she might want to marry. I agreed reluctantly, and after I got over my nerves it was quite a pleasant experience, riding through the fields in the sunshine.'

'Did something happen?'

'There was a man out with his dog. The dog got excited and spooked the horse. The horse ran, and at first I managed to hang on, but the path took us under a low hanging branch, and I did not duck in time.'

'That must have hurt.'

'I was lucky I was not seriously injured.'

'I did not know,' Simon murmured quietly, frowning. There was so much he did not know about his wife.

All these little stories from her childhood, her likes and dislikes. It wasn't surprising as he had spent no time with her, but despite his plan to keep a good amount of distance between them, he felt a flicker of sadness. His brother, Robert, had shared everything with Maria, and over the course of their marriage they had learned all those little stories, all the childhood anecdotes that build to mould a person into their adult form. 'We can walk if you prefer.'

Alice inhaled deeply and then shook her head. 'No, I wish to be able to ride. A sedate half an hour around Hyde Park will be a good way to get me over my fear.'

'Only if you are sure.'

She nodded and approached the smaller of the two horses, a docile mare that regarded her with hooded eyes. She took her time, stroking the horse's nose and then neck, talking softly to the animal. Alice might not have ridden for a long time, but she knew how to approach an animal to ensure the encounter was a calm one.

After a few minutes she looked around. 'I am not sure I am strong enough to pull myself onto her back.'

'I will help you.' He looped Socrates's reins over a fence-post and came up behind Alice, guiding her hands to the correct spot on her horse's back to help her to pull herself up. 'Put a foot in my hand, and I will lift you. Once you are high enough, you need to twist around and find a comfortable position in the saddle.'

As he moved closer he caught a hint of her scent and had to resist the urge to lean in farther. It was tantalising, a subtle mix of lavender and rosewater, and he had the sudden desire to press his lips against the soft skin of her neck. There was a spot just behind and below her ear that looked perfect for his lips, and he had to stop himself quickly as he realised he had almost leaned in to kiss it.

His body brushed against hers as she lifted her foot into his hand, and he quickly boosted her into the air. With his help she twisted lithely and was quickly seated in the saddle. He took a minute to help her position her feet and showed her how best to hold the reins, all while trying to ignore the urge to pull her out of the saddle and back into his arms.

He tried to reason it was only natural, this attraction he felt. He had been starved of companionship for a long time, and Alice was an attractive young woman. Never before had he dallied with a respectable unmarried woman, but on the night of the Midsummer's Eve ball nearly a year earlier, he had been unable to resist kissing her, even though he'd known better. That attraction, that deep desire, had not faded in the time he was away, although now it was even more imperative that he did not do anything to jeopardize the delicate balance of their relationship.

Once Alice was settled he pulled himself away and mounted his horse, glancing over to check his wife was not looking too nervous.

'Shall we start with a gentle walk down to the Serpentine?'

'That would be pleasant.'

He urged Socrates on gently and was pleased to see Alice doing the same to her horse, and after a minute he was able to fall into step beside her. They had to wind along a couple of tree-lined paths to get to the wide-open space of the more central area of Hyde Park, but before long they were side by side, riding towards the water.

'How are you finding it?'

'I am a little nervous,' Alice confessed with a self-deprecating smile, 'but I think I am beginning to enjoy it.'

'I am glad. We can stop at any time.'

They rode in silence for a few minutes, and each time he glanced across at Alice he could see she was deep in thought. He realised he knew so little of her hopes and her wants that he had no idea what she would be amenable to when they discussed their future. It was clear she understood they would not have a conventional marriage, even now that he had returned to England, yet it was hard to fathom whether she wished to continue her life completely separate from his or if she wanted companionship from him.

As they approached the sparkling blue water, he slowed and her horse followed his lead, and for a moment they took in the view without saying anything. It was a glorious day, and the park was wonderfully empty despite the pleasant weather.

'Is there somewhere we can go that is a little more private?' Alice said, leaning towards him slightly. 'I do not wish what we discuss to become gossip by this afternoon.'

'Of course. The park is vast. If you are happy to continue with our ride, we can find somewhere we will not be overheard.'

'Thank you.'

He led them away from the lake, pleased to see with every passing minute Alice's confidence was growing, the reins now held loosely in her hands as they allowed the horses to pick the pace. After ten minutes they were away from the people strolling by the water, and it felt as though they had this part of the park to themselves.

As he watched, Alice straightened in her seat as if gearing herself up for battle. He felt a stab of regret that they needed to have this discussion but also knew that once their expectations and preferences were out in the open, they could move away from the uncertainty that surrounded them both.

'You wished to discuss our future, Simon,' Alice said, glancing over at him but not holding his eye. He could sense her trepidation of the subject but was pleased she had initiated the conversation.

'I think we both need to know where we stand.'

'Do you wish to divorce me?' she said, her voice low. Simon was an experienced rider, but in his shock he almost fell out of his saddle.

'Divorce you? Whatever gave you that idea?'

She looked at him incredulously for almost a minute before replying. 'You married me thinking you would be dead within a few months, so that our union was an act of duty that would not really affect you. Now that you have been told you are not imminently going to be struck down, in fact you may never be in the way your brother and your father were, I expect you wish to return to your normal life to a certain degree.'

'I am not going to divorce you, Alice. That would ruin us both.'

'I would not try to stop you,' she said softly.

'Do you want me to divorce you?' he asked, unable to fathom how divorce had even entered her mind. Divorce was a messy and protracted affair, and he had only seen it occur a couple of times, and on each occasion neither party had come out unscathed. He found he was upset at even the idea of divorcing Alice.

'No,' she said quickly. 'Far from it. From the whispered conversations I have heard about when Lord Southerhay divorced his wife eight years ago, I can see it is a catastrophic course of events with both parties completely humiliated by the discussion of their private business in front of Parliament itself. I am aware if you divorced me my life as I know it would be over. I doubt I would ever marry again, and I wouldn't have children, a family. My own family would disown me. It would be the worst possible outcome.' She paused and then looked over at him, holding his eye. 'But I do understand if that is the path you wish to take. I am not what you had planned for your life, and if you now want to find a wife you actually want to marry, I will understand.'

'I am not that heartless, Alice,' he said, his voice low. He felt a flicker of anger that she would think so little of him and had to remind himself she had only known neglect and desertion from him. Divorce was a fate worse than death to many and happened only once in a generation in their social class. Yet surely she would understand they had entered into this marriage to save her from ruin, and he wouldn't callously abandon her now.

'Not divorce, then,' she said, nodding with relief.

'Not divorce, we can agree on that.' He paused, wondering how he was going to say what he had to. Despite not knowing Alice well, he did know she wanted a family one day. She had spoken of being surrounded by children, of a happy family life with a husband who loved her. He remembered how she had been with the two children in Hyde Park, sailing the model boat on the

Serpentine. At that image he felt the words stick in his throat. That was not the life he could give her.

'I may have been told by the doctors the headaches were not a harbinger of imminent death, but I still cannot know what the future might hold,' he said slowly, watching Alice's reaction. 'I may suffer the same fate as my father and my brother, and it could happen at any time. It has meant addressing my mortality each and every day, knowing this could be my last. I was eager to return to England to see my family and to take up my responsibilities once again, but it does not change the fact that one day in a few months or years I may have to leave suddenly again, or I may die without any warning.'

'That could be said for any of us,' Alice said softly. 'I do not mean to take away from the seriousness of your situation—of course your risk is greater—but none of us know what the future will hold. I may catch consumption from one of the children at the orphanage tomorrow and wither away within the next six months, or I could be thrown from this horse and crack my skull this afternoon.'

'You are not wrong. I know it is foolish to live one's life always thinking about whether today is the day you die, but I find it is not a thought I can change just by intention.'

Alice nodded slowly. 'I understand that,' she said, giving him a sad smile. 'Although, I wish it were not so.'

'It also means that I will not have children. I refuse to bring a child into this world who might suffer the same.'

He could see Alice had more to say, perhaps more to argue on this subject, but after a moment she pressed her lips together and nodded. 'I understand,' she said simply.

Looking at her intently he spoke a little softer. 'I know this is not the life I promised you. I offered a year or two of comfort with your reputation intact, and then perhaps a few months of mourning before you could start looking for a husband of your own choice. A man you wanted to marry and who would give you your family.'

Alice looked away, but before she did, he thought he saw tears in her eyes. He felt like a cad, ripping away her hopes for the future like this.

'I do not begrudge you being alive, Simon,' she said softly. 'Whatever that means for my future.'

They were kind words from a kind young woman, and for a moment he wanted to pull her into his arms, hold her close to him and tell her he would give her whatever she wanted, yet he couldn't do it. Their lives were destined to go in very different directions, and as much as he liked Alice, as much as he desired her and could see himself being happy with her if they lived a conventional life as husband and wife, it wasn't a path he could take.

He couldn't bring himself to voice the other reason he couldn't build a true relationship with her—it was buried too deep inside and he didn't like to examine it too closely—but there was a part of him that felt as though he were stealing his brother's life. He had the title, the properties, the place in Parliament, all the things his brother should be enjoying still. If he allowed himself to have a normal life with Alice, to treat her as his true wife, to have children with her, that would be a step too far in assuming the life that should have been his brother's.

Alice took a deep breath and seemed to brace herself for what she had to say next.

'I understand you do not want to have children, that you are concerned about passing to them whatever it is your father and brother were afflicted by. I also understand that means we cannot have an intimate relationship as is normal between husband and wife.'

He hadn't expected she would be so direct, but he was pleased that there was no ambiguity in her words. The last thing they wanted was to speak in metaphors and then both leave with a different understanding of what the future would hold.

'I am not sure what it is you do want, Simon. Do you wish for us to lead completely separate lives? For me to reside in Northumberland whilst you are in London, and then when you travel north we cross on the road when I am heading for London? Or do you want us to have a closer relationship, a friendship, a companionship? It is very hard to know what to suggest when I have no idea what it is you would be comfortable with.'

Up until he had arrived back in England, he would have said the first of her suggestions was the one that made the most sense, but now, even after spending just a few scattered hours with Alice, he wasn't sure he wanted to move around the country like ships passing in the night, barely acknowledging she existed. Whilst he was in Italy, his marriage had seemed an abstract concept, something that was very easy to put out of his mind, but now that he had returned it was far harder to ignore her, and he realised he didn't wish to.

'I propose a friendship, perhaps with time, even a companionship. We do not need to be tied to one another, if you wish to stay in London when I go to Northumberland, then there is no issue. If I wish to visit friends, then I will inform you, but there is no expectation that we conduct every aspect of our lives together.'

'That sounds agreeable,' Alice said. 'So we shall endeavour to at least keep the other person informed of our plans.'

'Yes,' he murmured. 'I know I left rather abruptly a few weeks ago when I travelled to Northumberland. I should have informed you in person. I was overwhelmed by my return home, but it is no excuse for leaving without bidding you farewell. I am sorry.'

'Thank you.'

They had ridden some way across the open grass now and were in a deserted part of the park. There was a good view over the green space up here, and for a moment Simon paused to take it all in. He felt a roil of emotion as he let his eyes take in the rooftops of London beyond the park. When he'd left England eleven months ago, he had thought he would never look upon this view, nor see his beloved Northumberland again either. His homecoming had proved more emotional than he had imagined.

'I have brought some refreshment. Shall we pause here and toast our marriage with a glass of lemonade?'

'That sounds lovely.' Alice smiled at him, and for an instant he had the urge to throw away every caution and pull her into his arms, to hell with the consequences. Quickly he pushed the thought away: he had given in to his desire once with Alice, and that had upended both their lives. He must control himself better around his pretty wife.

Chapter Thirteen

Alice tried to push away the desire she felt as Simon wrapped his hands around her waist to help her from her saddle. It was an impossible situation, and she had to do everything in her power not to make it worse.

She considered his offer of friendship, companionship perhaps, and realised it was better than she had feared but not what she had secretly hoped for. It was ridiculous to even think about, but deep down she knew she wished Simon had come racing back to London because he had suddenly realised he could not live without her. It was so far from the truth of the matter it was almost laughable. He did not want to live with her as most men wanted to live with their wives. He would treat her as a spinster relative, with kindness and perhaps even a little platonic affection, but there would be no intimacy, no love.

Alice pushed away the disappointment. This way was better. She could continue with her life here in London, travel to Northumberland to see Maria and the children as planned later in the summer, take her trips to visit her own sister. Sometimes Simon would be at home when she returned, sometimes he would not. Her life would not change substantially, and perhaps with a little time she would grow to enjoy this new phase.

She was determined not to become reliant on Simon's company, though. He had shown how quickly he could disappear and how little importance he placed on including her in his plans. She would have to conduct her life with this in mind, always wary that he could disappear at any moment.

With his hands around her waist, Simon steadied Alice as she slid to the ground. They ended up standing close, and Alice could not resist the urge to raise a hand and place it on his chest. Even through the layers of clothing, she could feel his heart beating, slow and steady underneath the subtle rise and fall as he inhaled and exhaled. She glanced up at him and saw him regarding her strangely, with an almost hungry look in his eyes, and she realised that desire for her he had shown on the night of the Midsummer's Eve ball had not disappeared completely. He was holding himself tight, coiled like a deadly snake ready to spring out at its prey, and she realised with a rush of satisfaction she was making him feel on edge.

She was pleased not at his discomfort but that she was not the only one struggling to deny she felt something more than a desire for friendship between them.

Alice allowed her hand to linger for another few seconds and then withdrew, stepping to the side to move around him, trying to pretend nothing had happened. Despite being a married woman of eleven months, she was still very much an innocent in the ways of seduction. However, people assumed she had at least had her wedding night with her husband, and it meant she was no longer shielded from some of the more delicate conversations held between married women.

She had no plans to try to seduce Simon: not only would she have no idea how to go about it but also it wouldn't be fair. She might not agree with his reasons for deciding not to have children, but it *was* his decision, and she would not trick him into any intimacy in the hopes that she might have the family she dreamed of. Instead she would work on making the life she did have as fulfilling as possible, and perhaps dreaming of her husband's lips on hers last thing at night when they went to bed.

Simon lingered by the horses for a moment and when he turned to face her, he looked composed with no hint of the desire that had flashed in his eyes when she'd stood close.

He took a blanket from the saddlebag on his horse and spread it on the grass, indicating for her to have a seat. She lowered herself to the ground, making herself comfortable on the soft wool of the blanket. From the saddlebag he also produced a large bottle of lemonade and a parcel that she suspected contained some of Cook's delicious biscuits.

He brought them over, indicating the lemonade. 'I forgot glasses,' he said with a shrug. 'We will have to drink from the bottle.'

'I do not mind. When I was young my parents would sometimes take us for picnics on the beach in the summer when it was a particularly hot day. We would walk across the dunes and find a quiet spot, spread out a blanket and enjoy our lunch with the sea lapping at the shore in the distance. My mother never remembered to pack glasses, and Margaret and I always shared lemonade straight from the bottle.'

'It sounds idyllic.'

Alice wobbled her head from side to side. She couldn't complain about her childhood, not when she compared it to the awful circumstances the children in the London orphanages and on the streets lived in, yet it had not been happy. There had been happy times, long summer days spent playing with Lydia and her sister, paddling in the sea and coming home soaked through with seawater, the winter storms where she and Margaret would creep to the empty attic room and watch the thunder and lightning light up the village and the sand dunes beyond. She had some fond memories, but there had always been an uneasiness in their house. Her father was strict, even more so than most parents she knew. He would bring out his cane if he thought she or Margaret had committed any more substantial infractions of his rules. Often the girls would be unable to eat their dinner because their punishment had split the skin on their hands.

Their mother had not been so coldly cruel, but she had expected quiet obedience from her two daughters and was quick to anger if they did not obey. It had not been a happy childhood, but she had been clothed and housed in comfort, with decent meals on the table.

'You have happy memories?'

'I used to enjoy the times I had playing on the beach with my sister,' Alice said, deciding not to mention the difficult feelings she had towards her parents.

'That is a well-practised answer. You are skilled at diplomacy, Alice.' He regarded her as he sat down. 'Am I to take it your childhood wasn't idyllic?'

She puffed her cheeks out and then blew out the air before shaking her head.

'It wasn't idyllic,' she said slowly. 'It wasn't terrible, but my parents were distant and cold, and I was always one step away from punishment. I cannot complain when I see what some children have to endure, but it is not the way I would want to bring my children up.' She glanced at him quickly before adding, 'If ever I have them.'

'It is perhaps why you are so interested in the work with children on the streets and in orphanages that the London Ladies' Benevolent Society does.'

'I think you may be right,' she said, taking the bottle of lemonade after he had popped out the cork for her. It felt strange to swig from a bottle in front of this man she barely knew, but she was thirsty, and after a moment she pushed away her reticence and took a delicate sip. The lemonade was delicious and refreshing, and she decided to forget about what she looked like or what Simon thought of her and took a long gulp of the beverage. 'Since I have taken over the helm I have steered the society towards projects that help women and children. We do a lot of fundraising and donate to many good causes, but there has been a definite shift to help the most vulnerable in society with our efforts.'

'I have been making enquiries,' Simon said as he sat beside her. The blanket wasn't huge, and he sat close without his position being scandalous. They were a married couple and there was nothing wrong with them sharing some refreshment whilst seated together in a public park, yet somehow when his hand brushed hers it felt as though they were doing something illicit.

'Enquiries?'

'Into your society. I am impressed. What you have managed to do in a year is nothing short of extraordinary.'

A subtle warmth diffused through her body, making her skin tingle at his compliment.

'It has taken up much of my time these last few months, but I feel like we are finally making a difference where it is most needed.'

She glanced at him and decided she would share a little more. He looked engaged and interested, and although she had vowed she would continue her life in the knowledge he might leave it at any moment, she did not have to petulantly shut him out of her world.

'Lady Kennington has identified a small orphanage close to the slums of St Giles that she thinks would benefit immensely from our patronage. Apparently it is a dilapidated building that takes from the poorest areas. I am planning on visiting later today to see whether we will be able to help.'

'I am sure any donations will be thankfully received.'

'I hope we might be able to offer more than that. Many of the ladies from the Benevolent Society are keen to do more than just fundraise. We have a mix of backgrounds and a wealth of expertise at our disposal. It will depend on who runs the orphanage, but I am hopeful we might be able to provide more than just money.'

'What do you mean?' He leaned forward, looking intrigued, and Alice felt a rush of satisfaction at his interest.

'One of the main limitations of many of the orphanages is the lack of support as the children get to the age when they are no longer eligible for a bed and a hot meal from the establishment. They may have rudimentary reading and writing skills, perhaps very basic arithmetic, and they will be trained to do a number of menial household jobs, but often it is not enough. People see they are from the orphanage and will not give them a chance, except in the very lowest paid positions.'

'I cannot argue with the truth of that.'

'I am not sure exactly what the answer is yet. Perhaps better schooling, perhaps a focus on certain trades and skills for when they leave the orphanage. I am hoping with a small establishment like St Benedict's we may be able to foster a system where some of our benefactors look to take in the young boys and girls when they reach fourteen and help to train them as maids and footmen. It may take a little patience, but I believe with the right people it could make the world of difference.'

'A little like your scheme to match the wealthier families with the poorer to provide support over the winter in Bamburgh.'

She felt her cheeks flush, finding that she was pleased he had remembered.

'It is an admirable idea, but it would be a big adjustment, asking these children to abide by the rules of a wealthy and prominent household.'

Alice shook her head vehemently. 'It is the perfect time to do it. They have been used to strict rules for years, being told exactly what they can do and when by the master or matron of the orphanage. It is better to take them from that environment, before there have been too many other corrupting influences.' She cocked her head to one side. 'You have borne witness to this scheme in action.'

He looked at her in surprise. 'I have?'

'Yes, in the young footman, Frank Smith.'

'He is a lad from an orphanage?'

'Yes. I had a long discussion with Miss Stick about whether she would be supportive of the idea of bringing him in to train up.'

'She was happy to do it?'

'Very happy. Miss Stick has a hard demeanour but a very good soul,' Alice said affectionately. 'We visited the orphanage together to talk to Frank and to check he would be a good fit, then he joined the household five months ago.'

'Five months ago he was an orphanage boy?'

'He was.'

Simon let out a low whistle. 'I would not have guessed.'

'Three times a week he spends an hour with either myself or Miss Stick to develop his reading and writing and arithmetic skills, and once he is secure in basic knowledge, we will discuss what he wishes to do with his life and hopefully be able to guide him in that direction.'

'That is an ambitious plan, Alice,' Simon said, looking at her in wonder. 'You think this will work?'

She shrugged. 'I think with Frank it will. He is a determined young man who has seen the worst of life at a very young age, and he is motivated not to end the same way his own parents did, in poverty, unable to support their family. I am not saying it is the answer for everyone, but perhaps it is enough to help a few.'

'Once Frank has gained the skills he needs to get a job elsewhere, you will repeat the process I assume?'

'That is the plan, whilst gently advocating for others to do the same.'

'What if it goes wrong?'

She put her hands a little behind her bottom and leaned back, tilting her face up to the sun underneath the rim of her bonnet. Her skin would burn if she stayed this way for too long, but a couple of minutes would not matter, and it felt so glorious to have the warmth of the sun on her face.

'You mean what if one of the children from the orphanage steals all the silver or brings the household into disrepute?' She shrugged again. 'It is the risk you take when you hire any servant. References can be forged, recommendations coerced. At least this way you know the person's background, and you can learn what they have been through.'

For a minute Simon remained silent, and then he nodded thoughtfully. 'I think the scheme has merit. It will be interesting to see what comes of it.' It was the first time he had spoken of being interested in something shared in the future, and Alice wondered if he would really stick around to see the results of her plans or if in a few months he would disappear again, his only correspondence a short note telling her he was gone.

'I am visiting St Benedict's Orphanage this afternoon. I will keep you updated on my progress.'

Simon frowned. 'I hope you do not plan to go alone. It is not in a salubrious part of the city.'

'I am meeting the matron of the orphanage. I hardly think my life will be in danger.'

'You should take someone with you.'

'Are you volunteering?' It was said in jest, but she saw Simon tilt his head to one side as he considered.

'I am. I have no plans this afternoon. I would be happy to accompany you.'

For a moment she didn't know what to say. Part of her felt unsettled: it was strange enough having her husband back in her life, sharing her home, but she had not expected him to have any involvement with the charity work she did too.

'Thank you,' she said eventually.

'As pleasant as this has been, we should head back home soon,' Simon said, rising to his feet and holding out a hand to help her up. She stood, her body bumping lightly against his, and for a moment she felt as though time stood still. The sensible part of her mind screamed for her to step away, to put some distance between them, but her body just would not obey. She wished she didn't feel this attraction towards her husband. He had made it perfectly clear there would be no intimacy between them, yet she yearned for him to kiss her, to trail his fingers over her skin and make her feel truly alive.

With great effort she stepped away, turning her back for a moment to compose herself. By the time she turned back, Simon had moved and was busying himself with the horses, seemingly unperturbed by their moment of closeness.

Chapter Fourteen

St Benedict's Orphanage was based in a run-down building that had been built on the very edge of the slums of St Giles. It was tucked between two equally rickety buildings, one of which leaned forward over the street as if threatening to collapse any moment. When they had stepped out of the carriage, Simon had looked up and down the street dubiously, wondering how likely it was that the whole row would collapse and crush everyone inside. Such tragedies were not unheard of in these areas where the buildings were poorly constructed in the first place and decades of hard use had chipped away at any structural integrity that might have once been present.

The inside of the orphanage was not much better. There were sloping wooden floors, small windows and a staircase that creaked ominously whenever anyone climbed it. The rooms were dark and draughty, and the accommodation consisted of one long, thin room for the boys and another of similar proportions for the girls. Downstairs there was a communal area set with tables where the orphans both ate and did their lessons.

Despite the grim conditions the children lived in, Simon had been pleasantly surprised when he met Mrs

Phillips, the kindly woman appointed matron of the orphanage by the board of governors. There were twenty-
four children under her care, all thin and pale, but neatly
turned-out with faces scrubbed and hair cut short to
guard against lice.

She had spoken passionately about the work she did
in measured tones but with an accent that made Simon
think she had grown up locally, perhaps even a child of
the slum herself once. She certainly was a good advo-
cate for the orphanage.

They were now sitting at the back of the room whilst
the children were finishing their lessons. All twenty-four
were taught together, despite them ranging in ages from
two to fourteen. They sat, boys on one side of the room,
girls on the other, the youngest at the front and the oldest
at the back. At the front of the room the teacher pointed
to letters and phrases written out, and the children had
to read out in unison what they said.

'Look,' Alice whispered, motioning to a few children
in the middle of the room. As well as reading the words
they were also copying them onto slate tablets. 'I think
they only have four slate tablets between twenty-four
children.' She shifted a little, leaning forward to see a
little better. 'That is something we could easily donate
funds for.'

As she sat back, her arm brushed against his, a fleeting contact, but it made him stiffen all the same. He
realised he liked this version of his wife. Here at the
orphanage, the naïve country girl he had married was
long gone; instead, there was an idealistic woman who
was determined to make a difference in the world. When
she conversed with the matron, she spoke with convic-

tion and confidence, a woman who was used to being listened to.

After a few more minutes the lessons finished and the children filed out of the classroom, some into the kitchen beyond to get started on helping to prepare the evening meal, others upstairs where no doubt some other work waited for them. They moved quietly, a little subdued, and Simon felt a pang of pity for those who had lost their families and now lived in this dull, monotonous life, although he supposed it was better than the alternative that waited for them on the streets.

'Thank you for your visit, Lady Westcroft,' Mrs Phillips said as she ushered the last of the children upstairs and came to stand with them. 'We are most honoured in your interest in our small orphanage.'

'I am grateful for your hospitality and your honesty,' Alice said warmly. Mrs Phillips had a positive outlook, but she had not glossed over the shortcomings of the small orphanage, letting them see the bad alongside the good. 'We have our next meeting of the London Ladies' Benevolent Society in two weeks. I will report back to our members, and I am hopeful we will be able to offer some monetary and practical support.' Alice paused, looking at the matron with an assessing gaze, then nodded as if making a decision. 'I am conscious of your years of experience, Mrs Phillips, and I am wary of charging in and suggesting changes that may not be helpful, despite our best intentions. I wonder if you might take some time to write down what you think might be helpful so I can present your thoughts to the other members, or consider if you were willing to even come and talk to the ladies yourself.' Alice held up her hands and smiled at the matron. 'I know you are terribly busy, but give it some thought, and let me know what you can manage.'

'I will, Lady Westcroft.' Mrs Phillips turned to Simon. 'It is a pleasure to meet you, Lord Westcroft.'

'And you, Mrs Phillips.' He inclined his head and then offered Alice his arm as the matron showed them out.

Their carriage was waiting outside, surrounded by a gaggle of curious children. Simon was about to gently shoo them away when Alice gripped his arm.

'Thank you,' she said, looking up at him with her pale blue eyes. She had a contented smile on her face, and Simon felt a desire to keep that smile on her lips for ever.

'What for?'

'I admit I have only had the one husband,' she said with a mischievous glance at him, 'and that husband only for a few days, but I have seen how other men treat their wives. They disregard their views, silence their opinions. Many other men would have insisted on taking the lead with Mrs Phillips, even if it were not their cause to lead on. You did not. You stepped back and allowed me to be the one to ask questions and be in control, even for that short amount of time.'

'Most men are fools,' he murmured. 'They do not listen long enough to their wives to realise what they have to offer the world.' He smiled at her, feeling a unfamiliar satisfaction. This past year he had lived a lonely life, and he realised with a jolt that spending time with Alice, with her kind manner and lively conversation, were just what he needed. Despite the urge he felt to stand on the street corner staring into his wife's eyes, he motioned to the carriage. 'Shall we return home before we become targets for every cutpurse in London?'

Alice inclined her head, but as they stepped from the kerb to cross the road to their carriage, a group of beggar children broke off from the main gaggle and surrounded them, clamouring for money.

There were a couple of older boys in the group, but most of the children were no more than seven. Out of the corner of his eye, Simon saw a man leaning against the wall of a building on the other side of the street, and suddenly he felt a cold chill run through him. The man was resolutely not looking at them despite them being in his direct line of sight. It was suspicious, and without saying anything Simon reached out to grip hold of Alice's arm, wanting to pull her closer to him.

He'd had a privileged upbringing with most of his childhood spent on the estate in Northumberland, but his time travelling had taught him to be vigilant and trust his instincts. He believed the human mind was very good at working out when there was something wrong: it was why people talked of following their gut. Right now his gut was telling him to get his wife out of this situation as quickly as possible.

Alice looked at him in shock as he wrapped an arm around her waist and propelled her through the crowd of children, into the carriage. They had almost made it to the door when one of the younger boys stepped in front of them and with lightning-fast speed whipped out a knife. He held it low so it was hidden from any casual onlooker by the press of bodies around them. Simon saw the boy's hand was shaking, the knife weaving from side to side. He was a pale, scrawny lad, his face grimy and his feet bare on the cobbles. He looked pitiful rather than threatening, and as Simon watched the knife he realised it was likely a distraction. Whilst their eyes were fixed on the blade someone else would be trying to pick his pocket or relieve Alice of anything valuable.

He spun, reaching out to grab the thin wrist of an even younger boy whose hand had slipped inside Simon's jacket. The boy cried out in fear, and after a second the crowd of beggars that surrounded them disappeared, the children scarpering in different directions, diving into alleyways or dashing around corners. Simon looked up, past the carriage, to see the man who had been observing them calmly walking away too.

Only he, Alice and the little pickpocket remained.

The boy struggled, wriggling and tugging at his wrist, desperation on his face as he realised there was no escaping this predicament.

'Stop it,' Simon said, his voice firm but not cruel. The boy looked only five or six, although it was hard to tell as he was clearly malnourished, his growth no doubt stunted by a poor diet.

The boy stilled, looking up at Simon for the first time with big brown eyes.

Next to him he felt Alice shift, but he dared not take his attention from the boy in front of him.

'I don't want to hang,' the boy said after a minute, tears forming in his eyes and rolling onto his cheeks, making tracks through the dirt.

'You're not going to hang,' Simon said, moderating his tone. 'How old are you?'

The boy sniffed. 'Seven.'

Simon grimaced. If he handed this lad to a magistrate

and insisted he be punished for attempting to steal his purse, the child could end up taking a trip to the gallows. Some judges were more lenient towards the younger children that appeared before them, but others looked to set an example to thousands of children who committed crimes each year just looking to fill their hungry bellies.

'What is your name?'

The boy pressed his lips together and shook his head. Alice crouched down, seeming not to notice as the hem of her dress brushed against the dirt of the cobbles.

'What is your name?' she asked this time, her voice soft as if she were talking to one of their nieces.

'Peter, miss.' The boy looked at Alice, and then the tears started to flow from his eyes like a river after a winter storm. 'I don't want to hang, miss. Please don't let him hang me.'

'You're not going to hang,' Simon said firmly. 'There was a man watching us. Tall, dark hair, green coat. Was he with you?'

The boy nodded miserably.

'He told you what to do?'

Again the boy nodded.

'What is his name?'

'I can't tell you. He'll gut me if I do, and that's even worse than hanging.'

'Is he your father?' Alice asked.

'No, my father's dead.'

'What about your mother?'

The boy's eyes darted to the side, and he shrugged.

'Your mother is alive?' Simon said, waiting for the boy to look at him again. He still held the lad by the wrist, knowing as soon as he loosened his grip, the young boy would disappear into the warren of streets that made up St Giles.

Peter nodded glumly.

'Do you live near here?'

Again the boy nodded.

Simon turned to the driver of the carriage who had hopped down from his seat to join them.

'Drummond, take my wife home. Ensure she is escorted safely all the way to the front door.'

Simon turned to Alice to see her frowning.

'You mean to send me back alone?'

'You will be quite safe with Drummond, in the carriage.'

'It is not my safety I fear for.'

He looked at his wife for a moment, realisation dawning. 'You wish to see where this boy lives too?'

'He is only seven, Simon, and clearly he was under the influence of that man who was watching us. I do not want to see him punished.'

'You think I do not mean it when I say I do not want to see him hanged?'

Alice didn't say anything, but her lack of denial hurt more than he thought possible. He might not plan to be a true husband to his wife, but to realise how little she trusted him was difficult to accept.

'I merely want to take this boy home to his family and have a quiet word with his mother. She may be pragmatic, she may not, but I cannot merely let the boy go,' Simon said, his voice low. 'He will be off through the streets and back into the arms of the gang that pressed him to pick my pocket.' He spoke sharply and saw Alice recoil slightly, but she did not retreat.

'I shall come with you, then.'

'Lead the way, Peter,' Simon said brusquely.

Sullenly the young boy led them through a maze of streets to a set of rickety steps that led up to a wooden platform.

'Up there,' Peter said, motioning with his head. The streets were busy and they were drawing curious looks, and Simon found he wanted to get this over with, deliver the boy back to his mother and get Alice home to safety.

They climbed the stairs, and Simon knocked on the door, hearing the sound of a crying baby inside before the murmur of a low voice. After a minute the door opened, and a young woman peered out. She was in her twenties, but already her face was lined and her skin sallow. She held a baby in her arms and was bobbing up and down to soothe it. Her eyes widened as she saw Peter, and she looked up at Simon fearfully.

'What has he done?' she said, her voice cracking.

'You are Peter's mother?'

'Yes. What trouble has he found now?'

'He was in the company of a number of other children and a man who seemed to be directing them to pick people's pockets.'

The woman's face paled, and she reached out for her son, a protective look on her face.

'Don't blame my Peter, please, sir. He's only seven, only a young boy. He's hungry, that's all. We haven't been able to afford much food these last few months, not since his father died. Please don't report him. They'll make an example of him, I know they will.'

To his surprise Alice stepped forward and laid a hand on the woman's arm.

'We are not going to report him. We just wanted to be sure he got home to you safely.'

'And to let you know he is running with a group of pickpockets. If he continues with them, the next time he gets caught, whoever catches him may not be so lenient.'

'You're not going to report him?'

'No.' Simon let go of Peter's wrist, and the boy slipped into the darkness of the room behind his mother, peering out from behind her with a stunned look on his face.

'Thank you, sir. I will make sure he doesn't do anything like this again.'

Simon nodded and then took a step back. There was nothing more they could do here. In all likelihood Peter would be back with the gang of pickpockets first thing tomorrow, choosing to risk his neck rather than endure the relentless hunger he must feel each and every day. It was an awful situation, but now the boy was home safe he had to hand responsibility over to his mother.

He gestured to Alice that they should leave, and she gave Peter's mother one final reassuring smile before they climbed back down the rickety steps.

They walked in silence for a few minutes, navigating the maze of streets until they stepped back out to where the carriage was waiting.

Once inside Simon settled back on his seat and watched the orphanage disappear from view as the carriage rolled away. He was still hurt by Alice's mistrust of him, and he knew he needed to address it lest it eat away at him.

Before he could speak Alice leaned forward and placed her hand on his. It wasn't an overly intimate gesture, at least not for a wife to a husband in normal circumstances, but even the most innocent of touches seemed to ignite something inside him and made it impossible to focus.

'Thank you,' she said, looking across at him and giving him a soft smile.

'You did not trust I would not hand the boy over to a magistrate,' Simon said, watching as Alice stiffened and then nodded slowly.

'You are right,' she said eventually, then let out a deep sigh. 'We do not really know one another at all, do we, Simon?'

'Have I ever done anything to make you think I am an unreasonable man?'

'No,' she said quickly. 'You have always done exactly what you said you would.'

'Then, why doubt me?'

'Do you know how many hours we have spent in one another's company?'

He shook his head.

'Eight. Eight hours. Three at the Midsummer's Eve ball a year ago, one in the weeks before our wedding and one hour after we were married, then three in the days since you have returned. I have spent more time with my hatmaker in the last year, and I absolutely loathe hats.' She was speaking fast now, and he saw the pent-up frustration in her eyes. Their ride through Hyde Park earlier had been pleasant and their discussion reasonable, but he realised much of that was because Alice had been holding back the hurt she was feeling at how he had abandoned her. 'How am I meant to know how you will react to a certain situation? How am I meant to trust your word? We are two strangers tiptoeing around one another, neither sure how the other will react.' She sniffed and turned her head away, blinking furiously. After a moment she turned back. 'I *know* it has to be this way, Simon. I can understand your reasons and I accept them, but it does not mean you can have it both ways. Either you stay distant, living your life without the complication of another's feelings or you allow me close, but if you choose the former you must understand you cannot have the perks without the drawbacks.' She sat back, her chest heaving and her cheeks flushed with colour.

'I thought we had come to an understanding in the park.'

'Friendship?'

'Yes. A decision we would both live our lives independently, but with consideration of the other person.'

She looked at him then, a fierce intensity burning in her eyes, and for a moment he thought he saw a flash of desire, but then she pressed her lips together and inhaled sharply.

'You chide me for not trusting you, yet trust must be built, as must a friendship. I thought that was what you were doing, accompanying me to the orphanage, trying to build some common ground between us, but perhaps I was wrong.'

'You were not wrong, Alice,' he said, sitting back and running a hand through his hair. 'God's blood, I'm trying. This is difficult for me as well.'

She snorted and shook her head, and he felt a swell of anger rise inside him.

'I grant you it is more difficult for you, to have me return alive when I had promised you your freedom, but I too am trying to navigate an impossible situation.'

She leaned forward, jabbing a finger in his direction. 'Do not imply I want you dead.'

'It would be far simpler for you if I were.'

'You think I am that cruel?'

Simon felt the momentary anger simmer and then die away inside him, and he lowered his voice.

'No,' he said quietly. 'Of course not. Forgive me, that was unacceptable.'

Alice looked at him, her eyes narrowed. 'Just because you do not think you deserve to be alive doesn't mean I would ever agree with you. I went into this marriage with my eyes open, and although it may not be exactly what you promised, I would never, ever wish you were dead so that I could have my freedom.' She paused to draw in a ragged breath. '*You* are not a victim here, Simon. You get to dictate how our lives continue. You have the position of power. You say we cannot have a normal marriage,' she said and snapped her fingers, 'so we do not have a normal marriage. You say we cannot have children—' another snap of the fingers '—no children. You say we will work towards a friendship.' The third snap seemed to pierce his very soul. 'Friendship it is.'

Her words cut through him, and he gripped the seat, trying to anchor himself as the world spun around him.

For a long time they were silent, and the carriage was travelling through familiar streets before Simon was able to speak again.

'What do you mean, I do not think I deserve to be alive?'

'It is true, is it not?'

He shook his head, but even to him the movement was unconvincing.

'When you left, your mother and your sister-in-law

were devastated. It was as though they were in mourning, and for two women who had lost so much already, it nearly broke them.'

Simon closed his eyes for a moment, knowing this was going to be hard to hear. He had known his departure to Italy would be painful for those who loved him, but at the time he had thought it would ultimately protect them.

'Your mother couldn't get out of bed for a week.' She held up a hand. 'I do not tell you this to punish you, to make you feel guilty, but I think it is important you realise the impact of your actions on those who love you.'

'I knew it would be hard for them, but I thought it better than the alternative.'

'When your mother was up to having visitors, I went and sat with her every day, and she told me all about you and your family. She told me of how you idolised your father, how he was a wonderful man who both you and your brother looked up to. She told me of how his death had ripped you apart. A boy of twelve needs his father, and you lost yours in one of the worst ways imaginable.'

The carriage was beginning to slow as they approached the house, but Simon knocked loudly on the roof and stuck his head out the window, telling the driver to loop around until he was instructed otherwise.

'You mourned him deeply, but you still had your brother. Your mother told me you loved Robert more than anyone else.'

'He was the best of men.'

'And she said you slowly were able to put your father's death behind you.'

'With Robert's help.'

'Robert, with the beautiful wife and the incredible daughters. The earl, the beloved landlord.'

Simon nodded. His brother had been the perfect earl, the right mix of family man and imposing figure of authority.

'Then he died, and you were thrust back into mourning again, but this time there was no beloved brother to pull you out of it, and what was more you were expected to step into his shoes, to take his place.'

'I could never take his place.'

'But you were forced to. You became the earl, you took his seat in Parliament, you inherited all his properties, you were made to live the life which, only a few months before, your brother had.' Alice's voice softened, and she reached out and took his hand. 'Your mother thinks it was too much for you to bear, the idea that you were taking the life that should have been Robert's.'

'It was his life.'

'And she believes somewhere deep down you don't think you deserve to be alive when two great men, your father and your brother, were snatched away from this earth so early.'

Simon didn't say anything. It felt as though his heart were being squeezed inside his chest, and with every passing second the pain became more intense.

'It is why you will not even countenance a traditional marriage with me,' Alice said, her voice so low it was barely more than a whisper. 'You think that is a step too far. You have no choice but to be the earl and to take your seat in Parliament and to be the landlord to your tenants, but you can choose not to allow yourself any happiness, not to take that final part of Robert's life, the role of husband and father.'

'You have clearly thought about this a lot,' he murmured.

'I have thought of little else this past year. Your family have been struck by such tragedy, it is impossible to fathom the sorrow you must feel, yet I pity you not just for the loss of your father and brother but for your resolution that you do not deserve the happiness that they once had just because only you now survive.'

'I do not want your pity.'

Her fingers danced over the back of his hand, and he glanced up involuntarily. Alice looked agitated, as if she were about to burst into tears, but he did not have the emotional reserve to even think about comforting her right now.

With an air of desolate determination, she blinked back the tears. 'You do not want anything from anyone, Simon. You want to walk through this world without your troubles touching anyone else, but we do not live in isolation. Every time you push people away, every time you run away from your problems, you are hurting someone else besides yourself. I don't want you to suffer, Simon, but I also want you to see that when you suffer so do the rest of us, each and every person who cares about you.'

Ever since his father's death, he had not wanted to be a burden. He had seen how the bereavement had devastated his mother, how much more responsibility his brother had had to shoulder. He had wanted to make their lives easier, and here was Alice showing him he had done the complete opposite. He knew she was right, that whilst he had tried to push away his own pain, he had inadvertently made things harder for the very people he was trying to protect.

Quickly he thumped on the roof of the carriage again, waiting for it to slow before he threw open the door and jumped out. It had not completely stopped, and he startled a couple who were strolling arm-in-arm down the street, but he found he could not bring himself to care. He slammed the carriage door shut and without another word strode off, desperate to put as much distance between himself and Alice as possible.

His head was spinning, and he drew in deep ragged breaths, wondering how she had so thoroughly summed up everything he felt about his brother's death and the life he now lived.

Chapter Fifteen

Alice hated the silence in the house as she paced the floor of the drawing room. She had not meant to upset Simon, but once she had started trying to make him see what he was doing to himself she had been unable to stop.

Now it was eight hours later and Simon was still not home.

'You've probably made him run all the way back to Italy,' she muttered to herself.

Alice wished she had held her tongue. Simon was still grief-stricken from the death of his father and brother and reeling from the uncertainty of whether he suffered from the same condition that might strike him down at any moment. What she had said in the carriage was like sticking a knife in an already-wounded man. She was not proud of her actions, even though her words had been true.

She groaned. It had come from a selfish place, a need to lash out, as she had realised that Simon was never going to see her as anything more than a burden. Perhaps one he could develop a friendship with, but a burden all the same. When he had been quietly supportive in the orphanage, she had understood how much she yearned for a deeper relationship with this man. As much as she could tell herself she wished to safeguard her independence and protect herself from him hurting her by disappearing again, deep down she knew she wanted more.

'You are a fool,' she chided herself. Her outburst had only served to push him away and hurt him.

There was a noise from outside, and Alice stopped her pacing immediately. She had sent the servants to bed long ago, resolving to wait up herself to see if Simon returned. It was past two o'clock in the morning, and she had almost given up hope.

Alice rushed to the front door and opened it, jumping back as Simon half stumbled, half fell inside. He twisted as he fell and landed on his bottom, looking up at her and giving her a lopsided smile.

For a moment Alice didn't move, too stunned to do anything more than stare.

'Good evening, my beautiful wife,' Simon said, slurring his words.

'You're drunk.'

'I may have had one or two little glasses of whisky.' He tried to stand, but his feet got tangled, and he ended up where he had started on the floor.

'I have been so worried about you.' She took a deep breath, knowing she would have to apologise again in the morning when he was sober, but needing to get the words out now as well. 'I'm so sorry for what I said, Simon. It was unforgiveable.'

He tried to stand again, and this time managed to get to his feet, stumbling slightly as he moved. Alice reached out and steadied him, and he wrapped an arm around her shoulder.

'You smell nice,' he said, burying his face in her hair and inhaling deeply. 'You always smell nice.'

'I think we had better get you to bed,' she said as he reached up and plucked a pin out of her hair.

'You have such beautiful hair.' With clumsy fingers he pulled out a couple more pins, allowing the soft waves to cascade over her shoulders. 'You should wear it loose all the time. You look like a goddess.'

'You are very effusive when you are drunk.'

He grinned at her. 'Truthful. I'm truthful when I'm drunk.'

'Do you think you can manage the stairs?'

'Of course,' he said, almost tripping over his own feet and looking up at her guiltily. 'Perhaps with your help.'

Slowly they climbed the stairs, pausing halfway up for Simon to rest his head on her shoulder and declare she had the prettiest shoulders in the world.

Once upstairs they started along the hallway, passing the door to the master bedroom that was still Alice's. Simon reached out for the door-handle and opened it, pulling her in that direction.

'You don't sleep here,' she said, trying to pull him back into the hall, but her small stature put her at a disadvantage.

'We should sleep together,' he murmured. 'We are married. There is nothing wrong with it.'

'Do not jest, Simon.'

'I am completely serious,' he slurred, looking at her intently. 'What man wouldn't want to fall asleep with you in his arms?'

He had pulled her farther into the room now, and Alice looked back dubiously at the door.

'You can sleep here tonight. I will take your bedroom.'

'Stay with me, Miss James.'

'Alice,' she corrected him.

She stumbled back and sat down on the edge of the bed, almost sliding off onto the floor. Twice he reached down to try to pull his boots off, and twice he missed.

'Let me,' she said, placing a hand on his chest to stop him from bending down again. He caught hold of her wrist, his fingers caressing the delicate skin. For a moment she did not move, allowing herself to enjoy the caress. These last few days she had found thoughts of her husband touching her had crept into her mind unbidden far more than she would like to admit. It was typical that it took far too many glasses of whisky for her fantasy to become reality.

Brusquely she shrugged him off and bent down to pull off his boots.

'Thank you,' he murmured, lying back on the bed.

'No, no, no,' Alice said quickly, knowing if he fell asleep like this he would be uncomfortable and his clothes almost certainly ruined. 'We need to get you out of your jacket and cravat at the very least.'

'You want to see me naked, Alice,' he murmured, a smile on his face but his eyes closed.

She remained silent, putting her energy into helping him sit back up and then manoeuvring the jacket from his shoulders. His movements were uncoordinated, and it took far longer than it should, but eventually he was just in his shirt and trousers.

'Let's get you into bed,' she said, figuring he could sleep comfortably enough in the remaining clothes.

'I'm not undressed,' he murmured, and as she watched, he pulled his shirt over his head revealing the toned torso underneath. Although she had only ever seen him clothed, Alice knew he had a lean, muscled physique. Even through the layers of his shirt and jacket, the few times they had danced she had been able to feel the power he held in his body. Now, though, with his upper body bared in moonlight, she paused, her eyes raking over his half-naked form.

Alice felt something stir inside her, and she had to resist the urge to reach out and trail her fingers across his skin. In the state he was in, he would invite her in, forgetting about all the reasons he did not want to be intimate with her, but she would not do that to him, no matter how much she craved his touch.

'Let's get you into bed,' she said again, adopting her best schoolmistress voice and trying to pretend she was completely unaffected by him.

Somehow she managed to get him standing so she could pull back the sheets and then help him climb into bed. As she leaned over to ensure the pillows were comfortable under his head, his arm reach out and caught her around the waist.

'Don't leave me, Alice,' he said, his touch gentle but firm.

'I'll just be along the hall.'

'Stay with me tonight. You are my wife.'

'In name only,' she said, regretting the sharpness of her words immediately, but thankfully Simon did not seem to notice.

'There's space for you right here,' he said, and with a firm pull he tumbled her into bed beside him.

Alice let out a low cry of surprise and was about to sit up when Simon rolled over and flung his arm across her, pinning her in place. His face nuzzled into her neck, his lips brushing against her skin.

'Have I told you that you smell delicious?' he mumbled.

'You did mention it on the stairs.'

He murmured something incomprehensible, and then with his lips against her skin and his arm thrown possessively over her body, his breathing deepened.

'Simon,' Alice whispered, wriggling from side to side, unable to believe he had fallen asleep so quickly.

There was no response. She stilled, considering her predicament. The right thing to do would be to slip out from under his arm and leave him to sleep alone. She could spend the night in his bed; his room was comfortable and his bed made up and inviting. Yet something made her want to stay. Alice knew Simon was only being affectionate because he was in his cups. Tomorrow in the cold light of day, he would probably regret his actions, but tonight he had wanted her. This past year she had craved affection, craved the touch of another person, especially whilst she was in London. At least in Northumberland she received the occasional embrace from her sister-in-law or nieces, but here she was the lady of the house and so far above everyone else in social status there was no contact whatsoever.

Alice closed her eyes for a moment and wondered if she were being completely foolish, but it was merely a cuddle, one warm body pressed against another, nothing more. Tomorrow she could tell Simon she had been trapped by his arm over her waist, and it wouldn't be entirely untrue.

Deciding she would allow herself to have this one chaste night with her husband in their marital bed, Alice closed her eyes and tried to quieten her racing thoughts.

In all his thirty-three years, Simon had only been blindingly drunk a handful of times, normally after celebrations where drink after drink had been on offer and his spirits high. He thought back to the night after his graduation, surrounded by friends, toasting the end of their time at university. The memory gave him a momentary warm feeling, and he luxuriated in it for a few seconds before returning to the matter in hand.

'You're not a young pup anymore,' he muttered to himself. Ten years ago he could have drunk twice as much and not felt the room tilt around him the next day, but now his body was protesting, and he would probably pay for his excesses the entire day, or at the very least until he could get a strong cup of coffee inside him.

As he lay in bed, eyes firmly closed to guard against the room spinning, he realised he was not alone. There was a warm body in the bed next to him, soft and smooth, and he was pressed at least partially against her.

His eyes shot open, and he took in the red hair spread across the pillow and the peaceful face of his wife as she slept. She looked contented, happy even, and as he watched, she burrowed farther down into the pillow, her body shifting and pressing against him.

For a moment Simon was too shocked to move. She was in a sensible cotton nightgown with a dressing gown overtop, but at some point in the night the material had ridden up to reveal her legs and, above them, the hint of her buttocks. Up higher his hand rested across her waist, fingers splayed, the tips brushing against her breast.

Simon felt a surge of desire almost overwhelm him. He had always found his wife attractive, but lying in bed next to her, her warm body pressed against his, was unbearable. He wanted to lower his lips to hers and kiss her until she woke, and then strip the sensible nightdress from her body and enjoy every inch of her.

A sensible man would move away, but Simon could not bring himself to roll over. With a great effort he thought back to the night before. Alice did not look like she had been ravaged, her nightclothes were not torn or discarded, and she slept peacefully beside him.

Slowly the events of the previous evening came back to him. He retraced his steps from his gentlemen's club where he had spent half the afternoon trying to drown out the echo of Alice's words with a bottle of whisky. Later he had moved on to less salubrious establishments and had continued drinking where no one knew him.

He remembered stumbling home and Alice waiting for him, the rest of the house in darkness, and finally he remembered her helping him upstairs to bed.

Gently he pressed a kiss against the back of her head. She couldn't know how much he desired her, how every day he dreamed about scooping her into his arms and making her into his true wife. It was torture being so close and being unable to act on the desire that surged through him.

She was right in her assessment of him the day before, although her delivery of the stinging truths had left a lot to be desired. He wouldn't allow them to become close for two reasons. The first was as he had told her when he'd returned: he did not know when he might suddenly die, killed by the same affliction that had suddenly taken his father and his brother. He did not want to build a relationship with Alice only to pull it all away from her when his inevitable death came.

The second reason was something he thought had remained hidden deep inside, this feeling that he had stepped into Robert's life. He had the title, the seat in Parliament, the estate and all the properties, the responsibility of being the earl. All the things Robert had relished and enjoyed. It would be too much if Simon had a happy marriage and children too, those things that his brother had cherished the most.

'Not so hidden,' he murmured quietly. It would seem his mother had guessed what stopped him from settling down as an earl was expected to, what drove him away from a conventional marriage to live a life of loneliness.

He wished it wasn't the case, and he knew Robert would never begrudge him happiness, but he couldn't help feeling as though he had stolen his brother's life.

Next to him Alice shifted and pressed herself even closer against him, giving a little sigh of contentment. He knew she wanted more from their marriage, that despite having built a life for herself here with her charities and position in society, she craved human touch and affection. He had seen the way she glanced at him, the desire in her eyes, and part of him responded in the same way.

With his free hand he reached out and gently stroked her hair, allowing himself to imagine for a moment a life where he gave in to his desire. Long mornings spent in bed together, snatched kisses in public, walking hand in hand through Hyde Park. Skipping dinner in favour of returning to the bedroom and trying to quench the insatiable desire they felt.

It was a tempting picture, and with her warm body pressed against him he almost gave in, but nothing had changed, not really. Alice might know of the pain and turmoil that raged inside him, but that did not lessen it.

She let out a soft sigh and then wriggled a little, and as he watched, her eyelids flickered open. She gave him a sleepy smile, not really registering she was pressed against her husband in bed, but after a few seconds her eyes widened, and she scrabbled to sit up, pulling the bedcovers around her.

He hair was loosed down her back, and he vaguely remembered leaning in and plucking some of the pins out the night before, yet he certainly wouldn't have had the dexterity to remove them all. That meant she had taken some out herself. Equally, even if he had been the one to pull her into bed, she would not have remained trapped indefinitely. At some point she had decided to stay, decided to spend the night with her husband, removed the rest of the pins from her hair and fallen asleep in his arms.

'Good morning,' he said, speaking softly, aware that soon his head would begin pounding from the aftereffects of the alcohol.

'Good morning,' Alice said eventually.

'Thank you for helping me to bed last night.'

She inclined her head, unable to meet his eye for a second. 'How do you feel?'

'Like I drank far too much whisky yesterday,' he said with a half-smile. 'Unsurprisingly.'

She looked at him, biting her lip and screwing up the bed-sheets in her hands.

'I'm so sorry,' she blurted out, a look of anguish on her face. 'What I said to you yesterday was unforgiveable. I should have kept my thoughts to myself. It is none of my business why you do not wish to have a conventional wife or a family. It should be enough that you tell me that you don't.'

'Nonsense,' he said softly. 'The way we entered into this marriage might have been unorthodox, but I cannot continue pretending I do not have a wife.' He reached out and placed his hand next to hers so their fingers were touching. 'If anyone has the right to talk to me of these things it is you.'

'I went about it the wrong way.'

'That I will not deny,' he said, softening the reproof with a smile, 'but I do not believe your intention was malicious. Indeed, I think it came from a place of affection, which is remarkable, given how I have held you at arm's-length since I returned.' He looked down now to where their arms touched and wished he could reach out and take her hand in his own, but despite the desire he felt, despite the affection and respect, he still could not rid himself of the belief that he did not deserve the happiness that such a union would bring.

Alice looked at him sadly. 'You do deserve happiness, Simon. I know it doesn't mean much coming from me, a near stranger, but I have listened to what your family have said about you this past year. I have heard of your devotion to your nieces and how you coaxed Sylvia from a very dark place after her father died. I have heard how you supported Maria and ensured she didn't have to think of the practicalities when she was left widowed with three young children.' She paused, looking at him almost pleadingly before pressing on. 'Then, there are your actions when it comes to me. We were both foolish at the Midsummer's Eve ball, but you would not have suffered the consequences, especially with your plans already made to leave England. Yet despite having an easy way out, you did not hesitate to upend your decision to ensure I was protected. You gave me your name and a life of comfort and opportunity. Do you know how few men would do that for a woman they barely knew?' She shook her head, not waiting for an answer. 'You swooped in and rescued me, Simon, from a life of shame and scandal, when my best hope was that a man I hated would consent to marry me. How could I not fall a little in love with you?'

This made him look up sharply, and Alice held up a placating hand.

'Do not fear, I do not deny over the past year I have dreamed of you returning from Italy, telling me you could not bear to be away from me, but since your return you have made it clear there will be no intimacy between us. We shall live our lives like two spinster siblings, chaste with a moderate affection. I have heard what you have told me over and over again.'

'I have been a little blunt, haven't I?'

She smiled at that. 'Perhaps I have needed the bluntness.'

'I cannot change how I feel about Robert,' Simon said.

'I know.' Her expression was sad but not surprised. He

felt a sudden surge of anger, directed towards himself. Here he was in bed beside a beautiful woman, a woman he had could not stop thinking about kissing, and all he had done these past few days was make her miserable.

'If you think you could allow yourself to be happy with someone else, I would understand,' Alice said softly. 'I know I was not the woman you would have chosen for a wife, and if you wish to take a mistress I will not object.'

'You doubt my attraction to you,' he said, his voice low.

She looked at him in surprise, and Simon felt something shift inside him. If he were to reach out and pull her to him, there would be nothing illicit about it. They were husband and wife, and Alice could not hide the fact that she was attracted to him. The only person standing in the way of the desire they both felt was him.

He felt the familiar guilt he was hit with every time he contemplated something enjoyable, but this time he pushed it down. He wasn't proposing he live a normal, full life with Alice, not like Robert had experienced with his wife, just that he and Alice enjoy the occasional bit of affection.

'Do not doubt my attraction to you.'

He looped a firm arm around her waist, feeling the warmth of her skin through the layers of her nightclothes. Alice's body was stiff for a second, and then she let out a little moan and relaxed against him.

Before he could talk himself out of it, Simon kissed her, a kiss filled with all the pent-up desire and passion that had been surging through him since his return. He gripped Alice gently, and manoeuvred her into his lap, loving the way she felt as she wrapped her legs around him.

Her lips were soft and sweet, and he kissed her deeply, as if searching for something he had lost long ago.

'You do not know how many times I have dreamed of doing this,' he said, pulling away for a second to kiss the soft skin of her neck. She shivered at the touch of his lips on her skin and pulled him closer.

He wanted to take his time and enjoy her, to show her pleasure in so many different ways, yet he also felt a frantic need to do this quickly in case the rational part of his mind took over at any point.

'Simon,' she whispered, invoking his name like he was a demigod. He kissed her again, long and deep, his hands caressing her back.

'This needs to come off,' he said, gripping the thin material of her nightgown. Without protest Alice slipped an arm from her dressing gown and then wriggled out of it completely. Now there was only her nightgown separating their bodies. She shifted on his lap, brushing against his hardness as she lifted herself up and he caught hold of the hem of the garment. Before either of them could come to their senses, he lifted the nightdress over her head and threw it on the floor beside the bed.

For a moment they both stilled, Alice with a look of apprehension in her eyes that reminded him that she might be a married woman in the eyes of society, but that she was still very much an innocent.

Slowly he lifted a hand and trailed a finger from the notch between her collarbones down between her breasts.

'You are beautiful, Alice,' he said.

Her instinct was to cover herself with her arms, wrapping them round her body, and he cursed himself for his part in making her feel unattractive or unwanted. Nothing could be further from the truth. Right now he could not understand how he had allowed himself to be apart from her for so long.

Gently he pressed her arms back to her sides and trailed his fingers over her chest again, loving the way her breath caught in her throat as his hand brushed against her breast.

'You're teasing me,' she said, a note of accusation in her voice.

'I am building the anticipation,' he said, smiling.

'Another way of saying *teasing*.'

'Would you prefer it if I just dove straight in?' he said, leaning forward and taking her nipple into his mouth, making her gasp with pleasure and shock.

Alice let out an incomprehensible moan, and he felt her body stiffen underneath him before slowly she relaxed, letting her head drop to his shoulder.

He pulled away, kissing her again and resuming his slow, gentle caress of her body.

'You have the softest skin I have ever felt,' he murmured, circling from the top of her chest around her breasts and back again. He repeated the movement again and again until he could feel the anticipation. Carefully he flipped her over so she was lying on her back on the bed, and he held himself above her, lowering his lips to meet her body. He took his time, trailing kisses across her breasts and over her abdomen as she writhed underneath him, the heat building between them.

He stroked her thighs as he kissed her, slowly coaxing her to relax.

'What are you doing to me?' Alice whispered as he

moved even lower, feeling her tense and push forwards involuntarily as he kissed her thighs.

He didn't answer her; instead, he trailed kisses up her thighs and then without any further warning kissed her in her most private place. Alice let out a shocked yelp, her hands scrabbling at his head.

'What are you doing, Simon?'

'I would have thought that obvious.'

'I did not know...'

'That you could be kissed there? No, I suppose you would not. Can I show you how good it can feel?'

With only a moment's hesitation she nodded, and Simon lowered his head, loving the way her hips came up to meet him. She was responsive to his every touch, and it wasn't long before he saw she was gripping the bed-sheets either side of her with her hands as if clinging on for her life.

Alice's breathing quickened and then she clamped her legs together, letting out a deep moan.

Simon raised himself up and pushed his trousers down, holding himself above Alice before he pressed against her. Slowly he entered her, feeling her body rise to meet his, and then he was fully buried inside her.

He held in place for a moment, his eyes meeting Alice's, and then he withdrew, knowing he had to go slow for her, but it took every ounce of his self-control. Gradually he increased the speed of his thrusts, lowering his lips to brush against hers and loving the way her fingers raked down his back. Beneath him he felt her tense and tighten and then let out a moan of pleasure as she climaxed, the look of ecstasy on her face and the tightness that engulfed him enough to push him over the edge.

Quickly he withdrew and finished on the sheets, even in the moment of passion in control enough to know he could not risk her getting pregnant.

He moved off Alice, coming in behind her and pulling her into an embrace. He couldn't see her face, but her body did not feel fully relaxed, and he wondered if she was already regretting their moment of intimacy.

Eventually she turned to face him, her eyes searching his for something he worried she would not find. Without a word she turned back, tucking her body close to his, and pulling his arm around her. She laced her fingers through his, and he held her tight.

Chapter Sixteen

$\iff$

Alice had been surprised that she'd slept again, a deep slumber that had not been disturbed by Simon rising at some point, and she was disappointed to find herself alone when she woke. She wondered if their intimacy had been enough to drive him away completely, out of London, perhaps even out of the country, she and glanced over at the little writing desk in the corner to see if she could spot a hastily scrawled note.

There was no note, and a few minutes later the door to the bedroom opened and Simon walked in carrying a tray of coffee and a couple of newspapers under one arm.

'You're awake,' he said with a smile.

Alice would never admit how much it pleased her that he was still here.

'What time is it?'

'After ten. I checked with Miss Stick, and she tells me you have no engagements until your dinner party with the Hampshires this evening.'

Simon was fully dressed, and he showed no outward signs of his heavy night of drinking, although once he had poured the coffee he took a tentative sip before deciding to take a full cup.

'I brought you the papers,' he said. 'We are mentioned in the gossip rag.'

Alice's eyes widened. She had been featured many times before, but in recent months only small comments about what dress she had decided to wear or who she had danced with, nothing more interesting than that, but from Simon's tone she could tell today was different.

'Third paragraph down.'

She let her eyes drift over the first two paragraphs quickly, then read aloud.

'*Lord Westcroft made a return to London this week, much to the surprise of society and to his wife. Lady Westcroft was left looking shocked at the Livingstones' ball when her husband waltzed in and swept her onto the dance floor. One has to wonder if the errant Lord Westcroft thinks of his wife at all—at the very least he does not seem to include her in his travel plans.*'

She eyed Simon carefully. It was more a criticism of him than her, and not entirely untrue even if it was an unflattering view of the situation.

'They are not wrong. I did just waltz into the Livingstones' ball and surprise you. It must have been unsettling for you.'

Alice blinked, pulling the sheets up a little farther to cover her nakedness. *This* was what they were going to talk about now? After everything that had happened yesterday and this morning?

Pointedly she set the paper on the bed and looked at him expectantly. Simon sipped his coffee, pretending he didn't feel her eyes on him and then sighed.

'You wish to talk about this morning.'

'We *need* to talk about this morning.'

Simon cleared his throat and then for a long time did not say anything at all.

'Simon,' she prompted him eventually.

'I spent a long time thinking yesterday after our…discussion,' he said slowly. 'And I have to acknowledge that on many points you are correct. I do feel guilty about living the life my brother should have, and I shy away from following the same path as him in the parts that are not essential. I had vowed never to marry, but when we met we set into motion a chain of events that led us to the altar. It did not matter too much, for the marriage was not to be like Robert's, not a love match.'

Alice hugged her knees to her, wondering if she was strong enough to hear what he had to say.

'I am not trying to punish myself, or you, in any way, Alice. I know my father's and brother's deaths were not my fault, yet I cannot help the guilt I feel that I am still here whilst they are not.'

'I understand that can be quite common amongst people where one person survives a tragedy when others close to them have died.'

'It was hard hearing that everyone close to me had worked out what was going on in far better detail than I had,' he said quietly. 'I think that is why I was so upset yesterday. I thought what I was doing wasn't affecting other people too much, but I was wrong.'

Alice felt like they were reaching some ultimatum, some declaration of how he truly felt and what he wanted from his future.

'I cannot deny the desire I feel for you, Alice. I think that was obvious this morning.'

Alice felt her heart sink. As unlikely as it was, she

had hoped for a declaration of love, a suggestion that they make their marriage a conventional one where they enjoyed each other's company to the fullest. She chided herself for getting her hopes up once again. She was too naïve in the ways of the heart, and she needed to start protecting herself better.

'What do you propose we do?'

Simon sighed. 'I am not sure we can live in the same house and not end up in a similar situation as we did this morning.'

'You wish to leave?'

'No,' he said quickly. 'I do not. Yet I cannot offer you what a husband should in these circumstances.'

Love. He could not offer her love. Even if he stayed, he would be holding part of himself back, making sure he held her at arm's-length to deny himself the happiness they could have.

She pressed her lips together, wishing she could find the words to tell him how she felt, how it hurt to have him stand here and tell her that, despite the fact they were married and they both desired one another and cared for one another, he could not allow himself to build a mutually loving relationship with her. She should reject his unspoken proposal, but she thought of how her body craved his touch, of how happy she had felt in the moments of their lovemaking.

She had entered into this marriage after Simon had told her he would be dead within the year and she would be free to marry a man of her choosing, a man who could love her. That wasn't going to happen now, and if the doctors had got things wrong it might never be the case. She had forty years of marriage stretching out in front of her with a man who could not love her, and she could not seek that comfort elsewhere. At least if they had a physical relationship, she could slake some of her craving for intimacy with Simon's touch.

'We continue as before,' Alice said, decisively. 'Companionship, friendship, they are our focus, but with the added benefit of sharing a bed whenever we both choose.'

'You would be comfortable with that arrangement?'

'We are married. There is nothing wrong with it,' Alice said firmly. 'We are both adults with desires and needs, and I think it safe to say we both find the other attractive.'

'Indeed,' Simon murmured.

'Then, it is settled. I know not to expect a declaration of love from you, and you are happy to give me the freedom I have enjoyed for the last year to make my own decisions.'

'I feel as though we should shake hands,' Simon murmured.

'There is no need for that,' Alice said quickly. Despite the agreement she had just proposed, she felt as though she needed some privacy to pull apart what she had just agreed to. It was all very well telling Simon that she would not develop feelings for him, but if she were honest she was well past halfway to loving him already, flaws and all. 'Now, I need to wash and dress. Could you ring the bell for my lady's maid?'

Chapter Seventeen

It was growing dark when they stepped out of the carriage in front of Mr and Mrs Hampshire's house, Simon offering her his arm. Alice felt the spark that flowed between them as her body brushed against his and quickly tried to quell it. She'd spent the day trying to persuade herself she hadn't made the biggest mistake of her life, and now she was beginning to believe their decision might actually be for the best.

Simon had been attentive on the carriage ride to the Hampshires after a note had arrived that afternoon, inviting him to join the dinner party, and Alice was enjoying his company. For the past year she had always had to arrive alone at events like this, and it was pleasant to walk in on her husband's arm.

It was not to be a large affair, and in the drawing room Mrs Livingstone ensured they both had a drink before dinner. There were five other guests, all people Alice knew fairly well, including Lady Kennington and her husband, and a wealthy couple in their forties who had moved to London from Bath a year earlier with their eighteen-year-old daughter, Emma.

'Emma is going to play for us,' Mrs Hampshire announced, showing Alice and Simon to a small sofa to listen.

Emma Finn was a talented pianist, and she played a few pieces perfectly with no music in front of her. Alice found herself relaxing, sinking back into the cushions of the sofa and into her husband. Simon had an arm behind her, resting on the back of the sofa, but after a minute she felt his fingers gently caressing her neck. At first it was an occasional touch, a gentle stroke as she shifted in her seat, but as the other guests became focussed on Emma at the piano, his touch became bolder, and he began tracing circles on the soft skin of her neck, just below her ear.

Alice felt as though every inch of her skin was taut with anticipation, and as his touch intensified she could not follow the music. All she could think about was Simon's fingers dancing over her skin, imagining him dipping lower.

All too soon the music finished, and Alice had to shake herself from the daze she found herself in.

They were not seated next to each other at dinner, as was the custom, but Alice found it hard to concentrate on anything but the fleeting glances she shared with Simon across the table. He was directly opposite her, and she had to keep reminding herself it was not polite to just stare longingly at her husband all evening. She'd had her reservations about their new arrangement, but trying to bury her attraction for him would have been futile.

'What did you think of St Benedict's?' Lady Kennington asked her as the main courses were brought out. Alice started to answer and then felt Simon's foot tap her own under the table. She forced herself to concentrate.

'It is well-run. I liked Mrs Phillips, the matron. She seemed sensible and kind, and the children were polite and clean. But the orphanage was in a dire state, and I think they have very little funds available to them.'

'It is a good cause, is it not?'

'Very good. I have asked Mrs Phillips to put some thought into what she feels would be helpful from the London Ladies' Benevolent Society.' Alice was about to say more, but Simon was gently caressing her leg with his foot, and she was finding it difficult to concentrate.

'Are you feeling well, Lady Westcroft?' Lady Kennington enquired.

'A little warm, that is all,' Alice said quickly, resolutely not looking at her husband.

The rest of dinner followed in much the same way, with Alice trying to concentrate on the conversation around the table but being unable to think of anything but the man sitting across from her, imagining he was pushing her back onto the bed and making love to her. It felt like the meal went on for ages, and Alice was pleased when it was time to move back to the drawing room, with the men moving to another downstairs room for drinks and cards. After a minute of listening to Miss Finn on the piano, she quietly excused herself, muttering something about the ladies' retiring room. In truth she needed some time to herself.

There were candles lit in the hall, but it was dark compared to the drawing room, and as Alice made her way to the stairs she did not even think to look in the dark corners. She gasped as a figure stepped out from the shadows by the stairs, gripping her by the wrists and pressing her against the wall.

'Simon,' she whispered, her heart pounding.

'You mean to torture me,' he murmured in her ear.

'Torture you?'

'You look ravishing tonight, and all I can think about…' He kissed her neck, making Alice gasp. 'You bring me somewhere I cannot touch you. I cannot even sit next to you.'

His lips were hot on her skin, and she felt a shudder of pleasure run through her body. It didn't matter that they were standing in someone else's hall, it didn't matter that at any moment someone could come out of one of the rooms and see them: all she could think of was Simon and where he would kiss her next.

'All I could think about all dinner was stripping you naked and lying you down on the dinner table.'

Alice gasped, picturing the scene. 'Not with everyone watching.'

'They would scatter soon enough. Good Lord, how do you always smell so good?'

'Simon, not the hair,' she said as he reached for one of her pins. 'I have to go back in there.'

He ran a hand down her side, over her waist and around to her buttocks and then lowered his lips to the bare skin of her upper chest. For a moment she forgot where they were and let out a moan that seemed to echo around the grand entrance hall.

'We need to get home,' he said, lifting his lips for just a second. 'Or we will never be invited to a dinner party with the Hampshires again.'

Before she could answer, he kissed her deeply, one hand still pinning both of hers above her head. He was gentle, but there was no denying he was much stronger than her, and she loved the way he held her against the wall, the cool wallpaper against her back.

'I will make my excuses,' Alice said, allowing herself one last kiss before she pulled away.

She paused before reentering the drawing room, aware that her cheeks were flushed and her clothes probably a little dishevelled. Thankfully, Miss Finn was still playing another masterful piece on the piano, and Alice was able to sidle up to their hostess and speak to her discreetly.

'I am awfully sorry, Mrs Hampshire, but I feel a little unwell. I think it best I return home.'

Mrs Hampshire looked at Alice with concern. 'You do look pink, my dear. Yes, go home at once, and get that housekeeper of yours to make a tincture.'

'Thank you for a wonderful evening.'

'Do you wish for me to send someone to accompany you home?'

'No, I am sure Lord Westcroft will be happy to come with me.'

Mrs Livingstone smiled indulgently. 'Of course. I forget you are still like newly-weds. Come, let us go fetch your husband.'

It felt like an eternity before they had bid everyone goodnight and the carriage had been brought round to the front door, but after a final wave to their hosts, Alice and Simon were alone.

Before he stepped up into the carriage Simon had a quiet word with the driver and then they were underway, travelling at a good pace through the quiet streets.

'I have instructed Drummond to keep circling around London until I alert him we wish to go home,' Simon said.

Alice's eyes widened, but before she could say anything Simon gently pulled her onto his lap.

'Where were we?'

'I think you were kissing me here,' Alice said, indicating the spot on her neck just below her ear. When he kissed her there it sent little jolts of pleasure all the way through her body.

'And I think my hands were here,' Simon said, slipping his hands underneath her and giving her buttocks a squeeze as he gave her a mock lascivious raise of his eyebrows.

She leaned forward and kissed him, losing herself in desire. It felt as though she were falling head first into paradise, and she didn't want to ever stop.

They kissed for a long time, then Alice shifted, snaking her hands down in between them to push at the waistband of his trousers. He gathered her skirts up, and soon there was nothing between them. Alice positioned herself carefully, feeling the wonderful fullness as he entered her, and then she was lost as their bodies came together again and again until she cried out, and wave after wave of pleasure flooded through her.

Simon lifted her off him quickly before he, too, let out a low groan of pleasure.

For a long while neither of them spoke.

'You make me reckless,' she said eventually.

'I think it is the other way round,' Simon murmured. 'Take the Midsummer's Eve ball. I have spent the last ten years carefully avoiding any scandal that might tie me to a respectable young woman. A few hours in your company and I'm suggesting midnight dashes through the gardens and kissing you far too close to the house.'

Alice closed her eyes and remembered that night. It was the night that had changed the course of her life. When things got difficult, all she had to do was remind herself that she could have been unlucky enough to be married to vile Cousin Cecil. This arrangement with her husband was unusual and certainly not what she would have chosen for herself when she was a young girl dreaming of her perfect man, but it was better than a lifetime of repression as Cecil's wife.

'You look serious,' Simon said, leaning forward and stroking her forehead between her eyebrows. 'What are you thinking about?'

'How the course of my life changed completely in the space of one evening.'

'It did, didn't it?'

'I suppose none of us can know what life has in store for us.'

They lapsed into silence, and Alice wondered if Simon was thinking about all the uncertainty in his life. She wanted him to see that he was not the only one who did not know what would happen. He might have the same condition that had killed his father and his brother, but equally he might not. Even if he did, it might not strike him down for decades. There were so many dangers in life; people were caught up in unpredictable scenarios all the time. Simon had reason to be more worried than most, but it did not mean she agreed with his approach to hold everyone he loved at a distance in hope that they would not suffer as much when he did die.

She looked at him and bit her lip. Despite her stern words to herself and her best efforts, she knew she was falling in love with Simon. She felt more than desire, more than physical attraction. She wanted more than he could offer her. It was a sure way to get hurt, but it wasn't something under her conscious control.

Chapter Eighteen

The next week passed in a blur with one day running into the next. They spent a large proportion of their time in the bedroom. Simon could not keep his hands off Alice, wherever they were. He sought her out in the drawing room or at the breakfast table, and she was always as happy to kiss him as he was her. As the week progressed they stopped pretending to even try to do anything else and gave in to the pleasure of acting like newly-weds.

'I need to get dressed today,' Alice said on the morning of their eighth day together. 'Mrs Phillips from St Benedict's Orphanage sent a note yesterday saying she had spent some time thinking about what would be really helpful to the orphanage. She invited me to meet with her for an hour or so this afternoon.'

Simon frowned. 'I have an appointment with my solicitor that I cannot miss this afternoon, to go over a few land issues that have come up during my absence.'

Alice trailed her fingers over Simon's naked shoulder and then lowered her lips to kiss it absently. 'It does not matter. If Drummond takes me in the carriage I will be perfectly safe. I will ensure he drops me off right outside.'

'One of those street children had a knife.'

'I think that is probably true of many people in our beautiful city.'

'None of them have threatened you.'

'That is true.' She considered for a moment. 'How about I take Frank Smith with me? He is young and strong, and his background means he is used to the tricks and schemes of the street urchins.'

'I would prefer to come with you myself, but I suppose that is a fair compromise. With Drummond and Smith, you can hardly get into too much trouble.'

'I promise to go straight there and straight back,' Alice said, smiling. 'No matter how many pallid pickpockets I run into and feel sorry for.'

'No pallid pickpockets, and no diversions.'

She leaned in and kissed him, feeling a thrill of anticipation for the day ahead.

'I shall be back home around five, then we have dinner with the Dunns later.'

'Then, I have plenty of time to persuade you we should send our apologies and have dinner at home.'

'You would choose to stay home every night of the week,' Alice said as Simon's arm snaked around her waist.

'Tell me you'd rather spend the evening with dull old Mr Dunn droning on about the time he almost joined the navy or Mrs Dunn trying to pretend she has early knowledge of the fashions coming out of Paris, and I will admit defeat now.'

'You are being uncharitable,' she said as he pulled her down for a kiss.

'You have a choice. Either we can spend the evening

with the Dunns or we can cancel and I will count how many times I can kiss your body before you beg me for something more.'

'You are not playing fair, Simon,' Alice said, mock reproval in her voice. 'You get to persuade me with kisses. Mr Dunn only gets his tales about the navy.'

He kissed her again.

'When the stakes are this high, it is best not to play fair.'

Reluctantly Alice stood and moved over to the mirror. She needed to go to the modiste today too, after postponing her appointment for a fitting of a new dress earlier in the week.

'I will consider your proposition, but now I am going to have to insist you leave. I have neglected my errands for too long.'

Simon stood, picking up his crumpled shirt from the chair where she had thrown it the previous evening, and pulling it over his head.

'You wound me with the ease with which I am cast out, discarded,' Simon said, his hand on the door-handle. 'Until tonight, my sweet.'

The rest of Alice's day was productive, but she had the feeling of wanting to rush through everything so she could return home to Simon. It was a ridiculous idea, for he wouldn't be home from the solicitor until after she had finished at the orphanage.

At three o'clock she instructed Drummond to take her to St Benedict's. Frank Smith sat on the narrow bench at the front of the carriage beside Drummond, primed to step in if there were any trouble.

The journey through London was uneventful, and

before long the carriage stopped outside the orphanage. It was an overcast day, and the slums looked even less inviting with their narrow streets in shadow.

'I shall be about an hour. Keep vigilant,' Alice instructed Drummond and Smith before knocking on the door of the orphanage.

Mrs Phillips welcomed her in and showed her through to the small room at the back of the building that acted as the matron's bedroom and office. It was sparsely furnished, with bare floorboards and nothing on the walls. There was a single bed in the corner of the room and two straight-back chairs by a little table. At the foot of the bed was a small trunk, and on the back of the door a hook for a coat. Mrs Phillips might be matron of the establishment, but her accommodation wasn't much more comfortable than that of the children in her care.

Alice knew the woman's role carried huge responsibility but did not attract a large salary, especially in a small, poor establishment like St Benedict's. Mrs Phillips would eat the same food as the children and might even be restricted in when and why she could leave the premises.

One of the girls brought in a heavy teapot on a tray with two cups, and Mrs Phillips served Alice.

'Thank you for coming, Lady Westcroft. I have been thinking about what you suggested,' Mrs Phillips said as she handed a cup to Alice.

They talked for more than an hour, discussing all the issues Mrs Phillips had noted down, from small things like the purchase of more slate boards for the classroom to much larger concerns such as sanitation and access to clean water. By the end of their discussion, Alice felt exhausted but excited to share Mrs Phillips's ideas with the London Ladies' Benevolent Society.

At five o'clock, she bid Mrs Phillips farewell and stepped out into the warm late-afternoon air. Alice was preoccupied, wondering how best to present all the issues to the other ladies and she stepped out into the street without looking.

It was uncommon to see people on horseback in this part of the city. Most people travelled on foot, and those who had to pass through preferred the safety of a carriage. She looked up too late: the horse was almost upon her, and Alice saw the rider pull on the reins sharply, causing the horse to rear up in fright. Hooves thundered past her face, missing by mere inches as a firm hand on her shoulder pulled her backwards to safety.

The whole incident lasted less than a few seconds, but Alice felt as though she had been running for a whole hour. Her heart squeezed in her chest, and her breathing was ragged and uneven. The man on horseback called something incomprehensible and probably unkind and carried on along the street as if nothing had happened.

As she regained her composure Alice turned to the person who had pulled her back.

'Thank you—' she began, the words dying in her throat. Standing very close, a malicious glint in his eye, was the man who had watched them the time she and Simon had come to the orphanage.

'You're welcome, miss. Can't have a pretty lady like yourself trampled under a horse's hooves, brains splattered about the cobbles,' he said, his voice low so only she could hear.

Alice swallowed and glanced down, feeling a cold

chill spread through her as she caught the glint of metal in his hand. He was holding a small knife in the narrow space between their bodies, the tip pointed at her abdomen. The metal was dull and looked well-used, and Alice thought she saw a crust of blood around the hilt.

'Don't call out,' the man said calmly. 'Your best chance is if those two fools on top of the carriage do not come over to see what is happening.'

Glancing up, she saw Drummond's face. As yet he was not climbing down from the carriage, but he was looking over at her with an expression of puzzled concern on his face. Alice knew it would only be a matter of seconds until he was climbing down to investigate why she hadn't crossed the road and got into the safety of the carriage.

'Now, I did not have to save your life there, miss, but I am an upstanding citizen, and I think a good deed like that deserves a reward.'

Alice nodded, wishing she had brought her coin purse so she could have just handed it over without any delay.

'I do not carry money on my person,' she said truthfully. It was foolish to carry money in areas such as this where half the population were desperate enough to steal if the temptation were right.

'That is a shame, miss. I suppose we'll have to think of something else.' He looked her over, grunting as he saw she was not wearing a necklace or earrings. The only jewellery she had was the wedding band on her finger. 'You'd better start with that gold ring,' he said, motioning at it with his knife.

Alice looked down, reluctant to part with the ring Simon had given her on the day of their wedding. It was symbolic of so much, and she did not want to part with it, but she knew compliance was the best way to walk away unscathed from this situation.

She reached down with her right hand to try to pull the ring off, grimacing at the resistance. As she worked on pulling it over the knuckle, she saw Drummond and Smith finally realise there was something wrong. They moved fast for men trained as household servants, dashing across the road to come to her aid. The man who was stealing from her glanced up and saw them coming, reaching out to grab the ring from Alice. As he did so, Smith arrived and went to throw his whole body weight at the thief. The culprit ducked under Smith's arm and quickly struck out, clearing a path through the middle of them. To Alice's dismay he disappeared into the crowd within seconds.

'Thank you,' she said, turning to Drummond and Smith. They were both looking at her in horror. Slowly, not wanting to know what sight awaited her, she looked down. A bloom of blood was spreading across her pale blue dress, staining the material and seeping out around the blade of the knife that was still buried in her abdomen. 'There's a knife,' she said, feeling her whole body stagger to the left at the sight of the blood and the thought of the wound that must be underneath.

Instinctively her hand gripped the handle of the knife, thinking to pull it out, but Drummond reached out to stop her.

'Leave it,' he said forcefully. 'We need to get you back home and then a doctor can remove the knife. Do not even think about touching it.' Her abdomen was starting to throb and hurt, and she marvelled that she had not felt the knife slide into her flesh.

Drummond lowered his shoulder and half carried, half dragged Alice to the carriage. Carefully he helped her inside, instructing her to lie across the seats and avoid any unnecessary movement.

The journey back home seemed to take for ever, with Alice feeling every jolt of the carriage and every corner they rounded. Drummond was driving fast, aware Alice was inside the carriage bleeding, and no doubt eager to get her home before she lost so much blood she breathed her last breath. Frank sat opposite her, looking young and scared, his arm placed strategically to ensure she did not tumble from her seat.

As the carriage slowed, Alice saw Drummond jump down calling out as he did so, and the next thing she saw was Simon's anxious face.

'Alice, what happened?'

She tried to lift her head, but the world tilted and shifted under her, so instead she closed her eyes and let someone else tell him.

Outside she could hear Simon ordering someone to run for the doctor and also the barber-surgeon. Alice tried to protest: she had heard terrible stories about these barber-surgeons and the things they did in terms of professional interest. She did not want to endure an agonising procedure, her only comfort a little strong alcohol beforehand.

Tears began running down her cheeks as Simon carefully looked back into the carriage.

'Stay here with me, my love,' he said softly, reaching

out and taking her hand. Now half the front of her dress was bloodstained, and it hurt every time she moved.

Simon carefully climbed into the carriage and slipped his arms underneath her, lifting her ever so gently. He moved slowly, his eyes fixed on her face so he could see if there was any increase in pain as he carried her. The hardest part was getting out of the carriage, but once he extricated them, Simon could move more quickly. He carried her into the house and straight up the stairs to the bedroom they had shared this past week.

Miss Stick helped to position her in bed, pulling back the bed-sheets and then tucking them around Alice's legs, and then she hurried out to organise anything the doctor might need.

Simon stayed with her, kneeling by the side of the bed as if he were a child saying his prayers, his hand holding hers tight.

Alice closed her eyes, feeling suddenly weary despite the pain.

'Stay awake, my sweet,' Simon said softly but firmly. 'It is important you stay awake.'

With great effort she forced her eyes open. They felt like they had heavy weights attached to her eyelids, and all she wanted to do was surrender to the pull of sleep.

A few minutes later she heard the doctor arrive, and Simon quickly explained the situation. She had not met the man before, having been in good health since arriving in London, and was pleased to see a reassuring, sensible face looking down at her.

'We need to remove Lady Westcroft's clothing so I can see the wound fully before I attempt to take out the knife,' Dr Black said, motioning for Miss Stick to come forward from her position by the door. 'We need scissors, as sharp as possible, to cut away the material. I dare not try to lift her garments over her head.'

Miss Stick returned a few moments later with sharp scissors and leaned over Alice. Her normally composed demeanour had cracked, and Alice could see tears in the housekeeper's eyes.

'Let me, Miss Stick,' Simon said quietly, taking the scissors from the woman.

He worked slowly but steadily, instructing Miss Stick to hold the material of her dress taut as he cut it. The bodice part of her dress was thicker and Alice felt the scissors jolt and stop a few times, but after a minute the fabric was laid open to reveal her chemise and petticoats underneath.

Despite her predicament, Alice felt a little self-conscious. No doubt in the course of his job Dr Black was accustomed to seeing the naked form, but the only man who had ever seen her naked was her husband, and she suddenly had the urge to cover herself with her hands.

'Be still, Alice,' Simon murmured reassuringly as he gripped the hem of her chemise and began sliding the scissors along the material. 'There is only you and I and Miss Stick here with the doctor.'

Once Alice's chemise was cut, Miss Stick hurried forward and arranged a sheet over her chest to help preserve Alice's dignity, and then the doctor stepped forward to look at the wound.

The dagger was still embedded in her abdomen at the level of her navel, but far to the right in the space between the bottom of her ribs and the bones that marked the top of her pelvis. With every movement the wound stung and sent a jolt of pain through her body. The doctor took his time inspecting the wound and then moved away from the bed to talk to Simon.

'I wish to hear,' Alice called, surprised at how weak her voice sounded. The doctor looked over, a serious expression on his face, but Simon placed a hand on the man's elbow and guided him closer to the bed.

'It will be dangerous to remove the knife, but we must for the wound to begin to heal,' Dr Black said, his expression grave. 'I believe the blade has missed the major organs and vessels, but as we remove it we may reveal a bleed that has been plugged by the knife, or there could be damage to the bowel underneath.'

'Is there anything we can do to decrease the risk?' Simon asked, his face pale.

'You must stay completely still, Lady Westcroft. Even moving a fraction of an inch could be the difference between life and death.' The doctor looked between Simon and Alice. 'I will prepare the needle for stitching the wound after. It will be painful, but I have laudanum in my bag which should ease you.'

'I do not want laudanum,' Alice said, thinking back to when she had hit the tree as a girl on horseback and bruised her ribs. The doctor then had given her laudanum, and she had fought terrible hallucinations for days. The alternative was significant pain whilst her wound was stitched, but she would take that over the painkiller any day.

'Very well.'

The doctor moved away and spoke to Miss Stick in a low voice, instructing her on all the things he would need. Simon returned to Alice's side, crouching down by the bed and holding her hand.

'You are brave, my sweet,' he said, lowering his lips to her hand and kissing the skin.

'I do not think I have a choice,' Alice replied with a weak smile. 'It was that man, Simon, that horrible man we saw with the gang of pickpockets.'

'He targeted you on purpose?'

'I think he was waiting for me outside the orphanage. He held the knife to me, in between my body and his so Drummond and Smith could not see it, and he was demanding my valuables, but I did not take anything with me. He asked for my wedding ring, and I was going to give it to him, but Drummond grew suspicious as to why it was taking me so long to cross to the carriage, and he and Smith rushed over. He grabbed my ring.' Alice looked down at her fingers where the ring had been, tears pooling in her eyes. 'Then he pushed past me and ran away. He must have lashed out with the knife when he pushed past me.'

'Do not worry about any of that now,' Simon said, stroking her hair from her face. 'Let us focus on getting you better, and then we can worry about the scoundrel who did this to you.'

The doctor returned to the bedside, a small tray of items in his hand. Alice glanced down at it and then wished she hadn't. There was a long needle on it, thick thread trailing from behind, as well as a couple of small knives and a pair of scissors. Thankfully Miss Stick returned at the same time, and Alice forced herself to watch the housekeeper's preparations rather than the doctor's.

'Are you ready, Lady Westcroft?'

'I am,' Alice said, taking a deep breath and closing her eyes. She tried to think of all the things that made her happy. The dappled sun through the trees in the park, the sound of the sea crashing against the dunes in Bamburgh on stormy nights, the giggles of her nieces and, of course, Simon.

He held her hand firmly as the doctor anchored the skin around the knife and then in a smooth, slow motion pulled it out.

Alice let out a low, wounded cry and then against her better judgement looked down at the wound.

Fresh blood welled out of the gash in her side, and she felt the room spin around her. Darkness pulled at the periphery of her vision, and she gripped Simon's hand harder, but she was unable to cling to consciousness.

Alice woke to pain much worse than what she had already endured. The doctor was leaned over her, piercing her skin with the needle. That hurt in itself, but even worse was the pain as he pulled the thread through after. She felt every inch slide through the fresh hole in her skin.

'You must stay still, Lady Westcroft,' Dr Black said, his voice authoritative. He turned to Simon and instructed, 'Keep her still.'

Alice felt Simon stand and lean over her, kissing her on her forehead. 'Stay still, Alice. You are doing very well. This will not take long, and then you can rest.'

She clenched her teeth and endured the pain, tears rolling down her cheeks, and it was a great relief when the doctor stepped away.

'She must rest. The knife was small, but unfortunately it was not clean. I worry the wound might fester.' The doctor glanced over at her, pity in his eyes. 'If she does develop a fever, then send for me. Otherwise I will call tomorrow to check on the wound.'

'Thank you, Dr Black,' Simon said, shaking the man's hand.

Simon approached the bed with trepidation. Miss Stick had tried to shoo him out of the room whilst she and one of the maids changed the bloodstained sheets around Alice, as deftly as they could without jostling her. He had acknowledged he was in the way but had felt unable to retreat farther than the chair in the corner of the room whilst they worked. Now they were finished, he pulled his chair closer to the bed and took Alice's hand in his.

Her eyes flickered open, and she gave him a weak smile, but her face was ashen, and underneath her eyes were dark circles. She looked terribly unwell.

Gently he kissed her fingers where they entwined with his and then sat back in the chair and waited.

Alice slept fitfully, every so often trying to turn in her sleep to get into a more comfortable position. When this happened he would spring forward and press her shoulders gently, holding her on her back so she did not pull at the stitches or disturb the wound.

'Please do not die,' he whispered time and time again. It was strange to be sitting here next to his young and normally healthy wife. A year ago he had been convinced Alice would outlive him, but here he was the picture of health and she was suspended in that awful void between life and death.

Periodically Miss Stick would knock quietly at the door and enter the room, taking her time to straighten the sheets and ensure Alice was comfortable. He saw real affection and concern in the housekeeper's eyes. In her short time in London, Alice had made an impression on so many people.

The housekeeper would also bring Simon trays of tea and press him to drink and eat a little, pouring out the tea and handing it to him, not leaving the room until he had taken at least a few sips.

The hours seemed to drag as Simon found he could not rest, not whilst Alice's future was so uncertain. Every so often he would place a hand on her brow, dreading he would feel the heat that would indicate the wound was infected, pus accumulating under the stitches.

It was dark outside when he finally nodded off to sleep, dozing fitfully in the armchair, waking every few minutes to glance across at Alice and then his head dropping down onto his chest.

Miss Stick offered to sit with Alice so he could sleep, but Simon had an irrational fear that if he moved, if he left her bedside, something terrible would happen. He knew it was not true, but he could not help feeling that way.

As the first rays of sunshine filtered through the gap in the curtains, Alice stirred, her eyes flickering open as they had through the night, but this time she seemed to focus on him.

'How are you, my love?'

She smiled at him weakly and tried to push herself up in bed. Simon laid a restraining hand on her arm.

'Everything hurts,' she said, her face contorting into a frown.

'I can send for the doctor if you would like some opium, or perhaps just the laudanum he offered you yesterday.'

'No,' Alice said quickly. 'I just need to change position. Will you help me?'

'Of course.'

She was light and easy to manoeuvre, and slowly they managed to get her sitting up a little more. He regarded her with a frown. She was still terribly pale, but it was good to see her alert and able to focus on him.

'I am awfully thirsty.'

'Would you like water? Tea?'

'Just some water.' He poured her a glass from the jug in the corner of the room and held it to her lips as she took small sips. 'Have you been here all night?'

'Yes.'

'That is kind. Thank you.'

'I could not have been anywhere else,' he said, hearing the anguish in his own voice. He didn't want to examine what it meant. He didn't want to acknowledge the deep panic he felt at the idea of losing Alice. It was as though she had buried into his heart and become part of him.

'I feel better knowing you are here,' Alice said as she closed her eyes and drifted off to sleep again.

Chapter Nineteen

Alice spent an entire week in bed, and by the end she could quite happily have never seen another pillow or bed-sheet again in her life. Around day two the wound on her abdomen had reddened and grown tight, pulling at the stitches. Dr Black had visited, a grave expression on his face, asking to speak to Simon privately after he had examined the wound. Later Simon had told her of the doctor's concerns of infection and that if the redness and swelling did not settle, he might have to snip the stitches to let the accumulated pus out.

Thankfully the swelling had not worsened and after another day began to subside, and Alice did not succumb to a fever as they feared she might.

Dr Black was cautious and had insisted she stay in bed for the whole week, but today was her first day of freedom.

'I see that glint in your eyes,' Simon said, shaking his head. 'Do not think you are going to be running around this house just because you have been given permission to get out of bed.'

'If I stay in this room one day longer, I think I will go mad.'

'Dr Black said you could get up and sit in the chair, not go charging round the house like an excitable dog who has not seen his master for days.'

Alice sighed. She had hoped to make it downstairs. It would be wonderful to sit in the drawing room, perhaps in a chair by the window as she watched people on the street outside go about their lives.

'Let me help you,' he said, and he leaned down so Alice could slip an arm around his neck. He lifted her smoothly and then helped her to gently set her feet on the ground.

It felt strange to be standing again, and for a moment Alice's legs felt weak and wobbly, but Simon was there, as he had been this entire past week. Not once had he left her alone for more than an hour, using the time when she slept to bathe and change clothes and conduct the urgent bits of business that could not wait.

She had grown used to his constant attention, and his presence had made a difficult week much more bearable. They had read together, he had taught her to play chess, he had told her of his childhood, of the happy memories with his parents and his brother, and she had shared more of what her life had been like growing up in Bamburgh. She had thought at some point he would pull away, especially when it became more and more certain that she would make a full recovery, his duty done. Yet he had not. Each morning he was there in the chair beside her bed, and each evening he leaned over to kiss her, passion bubbling under the surface, barely restrained.

It was a stark contrast to the week they had spent prior to Alice's injury, unable to keep their hands from one another. Yet despite her injury Alice found she had enjoyed this second week together almost as much. She had a deeper understanding of her husband now, and she felt he had truly relaxed around her.

He settled her into the chair they had positioned by the window and took a seat beside her then closed his eyes and let out a jagged sigh.

'Is something amiss, Simon?'

He shook his head, but for a moment he did not look at her.

'You do not know how worried I have been,' he said quietly. 'When I saw you with that knife sticking out of you...' He shook his head.

'I know,' Alice said, biting her lip at the memory of the panic she had felt when she had looked down and seen the knife in her for the first time.

'I thought you were going to die. People who get stabbed do not often survive, especially if they are stabbed in the abdomen.'

'I am lucky, I know that.' She reached out and gripped his hand, waiting until he looked at her to continue. 'But the worst is over. Dr Black said so. The wound is healing well, and in a few days he will come and remove the stitches. I will have to avoid heavy lifting and strenuous activity for a while, but it will not be for ever.'

'I know you are recovering well, Alice,' Simon said. 'And I am so grateful for your strength.' He fell silent again.

Alice opened her mouth to speak, trying to find the right words to gently prompt to see if the issue were how their relationship had changed again. In the few weeks since his return, they had moved quickly from tiptoeing around each other to friendship and then being unable to keep their hands off one another. This past week had been another change again, with Simon caring for her as any true husband would care for his wife.

She felt a flicker of hope and wondered if this last week had made him realise what was important in his life. Not for the first time her mind started to fire pictures of their perfect future together at her. She imagined them strolling hand and hand through London before spending a few hours together raising money and awareness for the orphanage. Then at the end of the day they would return home together to retire to the bedroom and enjoy one another's company in a more intimate way. She even dared to dream of children, a little baby of their own, a house filled with happiness and love.

Alice hadn't even dared to dream about such a future, but Simon had changed this week. He had stopped trying to hold her at a distance and instead allowed her to see every part of him.

Before Alice could find the right words to ask if perhaps his feelings towards her and their future had changed, there was a gentle knock on the door, and a moment later Miss Stick entered.

'You have a visitor, Lady Westcroft.'

Simon frowned. They had kept visitors away this past week so she could focus on recovery, but the room was filled with flowers from well-wishers. Miss Stick had been wonderful at gently guiding friends and acquaintances away, suggesting they visit in a week or two when Alice was back on her feet.

'Hardly a visitor,' Maria said as she burst into the room. 'My darling Alice, I came the very second I heard the news. Let me look at you.' Maria swept over and knelt before Alice, regarding her carefully, then laid a hand on her heart and let out a choked sob. 'You're going to recover,' she said, tears dropping onto her cheeks. 'Forgive me, but for the entire journey here I feared you would have succumbed to infection, and I would be arriving to a house in mourning.'

Alice gripped Maria's hands, wishing she could pull her into an embrace but wary of the strain on her stitches.

Maria stood, turning to Simon and hugged him. 'You must be so relieved.'

'It has been a worrying week,' he admitted.

'But I am well on my way to recovery now. The doctor insisted I stay in bed for a whole week, but today, finally, I have been allowed up.'

'Sit down, Maria,' Simon said, indicating the chair next to Alice's. 'I will arrange some refreshment. You must be thirsty.'

'I am famished too. The coach set off before breakfast this morning, and in my rush to get here I have not stopped for it since.'

'I will organise food and tea.'

Simon strolled out of the room as Maria settled in the chair. Alice felt a great happiness at having her sister-in-law here. Out of everyone from her old family and new, Maria was the one she had leaned on the most this past year.

'You must tell me everything that happened. How did you get such an injury? Was it through your work with the orphanages?'

'Indirectly. I was visiting one of them near St Giles, and a man tried to rob me. He wanted my wedding ring, and as I was trying to take it off my finger, the driver and footman who had accompanied me realised something was wrong. They rushed over, and in the thief's desperation to get away he stabbed me.'

Maria's hand went to her mouth. 'You must have been so frightened, Alice.'

'It didn't feel real, not until we were back here and the doctor was talking about pulling the knife out and stitching me up.'

'The wound is healing? It has not festered?'

'No. There was a day or two where we thought it might go that way, but thankfully the redness subsided and it has since healed well.'

Maria leaned forward in her chair and lowered her voice. 'And what of Simon? I didn't expect the look of devotion he was giving you when I first arrived.'

'Simon has been wonderful,' Alice said carefully. She knew how invested Maria was in her brother-in-law's happiness and how much she wanted him to settle down and allow himself to experience the same sort of wedded bliss she had found with Robert. 'He has barely left my side.'

'He was always a kind boy, sensitive too, although that is hidden underneath the layers of grief and the hard shell of an exterior he has to project in his role as earl.'

'He is kind,' Alice said softly. He was so much more than that. She thought of the way he had kept her entertained during her recovery, which was wonderful in itself, but she knew he had done it to ensure her the best possible chance of getting better. If her mind was stimulated and he did not allow her to grow bored, then she was more likely to follow the doctor's orders and stay in bed.

'You have not found it too difficult, having him back?'

'I cannot lie. It was a shock at first, but I think we have found a happy equilibrium together.' She bit her lip, wondering what their relationship would look like when she was fully recovered. Her injury had put a stop to the physical intimacy they had shared in the week before she was stabbed, but their relationship had not faltered as she had been worried it might. Instead it had flourished.

'He has not mentioned leaving again?'

'No.' Alice felt her heart squeeze at the thought. She had told herself she would not become too used to Simon's company, but she knew if he left now she would be devastated. These past few weeks, she had tried her hardest to remember he did not want a deeper relationship, but slowly and surely she had fallen in love with her husband.

She pressed her lips together and glanced over her shoulder, wondering if she should confide in Maria, but before she could say anything Simon walked back into the room.

'Tea and toast and cake will be brought up shortly,' he said.

'Perhaps you might carry me downstairs, Simon. There is more room in the drawing room, and I would like a change of scenery.'

He considered for a moment and then nodded. 'If you are sure. Just for half an hour, though, then I will carry you back up to bed.'

Alice didn't argue, excited by the prospect of leaving her room for the first time in a week. Carefully Simon leaned down and positioned his arms underneath her, lifting her up smoothly from the chair. He walked slowly, ensuring his footsteps did not jar or jolt Alice as she held onto his neck.

They made it downstairs without incident, and Simon settled Alice in a comfortable armchair, ensuring she had just the right number of pillows behind her.

'Thank you,' Alice said, beaming up at him.

'You're welcome.' He dropped a kiss on the top of her head and then moved away. 'I will tell Miss Stick to take the opportunity to change your sheets now you are out of bed. I am sure it will feel good to have fresh ones.' He disappeared, and once again Alice was left alone with Maria.

Maria stared after him and then rose from her seat and softly closed the door behind her.

'Is something amiss?' Alice asked, confused at their need for privacy.

'You're in love with him,' Maria said, her eyes wide. 'It is obvious with every look, every touch.'

Alice started to shake her head and then stopped. It was impossible to hide such things from Maria: she was astute in all areas, but in particular she had a very well-developed emotional intelligence.

'We have grown close these last few weeks.'

'I can see that,' Maria said, studying Alice carefully. 'You have forgiven him for abandoning you?'

'Yes.'

Maria looked at Alice cautiously, as if aware her next question was delicate, especially for a woman who was up for the first time in days and shouldn't be upset.

'Have you spoken of your future together? Has he said he wants to settle down with you?'

'We have spoken many times,' Alice said, shaking

her head a little, recalling their conversations in Hyde Park and later in the carriage and the again in the bedroom. Each had resulted in a different plan, a different conclusion. 'But we have agreed on nothing long-term.'

'I do not wish you to get hurt, Alice.'

'I know. I do not wish for that either.' She lowered her voice further so it was barely more than a whisper. 'I have tried my very hardest not to fall in love with Simon these last few weeks, but I fear I have been unsuccessful. At first I tried to keep my distance, and then I told myself we could be close just as long as I remembered not to fall for him. I was very resolute at first, but he has a way of burrowing into your heart.'

'He is very loveable,' Maria said with a sigh. 'But so are you, and you deserve to be loved, Alice.'

'I cannot force him to love me,' she said quietly, wondering if she was mad to think that perhaps he did love her. Over the past week he had certainly been devoted to her care and recovery, and every time he came into the room he smiled broadly, a smile that told her he was pleased to see her. She thought maybe he did love her: he was just too stubborn to admit it, still ruled by the guilt of taking over every aspect of his late brother's life.

'He is a fool,' Maria said suddenly, anger flaring in her voice. 'I love you both dearly, but until I saw him with you today, I could not imagine how you would be together, yet you are perfect, you complement each other in exactly the right ways. It is an incredible turn of events, marrying a stranger and ending up with the one person you are destined for in this life, and if he squanders this chance of happiness, he is a complete and utter fool.'

'I think the problem is he feels he shouldn't be happy.'

'Silly boy,' Maria said, biting her lip and shaking her head at the same time. 'Do you want me to talk to him?'

'No,' Alice said quickly. She needed to step carefully with Simon; the last thing she wanted was to push him away. If he was made to confront his feelings for Alice too soon it might scare him away. It would be better to let things build, for him to see there was no point denying the love and happiness they brought to one another.

'If you are sure?'

'I am sure.'

'You two look deadly serious,' Simon said as he re-entered the room.

'We were discussing Alice's injury. It sounds horrific,' Maria turned to Alice and leaned over and squeezed her hand. 'You should return to Northumberland, where it is safe, as soon as you are well.'

Alice smiled. Maria had a motherly, protective instinct that sometimes went a little too far, but it came from a place of affection and love.

'I hardly think Alice need quit London for good,' Simon said quickly, 'just avoid certain areas.'

'I can't stay away from St Benedict's Orphanage for ever. The London Ladies' Benevolent Society has great plans for that place.'

'You are incorrigible,' Simon muttered. 'You were stabbed outside its doors, and still you will not give it up.'

'It is a worthy cause.'

Simon shrugged. 'I am going to invoke my privilege as husband and insist you do not go there ever again unless I am by your side.'

'I will agree without argument, as long as you make yourself available to me whenever I wish to visit.'

'I can see no problem with that,' Simon said softly.

* * *

Two hours later Alice was back in bed, resting. She had not wanted to admit she was fatigued by the short spell she had spent downstairs, but as Simon had carried her back up to the bedroom she had leaned in close to him and nuzzled her face into his neck.

'Was it too much for you, my dear?'

'No,' Alice said quickly, 'just enough. I am a little tired now, but I enjoyed seeing a different view of these four walls.'

Simon helped her to get comfortable in bed and then made to sit in the chair next to her.

'You should spend some time with Maria,' Alice said, trying to stifle a yawn. 'It will do you good to get some fresh air, and I can hardly accompany you out anytime soon.'

'What if you need anything?'

'I am sure Miss Stick will be more than happy to check on me at regular intervals, and I have a loud voice to call out if I need something desperately.'

A day ago he would have dismissed the idea immediately, but Alice's strength was returning quickly now, and he realised it would be good to get outside and enjoy some fresh air.

'If you are sure?'

'I am. In fact, I insist.'

Half an hour later he and Maria were on horseback, riding side by side towards the park. Maria was an excellent rider, confident and at ease around the horse he had chosen for her, even though she had never ridden it before. It made Simon think back to the pleasant ride he had shared with Alice a few weeks earlier. They had still been feeling their way through their relationship at that point, wondering if they could even live companionably in the same part of the country. Now the idea of living apart from her made him feel a little sick.

'Thank you for coming down. I know Alice enjoys your company immensely.'

'I packed my bags as soon as I received the news she had been hurt.' Maria paused before continuing mildly, not looking at him. 'I was worried she would be gravely wounded with no one who cared about her to look after her.'

'I am here,' Simon said quietly. He had known Maria a long time and knew she wasn't lashing out to hurt him and would get to her true point soon.

'Yes, you are, but when I last saw you we spoke of your wife who you had left in London after not bidding her farewell. You told me you did not know what you planned to do with her, but that you would try to accommodate her wishes, unless of course she wished to have a true and full marriage with you.'

'I was young and naïve.'

'It was four weeks ago, Simon.'

'A lot has happened in four weeks.'

'Evidently. I rush down here thinking Alice might be all alone, and I find you devoted to her comfort, the very picture of a loving husband.'

'Would you rather I abandoned her?'

'Good Lord, no. This is exactly what I have always hoped for you. Marriage is a wonderful gift if done right, and I think with Alice you have the chance to build something truly special.'

He remained silent. It was difficult to deny the feelings that had grown inside him over the past few weeks. He had always felt an attraction to Alice, but the more time he spent with her the more he realised he liked her too. She was kind and generous and entertaining to converse with. She had an opinion on most matters of politics or social dilemmas. Added to that was her natural warmth, the way she could get virtual strangers to trust her, to feel like treasured confidants.

'I do not know *exactly* what I feel for her,' Simon said, acknowledging how difficult this was for him. He had enjoyed the time spent in Alice's company, but with it had come guilt. Guilt that he was happy, living his life, whilst Robert was long gone.

'Perhaps you don't need to know. Perhaps it is enough to realise you make one another happier together than you are apart.'

Simon looked down at the reins in his hands, glad that there was the distraction of riding that meant he did not have to look Maria directly in the eye as they spoke.

'I cannot just banish what I feel about Robert,' he said eventually.

'I know. I doubt it will ever leave you completely, Simon, but you knew Robert better than anyone else. He loved you so much, and he wanted you to be happy. That would never have changed, and I know if he is looking down on us now he will be shouting for you to stop being so pigheaded and stubborn, to stop using his death as an excuse not to live your own life.'

'He was the best of brothers.'

'He was, and we were lucky enough to have time with him in this world.' Maria reached across the gap between them and grasped his wrist, waiting until he looked at her to continue. 'Honour his memory in the way he would have wanted it. Live your life as he would, being fair and kind and conscientious. Love with all your heart. That is a greater tribute to Robert than hiding away and never allowing yourself any happiness.'

For a long time they rode in silence, Maria content to sit quietly in her saddle to give Simon the space to think on what she had said. He knew in many ways Maria was right. Robert had only ever been thoughtful and generous; he would not begrudge Simon any happiness. The feeling of guilt—that he was stealing the life Robert should have had—had come directly from himself. It was a conviction that was difficult to shake.

Yet here he was considering an alternative. As they rode through the park Simon allowed himself to imagine what his life could be. Waking up to the woman he loved, taking long, leisurely strolls whilst they discussed anything from their families to what the latest law to pass in Parliament meant for the wider country. Then home to tumble into bed together. It was an enthralling glimpse into what the future could be.

'Lord Lathum and his wife have just had a baby,' Maria said suddenly.

Simon was pulled back to the present and looked at his sister-in-law in confusion. He barely knew Lord and Lady Lathum.

'I am pleased for them.'

'They are healthy. She is not yet eighteen, chosen for her childbearing potential and sizeable dowry, I am told,' Maria said, turning her horse around so they could start the walk back to the house. 'He is your age, certainly no older. There have been no problems in the family previously, but their child has been born with an unnaturally large head and an extra finger on his left hand.'

Simon blinked, wondering what point she was trying to make.

'You have lost me, Maria,' he said eventually.

'Let me speak plainly.'

'Please do,' he murmured.

Maria pressed on, ignoring him. 'I am hopeful that in the course of the next few weeks you will see the only sensible thing to do is to commit to a full and happy marriage with the sweet young woman you decided to marry last year. You will be blissfully happy, but for your wife at least there will be one thing missing from your union.'

'Children,' he said, his face darkening. He knew how much Alice loved children. She spoke of their nieces with such affection, and every time they passed a young child with their nanny or nursemaid in the street, her eyes lit up. She had a patient and caring nature, and instinctively Simon knew his wife would make a wonderful mother.

'Yes, children. Alice has never come out and said she wishes a house filled to the brim with children, but I can see it in her eyes.'

'That is one thing I will not be persuaded to change my mind on.'

'Lord and Lady Lathum should have had a healthy child. The odds were in their favour, yet they are devastated their firstborn son has not been born healthy.'

'I do not get your point, Maria,' Simon snapped.

Luckily Maria did not offend easily, and she ignored his abrupt tone.

'None of us know what the future may hold.'

'That is exactly what Alice says.'

'You may drop dead tomorrow or you might live until you are a crotchety old man of ninety. Take Alice as a wonderful example. She is young and healthy, but if that knife had been thrust in with a fraction more force or an inch higher, it would have hit her liver, and Alice would have bled out on the streets of St Giles.'

Simon grimaced.

'I have said enough,' Maria said and nodded in grim satisfaction. 'I know you do not wish to discuss it with me, but I owe it to Alice to at least try. I love her like a sister, and I would hate for her to find happiness with you only to realise that very happiness was stopping her from having the family she dreamed of.'

'It isn't as if she can choose not to be married to me. She cannot suddenly decide to go and make a future with another man, a man who does wish to have children.'

'Of course she can,' Maria said, shaking her head. 'Perhaps not within the social circles we move in, but there are plenty of women who reside with a man who is not their husband, someone who provides a home for them, love, children.'

'You go too far, Maria,' he said wearily. 'Alice would not do that.'

'No, she wouldn't,' his sister-in-law said quietly. 'You are right, but perhaps it serves to remind you that in saying you will never have children, you are also saying she will never have children. *You* are making a significant decision about Alice's future and expecting her to accept it without discussion.'

'We have discussed it.'

'Telling her you will never father a child and discussing the issue are not the same, Simon,' she chastised gently.

'I need some time to think,' Simon said, aware he sounded unforgivably rude, but his head was spinning, and he had the sudden urge to be alone. He needed time to work through everything Maria had said to him. The last thing he wanted was to make Alice unhappy.

'Of course. I will return home and check on Alice. You take all the time you need.'

It was almost dark by the time Simon dismounted outside the townhouse, handing Socrates's reins to the groom and looking up at the window of the room where Alice was recuperating. He was eager to return to her side. For the past week they had spent hardly any time apart, but he knew he would have to hold his tongue and perhaps even lie to her about what he and Maria had discussed that afternoon.

On his ride through Hyde Park after Maria had left him, he had turned over their conversation, examining it from each possible angle, until his head had started to throb. He had been unable to concentrate, so he had dismounted and sat on a bench overlooking the lake, trying to think of nothing but the ripples on the water in front of him.

As he sat, he had come to a realisation, one that he wished to share with Alice, but he knew she was not up to it yet. It might be weeks before she was strong enough to hear what he had to say, and the last thing he wanted to do was set her recovery back by any degree.

'I missed you,' Alice said as he knocked on the door and entered. Maria had been sitting by the bed, but she rose when Simon entered and murmured an excuse to go. Simon caught her by the hand as she walked past him, and Maria paused.

He smiled at her, squeezing her hand gently, and she searched his eyes for the answer to an unspoken question, and then she reached out and embraced him. Maria was the only person who could speak to him so freely and he would forgive in a heartbeat.

When they were alone, Alice looked at him curiously. 'What was that about?'

'Whilst we were out, Maria reminded me what a fool I was being.'

'A fool?'

'Yes.' He leaned down and kissed Alice on the forehead. 'It does not matter, my sweet. You rest, and I will tell you everything when you are recovered.'

Chapter Twenty

Three weeks later Alice stepped out of the door for the first time in a month. Her stitches had been removed by Dr Black, and she was declared fit to start building up to her normal levels of activity. To her dismay she had lost some muscle whilst invalided, and she knew it would not be an easy feat to get back to rushing around London, attending to her various commitments.

Alice was determined to make a good start and today had suggested she and Simon step out for a short walk around the local streets. It was early, only a little past nine o'clock in the morning. Alice had chosen this time deliberately for two reasons. The first was to avoid the jostling of people walking on the pavements later in the day. At nine o'clock most wealthy people were still at breakfast or readying themselves for the day, so the streets around Grosvenor Square were quiet. The second reason was that she did not wish to encounter any of her friends and acquaintances when she left the house for the first time. She was excited to get back to normal, but she did not particularly want to stop to reassure people she was recovering well multiple times on her walk.

'Are you ready?'

She breathed in deeply and then nodded. 'I am ready.'

'You will tell me if you start to tire?'

'I promise.'

They set off at a sedate pace, walking as you would if accompanying an elderly relative out and about, but after she had got used to moving outside again, Alice found she did not mind ambling along. She was pleasantly surprised to find her wound did not pull too much when she walked. Dr Black was right: the skin had knitted together beautifully, leaving her with a neat scar that he assured her would get smaller with time.

Simon was quiet as they walked ,and Alice wondered what he was thinking. He had been attentive these last few weeks, but sometimes she thought he was distracted, staring off into the distance for some time before focussing his attention in the room again. Once or twice she had panicked that he might be thinking about leaving again, finally fed up of life in London, life with her. Quickly she had pushed away the thought. Alice was trying to enjoy what time they did share and not think too much on the future, despite wishing Simon would fall to his knees, declare himself a fool and tell her he had loved her since their very first kiss.

They turned at the corner, planning on doing a small loop around the local streets before ending up back home. As they crossed the road to start on the second side of the square, a man in the distance called out.

Alice was horrified to find she stiffened, unable to move for a second. It was her first time out since the attack, and although physically she was more than ready, she did feel a little apprehensive.

The man in the distance called again, waving jovially.

'Northumberland,' the person shouted, taking his hat from his head and waving it.

'I take it you know that man?'

Simon frowned, looking hard at the man before shaking his head. 'It sounds like I should know him, but I do not recognise him.'

'He's coming over. Perhaps he will introduce himself to me.'

The man approached quickly, and then when he was five feet away he stood stock-still and looked at Simon strangely.

'My apologies, sir. I thought you were someone else.'

'We do not know each other?' Simon asked.

'No. I thought you were the Earl of Northumberland, an old friend of mine.'

'I am the earl,' Simon said, his voice dropping low.

'The Earl of Northumberland?'

'Yes. You must have known my father or my brother.'

'I knew Robert,' the man said, looking a little uncomfortable.

'My brother. He died a few years ago.'

'My deepest condolences. I apologise profusely for the misunderstanding. I have been out of the country some time, and I had not heard about your brother's death. You are very much like him in looks and countenance.'

Alice sucked in a sharp breath as she felt Simon sway almost imperceptibly beside her. She wanted to pull Simon away, to stop him from hearing the man's words. She knew he found it difficult to hear how similar he was to Robert. It brought to the fore the feelings that he had stepped into his brother's life, replacing him in every way.

'It is an easy mistake to make,' Simon said, nodding to the man before turning away.

'We can return home,' Alice suggested as they began to put space between them and the man.

'There is no need. I am perfectly fine.'

'It was an unsettling encounter. It is not weakness to admit you are a little upset.'

'I am not upset, I am not unsettled. I told you I am fine.'

Alice fell silent. Her husband was far from fine, no matter what he told her. He started walking a little quicker now, his head bent and his eyes darting from side to side. At first Alice tried to keep up, but as they walked faster the movement pulled at her scar, and after a couple of minutes she slipped her arm from his and stopped. Simon did not notice, at least not for a good few seconds, and when he did finally look up and around, it was with an air of barely suppressed irritation.

When he spotted her, he returned quickly.

'I think I want to return home,' she said, looking back over her shoulder at the way they had come.

'Of course.' He offered her his arm, but Alice waved it away, plastering a wide smile on her face. 'I am fine, Simon. I will walk home by myself. I am sure you have other things to do.'

For a moment she thought he would brush off her suggestion and escort her home, and they would return to their normal routine of the last few weeks, but instead he nodded, turning absently away from her.

Alice felt her heart squeeze and then shatter. Everything had been going so well, and then with one reminder of the brother whose place he had taken, Simon had completely regressed. Of course she did not mind if he showed emotion, if he leaned in and told her how difficult it was when he was mistaken for the brother he had loved so much: they could have shared that sadness. But instead he had blocked her out completely.

Quickly she turned, walking away before Simon could see how distressed she was.

The footman opened the door, surprise on his face that she had returned alone. Alice hurried in and struggled up the stairs to her room, forcing herself to remain calm. Simon had been upset, that was all, and she did not begrudge him some space to work through the emotions he felt at being mistaken for his brother. She would rather he talked to her about it, but she could not force that.

'Be calm,' she told herself, resisting the urge to pace over to the window and see if Simon had changed his mind and was returning.

For hours Simon walked, without sparing a thought for where he would end up or what direction he was travelling in. He thought he knew London well, but the streets passed in a blur, with the buildings getting smaller and closer together as he moved farther away from the centre of London to the poorer outskirts. At some point early on he must have crossed over the river, for when he stopped walking hours later he was well south of the Thames, but he did not have any recollection of doing so.

It was the fading light and lengthening shadows that brought him back to his senses. For a long time he had walked, head bent, trying to gain control of all the awful thoughts running through his mind, but he felt completely overwhelmed.

He took a moment to look around him, feeling as

though he had just come out of a trance. He was out of the city proper, the roads widening and only a few scattered houses on either side. Vaguely he recalled travelling by this road on a few occasions: it was one of the few that led out of London to the south, the route travellers to Sussex would take to start their journey to the coast.

Now he had stopped he was aware of the ache in his legs and feet. He was an active man, often walking for hours in the Tuscan hills in the last year and enjoying long, physically challenging rides on horseback as well, but he realised he must have been walking for at least six or seven hours. His mouth was dry, and he longed for something to quench his thirst. In the distance he could see the smartly painted swinging sign for one of the inns that were dotted along the main routes out of London to provide shelter and refreshments for weary travellers.

It only took him a couple of minutes to make his way to the inn where he was welcomed by a middle-aged woman with a smile and the offer of ale. He ordered and was thankful when the drink arrived, downing half the tankard as soon as he raised it to his lips.

Thankfully the inn was quiet, and Simon had found a corner table to himself so he was able to nurse the rest of the ale in peace, undisturbed by the few other patrons.

After a moment he closed his eyes, feeling awfully weary. He could not quite believe he had been walking for so long.

'Alice,' he murmured, thinking of how he had just abandoned her in the middle of the street when he was meant to be escorting her. It was inexcusable, yet he had been unable to act in any other way. When the man had approached them, mistaking Simon for his brother, he had felt as though he had been shot through the heart. Every day he woke up wishing his brother were alive, feeling guilty that he got to continue with life when Robert did not. Ever since his talk with Maria, he had spent each day fighting so hard to push the feeling away, to convince himself he was something more than an imposter living the life his brother should have had. Then the feeling had come rushing back in an instant with one innocent little mistake.

For a minute Simon cradled his head in his hands, trying to unpick the tangled web of thoughts and mess of emotions jumbled inside him. It had been one of the reasons he had walked for so long: as soon as he stopped, the sorrow and despair threatened to overwhelm him, but he knew the answer wasn't running for ever.

He took another large gulp of ale and motioned for the barmaid to bring another over. He would only have the one more—the last thing he needed was to lose control of his senses.

Simon sat back in his chair and watched the other people in the room for a moment and then drained the last of the ale from his tankard. He knew he had to let his thoughts in, to acknowledge the pain he was feeling, the doubts, but part of him wanted to keep pushing it away.

'Here you are, sir,' the barmaid said, placing the ale down in front of him. 'Anything else I can get you?'

'No, thank you.' He tried to empty his mind as he stared into the full tankard of ale, but his thoughts were still racing. These last few weeks he had been pretending everything was all right, that he wasn't about to fall apart any moment. He had felt real happiness with

Alice, a sense of contentment that he now feared he did not deserve.

His mind brought forward an image that he often saw in those quiet moments when nothing else was happening. It was of Robert and Maria at their wedding, coming out of the church with their heads bent together. The image was as clear to Simon as if he were looking at a painting, even down to the blissful expressions on their faces.

He'd felt that same bliss when he'd been walking arm-in-arm with Alice, that same contentment. In his mind he had been planning what their future might be like, pushing aside the doubts that plagued him about how long he would live.

Deep in his chest he felt a throb of pain. For the last few weeks he had been lying to himself, pretending he was worthy of something he was not. If he pursued a relationship with Alice, he would be seeking that same happiness his brother had enjoyed, that same ideal of family life. If he followed his heart, he would be stepping into Robert's shoes completely, choosing a contented, domestic life.

'I can't be you,' he murmured, low enough not to attract any attention. 'I can't take your life.'

Morosely Simon stared into his ale, not knowing what was for the best. He couldn't just abandon Alice—that would be cruel—but he didn't know what he wanted from his life. He could either pursue happiness and lead a life plagued by guilt or accept that he couldn't be with Alice, despite falling for her these last few weeks.

Twenty-four hours later Simon was not back, and Alice's mild concern had turned to devastation and anger.

After everything they had been through, he had left again, disappeared without a word. She understood the strong emotions he felt around inheriting his brother's title, and if he had been here in the house she would have given him space to work through how he was feeling.

The problem was he wasn't in the house. He hadn't even sent a note to let her know where he was or how long he was planning on being absent. He could be half-way to France by now or boarding a boat for any part of the world he desired. The last time he had felt over-whelmed, he'd run away, fleeing the country. She wasn't entirely convinced he wouldn't do the same this time.

'I will not stay here, perpetually waiting,' Alice murmured, and decisively she crossed to the corner of the room and pulled the bell cord to summon the maid.

A minute later she appeared at Alice's door, bobbing into a little curtsy. 'What can I do, my Lady?'

'Ask Miss Stick to have my trunk brought up to my room and to get Drummond to ready the carriage and the horses.'

'Yes, my Lady.'

Alice began pulling her dresses out and quickly started to fold them. She did not care that they would be creased in the trunk, she could have them steamed when she arrived in Northumberland. All she cared about was getting away from London and away from Simon.

'Alice, the maid said you were packing to leave,' Maria said as she came into the room.

'I am planning on returning to Northumberland immediately.'

Maria raised an eyebrow in question.

'He's gone, Maria. Yesterday when we were out walking, an old acquaintance of Robert's thought Simon was his older brother. It upset him, and he left almost immediately. I thought he would walk about for a while to think about things and then he would come home.'

'But he didn't return?'

Alice shook her head miserably. 'I have no idea where he is or if he is ever coming back.'

'Of course he is coming back, Alice. He loves you.'

'Does he? He has never told me so. He looks after me, treats me as an equal, but he has never been able to say that he loves me.'

Maria chewed on her lip. 'You are set on leaving?'

'I am, just as soon as I am packed.'

'Then, I will come with you. It would not be right for you to travel on your own after such an injury.'

'Are you sure?'

'Of course. I tire of London, especially as my girls are in Northumberland. I will return with you. Perhaps you can stay with me and the girls for a while. I do not think you should be on your own.'

'I would like that,' Alice said, suddenly feeling weary. She wanted to collapse on the bed and cry until she had no more tears to shed. She had allowed herself to believe Simon loved her, even if he could not bring himself to say it. She'd thought it was just because he found it difficult to acknowledge he was finally allowing himself to experience a little happiness.

'Come, Alice. I will make the arrangements. In a few days we will be back in Northumberland, and Simon will have to deal with an empty house here when he does emerge from wherever he has taken himself.'

Morosely Alice nodded and allowed herself to be cajoled and organised into getting everything she might possibly need for a summer spent in Northumberland.

Chapter Twenty-One

Simon climbed the last of the winding stairs, gripping the handrail as his foot struck the top one. He considered himself to be a fit and active man, yet even he was a little out of breath as he emerged into the cool late-afternoon air. It had been twenty years since he had last climbed the three hundred and eleven steps of the Monument, situated close to the magnificent St Paul's Cathedral. It had been one of his father's favourite places in London, and when he was young his father would often pay the entrance fee for him and Simon and then race his son up the stairs to the top. Once up there they would pick a spot on the narrow platform and stare out over London.

His father used to enjoy pointing out the magnificent buildings of the city, but for Simon it was the peace and the companionship he cherished the most. This was something that was his to share with his father, a sacred place where he could feel at peace.

Robert had offered to take him up the Monument once after their father had died, but Simon declined, wanting to keep his memories unsullied.

Now he stood alone, wishing his father and brother were by his side. There had been so much grief over the years, along with so much fear. It was hard to think about both. Despite his loving family, despite the best efforts of his mother and Maria, he had suppressed both his grief and his fear, pushing them deep down inside him where they had grown and got horribly out of control.

Up here, with the wind whipping at his face, he felt a moment of clarity after a difficult twenty-four hours. When he had been out walking with Alice and the man had called over to him, it had felt like his worst fear had come true, that someone had proved Simon had stolen Robert's life. Of course, now he looked at it rationally he could see that wasn't the case. It was merely an old acquaintance of his brother who had been momentarily confused by a family resemblance. Yet still he felt as though it had caused a monumental shift inside him, forcing him to confront his own fears and limitations. These last few weeks he had pushed aside his doubts about his happiness and his future, but they were still there, waiting to surface.

He closed his eyes, trying to empty his mind of everything but his doubts about the future, but as always it was the past that clung on, haunting him. The memory of his father came to him, but not the happy times, not the time spent exploring the countryside or strolling along the beach. Instead he was confronted by the terrible image of his father rising from his desk in his study, smiling as Simon hurried towards him, ready to impart some important fact about his day. Simon remembered how his father had stiffened, his face becoming a mask, then without any other warning he had dropped to the ground, dead before Simon could even utter a word.

Simon felt the sting of tears in his eyes. The moment of his father's death was crystal-clear in his mind: he could remember every expression, every miniscule movement, until there was nothing more. The period after was a blur, an overwhelming maelstrom of grief and shock that he had never properly recovered from.

Thoughts of his father's death led his mind to Alice and the panic he had felt when she had been stabbed. In the immediate aftermath, he had functioned by seeing to the practicalities, and as the days became weeks he suppressed the fear and desperation, trying to pretend the feelings weren't there. Yet he knew they bubbled under the surface, just waiting for an opportunity to get out. When he had seen the blood seeping through her dress he had felt a cold dread, a certainty that he would lose her just like he lost the other people most dear to him. The thought had plagued him for weeks, even as she recovered and it became clear she would not die from her wound.

'It is all such a mess,' he muttered to himself. He wished he were free to love without consequence, to live his life without fearing death but also in the shadow of the grief that had haunted him for years. He wanted to welcome in the love he felt for Alice, but he knew with that love there came the possibility she might one day be hurt, and one day he might lose her too.

'What would you do, Father?' Simon asked, gripping the railing. His father had always seemed so wise, contemplating Simon's questions and dilemmas with a serious demeanour, but always his answers would contain a little humour, something to show his son life was for enjoying as well as doing your duty.

He knew what his father would say. He could even

hear his deep, melodious voice as he urged Simon to live his life, to grab any chance at love, at happiness. Robert would tell him the same.

Simon felt the tears welling in his eyes. He did know how lucky he was to have been loved by two such incredible men. His father with his kindness and his patience, and Robert who had always been the sort of older brother everyone wished was their own.

He wondered how Robert would have coped if their lives were reversed, if Simon had been the one to die at a young age and Robert had survived. He knew the answer immediately. Robert would have gathered his family around him and ensured he made the most of every moment with his beautiful wife and children. He wouldn't have run away or spent his time wishing for things that could never be. He wouldn't have dwelt on questions he would never know the answer to or wasted his time worrying those he loved would be taken away.

'You have been a fool,' he murmured to himself, but even as he said the words he felt a flicker of rebellion inside him. For once he looked upon himself with kindness and compassion and reminded himself he had still been a boy when his father died, and although he was well into adulthood when Robert passed away, the sudden shock of his death would be enough to traumatise anyone.

Simon straightened, feeling a resolve like nothing he had experienced before. He knew it would not be a simple matter to start viewing himself with kindness, but he was going to try. There would be no more thoughts that he was less worthy than Robert, no more self-accusations that he was trying to step into his brother's life.

The first thing he had to do was make things right

with Alice. He had treated her terribly, unable to stop himself from showing her love and affection, but always holding back from telling her he loved her. It was cruel to keep her on edge and uncertain, and although that hadn't been his intention, it was no doubt the result. He could see now he had been holding part of himself back from her these last few weeks, not only because he felt guilty for feeling so happy but out of fear of giving his heart only to lose someone else he loved. It was understandable given his losses, but he hoped she could forgive him for pulling away when she needed him the most.

Taking in the view one last time, he turned and made his way back to the spiral staircase and then descended quickly, his feet clattering on the stone steps.

Back home the door was answered by a confused Frank Smith who looked at Simon as if he had grown an extra head.

'Where is Lady Westcroft?' Simon said, looking to the stairs and wondering if she was still resting from their trip out that had been cut short the day before.

'Lady Westcroft, my Lord?' Smith said, glancing over his shoulder.

'Yes, Smith. Where is my wife?'

'She left, my Lord. Her and the other Lady Westcroft.'

For a moment Simon could not move.

'Ah, you are home, my Lord,' Miss Stick said, emerging from the darkness of the stairs that led to the kitchen below. 'The Ladies Westcroft left a little earlier this morning. They took the carriage with Drummond and were heading for Northumberland.'

Simon reached out and steadied himself against

the wall. She'd gone. After everything he had put her through, she had finally had enough and left.

He did not blame her. He had behaved terribly yesterday, abandoning her when she was at such a low point. That would not be the worst part for Alice, though. Recently he had let her think that she could rely on him, and when she had started to trust he would not leave her again, he had disappeared without any regard for her.

'Will you pack for me, Miss Stick? I must follow my wife immediately. I will go and saddle Socrates.'

'Of course, my Lord.' Miss Stick hurried upstairs, and Simon made his way to the small stables. If he were quick, he would catch them on the road, although he would prefer privacy for what he needed to say to Alice.

It was a journey filled with peril and disaster. Only five miles out of London, Socrates threw a shoe. It was on a quiet stretch of road, a good mile out from the nearest village. Simon dismounted immediately and led Socrates by the reins to the village, hoping they had a farrier.

The farrier was able to fit Socrates with a new shoe, but the whole process took much longer than it should have. Simon wondered if the farrier was in league with the local tavern-keeper, for he delayed and delayed until it started to get dark, then suggested Simon rest Socrates overnight whilst he lodged in the tavern.

The next morning was no better with Simon coming upon an overturned carriage. The front wheel had splintered and flown off, and the carriage looked to have been dragged for some distance before the horses had been brought under control. Thankfully there were no fatalities, but one of the occupants, a young boy of eight, had fallen awkwardly on his arm, and the limb was bent at a strange angle.

Once he was satisfied no one else was badly injured, he put the boy on his horse and allowed him to ride to the next town where Simon sought out the local doctor and paid for his services. It meant he didn't begin his journey proper until after lunch and the distance he could cover before nightfall was limited.

When the third day of his journey dawned, he had only travelled fifty miles out of London and still had the prospect of many days ahead of him. It also meant the likelihood of catching up with Alice and Maria was very low, even though he could travel much quicker on horseback.

His third day of the journey was uneventful, but on the fourth disaster struck again as the inn where he was staying caught fire. He spent the morning stripped down to his shirtsleeves in a chain of men and women passing buckets of water from the river to throw on the blazing inn roof.

They were there for hours, and by the time the flames were under control the tavern had been decimated and half collapsed in on itself. Thankfully, due to the tireless efforts of everyone involved, the fire had not spread to any other buildings in the village.

Simon continued on his way much later that day, feeling as though his journey was cursed.

He arrived at Westcroft Hall in the early afternoon of a blustery, overcast day. There was a chance Alice had decided to go straight to one of the other properties he owned or to stay with Maria, but he felt she would have returned here first.

The door was opened by one of the young footmen who quickly took Simon's jacket and hat.

'Is my wife in residence?'

'She is, my Lord. She arrived yesterday.'

'Where is she?'

'I am here, Simon,' Alice said, her voice cool, with none of her usual affection.

He wanted to rush to her, to pull her into his arms and kiss her as if it were his last day on earth.

'I will ask Mrs Hemmings to prepare a bath.'

He looked down at his soot-stained clothes and grimaced. In his hurry to leave London he had packed light, but both his shirts had ended up grimy after the day spent fighting the tavern fire.

'Thank you.'

Alice nodded, holding his eye for just a second, and then she turned to leave.

'Alice,' he said, closing the space between them. 'Wait.'

As she spun to face him, he saw the sadness in her eyes and hated that he was the cause of it.

'Forgive me,' he said, his words quiet but clear. 'Please forgive me.'

There was a flare of something conciliatory in Alice's eyes, and then she looked away. 'I don't know if I can,' she said quietly. Without any fuss and without looking at him again, she walked away.

Chapter Twenty-Two

Alice had the urge to walk out of the house and keep walking. She wanted her face to be whipped by the wind, her hair flying loose about her shoulders and her skirt battering her legs. There was nothing quite like the wind as it hit the dunes on this part of the coast, and she felt the need to feel the cleansing sting as it brought colour to her cheeks.

She had not made any promises to listen to what Simon had to say, although she knew at some point they would need to discuss the future. They were still married: nothing could change that. It was only Alice's hopes and dreams and expectations that had changed.

Before she could change her mind, she grabbed her bonnet from its place close to the door, secured it tightly under her chin and then slipped out of the grand house. There was a path through the grounds that led to a narrow lane, and a twenty-minute brisk walk would bring her to the beach.

It had been a shock to see Simon so soon after she had arrived back in Northumberland, less than a day after she and Maria had pulled up in the carriage. Maria had reiterated her invitation to Alice to stay with her, but in the end Alice had decided she wanted a few days alone. She felt as though she were in mourning, experiencing a sadness for the loss of the dream she had woven around their lives.

Now with Simon back, she did not know what to think. He must have left London soon after they had and raced up here to speak to her, but that did not mean anything had changed—not really.

As Alice stepped onto the sand, she felt a powerful sense of being home. She loved London, loved the crowds and the sense that there was always something going on, but Northumberland was where she felt she belonged.

She climbed over the low dunes and walked along the beach a little, pleased to see she had the wide expanse of sand to herself. It was hardly weather for the beach, with the wind whipping up the sand every now and then so that she had to shield her eyes.

She chose a spot near the dunes where she was sheltered from the worst of the wind and made herself comfortable. What she loved most up here was the wide expanse of the sea. The water was always dark, the sand golden white, the sky changing with the seasons, yet one thing that never changed was the horizon. When she looked along the beach in either direction, as far as the eye could see was the flat line of the sea on the horizon, as if beckoning her to new adventures.

Alice sat for a long time, trying not to think of anything.

'I thought I might find you out here,' Simon said, surprising her. She hadn't thought he would follow her down to the beach.

He looked much fresher now after a bath, the soot washed from him and the grime scrubbed from his hair.

'I like the solitude on the beach, that sense that you are the only person in the whole world when you look out to sea.'

'It is beautiful.'

'Was your journey too strenuous?'

'It was not the most straightforward.'

'Was that soot on your clothing?'

'An inn I was staying at caught fire. I stayed to help put out the flames, but it was an old timber building, and the fire was relentless.'

Alice's eyes widened. 'Were you hurt?'

'No. Thankfully, no one was. The fire started when the innkeeper was cooking breakfast, so most of the guests were up, and there was time to rouse those who were not.'

'Did it spread to the rest of the village?'

'No.'

'That is something.' Alice shuddered. 'I always had such a fear of fire when I was a child. I used to fall asleep scared one of our neighbours would leave a candle burning and the whole row of houses would go up in flames.'

'I had never before seen a fire like this one. It was a destructive force, ripping through the building at such a speed you cannot imagine. It felt as though one minute there was a building with four walls and a roof, the next it was just a collection of timber supports left, sticking up from the ground with nothing to hold onto them.'

'I am glad you were not harmed,' Alice said, fixing her gaze again on the horizon.

He placed his hand on the sand next to hers, and Alice

felt the familiar spark travel through her as his finger brushed against hers.

'How are you? Has your wound completely healed?'

'It still pulls a little when I walk quickly, but apart from that it seems well healed.'

'I am glad.' He paused and then pressed on. 'I am sorry, Alice. Leaving you like that was unforgiveable.'

She shrugged, not meeting his eye. 'I should not be so upset. I should have expected it.'

'No,' he said sharply. 'I do not want you to expect such a thing.'

She turned to him, tears in her eyes. 'In London, after I had been injured, I thought that maybe something had changed between us, that maybe there was a chance that you could love me.'

There was pain in his eyes in response to her words, and he pressed his lips together so hard they went completely white. She realised how close he was to losing control and tentatively laid a hand over his. No matter how much she was hurting, she did not want to see Simon suffer like this. He had suffered enough in the last twenty years to last a lifetime.

'Can I tell you something? I know I have no right, but can I ask for your indulgence one last time before you decide what you are going to do?' He spoke quietly, but Alice could see he had control of himself again.

'Yes.'

'For twenty-one years I have been in mourning, but for the past five years I have felt as though I do not deserve to be here. I have hated every step I have had to take in Robert's shoes, every one of his duties I have had to shoulder. I have felt unworthy, and it has drained my very soul.'

Alice saw the anguish in his eyes and realised how much he had been suffering. She wanted to fold him in her arms and kiss him until he forgot the darkness, despite everything they had been through, but she knew he had to get this out in the open. Only then might he be able to begin to heal.

'Added to that is the fear that I will be struck down by the same condition that killed my father and my brother. I didn't want to die, didn't want my life to be over, but I felt like it was inevitable given how two good men, *better* men, had already been taken.'

'Not better,' Alice murmured.

'I have been hiding away, scared of dying but not feeling worthy of the life I had. The only way I knew how to cope was to push people away. Then I met you.' He flicked a glance at her, and she gave him an encouraging smile. 'That night at the Midsummer's Eve ball, when I met you I felt something shift. I was happy for the first time in a long time. It was as though you wakened something inside me.' He shook his head ruefully. 'Then I reverted back to my old ways and ran away, thinking I was sparing everyone the pain I felt, not realising I was only causing more of it.'

He turned to her, and Alice gave him an encouraging nod. She could feel the tears running down her cheeks as the wind whipped at them, but she didn't wipe them away.

'When I returned I did not know how we would live as husband and wife, but as soon as I saw you again I began falling in love. I fell hard and fast, even as I tried to pretend I felt nothing.'

Alice felt her eyes widen. She hadn't expected him to be able to say he loved her. For the first time since he had arrived in Northumberland, she allowed her mind to begin racing, to wonder if perhaps they had a chance at a future.

'You were like a magic potion, Alice. As you drew me in I started to realise little by little how terrible I had been feeling, how badly I had been treating myself, and how badly I had treated you. It was liberating to allow myself pleasure, to seek out enjoyment in things and realise that the guilt I was feeling for surviving when my brother had not was irrational. You did all of that. You showed me what it was to love and be loved.'

He reached out and stroked her cheek, and Alice felt a warmth flood through her body. She wanted to kiss him, to embrace him, but she knew it was important he say everything he needed to.

'When you were stabbed, I felt as though my world were ending. I didn't know how I would cope without you, even though I could not admit it to myself. I got so scared at the thought of losing someone else I loved. I tried to push everything down, to deny what I was feeling. Then when that man approached us in the street, mistaking me for Robert, it was as if every worry from the past came crashing back. I was overwhelmed. Suddenly I felt like a fraud, as if all the progress I had made was not real.' He shook his head. 'I am so sorry for abandoning you then, Alice. It was the worst possible thing I could have done.'

'Where did you go?'

'I walked the streets for hours, and then the next morning I went up the Monument. It was a place I used to visit with my father when I was young, and I realised I needed to properly clear my head, properly address what had happened.'

'That was when you came up with all of this?'

'It was the start. The journey here gave me a lot of time to think as well.'

Alice fell silent, her fingers drawing patterns in the sand by her sides.

'And now?' she asked eventually.

'Now I throw myself on your mercy, Alice. I love you with all my heart. Your smile lights up my world, and your laughter soothes my soul. I will do anything in my power to make you happy every day for the rest of our lives.'

'You want us to live as husband and wife?'

'Yes. More than anything.'

Alice felt her heart jump in her chest. Nothing was certain in life, but her main fear of giving her heart to Simon was that he would one day soon abandon her again. Now that he had acknowledged the reasons for his actions these past few years, she doubted he would act in the same way.

'I love you, Simon. I fell in love with you on the night of the Midsummer's Eve ball, and I have been pining for you ever since.'

'Do you think you can give me another chance?'

Alice closed her eyes and thought of all the reasons it might not work, then pushed them away. She loved him and he loved her. That was all they needed. Anything else they could work through together.

'Yes,' she said, leaning forward and kissing him.

'I have a question for you, one I hope you will say *yes* to.'

She frowned, puzzled.

Carefully he took something out of his jacket pocket and held it up so the light glinted off it. 'Alice, will you do me the honour of continuing to be my wife?'

'Is that my ring?'

'Yes.'

'How did you get it back?'

'The scoundrel who stabbed you was caught and brought before the magistrate a few days later. It seems he was wanted for a whole string of crimes. I talked to the magistrate, and they allowed me to search his possessions. He still had the ring on him when he was arrested.' He held it out. 'I will understand if you wish to have a different ring. We can choose one that does not have such memories associated with it.'

'No,' Alice said quickly. 'That is my wedding ring. That is the ring you placed on my finger when we married.'

Simon smiled and carefully slipped it onto the ring finger of her left hand.

'My beautiful wife,' he murmured and then leaned in and kissed her.

The wind whipped Alice's hair about her face, and the sand coated her skin, but Alice barely noticed. She was lost in the kiss of the man she loved, the man she had fallen for that very first night she had met him on a magical Midsummer's Eve.

Epilogue

Northumberland, Midsummer's Eve, 1818

Alice adjusted her mask, ensuring the ribbons were tied securely behind her head, and then she stepped out into the middle of the ballroom. The guests had been arriving for the last half an hour, and now Westcroft Hall was filled with chatter and laughter and music. Most people were wearing masks, delicate demimasks that barely concealed their identities, but it added to the sense of excitement.

'Good evening,' came a low voice from behind her, and Alice spun, a shiver running down her spine. Simon was standing there, dressed in a black jacket and gold cravat, easily the most handsome man in the room. 'May I have this dance?'

Alice inclined her head, and they walked to the dance floor to share the first dance of the evening.

Everyone was watching, but for Alice it felt as though they were the only two there, twirling around the ballroom as they did when they were the only two people in residence. For the duration of the dance she gazed into

Simon's eyes, and even as the music swelled and then died away, she found it hard to tear herself away.

'You're going to tell me I cannot have the next dance with you now, aren't you?' Simon said, a smile tugging at his lips.

Alice leaned in closer. 'If it were up to me, I would dance every single one with you, but we must fulfil our duties as host and hostess.'

'Can I tell you a secret?' Simon said, leaning in so his lips brushed against her ear.

Alice nodded.

'I would be willing to be labelled the worst host in the history of society balls if it meant I got to spend my evening only with you.'

'That is hardly a secret,' Alice said. She had the urge to kiss him and found her body swaying towards him.

'*Everyone* is watching,' Maria said as she glided over gracefully. 'If you ravish your wife here in the middle of the dance floor, you will never be able to show your faces in society again.'

'I would never,' Simon said, his eyes still locked on Alice's. 'A mere kiss, however...'

Alice felt helpless to resist and even began rising up on tiptoes until Maria gripped her arm.

'I am borrowing your wife, Simon. I'll give her back to you once you are no longer the centre of attention.'

Maria slipped her arm through Alice's and led her from the dance floor.

'This is marvellous, Alice. The most incredible ball I have ever been to.' Alice flushed with pleasure. It had been Simon's idea to host a ball on Midsummer's Eve, two years from the date they had first met, but Alice had been the one to remember all the details that had made the last ball so special and then to add in many more of her own.

The ballroom was beautifully decorated with fresh flowers spilling out of vases on tables and plinths around the room. Candles twinkled in the chandelier above their heads and in the sconces around the walls. It made the whole room look like a magical faerie glade, and their guests had embraced this theme with the women wearing floaty, flowery dresses and even some of the men tucking a rosebud or similar boutonnière.

The ballroom was not the only room that was decorated. They had decided on a woodland theme for each area, and it meant the entrance hall had garlands of leaves strung about it in a criss-cross pattern, making it look like their guests were entering the house under a canopy of trees. They had also opened up the drawing room as a quieter, cooler alternative to the ballroom, and for here Alice had sourced dozens of ferns that gave the room a calming atmosphere.

'The girls begged me to let them come and see the room decorated and everyone in their masks,' Maria said as they made their way through the crowd of people. 'I brought them down a little earlier, and I think Sylvia is convinced you are some sort of magical creature, placed in our family to bring us good luck.'

Alice flushed. The past year had flown by, and she and Simon had split their time between London and Northumberland, but by far her favourite part was spending time with their beautiful nieces.

She placed a hand on her swollen belly, looking down anxiously for a moment. They had discussed the subject of children of their own again and again in the early days after Simon's return. Simon worried about passing on whatever his father and brother had died from to any child of his, but as time passed he had also acknowledged that this was another unknown, something that might never come to pass, very much like his own risk of sudden death. They had agreed to put the subject to one side for a year or two and focus on the charity work Alice spent much of her time devoted to and touring the Westcroft properties to ensure everything was in order after Simon's long period away. They had continued to find it difficult to keep their hands off one another, but they took precautions. Fate had another idea, and a few months earlier Alice had realised she was pregnant.

In a way it had been better happening like this, the decision taken out of their hands. It was no one's fault, no one's decision, and as Alice's belly grew, their excitement for starting a family of their own did too.

They had returned to Northumberland a month earlier to prepare for the Midsummer's Eve ball and now planned to stay here until well after Alice had given birth. Alice wanted the reassurance of Maria's presence, and also she felt less nauseous when she could breathe in the fresh sea air rather than the heavy odours of London. Her own sister was planning on making the long journey up from Devon in a few months so she could also be on hand, which would also allow Alice to spend some precious time with Margaret and her little son.

They moved from group to group, exchanging pleasantries with their friends and neighbours, until Alice heard the first notes of a waltz and felt a hand on her shoulder.

'You promised me this dance, my love,' Simon said, his voice low and seductive.

This time he led her not to the dance floor but to the terrace beyond where there were lamps set along the stone balustrade and couples strolled arm-in-arm. They had been blessed with perfect weather for their ball. There was not a cloud in the sky, and hundreds of stars twinkled, helping to illuminate the terrace and the gardens beyond. Simon pulled her close, placing one had in the small of her back, and then they fell into step. Alice's heart soared as he twirled her and caught her and guided her across the terrace. When they danced like this, it always felt as though their bodies moved as one, perfectly synchronised like two swans gliding across a calm lake. As with the ball two years earlier, they had quite the audience by the time they had finished dancing, but everyone looked on indulgently, seeing nothing more than a young married couple enjoying the first flush of wedded bliss.

'This is the part where I should lead you into the garden,' Simon said, leaning close so his lips were almost touching hers.

'I think that might raise a few eyebrows.'

'You're right. Perhaps I should do this instead.'

He grinned at her and then closed the distance between them, brushing his lips against her own. The kiss was passionate but brief, even Simon knew he could not seduce his wife in front of sixty of the wealthiest and most influential people in Northumberland.

'This ball is perfect,' Alice said, rising up on her toes to whisper in his ear. 'But now I cannot wait for it to finish so we can retire upstairs.'

As Simon took her hand in his own, Alice rested her head against his shoulder and looked up at the stars, enjoying the perfect moment on a perfect night.

* * * * *

A Cinderella To
Redeem The Earl
Ann Lethbridge

MILLS & BOON

In her youth, award-winning author **Ann Lethbridge** reimagined the Regency romances she read—and now she loves writing her own. Now living in Canada, Ann visits Britain every year, where family members understand—or so they say—her need to poke around every antiquity within a hundred miles. Learn more about Ann or contact her at annlethbridge.com. She loves hearing from readers.

Visit the Author Profile page
at millsandboon.com.au for more titles.

Author Note

I hope you enjoy your visit to my vision of Regency England. As always, Damian and Pamela feel like family members, and it is with regret I must close this small chapter of their lives that intersected with mine for a few months. If you are interested in learning more about me and my books, please visit my website at annlethbridge.com. Do not hesitate to drop me a line. I always love to hear from readers.

DEDICATION

This book is dedicated to my greatest supporter—
my husband, Keith. Always and forever.

Chapter One

With a growing sense of dismay, Pamela gazed at Rake Hall, the address of her new employer, the Earl of Dart. Lit only by the moon. What must have once been a fine manor house built in the Palladian style was now a ramshackle hulk of boarded up windows, overgrown ivy and shrouded in darkness.

Clearly, the sly grin on the innkeeper's face in the village of Rake had been a warning Pamela should have heeded. Not to mention the sniggers from a couple of the patrons in his taproom when they overheard her asking for its direction.

At the time, she had ignored the worry that had niggled in the corner of her mind. After all, the agency had been quite glowing in their recommendation. Not to mention the offer of a fabulous salary. This would definitely be a step up in her career as a cook.

On the other hand, if she hadn't been quite so desperate to find a new position after her third argument with the head chef at her last post, she might have wondered at the generosity of the offer.

It had come at a moment when she feared she might be dismissed without a reference, having tossed out one of the head chef's desserts because she had been quite sure he had used rancid butter, likely in order to pocket the funds provided to purchase fresh.

The chill of the evening caused her breath to mist before her face. Fortunately, the brisk two-mile walk had kept her warm, but there was no denying winter was just around the corner.

Having to walk should also have been a warning sign that all was not well. She ought to have been met by some sort of transportation from Rake Hall. But, no. The best she had got from the innkeeper was directions to the manor house and an oily smirk.

Now she was in two minds as to whether to cut her losses and run.

She glanced up at the sky sprinkled with stars. Even by the light of a full moon, she did not fancy the long walk back to the village. And what would she do when she got there? She had no funds to pay for board and lodging. Would she sleep under a hedge like the vagrants she had pitied over the years?

She shifted her valise to her other hand, flexing her arm for ease. Well, she had walked this far, she wasn't going to turn back now. Besides, she had used her advance of a week's salary to pay for her travel from Cornwall. At the very least, she needed to work that off.

Very well. In for a penny, in for a pound.

As advised by the agency, she made her way around to the back of the house and across the courtyard between the house and the stables. To her relief, things looked a little less run down on this side of the house and the glow of candles in a couple of windows seemed welcoming.

A lantern beside a low heavy oak door guided her steps. She put down her valise, clenched her fist and banged hard.

After a long pause, and right at the moment she plucked

up the courage to bang again, she heard the click of footsteps on flagstones inside.

The door swung back.

A startlingly handsome man of dishevelled appearance, his necktie loose and his coat an embroidered grey waistcoat with buttons undone, opened the door and held up a lamp.

His dark eyebrows drew together at the sight of her. 'Yes?'

Oh, Lord, what sort of house was this? Not a very well-run one if he was any example. She straightened her shoulders. 'I am Mrs Lamb, the new cook.'

His eyes widened as if he was surprised. He leaned one shoulder—one impressively broad shoulder—against the door, crossed his shirt-sleeved arms over his chest and his lips curled in wry amusement as he looked her up and down. His smile turned appreciative and devastatingly attractive. 'Are you now?'

Her heart did an odd little flip-flop accompanied with a strangely girlish sensation of excitement. She hadn't felt this way since the first time Alan had kissed her on one of their long walks. *Alan.* The pain of loss hit her anew, followed swiftly by a sense of shame at her untoward reaction to this fellow.

For a moment she had trouble speaking. 'The agency sent me,' she forced the words out. 'I have a contract.'

His eyebrows rose. He nodded his head slowly, his gaze pursuing her as if she was an insect under a microscope. 'You were expected two hours ago.'

Who was this person? The butler? She hoped not. If she wasn't mistaken, he had imbibed a little more than he should have and was far more arrogant than he ought to be. She lifted her chin. 'The mail was late. Still, I expected a conveyance to be awaiting me.'

'Did you now?'

Handsome or not, she wanted to take him by those elegant shoulders and give him a good shake. 'I most certainly did. That valise is heavy. May I speak to the housekeeper?'

'You may not.'

Shocked at his denial, she stepped back. There really was something wrong here. 'Why ever not?'

'Because we don't have one.' He stepped back and gestured for her to enter. 'Come.'

When she didn't move, he glowered and gestured impatiently. 'Inside.'

The man's peremptory tone was not a good sign at all.

Heaven help her, she really didn't have a choice.

Feet dragging, she walked past him into the house. The strong smell of brandy wafted on the air along with the heat from his body in the confined space of the narrow entrance. She sidled through, far too aware of his masculine presence for comfort.

Her breath caught in her throat. How could she find him attractive after his rudeness?

'This way,' he said, and squeezed past her again, his shirtsleeves brushing against her. Shivers darted down her back. Reproach rippled through her. How could she respond to this man in this manner? Perhaps Alan had been right.

She pushed the thought aside. She had far more important things to be concerned about. Such as exactly what sort of household she had arrived at.

Apparently, completely unaware of their physical contact, he plucked a lamp from a small hall table, and led the way down a set of stairs into another narrow corridor. He paused at a doorway and the lamp afforded her a glimpse of an enormous kitchen, all neat and shiny.

Pamela peeped in and glanced around in awe.

'This is the main kitchen,' he said. 'Yours is this way.'

Puzzled, she followed him as he held the lamp high to help them see their way. He turned into an even narrower corridor which ended in what was only a slightly larger kitchen than the one in the cottage she and Mother had rented for a short while after her beloved scholarly father died suddenly, leaving them destitute.

A week after his death, her hopes for marriage and a family with her fiancé Alan had been dashed—her parents had informed her of the terrible news of his death by a fluke accident. What an idiot she had been to let her passion overcome good sense and anticipate their wedding vows. Having grown up in a vicarage, she'd been taught better. But then, whoever would have predicted he would be killed by a runaway gun carriage?

Her world had tumbled about her ears. No longer marriageable because she had let herself be ruined, and not penny to her name, she had thought that not even her connections could overcome such disadvantages. She and her mother faced a life of poverty.

Until her mother married a widower she had described as a beau from her salad days within a few months. While the speed of her mother's marriage had been a surprise, the fact that she had chosen a wealthy husband had not. Mother had been very disappointed by her father's lack of ambition and his tendency to give their money to people less well off than himself. Pamela often wondered if their blazing row about money she'd overheard a few days before his death had been part of the cause of his fatal apoplexy.

Certainly, her mother's new husband was wealthy and a peer, and just as keen as her mother to see Pamela wed to one of his friends, a rather elderly bachelor, who was in need of an heir.

After enduring a Season in London as a debutante and with her suitor likely to make her an offer at any moment, she had done the only honourable thing she could think of: she'd fled London and hired herself out as a cook.

And why not? She loved to cook and was good at it, too.

While her mother had tried to discourage her visits to the kitchen, seeing it as beneath one of her station, her father had not minded and the cook at the vicarage had been only too pleased to pass on her skills to so willing a pupil. Together they had preserved fruits and vegetables, made pastries and pies and custards as well as roasted and fricasseed all sorts of meats. She had even begun experimenting with her own recipes. Not to mention that it saved the family money since they did not need to hire extra help.

Her interest had certainly proved fortuitous after she and her mother had been forced to leave the vicarage to make room for the new incumbent. Pamela had discovered she loved being in charge of her own kitchen. However, the moment her mother married again, all that was over. Pamela was back to being someone who was meant to care only for the latest fashion and how many invitations she received in a week.

A tug at her heart made her breath catch. A sense of betrayal. Nothing she said, no excuse or request for delay, dissuaded her mother from insisting Pamela marry the man she had chosen. When Pamela finally told her mother she could not bear the idea of being touched by such an old man, her mother said she was being ridiculously missish. That was when she knew her fate was sealed, unless she took matters into her own hands. Now she was in charge of her own future.

And yet sometimes, like now, she felt lost. She felt a yearning for her old life. For family and the comfort of home.

No. She would not think of that now. This kitchen was *her* domain. She glanced around. Unwashed pots filled the sink. The stove needed a good scrub. And on the scarred wooden table running down the centre, sat the remains of a roast that was little more than a charred lump.

'It used to be the summer kitchen,' he pronounced. He gestured at the table. 'The last cook was a bit of a disaster.' His chuckle sent a pleasurable tremor down her spine. Heavens above, this really would not do. She frowned, but whether at her reaction to him or at the mess, she wasn't exactly sure.

She pulled herself together. 'A mess indeed, Mr—I am sorry I did not catch your name.'

A mischievous grin lit his face. Her insides fluttered. 'I didn't give it. I am Dart.' His words stopped her cold.

Dart? Why on earth was the Earl of Dart answering his own door? What sort of establishment was this that he had no servants?

It certainly looked as if the last cook had left in a hurry. Perhaps she had jumped from the frying pan into the fire.

'My lord.' She sketched a curtsy. 'I am curious as to why you use this kitchen when the other is so much better?'

He shot her a hard look. 'I hope you do not plan to question my every decision.'

Taken aback at the swift change in his demeanour, she stared at him.

'I do a great deal of entertaining,' he said in more moderate tones as if he regretted his outburst. 'When my guests are here, a chef comes from London to prepare their food. Your job is to feed the servants who wait upon my guests, as well as send food out to their coachmen and grooms in the stable block.' He paused. 'And, upon occasion, feed me and Monsieur Phillippe, when I am here and not entertaining. Any more questions?'

'Yes.'

His frowned deepened.

'Where are my quarters? I have had a long journey and I need to rest.' She glanced with distaste at the kitchen. 'I will start work on this mess first thing in the morning.'

His unwilling chuckle lightened the atmosphere, though she had no clue why he thought what she had said was humorous. 'Your quarters are this way.'

He led her further along the narrow corridor through an antechamber and into the room beyond. The lamp revealed a chamber that boasted a narrow bed against one wall and a table with two chairs in the corner.

He lit several candles in strategically placed holders. 'This chamber backs on to the kitchen hearth. It is cosy in the winter and too hot in the summer, but there are lots of windows to open.'

There were indeed. A set of French doors led to somewhere outdoors. He pulled a set of heavy curtains over the glass. 'Better to keep these closed at this time of year.'

He glanced down at her valise. 'I will leave you to settle in.' He headed for the door.

'Wait.'

He turned back with a glare. He really did not like to be questioned. 'What is it now?'

'I have an offer of employment from the agency detailing salary and terms that requires your signature.'

'I will meet you in my office tomorrow, at ten, to finalise the details.' He sounded completely uninterested, but given that the offer was for what she considered an exorbitant salary, she was determined to have the contract signed and sealed.

'Very well. I will attend you at ten. Also, how many people require breakfast tomorrow morning, where and at what time?'

He huffed a sigh. 'Two. Me, Monsieur Phillippe, in addition to yourself. Something simple laid out in the servants' hall will do. By tomorrow afternoon there will be fifteen additional staff. They will require dinner at six, then will return to London before morning. They return again on Friday. They will require meals two evenings each week. I hope that is clear?'

Only two evenings each week? All that money for so little work? What was she to do the rest of the time?

Her earlier misgivings returned in a rush.

Damian frowned as he strode back to his study. *Mrs* Lamb, as she called herself, had not been quite as anticipated. When he had hatched his plans to take revenge on her and her family, he had not expected to discover her hiring herself out as a cook. He had also expected her to be delicate, less confident and easily influenced.

Until recently, his only experience with gently born ladies had been his mother, who had suffered greatly at their reduced circumstances. Her brave attempts to pitch in had been endearing, but more of a hindrance than a help. Her idea of adding to the family coffers had been to take in mending, but then had required his father to hire a woman to provide assistance. An expenditure they could little afford.

His father, who did his best to protect his wife, had not had the heart to tell her she was costing him money. Her sensibilities had been very delicate.

At first meeting, it seemed that Mrs Lamb was made of sterner stuff, both resilient and competent, which rather contradicted the tepid reference he'd received from the chef at her last place of employment. The reference had accorded with his expectation of a spoiled little miss, who, not getting her way over something ridiculous, had run off to be a cook, to blackmail her family into giving in.

But time would tell which of these was true.

He certainly had not expected to find her quite so lovely, or feel a tug of attraction. Until now, he had found most of the *ton*'s ladies not to his taste, being far too empty-headed and ingratiating.

Fortunate indeed. Had he found the spoiled miss repulsive, it might have made undertaking her ruin more difficult. Rubbish. Nothing would stand in his way. He controlled his future, whether it be divesting a young man of a fortune by the turn of a card, or tempting a woman to let down her guard. Every move he made was thought out and based on full knowledge of the risks.

The hard scrabble of the many years of gaining a fortune in the mean streets of Marseilles had taught him to identify what he wanted and focus his all on getting it.

He'd learned from the best, first as a lad, running errands for one of Marseilles's notorious criminals, and later setting up his own illegal gaming hell, which attracted a better class of gambler, where he made sure the gaming was honest and the premises discreet enough to attract the wealthiest of customers.

So it would be with his plans for Mrs Lamb. Pamela. Such a soft name for such a sharp-edged female. Well, pretty soon he'd blunt her blade and have her eating out of his hand, when and how he decided.

It was inevitable.

A twinge of guilt took him by surprise.

Guilt? Or pity?

Impossible. There was no way he would entertain second thoughts. Her father had ruined his family so she could live off the fat of the land while they languished in misery in France. She, and the family of the other man who had profited from the fraud perpetrated on his father, were going to suffer the same fate.

He deliberately recalled his father's agony as his mother wasted away from some horrible disease in what was little more than a slum. It was the night she died that Damian had learned who had brought about his family's downfall and made him promise to avenge his mother's death.

After her death his father lost all hope. Night after night he drank himself into oblivion until he finally succumbed.

If only Damian had been able to do more, provide more, he might have been able to save them both. The guilt of it racked him. He could have done more if he had not let his scruples get in the way. He'd been offered a chance to participate in a lucrative robbery, but the sight of the pistols and knives to be used if anyone got in the way had deterred him. At fifteen he still had notions of honour and right and wrong.

Until the night his mother had died and he learned the truth about the way his father had been lured into debt by a man he trusted and then who denied any knowledge of the plot and refused to help.

If Damian had taken the opportunity, his parents might be alive today to enjoy their old age in security and comfort. All he could do now was keep his promise to his father and bring to justice those who had profited from their downfall.

He hardened his heart against the fleeting memory: a fascinating dimple in one soft cheek when a small smile curved her lips.

He cared nothing for her innocence or her reduced circumstances. *He* had been innocent, before he had been forced grow up among the stews of Marseilles. Innocence had offered *him* no protection. Scruples were nothing but a dead weight.

He entered what had once been his father's study—his own study now. It smelled of mould and dust. One day he would restore the house to its former glory. Perhaps. Or maybe, once his goal was accomplished, he would leave it to rot and move on. Only bitter memories and regrets remained for him here.

There was no need to think about the future. Right now, he had to focus on the task at hand. Bringing his enemies to their respective knees.

The thought usually warmed him. Tonight, it left him feeling hollow. Perhaps because there was much left to be done and he wanted it over.

Pip, his friend who had helped him survive the streets of Marseilles, was one of those rare fair-haired men from the north of France. Glass in hand, he pushed his lanky six-foot frame from the overstuffed chair beside the hearth and went to the desk. 'Brandy, *mon ami*?' he asked.

Damian sighed. 'Brandy would not come amiss.'

Pip poured him a generous serving from the decanter. They chinked glasses and Damian gestured for Pip to sit. They had been together for so long they needed no ceremony. Pip was his partner in some would call it crime—Damian called it justice.

'Everything is ready for tomorrow evening?' Damian asked.

'Of course.' Pip's French accent was hardly discernible. Barely twenty-five and smart as a whip. That was what living on the streets since birth did for a chap.

Damian had been lucky to meet the younger man or

the streets might have eaten him alive, he had been such a Johnny Raw. He still didn't know what had moved Pip to befriend him rather than take advantage of his naivety. Together they had run rings around the local gendarmes.

But that was in the past. Now, after years of living in the backstreets of Marseilles, he was home. And he was well on the way to accomplishing all he had dreamed of these past fifteen years: revenge.

A return, with interest, for what had been done to him and his family by two self-serving noblemen. It wouldn't happen overnight, of course. But his plans were well underway. Already, news of the exciting new club called The Rake Hell, a short drive from Mayfair, had spread far and wide among the younger members of the *ton*.

Pretty soon, his fish would be in his net.

'The cook has arrived,' he said.

Pip cocked an eyebrow. 'Is she as you expected?'

'More or less.' More and less. More beautiful. Less pliable, but not invulnerable.

'We will have no more complaints from Chandon about feeding riff-raff who don't appreciate his talents,' Damien said. 'If she is half the cook she claims to be.'

Pip chuckled. 'The staff will be pleased if it is so. The meal Betsy cooked last week wasn't fit to feed to a pig. How many will attend this week?'

'At least thirty, by my reckoning. About a third of them female companions.' Up from the twenty last week. 'Now I wait for the other one to fall into our net and the real game can begin. In the meantime, we are making a fortune. The future bodes well.'

'You are a lucky devil, Damian.'

'So they say.' His luck at the tables was legendary. He was counting on it to hold.

After the successes of the past few weeks, every gentleman in London would do anything to receive one of his prized invitations to an evening at the exclusive Rake Hell Club. It catered to only the richest and most well-connected members of the *ton*—and their vices. Their need for excitement and titillation. Like children.

To Damian, the tables were the most important part of his venture, but the draw for his patrons was the club's exclusivity and its upstairs rooms. A sprat to catch a mackerel.

'Is the cook aware of the sort of house she's come to?' Pip asked.

'She has no reason to know anything apart from that she cooks only for the staff.'

'But servants talk, *mon ami*. Everyone working here is known to us. Is loyal to us. This cook is a whole different story. Will you be able to keep her from going to the authorities?'

He shrugged. 'She needs money or she would not have taken the lure. Besides, there is nothing illegal about what we are doing.' Although they walked a very fine line and it would not take much to tip them over on to the wrong side of the law.

Pip sipped his brandy. 'Let us hope you are correct. I look forward to meeting this cook of yours.'

A spark of something hot rose in Damien's chest. Anger? Since when did he care about Pip's legendary romantic adventures? Nonsense. He merely didn't want Pip causing his plan to go awry. 'This is one female I insist you stay away from.'

A charming smile broke out on his friend's face. 'She is so lovely, then?'

'Ugly or fair, it is all the same to me. I don't want you getting in the way of our plans.' He caught the twinkle in his friend's eye and relaxed. 'Stop roasting me, I will deal with her.'

Pip tossed back his drink. 'It shall be as you request. I bid you goodnight. Tomorrow will be a busy day.'

Tomorrow would be a good day. Everything was coming together exactly the way he had planned.

Pamela dried her hands on a cloth and inspected the fruits of the labour she had started at six that morning. The little kitchen—her domain—sparkled. The wooden table top shone, as did the floor, the copper pots hanging from the wall rack gleamed and the stove had been scrubbed inside and out.

Four hours of hard work and well worth it.

To her delight, the pantry was exceedingly well stocked with everything she would need for at least two weeks. Now she began to explore the rest of her surroundings. Since the house was built into a small rise, while she had come downstairs from the front door to reach the kitchens, at the back of the house, it was above ground. The kitchen windows looked out over a herb and vegetable garden, long neglected.

Following the corridor, she had walked down the previous evening, she passed the servants' hall where she had laid out breakfast for three as ordered and opened the back door to the outside. This was how one accessed the garden and a collection of buildings for storage, smoking meats and laundry. Which had her wondering who was responsible for washing the linens.

Another question to ask her employer when she saw him in…not very many minutes' time.

Time to get ready for her appointment. At the thought, her heart gave an odd little skip. Not afraid, but a kind of eager anticipation. It really would not do. She must not let herself find him attractive. He was her employer. She peeked into the servants' hall and was disappointed to see no signs that Dart or Monsieur Phillippe had availed themselves of the breakfast she had laid out.

She had wanted his reaction to the food. She wanted to make a good impression. But alas, apparently the exceedingly handsome, somewhat brooding Earl of Dart clearly was not an early riser.

The more she thought about him, the more she wondered at the strangeness of his abode. Opening his own door. Hiring his own servants. And the odd arrangement regarding meals for the servants and guests.

She had heard that some members of the nobility were eccentric and she had an uncomfortable feeling about this one. Well, as long as he left her in peace to do her work, she didn't see why she would have a problem with his foibles.

Returned to her kitchen, she took a deep steadying breath, hung up her apron and glanced at her reflection in the bottom of a pot.

She smoothed a stray lock of hair back into her bun. Neat as a pin, like her kitchen. Satisfied, she climbed the stairs and pushed open the baize door into the main entrance hall.

Where was Dart's study?

She walked along the corridor to the right and peeked into the first room she came to. She could not believe her eyes. The floorboards were rotted and haphazardly patched, a broken chair lay on its side and odd bits of wood covered many of the window panes. If she wasn't mistaken, those were mice droppings all over the floor.

She tried the next room and found it worse.

Perhaps the other wing… She retraced her steps back to the entrance hall.

'Are you looking for something?'

Her heart gave a startled thump.

She spun around to see a young fair-haired man strolling down the grand staircase. An Adonis of a young man, no less.

She took a quick breath. 'Yes. I am seeking my employer. Lord Dart.'

The young man tilted his head and let his gaze roam from her head to her heels.

'Yes, of course,' he murmured. 'The cook.'

Her face heated. 'You have me at a disadvantage, Mr...'

He beamed winsomely. 'I am Phillippe. My friends call me, Pip. But then I only have one friend.'

She did not trust that charming smile for one moment. This was the Monsieur Phillippe Dart had spoken of the previous evening. 'Do you know where His Lordship is?'

'Bien sur,' Monsieur Phillippe said.

'Would you care to share the information?' she said coldly.

'So haughty a cook. Interesting.' He gestured to the other corridor. 'You will find him in his study.' He frowned. 'Do you offer breakfast, or should I help myself as usual?'

Something about this young man annoyed her. 'You will find bread and cheese and fruit laid out in the servants' hall. I was not asked to provide a hot meal until this evening.'

He nodded and walked off whistling. Very annoying indeed. And if he was responsible for the mess she had just cleaned up—he'd clearly stated he had been helping himself to her kitchen—she wanted to get back to her domain as soon as possible to keep an eye on him.

She hurried down the corridor. The set of large, ornately carved double doors she came to first did not look as though they would lead to a study, but she opened them anyway.

She gasped at the sight of gilt and glass and tastefully arranged tables arrayed around the rooms. It was one of the most sumptuous rooms she had ever seen in her life.

Nothing like the shambles in the other wing.

It looked as though it was set for a ball or a rout. Or a card party, perhaps, but on a very grand scale.

She backed out and continued along the corridor. Further along, a door lay ajar. Perhaps this was where she would find the elusive Lord Dart.

She pushed the door open and there he was, seated at a desk, wearing a pair of spectacles on the end of his aristocratic nose. He wore a tweed coat and belcher handkerchief at his throat. The uniform of a gentleman farmer. And he wore it with impeccable style.

By comparison, she felt suddenly dowdy.

As was right. After all, he was an earl and she merely a cook.

The room, however, was nothing like the luxurious ballroom. The furniture had seen better days and the air had a stale smell.

He looked up upon her entry, removed his spectacles and pushed to his feet.

That she had not expected. Courtesy to the lower orders was rarely observed in her experience.

She dipped a curtsy. 'You said we should discuss the terms of my employment this morning.'

'I did. You found everything to your satisfaction with your new quarters?'

Startled, she stared at him. Most of the employers she had come across since leaving home hadn't cared a farthing whether she found her quarters, let alone if she found them satisfactory. 'They are perfectly adequate.'

They had, in fact, been deliciously cosy and the bed had been so comfortable she had drifted to sleep in an instant.

He indicated a chair in front of the desk. 'Please, be seated.'

She hesitated. Then took the chair offered.

'You have the contract for me to sign?' he asked.

She laid the sheaf of papers on the desk. 'The agency contract.'

He perused the paper. 'All seems in order.'

He didn't even blink at the ten pounds per week the agency had proposed and she had wondered if he might argue about it, as had happened before when an employer discovered her youth.

An uneasy feeling rippled down her spine. Everything about this man—this house—seemed out of kilter with her experience. Perhaps accepting this position, no matter how lucrative, was a mistake.

But then everything she attempted seemed to be a mistake. Such as giving herself to Alan and trusting her mother to have her happiness at heart.

Unfortunately, each new undertaking she had embarked on had proved to have drawbacks.

It seemed this one might be no different.

The question was—would the drawbacks be untenable?

Chapter Two

Damian eyed the young woman sitting calmly before him. For someone who had chosen hard work after being raised in the lap of luxury, she seemed remarkably sanguine.

The self-assurance of the overprivileged miss. It seemed she hadn't learned her place. Or was she merely playing at being a member of the lower orders? Was her family supporting her, while they let her play with her patty pans?

He wouldn't be surprised.

He scrawled his signature at the bottom of the contract and handed it back.

'I had expected to find I would have a scullery maid to help,' she said.

Aha, here it was, just as he had expected, the lady needing someone else to do the real work. 'I doubt there is enough to keep two people busy.'

Her lovely mouth tightened. 'It took me four hours to clean the kitchen this morning, My Lord. A cook does not normally undertake that sort of labour. Why don't I seek help from a woman in the village for the days each week your household is in residence? It will not cost that much.'

He felt a sense of disappointment. As if he had wanted her to be different. Which was nonsense, of course.

'If the work is too much for you, perhaps I need to look for someone else.'

Her soft grey eyes focused on his face.

Dammit it. She was going to call his bluff.

She straightened her shoulders slightly, a stiffening of her resolve no doubt. But what was it she had decided?

'Very well,' she said briskly.

He let go the breath he hadn't realised he was holding and nodded.

'I will see how it goes,' she continued. 'I reserve the right to revisit the issue if necessary.'

If necessary. He could not help but admire her gall. But having passed one hurdle, he wasn't going to erect another. 'As you wish.'

She rose to her feet.

He stood up and opened the door. She paused on the threshold and glanced up at him. 'And I am not required to feed your guests?'

Oh, yes, she really did not want to work too hard. She was exactly what he had expected.

He narrowed his eyes. 'No. My London staff will take care of their needs, you have no need to worry that you will be overburdened.'

'I see. Thank you.' She turned and walked away. Her stride was purposeful, but exceedingly feminine. Quite enticing, in fact. Womanly and elegant at the same time. He muttered a curse under his breath.

He had the odd feeling she would prove to be more of a challenge than he had expected. Now if he could only figure out why that would be, he could solve the problem.

He glanced down at the papers on his desk. Some bills from tradesmen, an estimate for a new roof on the east wing from a local carpenter, and a bill for feed, which reminded him—he had planned to visit his horses this morning.

He put on his coat and headed across the courtyard.

In the stables, he found Pip in his shirt sleeves, already at work. No point in hiring a stable master and grooms when the animals were only here a couple of days a week, so he and Pip took on those duties.

The same logic did not apply to his cook, of course. Her wages were a small price to pay for the punishment he planned to exact.

He glanced at the bay standing patiently under Pip's ministrations. 'Is Caesar all right?'

Pip straightened. 'He seems fine. I was worried he had the colic last night, but everything is right this morning.'

'Glad to hear it.' Damian picked up a pitchfork and began mucking out the stall.

'I met your cook,' Pip said.

An odd sensation tightened his gut. Damian straightened his forkful of manure and regarded his friend. 'Did you?'

'On her way to see you. *Une belle petite fille, mon ami.* Be careful she does not turn the tables on you.'

He grunted and heaved the load of stinking straw into the barrow. 'Unlikely. She's not my sort of female at all.' He preferred the earthy experienced type who expected nothing but a generous gift at the end of an association.

Pip chuckled. 'You are right, of course. She struck me as very prim and proper. Perhaps she is more my sort.'

Damian snorted. 'Prim and proper would have *you* running for the hills. Prim and proper is looking for marriage.' He was banking on it. He leaned on his fork and glowered at his friend's grinning face. 'I meant what I said. Stay well away from her. This is mine to finish.'

Pip grimaced. 'You don't have to warn me off. I am not in the market for a wife, I assure you.' Pip put away his brushes and tossed a blanket over Caesar. 'You, however, are a different story. A nobleman needs an heir, does he not?'

Damian grabbed the barrow's handles and lifted it. This conversation was pointless. 'The title is nothing but a means to an end. And when that end is accomplished, I'll have no use for it.' He stomped out into the yard and tipped his load on the manure pile.

Behind him he heard Pip's laughter.

Damn him.

He could laugh. But Damian had decided long ago he cared nothing about the title or the duty it entailed. He had set himself one purpose in life and that was to make those who had caused him and his family to suffer humiliation and degradation suffer it tenfold in return.

Nothing would ever get in the way of that, even if it took him the rest of his life.

He certainly didn't want to marry. Women came with a whole set of expectations of their own. And if you failed to meet them, they did not take it well. His own mother had died of a broken heart, her sensibilities weakened and living in squalor too much to cope with after his father's failures.

Their family had lost everything because Father had believed the smiles and promises of a couple of noblemen he admired and who hadn't hesitated to use his admiration to their advantage.

Now the tables were turned. He, Damian, was the one the *ton* admired and fawned over. And he would have no hesitation in turning the tables on them and their offspring when the time was right.

He gazed across the courtyard at the house he had lived in until he was ten. The last twenty years had not treated it kindly. The bailiffs had taken anything of value that was not nailed down, but since it was entailed, it could not be sold to clear their debts. His family had been forced to leave England or face debtors' prison. Over the years several renters had come and gone and ultimately it had been abandoned to its fate. The cost to put it right would be enormous.

The estate belonging to the title he had recently inherited he would sell at the first opportunity, if anyone would buy it. He didn't give a damn. He would have loved to have sold it all—this estate, this house—and be rid of the financial and emotional burden, but its entailment meant he had to make do.

Once his plan had borne fruit, it could fall down for all he cared. He and Pip had set their sights on a new life in the New World.

The staff who had arrived earlier in the afternoon was a strange lot indeed. Pamela had expected housemaids and footmen and, indeed, when they had arrived, they had apparently gone about those sorts of tasks in the upstairs rooms, but the chattering jolly bunch who had come down from their quarters for dinner were like no servants she had ever seen.

The men wore the powdered wigs of footmen to be sure, and a livery of sorts, but rather than being of all the same discreet colour designed to fade into the background, their coats were bright blues, reds and greens and embellished with quantities of gold braid.

The women wore evening gowns and elaborate coiffures and glittering jewellery at throat and wrist. Stones made of paste, no doubt, but they sparkled in the candlelight of the plain servants' dining hall. And they all carried masks.

At the direction of the head footman, who had introduced himself as Albert, his underlings carried the tureens of stew from the kitchen to the table. She joined them, seating herself at one end of the table with Albert at the other.

The moment Albert finished saying grace everyone helped themselves to stew and fresh baked bread.

She turned to the young woman beside her, who was tucking in with apparent relish. 'I expect you will be busy when the guests arrive?' Dressed as she and the other women were, Pamela could not imagine their tasks were limited to bed making or fire lighting.

The girl eyed her up and down somewhat suspiciously, Pamela thought. 'Ain't that the truth?' She broke apart a slice of bread and dipped it in the gravy. 'Good grub for a change.'

A woman further down the table shot her a glare. 'Anything is better than what you got at the workhouse, Meg,' she called out.

A tall handsome young man in a red coat seated on the other side of Pamela chuckled. 'Don't take any notice of Betsy, down there. She's cross because you are a better cook. I'm Johnny, by the way. How do you do?' He raised his voice. 'Isn't that right?'

There were mutters of agreement around the table.

A sudden silence descended and people rose to their feet. Surprised, Pamela glanced up to see His Lordship in the doorway.

Clearly dressed for the evening in a black form-fitting coat that showed off his broad shoulders and lithe body, a dazzling white cravat with an emerald glinting in its folds and an emerald-green silk waistcoat, he looked gorgeous.

Her stomach gave an appreciative little flip. She was horrified to notice similar reactions on the faces of the other women.

'Please,' he said with a charming smile, 'sit down. Do not let me interrupt your meal.'

Everyone resumed their seats.

Pamela schooled her expression into one of cool enquiry. 'May I be of assistance, Your Lordship?'

Albert frowned, as if he thought she should not have spoken.

'I came to assure myself all is satisfactory,' Dart said. His gaze took in the table and the food before falling on Albert.

'Mrs Lamb has done us proud, My Lord,' Albert said.

Others at the table nodded their agreement.

Pamela could not quite believe her eyes and ears. What nobleman ever came to the servants' hall to ensure his staff was well fed?

His Lordship sent a glance of approval in her direction. 'It certainly smells wonderful.'

It seemed she had passed muster. Was that what this was all about, him checking up on her performance of her duties?

'Would you care to try it?'

He hesitated. 'Perhaps another time.'

The clock on the wall struck six. 'Come on, you lot,' Albert, said. 'Finish up. There's a lot to do before the chickens arrive.'

'Chickens?' Pamela said. Her voice was lost in the scraping of chairs on flagstones and the general hubbub.

Or perhaps not. 'Birds ripe for the plucking,' Johnny said in a low mutter, leaning close as he got up.

His words had a distinctly ominous undertone. She glanced over at His Lordship who stood back to allow everyone out of the door.

A strange sensation curled in the pit of her stomach. There was something not quite right here. Something she did not understand. Something she had the feeling she should have been told before she accepted the position.

There was no chance to ask any questions. In moments, the dining hall was empty, His Lordship having followed them out.

Pamela huffed out a breath, stacked the plates and carried them to the kitchen sink.

She might be inclined to find out just what was going on here. And if it was something unpleasant, as she was starting to suspect? She would have to decide if she would go or stay.

Leaving would require she pay a heavy penalty for breaking her contract. And the employment agency might refuse to send her any more offers of work.

That would not be a good outcome.

If she could not find other work, she would have to return home—to her mother and the prospect of accepting her elderly suitor.

She finished clearing the table and headed back to her sink.

A portly man in a chef's hat was standing at the stove with a ladle in his hand.

'Good evening,' she said.

The man turned. His face reminded her of a jolly elf, rosy red cheeks, brown eyes and hair which was clearly receding. His mouth turned down at the sight of her. 'Who are you?' His tone was definitely belligerent.

She eyed him calmly. 'Mrs Lamb, the new cook. And you?'

'Chandon. His Lordship's chef.' He took a sip of her stew. 'Adequate. Fit for those who serve.'

'They seemed to like it,' she said, trying not to let him bait her into saying something she would regret.

'They know nothing.' He stalked out.

He was wrong. Her stew was more than adequate. It

was delicious. Her father, who liked his food, had said so. Chandon was another of those men who feared female competition.

Well, this was her kitchen. Her domain. Next time he set foot in it, she would demand his departure.

She filled her sink full of dishes with hot water and soap and began the mindless task of washing up.

The sound of horses' hooves and carriage wheels crunching on gravel came from outside.

His Lordship's guests, no doubt. Along with their coachmen and grooms, who also required an evening meal.

They would definitely appreciate her stew, Chandon be hanged.

Damian surveyed his domain.

Now the obligatory meal was over, the tip of the hat to a legitimate house party, here, in the gaming room, he felt comfortable and in control.

The rattle of die and the clink of glasses amid the chatter and laughter played like a perfectly conducted symphony. Every table overflowed with players watched over by his female croupiers, smiling and nimble, while the footmen moved through the throng with trays of the very best champagne.

The more the pigeons drank, the more they played. The more they played, the more money he made.

A movement at the door caught his eye. A brief flash of drab skirt whisked out of sight.

What the devil?

There was only one woman in this house dressed in dreary grey. He passed through his guests, smiling and bowing, showing no sign of the anger building inside.

Pip, currently entertaining a couple of ladies at a game

of vingt-et-un, glanced up as he passed. An eyebrow rose in question. *Something wrong?* the look asked.

Nothing he couldn't deal with, he replied with a tilt of his head. They had been communicating with these silent signals since they were lads when the gendarmes would have carted them off to jail had they discerned the tricks they were up to.

Outside in the corridor, there was no sign of his quarry. He walked quietly along the hall to the nearest room, the library. He pushed at the door and it swung open.

On the other side of the room, his cook, in her prim grey gown and severe cap, was staring up at a portrait of one of his female ancestors in powdered wig and Elizabethan ruff, trying, no doubt, to give the impression she was completely absorbed. The tension in her shoulders indicated she was fully aware of his presence.

He stalked across the room and stood inches behind her. The severe bun beneath her cap meant her nape was bared to his gaze, soft and white and vulnerable. How would her skin feel against his lips? Would she shiver if he kissed her? Or would she turn and slap his face?

'Mrs Lamb,' he murmured.

She swung around as if startled, then backed up when she realised his nearness.

'My Lord?' Her voice was breathy, a little shaky as if her heart was beating too fast for comfort.

'Was there something you required?' he asked.

'I…er… I was wondering if the staff would require supper at the end of their day?'

Quick-witted, then. It was a perfectly reasonable explanation, even if it wasn't the truth. But then he hadn't expected the truth from her father's daughter. Deceit ran in her blood.

'There will be plenty left over for them once my guests depart, should they feel the need.'

'Oh, I see. Thank you.'

She made to move around him. He cut her off. She frowned.

'What was your real purpose for being in this wing of the house?' he asked.

She lifted her chin in a little show of defiance, but pink stained her cheeks. Guilt at being caught in a lie? 'I was curious.'

'You know what curiosity did?'

She looked him right in the eyes. 'I am not a cat, My Lord.'

And not a meek little mouse either. But then she hadn't been raised to be meek, unless she was dealing with someone she considered her better, or a good marriage prospect. 'I see. Is your curiosity now satisfied?'

She hesitated.

What would she say next?

'Why would members of the *ton* drive all the way out here to gamble when there are plenty of hells and whatnot close to hand in London?'

Interesting that she instantly saw right to the hub of the matter. 'Why indeed?'

She shot him a piercing stare. 'That is hardly an answer.'

'I don't answer to you, Mrs Lamb,' he said in bored tones. 'I fail to see how it is any of your business, to be honest.'

She flinched slightly, but, to his surprise, held her ground. 'It is my business if you are engaged in some sort of nefarious activity.'

Devil take it, did she think to cause trouble? He closed the gap between them once more. She held her ground, but her hands tightened convulsively at her waist.

'As far as I know, house parties are not outlawed in England,' he said evenly.

'I—no. It is rather reprehensible for a nobleman to be setting up a gaming establishment, however. Relieving people of their money.'

And it wasn't reprehensible to defraud a gentleman of his fortune as her father had done? 'This is not a gaming establishment. Everyone here is a guest, invited to spend an evening among their peers, enjoying each other's company and playing cards or die to while away the time.'

Her expression said she did not believe a word of it. 'At every one of the tables a member of your staff holds the bank. How is that different from a gaming establishment? Everyone knows that the bank almost always wins.'

'Unlike most gaming establishments, this house plays fair. While the odds are naturally stacked in favour of those who hold the bank, those who gamble here have a fair chance of winning large sums of money.'

Her lips thinned. 'Only to lose it all again the next time.'

How dare she look down on him? 'Do you think they would not be gaming elsewhere under much less favourable circumstances, if they were not gambling here?'

Her shoulders slumped. 'I suppose not.'

Surprised that she acquiesced so readily to his logic, he stepped back and gestured for her to leave. 'Now you have satisfied your curiosity, I would prefer it that you return to your domain and leave my domain to me. Is that clear?'

'Very clear, My Lord.' She looked as though she wanted to say more, inhaled a deep breath and marched out.

He watched her go. Felt the tug of his heart again. Pity? Regret that she would eventually receive her comeuppance at his hands?

How was it possible?

Had her father felt any regret about what had happened to him and his mother? It was only right that the daughter suffer a similar fate.

He strode back to the chatter and laughter in the ballroom. Everything was moving along very nicely. Nothing and no one would stop him from dealing justice to those who deserved it.

Chapter Three

Pamela stretched and snuggled back beneath her covers. She hadn't been this cosy since she had been forced to leave her bedroom at the vicarage behind.

In those days her dreams had been full of Alan, her future husband. Both sets of parents had approved their marriage and she had romanticised her future as a soldier's wife. His death, an accident while on manoeuvres, had been a terrible shock, not the least because they had anticipated their wedding vows. An awful truth she would have to admit to any man who might propose marriage in the future. She shook her head at her foolish thoughts. As if that was ever going to happen. Marriage was out of the question.

She was now an independent woman, earning her own living. It wasn't quite as easy as one might expect, but it provided a good deal of satisfaction.

Somewhere in the distance a cockerel crowed. She had work to do. A kitchen to ready for the next onslaught of His Lordship's 'servants', people who earned their keep by turning cards and rolling dice in the employ of a man she didn't trust an inch. She grimaced. She did not believe a word of his explanation the previous evening and not just because he had made her stomach flutter in a most inappropriate way.

That he had done on purpose. Standing so close. Looking down at her as if she was a mouse to be gobbled up by a cat.

She could not help recalling how handsome he had looked in his evening clothes, the way he'd surveyed *his domain* as he called it. He'd looked elegant and devastatingly charming when he'd smiled at one of his guests. Her stomach fluttered anew.

Dash it. She would do very well to avoid him if that was the sort of reaction he caused.

She forced herself to throw the covers back, but instead of the usual chilly air of a servant's attic, the room was warm and welcoming.

She lit a candle and prepared for her day.

As she washed and dressed, she found herself humming. She paused. What was that song?

A waltz. How odd. She must have heard it the previous evening.

She brushed her hair and pinned it neatly under her cap, then went to prepare the breakfast table in the dining hall. Most of the houses she had worked in fed the servants early in the morning, before they began their duties, but here there were no servants except her. All she had to do was prepare a breakfast for the Earl and his friend Monsieur Phillippe.

At the kitchen door, she halted on the threshold. Her heart gave an odd little thump.

Oh! What on earth was *he* doing here? The Earl himself.

'Good morning, Mrs Lamb.'

She glared at him. 'I hardly expected to see you so early this morning, My Lord.'

He blinked and shook his head as if to clear it. No doubt he had imbibed too much the previous evening. 'Really—why not?'

'If I am not mistaken, your guests did not depart until the small hours, which means I expected you to be still abed. Now if you will excuse me, I have breakfast to prepare.'

'That is why I am here—I am starving.'

'Breakfast will be available in the servants' hall shortly, as per your instructions.'

He gave her that charmingly boyish smile, the one that caused her mind to go blank and her heart to flutter. 'I am hungry enough to eat a horse right now.'

He sounded like a wheedling lad instead of the arrogant nobleman she knew him to be. But she could hardly deny a meal to her employer.

'Very well. Would scrambled eggs suit you?'

'A bit of bacon with it wouldn't go amiss.'

She couldn't hold back a chuckle. 'Very well, bacon and coffee. Shall I bring it to the servants' hall or...?' There had to be a dining room, she just hadn't seen it.

'I don't want to put you to any trouble,' he said, almost meekly. 'I can eat here.' He sat down at the end of the kitchen table.

Meek? Hardly. This man would never be anything but demanding and commanding. And his presence in her kitchen unnerved her. 'I have a great deal to do this morning.' Oh, dear, that sounded a bit rude.

He seemed to take it in stride. 'Then you should not waste your time bringing me a tray.'

He was clearly determined to have his way. And she did have a great deal to do. Instead of arguing, she needed to give him his breakfast and send him on his way.

She gathered her supplies from the pantry and set out what she needed. She would have to wait to break her fast until he was gone.

As she worked, he sat silently watching. She tried hard

to ignore his presence, but failed. Her hand shook as she poured coffee into a mug for him and one for her.

She passed him the cream and sugar, which he refused. She added generous dollops of each to her own cup.

The fire was now hot enough for cooking and so, after a few sips of coffee, she fried the bacon, scrambled two eggs and cooked two slices of toast.

'That bacon smells delicious,' he said as she served him.

'It is excellent,' she replied. 'Not too lean, but meaty.'

She handed him a knife and fork and a napkin and began scrubbing down the stove.

'Where is your home?' he asked.

'My home?' The question took her aback. She turned to face him.

He picked up his coffee cup with one eyebrow raised. He wanted an answer.

'I grew up in a small village in Kent, Bexley.'

He nodded slowly. 'I see.'

'And you?' she asked feeling emboldened by his interest.

'Here, at this house. And in Marseilles.'

'France. I have never travelled outside England. How interesting it must have been.' She turned back to her work.

'Interesting is one word for it.'

'What word would you use?'

'Educational.'

There was a tinge of wryness in his tone, but she could not read much in his expression when she glanced back at his face. 'Travel broadens the mind, they say.'

He chuckled and there was a warmth in that soft sound this time. Her stomach gave a little hop.

Most unnerving.

'They do say so indeed,' he said and bit into his toast

with strong white teeth. Why did he have to look so gorgeous simply chewing on a bite of toast?

She forced herself to turn back to her work. Keeping her hands busy meant she would not be tempted to stand gazing at him like a besotted fool.

By the time she had cleaned the top of the stove, His Lordship was rising to his feet. To her surprise, he took his plate and cup to the sink, passing close behind her. She froze, but he did not touch her or even seem to notice.

'Thank you for accommodating me,' he said.

'You were quick,' she said, then wished she had bitten her tongue. It was not her place to comment on his speed and she could not help but feel pleased that he had enjoyed his meal. She put a pan of water on the hob to heat for washing up.

'I learned early to eat fast or risk going hungry,' he said, seemingly unperturbed.

'At school, I suppose,' she said. She'd heard that some of the schools the boys attended were quite beastly.

His chuckle had a bitter edge. 'I suppose you could call it a school.'

Puzzled she turned to face him, but he was already halfway out of the door and did not turn back to explain. What on earth could he mean by that cryptic comment?

Replete from the delicious breakfast, Damian made his way to his study. He needed to tally up last night's income. Setting up Rake Hall had cost him a pretty penny, but it was starting to pay for itself.

He sat down at his desk and pulled out the tin box containing money and vowels.

He paused for a moment, thinking about breakfast. He could not recall when he had enjoyed a meal more.

The eggs were light and fluffy and seasoned just right, the bacon curled at its crispy edges and she had presented him with some perfectly browned toast, butter and preserves to finish it off.

But more than that, he had enjoyed watching her work. The swift sure way she beat the eggs, the turning of the bacon and the toast at just the right moment.

She knew her business.

Which, when you thought about it, was exceedingly odd for the daughter of a vicar and the cousin of at least one earl and a couple of barons. Daughters of the nobility did not know how to cook as a rule.

His investigations had revealed that the vicar had not left his family well off when he died, which was strange in and of itself, but somehow, he had not expected her to support herself by her own industry. Her mother certainly had not, marrying at the first opportunity. It was odd that the daughter had not chosen the same path to comfort.

Fortunate, given his plan. And that was *not* a pang of regret.

He had buckled down to work and by midday had finished.

Time to check in with Pip. He stretched his arms over his head. Paperwork: it was the bane of his life. A necessary evil. He shrugged into his coat and strolled out to the stables.

He met Pip in the courtyard on his way into the house.

'Good morning.'

Pip grinned and shook his hand. '*Bonjour, mon ami.* Are we rich?'

'Not yet.' He grimaced. 'We still have some way to go before we have recovered our investment. But we will. A few more evenings like last night and you will never need to work again.'

'Good. You have no need to check on the stables, if that is where you were going. All is under control.'

'Then you have no need to check in on the kitchen.' Now why the hell had he added that?

Pip's eyes gleamed with amusement. '*Bien sur*. I will be heading back to Town once my bag is packed. Will you come with me?'

'No. I will return in a couple of days. There are a few things here that require my attention. I noticed another leak in the roof. It would not do to have the ceiling fall down on our patrons.'

The smile on his friend's face became more mischievous. 'Or on the new cook.'

Damian let the comment pass. He was used to Pip's teasing. Or at least he should be, but he still felt a surge of irritation at his friend's obvious interest in Mrs Lamb. 'Well, if there is nothing for me to do in the stables, I'll take my walk around the property and see what other repairs are needed.'

Pip nodded. 'Very well. I look forward to seeing you in London in a few days.'

Damian meandered across the lawn with no clear destination in mind and found himself approaching the orangery—a glass structure set facing south against the wall along one side of the formal gardens.

He frowned. Someone had left the door open.

He hadn't been in the building since he had returned from France. Nor could he recall whether, the last time he had passed by the building, the door had been open or closed.

Perhaps the door had been left ajar years ago when his family fled for the Continent.

The dark sky made it gloomy inside. That and the smell of rotting vegetation. Bare branches added to the sense of death.

To his astonishment, Mrs Lamb was poking around in one of the large containers at the far end. It contained a small tree sporting the only green leaves in the building. She was the last person he wanted to meet.

Or was she? He sauntered between the rows of clay pots, the carpet of dead leaves crunching underfoot, wondering how long it would be before she noticed his approach.

She glanced up as he drew near. 'Oh. It is you.' Displeasure filled her expression.

What had he done? 'Why are you in here?' He sounded a little more brusque than he intended.

'It is an orangery. I was looking for oranges.' She must have seen his disbelief because she continued, 'I thought to make some marmalade.' She shook her head. 'Unfortunately, most of the trees are dead. They have been left without water.'

Another act to lay at the feet of his enemies. Dead fruit trees. Not the worst of their crimes, to be sure.

She tipped her basket towards him and in the bottom sat three small oranges. 'I did find this one tree with fruit. There is water dripping down from somewhere. It kept the tree alive. Let me show you.'

She spoke as if she had found a treasure.

Bemused, and very slightly enchanted by her enthusiasm—only very slightly—he followed the direction of her pointing finger.

'I think the water must come in somewhere up there.'

The glass panes above their heads were filthy, but he

could indeed see streaks in the dirt cause by trickling water. Higher up the glass was cracked.

He grimaced. 'Something must have broken the pane. Perhaps a tree branch in a storm.'

She gave a little shiver. 'Indeed. Well, I suppose it is an ill wind. The other trees are truly dead, but this one can be saved, if you've a mind.'

About to say it wasn't worth the trouble, the hope in her voice gave him pause. 'Perhaps.'

She tipped her head. 'Don't you care that this poor tree has struggled onwards in the face of terrible neglect?'

'There are other things more important than an orange tree demanding my attention at the moment.'

Disappointment filled her expression. 'Your house parties.'

'Indeed.'

She made a face of distaste. 'As you wish.'

How was it possible she could make him feel guilty about a tree? And what right had she to judge him about his way of making a living? Damn her. If not for the actions of her father, it would never have been necessary.

'I shouldn't think those oranges are worth the time. Better to put them in the slop bucket.'

'Well, I don't know about you, but I like marmalade with my toast and, since it is my time, I—'

'Time I pay for is *my* time,' he said mildly, but still she shot him a glare.

'You do not pay for all of my time. There are hours that belong to me, My Lord.'

Should he point out that the sugar she would add to the fruits, the wood she would use for the stove and the pots and pans and jars were all his? He opened his mouth.

Off in the distance, thunder rumbled.

Mrs Lamb froze. 'A storm?'

Genuine fear. The desire to put a protective arm around her shoulders took him by surprise. He restrained the urge. 'Yes,' he said, coolly, unfeelingly.

She glanced upward with a shiver. 'Excuse me. I will return to the house.' She moved past him.

The clean smell of soap blended with, of all things, the scent of orange filled his nostrils. A surprisingly enticing combination. The desire to inhale more of it had him following her, the rustle of dead leaves marking their passing. Outside, she pulled her shawl over her head, picked up her skirts and ran for the house.

Only by strength of will did he refrain from following to ensure she arrived safely.

Devil take it.

Never mind the orange trees. Lives had been ruined and that required payment.

To Pamela's relief the storm that had threatened earlier in the day had passed by with only a few distant rumbles. She'd spent until mid-afternoon organising the kitchen cupboards and preparing dinner for her employer—since he had not left with Monsieur Phillippe—a roast of beef and a selection of vegetables along with a game pie and some soup. To be served in the servants' hall.

It really was not right that a titled gentleman should eat in such lowly quarters, even if he was the only person dining.

She removed her apron and, taking the ring of keys she had discovered in a drawer, set off to explore the house, to see if she could discover a more suitable dining room.

Clearly the ballroom and the dining room used for his guests were too large. His study was unsuitable since it lacked a proper table, so she wandered along corridors, peeping into each room she passed. The library she had visited yesterday was devoid of any furniture and the empty shelves were covered in dust.

Without much hope, she threw open the last door along the wing and peered into a dark room with chinks of light showing here and there through the shutters along one wall. She picked her way across and with a little effort opened one of the heavy wooden shutters to reveal a magnificent view of the park.

The room was not large, but it was exactly what she had been seeking. Pleasant surroundings and no dust. A drawing room. No doubt the table in the centre was intended to be used for playing games of chance rather than for eating, but with a table cloth, it would perfectly adequate for one or two diners.

She threw back the rest of the shutters. Given the state of most of the house she was surprised to find this room in such good order. The only drawback was its distance from the kitchen.

A problem she could solve, surely?

If she got everything ready beforehand and put all the hot items on one large tray, perhaps it would work.

And when Monsieur Phillippe was also in residence, he could do the fetching and carrying.

It was exceedingly strange that neither one of them had a valet and His Lordship did not keep at least one footman to take care of the house. Instead, they ferried servants back and forth from London at what must be a considerable expense. If the gambling was not illegal, as His Lordship claimed, then there must be something else nefarious going on.

She recalled the way Meg and the others had laughed

about the upstairs rooms being ready. Perhaps it was there she would find her answers.

She picked up the keys from the table where she had put them while she opened the shutters and made her way to the narrow staircase at the end of the hall.

She hesitated. It really was none of her business.

She glanced down the staircase. Was it possible there was a shorter route to the kitchen beneath the courtyard? If so, it would make using the room a great deal more convenient. Would it not make more sense if she explored in that direction instead?

His Lordship might say everything was above board, but, from what she had learned over the past several years, many men said anything to get their own way.

Like her stepfather trying to push her into a marriage with his friend, a man old enough to be her father. She quelled a shudder.

Before she could change her mind, she ran upwards. A quick glance was all she would need to satisfy her curiosity and hopefully put her mind to rest.

The first door she came to did not open when she turned the handle. Locked.

She tried first one key, then another. None of them fit. Bother.

'Can I be of assistance?' a deep voice enquired.

His Lordship. Her heart sank. She turned to face him. To her surprise and relief, his expression was one of interest, not anger.

'I…er… I was seeking a place where you might dine, other than the servants' hall.'

A dark brow winged upwards. 'Among the bedrooms?'

Dash it. 'No. I found the perfect room downstairs and

then came up here, curious about something one of the maids said.'

He drew closer. 'What sort of something?'

She tried to ignore his proximity, the way he loomed over her, the way he made her feel overwhelmed and breathless.

It was hard to ignore when her heart galloped so hard.

She took a deep steadying breath. 'It wasn't so much what she said, as the way she giggled when she was asked if the bedrooms were ready. It struck me as odd since you said your guests were not staying the night.'

A rather mischievous smile curved his lips. 'I can see how that would pique your interest, Mrs Lamb. Why she would giggle, I cannot guess, but these rooms are used by my guests when they require a little privacy. They are generally called retiring rooms, *n'est ce-pas*?'

Oh. Retiring rooms, where a lady must go to use the necessary. And possibly a gentleman, too. It was so obvious, why hadn't she thought of it? Was she so determined to see problems at every turn in regard to this man? 'I see. Thank you. Well, if you will excuse me—'

He reached out a hand. 'Where did you get the keys?'

Swallowing, she glanced down at the ring of keys clutched in her hand. 'I found them in a drawer in the kitchen.'

'May I see?' His tone brooked no argument and, indeed, why would she argue? This was his house after all.

She held them out.

His wary expression cleared. 'Those are for the cellars. Now, you said you had discovered a suitable dining room. Would you care to show it to me?'

As if she had any option.

He shepherded her towards the staircase. Not that she

had any objections to showing him. She was pleased with her find.

'This way,' she said.

He followed her downstairs and along the ground floor corridor. She opened the door to the small chamber. 'What do you think?'

His silence caused her to look up. The genial expression had been replaced with…sadness?

How ironic that this woman had declared this room as perfect. This had been his mother's favourite place to spend her days with her needlework or taking tea with her friends. It was the room whose loss his mother had bemoaned constantly in their draughty two-room apartment in Marseilles.

When he first returned to the house, Damian had suffered an urge to restore this chamber to its former glory. His memories of the house and park were vague, but this room remained etched in his mind by way of her description. He'd done his best to recreate it and had been pleased with the result.

Even so, whenever he entered this room, he felt the pain of loss. That his mother had not lived long enough to return here, to redo it herself, saddened him.

He should have left it well alone. It had been pointless and he couldn't step foot in it without remembering her, and now this woman wanted him to eat in here. Damien tamped down his emotions. Or at least he attempted to sound calm.

'It is not a dining room.'

'No, but…' she opened one of the shutters '…the view of the park is quite lovely and the table, while small, would work for two people. I would cover it with a heavy cloth so the wood is not damaged—'

'I will dine in the servants' hall as previously arranged.'

She spun around, obviously surprised and obviously planning to attempt to make her case.

His frown must have stopped her words, because she closed her mouth and folded her hands at her waist. 'Very well.'

What the devil did she have to be disappointed about? 'What does it matter where I eat as long as I do eat? You cannot tell me this is more convenient, for I am not a fool.'

'No. No, indeed,' she said hastily, edging towards the door. 'If you wish to eat in the servants' hall, it is of no matter to me.'

Damn it all. This was not what he intended to happen. He was supposed to be charming her, not acting like a bear with a sore head.

He strode to the window and looked out. In his mind's eye he saw himself as a small boy running across the expanse of lawn trailing a kite, or sitting astride his first pony being led by a groom. But he no longer knew if these idyllic mental pictures were memories or merely stories told by his mother.

His clearest boyhood memories were of the stink of Marseilles's streets lined with tenements and running with filth. Of stealing pocket handkerchiefs to buy food. More recently they were of making money gambling in taverns until he had enough saved to buy an establishment of his own.

He heard a sound behind him. She was leaving.

'Wait.'

He turned back to face her. She straightened her shoulders as if bracing against more of his ill humour. 'I will eat in here.'

Surprise crossed her face. 'If you are sure?'

'Why not? As you say, the surroundings are far more

pleasant than downstairs. I will even show you a shortcut to the kitchens, if you wish.'

'That would be most helpful, thank you.'

'I am pleased to be of use.' He could not keep the wry note out of his voice.

She stifled a chuckle. He grinned at her. 'Come on. It's this way.'

He guided her down the stairs. After lighting one of the lamps set on a chest at the bottom, he led her along the gloomy tunnel he had discovered when exploring the wine cellars.

She shivered.

'Not afraid, are you?' he said recalling her previous re-action to thunder.

'Not at all. Just a little chilly.'

Yes, it was a great deal cooler down here and damp, too. He resisted a sudden urge to give her his coat and picked up his pace instead. 'It won't take long.'

'This goes under the courtyard?' Her voice echoed off the brick-lined walls.

'It does.' As they neared the end, he pointed to the doors on either side. 'These are the wine cellars. They used to be full of wine sent down by my father and his father before him. All gone now, apart from what I have purchased my-self. Everything from before was sold off to cover my fa-ther's debts.'

'Oh, dear,' she said. 'Was he also a gambler?'

He gritted his teeth at the implied criticism. His father had never gambled a penny in his life until her father had tempted him down the road to hell. 'He certainly had a run of bad luck. But he wasn't what you would call a dyed-in-the-wool gambler, no.'

'I am sorry. It is none of my business.'

It *was* her business. But she did not need to know that yet. He pushed open the door at the end. 'And here we are back at the kitchens.'

She looked up at him with a smile. 'That is indeed a much faster way. I can deliver your food much more easily. Thank you.'

He smiled back. 'My pleasure. Now if you will excuse me, I have some business that requires my attention elsewhere.'

'Of course.' She dipped a little curtsy.

A mad idea bounced into his head. He hesitated. When had he become so tentative? He always followed his instincts. They never let him down. 'Since there is no one in residence at the moment, apart from you and me, you may as well join me for dinner.'

Her mouth dropped open. 'I could not. It would not be right.'

The more he thought about it, the more he liked the idea. 'Where is the sense in us each dining in a solitary state, using up candles in two rooms instead of one, when it would be far more economical to dine together?'

'It isn't appropriate.'

He sensed her weakening. 'Who is to know? I won't tell if you won't. Either dine with me in the drawing room or provide my dinner in the servants' hall and dine with me there. I am not asking.'

She huffed out a sigh. 'Very well. I will dine with you in the drawing room, if you insist.'

'I do.'

Before she could change her mind, he walked away. For

several moments, he felt her watching him, as if trying to understand the reason behind his invitation.

The wariness in her face after he had made his suggestion warned him he would have to tread very carefully if he was not going to scare her off.

Having dinner with her employer was the stupidest thing she had ever done.

She should have left the issue of where he dined well alone and she would not be in this mess. But, no. She had to interfere.

She had already got a fire going in the drawing room, lit the candles and set the table. Now all that was required was the food.

She eyed the trays she had prepared to deliver to the dining room. Three trays, each platter with its own cover. By the time she had delivered all three, no doubt the dishes on the first one would be barely lukewarm.

Oh, yes, a very stupid idea.

And then there was what she was wearing. She had been torn between her usual serviceable grey gown and the gown she wore to church. A rare occurrence since she had been in service. The pale blue muslin had won out, but now she was regretting her choice. Too late to change. She slipped a shawl around her shoulders to keep out the chill in the tunnel and picked up the heaviest of the three trays.

'Here, let me help you.'

She almost dropped the tray in shock.

He grabbed it.

'I can manage,' she said, hanging on to it a second longer than she should have.

'I am sure you can.' He smiled at her. 'But it occurred

to me that you might need to make more than one trip, unless you had some assistance.'

He looked lovely in his evening clothes. Suddenly she was very glad she had chosen her best dress. She could not help smiling back.

'Thank you.'

He picked up the second tray, easily holding each tray in one hand, whereas she had struggled with the weight using both of hers. 'Can you manage the last one?' he asked.

'Of course.'

'Good, then we can make it in one trip, if you would be so good as to get the door.'

And so, with her opening doors for him, they made their way to the little drawing room.

'If you would put your trays on the sideboard, there by the window,' she said as they entered the room, 'I think we can serve ourselves.'

He glanced around. 'This all looks very cosy.' He set the trays where she directed. 'What delights do you have in store for me?'

She swallowed. Tonight he was clearly trying to be pleasant. Trying? He was devastatingly charming.

In the hopes of impressing him with her skill, she had thought most carefully about the menu. After all, feeding him was a great deal different than feeding his servants.

'Would you care to pour yourself a libation,' she said, 'while I make things ready?'

She had set decanters of brandy, sherry and madeira on a small circular table beside one of the armchairs beside the hearth, where a fire burned merrily.

He walked over to inspect the offering. 'Sherry for you?' he asked.

Startled, she almost dropped the platter of vegetables.

'Oh, no. Nothing for me, thank you. I will have water with dinner.'

Carefully, she organised the dishes on the sideboard and turned with a smile. He was watching her, while sipping on what must be sherry judging from the glass he was holding.

'I hope the sherry is to your liking,' she said. 'I found it in the cellar you pointed out earlier.'

'It is a very good sherry,' he said, smiling at her. 'I selected it myself.'

She felt her cheeks heat. She resisted the temptation to press her palms against them, to cool them.

'Yes, of course. I beg your pardon.'

'No need to apologise,' he said cheerfully.

She finished laying out the dishes. 'We can eat whenever you are ready.' She gestured to the plates.

He set his glass down beside the decanters and strolled over to inspect her offerings. 'I say, this looks marvellous.'

He seemed to be in the mood to be pleased. She began to relax.

'If you would carve the beef and the chicken, and then help yourself to the other dishes, I think that would work very well. There is white wine in the cooler, or red wine, if you prefer.'

'Wonderful,' he said. He carved thin slices of the meat and put them on a plate, which, to her shock, he handed to her.

'Oh, but—'

He chuckled. 'Fill your plate with vegetables, Mrs Lamb, it would be a shame for everything to get cold while you dither.'

She repressed a smile and did as instructed. It was no good standing here arguing about protocol.

She took her plate to her place at the table and, to her

surprise, he was there, pulling back her chair, helping her to sit. She could not remember the last time she had been treated like a lady.

Her heart picked up speed. She sat and smiled up at him. 'Thank you.'

She waited for him to fill his plate and sit down.

He poured water for them both and then chose the white wine from the cooler and, without asking, poured them each a glass. 'You have gone to a great deal of trouble, Mrs Lamb. Thank you.' He raised his glass in a toast. 'To the chef.'

Once more her cheeks felt hot. She picked up her glass of wine and tilted her head in acknowledgement of his toast. They both sipped.

The wine was delicious. Crisp and cold and slightly fruity.

'Bon appetit,' he said and began to eat.

Her heart felt so full, she wasn't sure she could eat a bite. But she had to, or he would wonder if there was a problem.

She cut into the chicken and was pleased to find it juicy and tender. The scalloped potatoes were cooked just right and the vegetables were perfect. She gestured to the small gravy boat. 'Would you pass the gravy?'

'I most certainly will. Can you pass the mustard, please?'

For a moment or two there was silence as they both took the edge off their hunger.

Abruptly, he put down his knife and fork. 'Good Lord.'

She froze. Was something wrong?

'This is far beyond anything I expected.'

'I beg your pardon.'

'This food. It is delicious.'

He sounded so disbelieving, a surge of anger rose up

from somewhere deep inside. 'Why would you be surprised?'

'Because you are—' He stopped and shook his head.

'Because I am what? A woman? You did not think a woman would be able to cook as well as your fancy French chef?'

A guilty expression flashed across his face. He gave her a shamefaced smile. 'I apologise. I must say, this meal is as good as, if not better than, anything Chandon has prepared over the past year. In my experience, all the best chefs are men. And usually French.'

She had the feeling he wasn't speaking the entire truth. His reaction had been too extreme to match his reason.

But she was pleased by his compliment. She could hardly argue with his praise, even if something about it did not feel…honest. On the other hand, she was quite prepared to take issue with his premise. 'I learned how to cook from a woman, actually. We females are not as incompetent as some men seem to believe.' She hadn't meant to sound quite so stiff or so censorious. 'I am pleased you are enjoying the fruits of my labour.' That was hardly better.

He picked up his knife and fork. 'I am indeed.'

Damian covertly eyed his dinner companion. He had stupidly ruffled her feathers, when he had intended to enchant her.

What was it about this woman that caused him to lose his grip on his famous ability to charm birds out of trees? There wasn't a woman in London who wasn't susceptible, so the story went.

Pip would laugh his head off, if he knew how he had fumbled this one so badly.

'You are right, my dear Mrs Lamb. Women are often underestimated.'

'By men.'

He looked up and saw she was staring at him narrowed eyed, daring him to contradict her. Challenging.

He liked a challenge.

He finished his mouthful. 'Are you saying that women do not encourage us males to think of them as weaker, less able, more in need of protection? Indeed, do not ladies like to think of themselves as the weaker sex, both physically and mentally?'

Her spine straightened. 'Are you blaming women for their subjugation?'

'It was a question.'

'It was men who made the laws that define a wife as an extension of her husband, rather than a person in her own right. It was men who decided that an older daughter would be pushed aside by a younger brother.'

These were truths for which he had no answer. He had not thought about them terribly much, either. 'Do you have a brother?' He knew very well she did not, but she would not know that.

'No. I am an only child.'

'So you were not pushed aside?'

'No. But I knew girls who were. What I could not understand was their meek acceptance of the situation. Or their willingness to marry whomever their father picked out, even if they loved another.'

He really had not expected her to be quite so militant. 'This is a friend you are speaking of.'

'Yes. A friend who gave up any chance for happiness, though she would never admit it.'

'Because she did not stand up for herself, in your opinion.'

She gave him a suspicious glance, as if to see if his intention was to mock her opinions. Seemingly satisfied, she nodded. 'She could have said no. Under the law, one cannot be forced into marriage.'

'I think you are the sort of woman whom no one could force into anything. I admire your courage.'

A pained expression crossed her face. 'Sadly, I do not believe I am at all courageous.' She began eating again, as if to forestall herself from saying any more. He decided that it was best to change the subject.

'And where did you learn to cook so masterfully?'

'At home.'

'Without wishing to pry, I would say that you were brought up to be a lady, rather than a cook.'

She frowned, looking worried. 'Why would you think so?'

'You are well educated, well spoken and well versed in the finest of table manners, for a start. And I noticed that among the items in your room is an embroidery hoop already decorated with the finest of stitches. Your family was never among the poor.'

She pressed her lips together, clearly deciding how much to admit. 'You are observant, sir. It is true. My father was a gentleman. I learned to cook because I discovered a love for creating good food at a young age and I was indulged enough to be able to follow my passion. Now it is no longer a hobby, but the way I earn my bread, I am fortunate that passion and necessity collided.'

He raised his glass and smiled at her. 'No, my dear Mrs Lamb, I believe it is I who am fortunate.'

Her eyes widened. A smile curved her lips. In that moment pleasure and beauty shone in her face. 'Thank you, My Lord.' She picked up her glass and drank.

He leaned back in his chair, replete with fine food and fine wine and finally able to relax. He had made her smile.

She cleared the dishes from the table and set them on the buffet.

'Let me help you with that,' he said. 'Would you like me to help you carry them to the kitchen?'

'No need. I will collect everything in the morning.' She offered him a shy glance. 'I have one last treat in store, if you would care for dessert.'

Dessert? It was she who looked like a sweet treat in her gown the colour of forget-me-nots. Good enough to eat. 'You are spoiling me.'

She rose and went to the buffet table. She bent to open its doors, presenting him with a view of her derrière, a beautifully rounded firm little bottom that he could imagine naked— He cut the thought off. What the devil was wrong with him?

She opened a door to reveal another, smaller cooler.

'May I assist you with that?' He was pleased that he sounded calm. Unaffected.

She glanced over her shoulder with a provocative smile. His heart skipped a beat.

'I can manage, My Lord.' She removed two small dishes, bumped the door closed with a seductive swing of her hip, leaving him dry mouthed, and brought the dishes to the table.

He forced himself to look at what she had placed before him and not the curves of her body that had just sent his body into a frenzy of lust the like of which he had not suffered since he was a youth.

'Ice cream!' he said, unable to resist grinning like a schoolboy.

'Lemon ice, actually,' she said as she sat down, 'with a touch of orange.'

'Made from the oranges in the greenhouse?'

She beamed. 'Yes. How did you guess?'

He thought about it for a moment. He recalled their conversation, about her desire to save that tree. 'You want to prove to me that the tree is worth saving.'

'Oh, dear, am I so easily read? Please, try it. Tell me what you think?'

'About the tree?' he teased gently.

Her light laugh made his body hum. 'No. About the dessert.'

While she watched him closely, he dipped his spoon into the oval yellow ice with a swirl of orange running through it. The taste was heavenly. Tart with a touch of sweetness and he could definitely distinguish both flavours. 'It is delicious. Ambrosia.'

She nodded, clearly satisfied with his reaction. And he felt supremely glad that she was happy.

He smiled wryly at himself. This was what he had wanted, wasn't it? To gain her trust. To seduce her the way her father had tempted his down a ruinous path.

He finished the dessert. 'Thank you. That was indeed a treat.'

She took those dishes from the table and stacked them neatly.

She glanced over at the table with the decanters and glasses. 'I expect you would like to partake of your port now.'

Was she trying to escape him? He wasn't ready to let her go just yet.

'Won't you join me?'

She looked shocked.

Damn. 'If you do not wish to partake of port, then I would be happy to join you in a cup of tea.'

Confusion filled her expression. 'I did not think of bringing a tea tray, My Lord. I presumed that once dinner was over...'

'I have an idea. Why don't we carry the dishes back to the kitchen and have tea there?'

She looked doubtful. 'Are you sure?'

'It is the perfect solution. That way I can help you with the dishes and we can have a perfect ending to a delicious meal.' He got up and started putting the leftovers on a tray. Somewhat unwillingly she filled the other tray.

'Ready?' he asked.

Chapter Four

With the dishes all stacked neatly in the scullery out of sight, Pamela concentrated on making tea for His Lordship, who had disposed himself on the settle beside the large hearth where she baked her bread.

She poured the boiling water into the teapot and waited the requisite number of minutes.

His Lordship, gazing into the fire, clearly deep in his own thoughts, looked a little sad. Or was that just her imagination?

Why on earth had he wanted to take tea in the kitchen? It felt strange. Almost scandalous.

Of course it was scandalous. Single women didn't entertain single men like this. *Be honest.* Dinner had been scandalous.

But then she wasn't a 'single' woman, was she? While she might never have been married, she used a married woman's title and she wasn't exactly an innocent. If she had been, she might have seriously considered her mother's suggestion that she marry.

But she'd foolishly let her heart rule her head, let passion overcome good sense and given herself to the man she had expected to marry, Consequently, there was no point thinking about making any kind of marriage, let alone a good one. And besides she was perfectly happy as a cook.

On the other hand, she was nobody's fool and she was beginning to wonder if His Lordship had some sort of ulterior motive for insisting she eat dinner with him, then inviting himself to tea in her kitchen. Unless he was as lonely as he looked at this moment.

How could a man in his position be lonely?

She poured the tea and took it over. He glanced up with a faint smile. 'Thank you.'

He patted the seat beside him. 'Please, make yourself comfortable.'

Sit beside him? 'I—'

'I do not bite, Mrs Lamb.'

She winced. Now he sounded offended. 'Very well.' She fetched her cup and sat down making very sure to leave a few inches of space between them. The settle was certainly a good deal more comfortable than the bench at the table.

He stretched out his legs. 'This reminds me of my youth. We always sat around the hearth and had tea on cold days.'

'Did you toast bread over the fire?' she asked. 'I love hot bread toasted on one side with the butter melting into it on the other.'

He grinned boyishly. 'Me, too. Nothing tastes like bread you have toasted yourself.'

'I was never allowed to hold the toasting fork. Father said it was too dangerous.'

'Oh, I was official toaster in our home. Mother said I made a better job of it than Father. I had more patience. He always held the bread too close to the flames, trying to hurry it along.'

She grimaced. 'Burned edges.'

'Exactly.'

They both laughed and sipped their tea in a comfortable silence.

'Thank you again for a wonderful meal,' he said. 'And for granting me your company. I don't know when I have enjoyed an evening more.'

She looked at him askance. 'More than your parties with all your guests? I find that hard to believe.'

A thoughtful expression crossed his face. 'You are right.'

A little pang of disappointment took her aback.

'I do enjoy my guests,' he said. 'I suppose what I am trying to say is that I enjoyed this evening in an equal but different way.'

Indeed, it must be very different. His party had been a hubbub of laughter and excitement. Even she could see that from her brief glance through the door. But it was kind of him to say he had enjoyed this evening. 'I have had a very pleasant time also, though I really do not think it is something we should repeat, since it is not really appropriate.' There, she had said it. Much as she hadn't wanted to, it was the right thing to do. She didn't want him getting any false notions, thinking she was fast, or available, or something. Just thinking about it made her feel hot.

'There won't be much opportunity,' he said with a chill in his voice. 'I will be heading off to London in the morning.'

Had she made him angry? If so, it was for the best.

'To make arrangements for your next party, I suppose,' she said. 'To pluck more chickens.'

He glared at her. 'Indeed.' He got to his feet. 'I will bid you goodnight, Mrs Lamb.' He bowed, put his cup on the table and left.

She sighed. Why could she not keep her thoughts to herself? They had enjoyed a perfectly respectable dinner and then she had ruined it. No doubt he was regretting giving her a job and would be looking for a replacement.

No. It had been the right thing to say. To remind herself of his true colours. To stop herself from falling for his charm.

Because falling for his charm would be a very easy, and a very stupid, thing to do.

She took the tea cups through to the pantry. Should she do the dishes before bed or leave them until morning?

If His Lordship was off to London after breakfast, she would be here all alone. And she would need to be up early in the morning to ensure he had breakfast before he departed. Besides, it would give her something to do tomorrow.

The dishes could wait.

She picked turning down the lamps, picked up her candlestick and headed for bed.

His Lordship had indeed headed out for London early in the morning. Pamela surveyed the breakfast she had prepared. No plates or utensils had been used. He had seemingly taken a couple of bread rolls and departed.

She went to the buffet and helped herself to scrambled eggs and bacon. She might as well enjoy the fruits of her labour, even if he had not.

She should not have bothered with the eggs. He had told her he wanted very little prepared in the mornings.

A rap on the kitchen door startled her.

Who could that be?

She went to the door to find one of the shopkeepers from the village. 'Good morning, missus,' he said doffing his cap. 'Dobbs at your service. Dobbs Greengrocers.'

She eyed the box clutched in his arms. 'I didn't order anything.'

'Came by way of His Lordship,' the man said.

'You better come in.'

He put the box on the table. 'Will there be anything else you will be needing?' he asked, glancing around.

She thanked heavens she had got the kitchen cleaned up from last night's dinner. Village gossip was notoriously cruel. Any sign that the new cook wasn't up to scratch would be reported immediately.

'Not at the moment, thank you.'

'You only has to send word, missus, and I'll do my best to accommodate. His Lordship said as how you wanted to make preserves. Took a few days to get them oranges, but I found them, so I did.'

'Oranges!' Her heart gave a little jump.

She could scarcely believe he had been so thoughtful.

It was three weeks since Pamela had arrived at Rake Hall, or Rakehell's Hall as she learn that the locals called it. The arrival and departure of the London servants, the master of the house, and his guests twice a week had become routine.

She had become acquainted with the members of the London household and they now treated her as one of their own.

She had not dined with His Lordship again, though she had served him and Monsieur Phillippe dinner in the drawing room twice since that first evening.

She glanced at the kitchen clock as it struck four. At any moment, she would hear carriages on the drive and the house would be full again. Today she had made a suet pudding with beef and kidneys and all kinds of vegetables as well as fresh bread and a treacle tart for dessert.

Albert loved her sweet desserts, as did most of the others, and Dart spared no expense to keep his household happy. Lord Dart was unusually solicitous about the welfare of his servants, she had noticed. And they were all devoted to him. Never a complaint or a cross word had she heard from any of them. Was that his way of ensuring they kept his secrets?

The sound of horses and wheels on gravel wafted through the window. She checked her cap and apron. All neat and tidy. Not that His Lordship ever noticed her appearance, since he entered the house by the front door. She made her way outside into the stable courtyard to greet the arrivals.

'My dear Mrs Lamb,' Albert said. He was always the first to step down. 'You are looking well.' He, on the other hand, was looking anxious.

'Is something wrong?'

'Betsy took off this morning. She said her ma was sick and she had to go tend to her. Then Giles twisted his ankle and had to be left behind. So I'm short-handed. We can manage without one, but two will be difficult. I'll have to leave one of the tables empty. It would have to be Betsy. She's always very popular with the punters.'

The other servants were climbing out of the carriages and heading into the house.

'Now what?' Albert said, glancing behind him. 'Lord have mercy. Meg, what the devil is wrong with you?'

Meg was bent double, her hand pressed to her stomach with one of the other girls hanging over her.

'It's her monthlies,' the other girl said. 'Always takes her bad.'

'Shut your mouth, Sukey,' Meg said. 'I'll be fine. I just got rattled about in that there box on wheels.'

Albert looked grim. 'Hurry along then. Lots to do before dinner. Sukey, you will have to take on Betsy's work.'

The girl, Sukey, looked back over her shoulder from where she was bent over Meg. 'And this 'un's, too, I should 'spect.' She didn't sound happy. 'I'll do me best, Albert, but you should've brought another girl.'

''Ow could I get another girl, when I didn't know I was going to be missing one? I ain't a bloody mind-reader.'

'Can't I help?' Pamela said, feeling sorry for him and for Sukey. Over the past few weeks she had learned that His Lordship was a stickler for everything being just so for his guests and the staff never wanted to let him down. They really cared about his good opinion.

Albert blinked. 'You've got your own work to take care of, Mrs Lamb.'

'My work is all done. Everything is prepared. I can do nothing more until after you have eaten and, even then, the cleaning up can easily be left until tomorrow.'

Sukey left Meg, who, arms wrapped around her waist, plodded her way up the steps into the house, and came back to Albert. 'I can manage the extra rooms, Albert, truly I can, but why not let her help at the tables tonight. The punters will like a new face to flirt wiv, you know they will. You know how His Lordship hates an empty table.'

This last apparently clinched the matter for Albert. 'All right, but you will have to help Mrs Lamb dress. Hopefully you can find a good costume.'

The parties at Rake Hall were always masquerades.

'Ooh, perfect,' Sukey said. 'You and me will have a quick bite, Mrs Lamb, then I'll take you up to the dressing room.' Sukey put her arm through Pamela's and they walked inside. 'I am sure we have something to fit.'

'Teach her how to deal the cards, too, Sukey.' Albert called after them.

Pamela felt a smidgeon of doubt, a slight sinking feeling in her stomach. She had never attended a masquerade. Father hadn't thought them at all proper for a young lady.

But then, she wasn't a young lady any more. Nor was she 'attending'. She would be safely behind a card table.

Damian glanced around the ballroom. Everything was as it should be. Guests floating around in masks and outlandish costumes, this week's theme was set in Versailles under Louis XIV, the Sun King. The tables buzzed with the rattle of dice boxes, the chink of tokens and coins, and the cries of winners and losers. Masquerades were always popular among the *ton*. For some reason they liked dressing up. As usual, he wore a mask as a nod to the event, but kept to his usual black evening coat. It made it easier for his guests to find him, should they have need.

One of the tables seemed particularly crowded. A cheer went up and he strolled over to see what was holding his guests' interest.

The woman dealing cards wore an elaborate grey powdered wig, a gold mask that covered her face from her forehead to her lower cheeks and a gown of gold tissue that skimmed the rise of her breasts. She shimmered under the light of the chandelier above her head.

Her hands handled the cards with a graceful elegance and skill he had never seen among any of his ladies. Her smile, a mysterious curve of full lips, emphasised by the small black spot at their corner, seemed to hold the gentlemen at the table completely enthralled as she encouraged them to risk their chips.

Vingt-et-un was always one of the most profitable games and, judging by the chips at her elbow and the growing pile of vowels, tonight would be even better than usual.

As she glanced up and the lovely grey eyes regarded him briefly, the breath left his chest in a rush. What the devil was Mrs Lamb doing dealing cards?

He felt a strong urge to haul her out of the room by her arm and demand an explanation. He clenched his hands at his sides. To do anything so rash would invite unwanted comment.

Her eyes widened as if she sensed his anger, then she smiled at him and her eyes twinkled with mischief. Devil take the woman, she was enjoying herself.

And why would he feel anger when she had played right into his hands? What did it matter that every red-blooded male in the room was ogling her with lascivious interest, when he had now started her down the path to ignominy?

It could not have worked better than if he had planned it.

He smiled back, bowed slightly and moved on. Phillippe, dressed as the Sun King himself, sidled up to him. 'Your cook is making *l'impression grande*,' he said softly.

'You knew she was here and didn't think to say anything?' He tamped down his temper once again. What the hell was the matter with him?

Phillippe shrugged. 'The staff is in your care. I assumed it was by your orders.'

Of course he should have known. Albert was the one who should have informed him. Well, he knew now and there was no more to be said about it. It would be many more hours before tonight was over, and a plan began to form for how he might use the time to his advantage.

As the evening wore on, Damian noticed that although the crowd around Mrs Lamb's table ebbed and flowed somewhat, it was always the busiest. It was the younger crowd who seemed to be drawn into her orbit. For the most part these young men were harmless, though not above sowing their wild oats in any available pasture.

He drew closer. He was surprised at how comfortable

Mrs Lamb looked in her new role as she deftly dealt a hand to those sitting at the table. A king of hearts landed face up in front of her.

The men around her groaned at the sight of the royal card.

'Your bets, please, gentlemen,' she said calmly.

'How about a kiss for luck?' the lad on her right said.

Damian frowned, ready to step in if this sort of loose talk made her uncomfortable.

Mrs Lamb laughed lightly. 'How about you make your wager, or give up your place to a gentleman who will, Lord James? You know full well I do not play favourites.' Her tone was friendly, but firm.

Lord James grinned good-naturedly. 'It was worth a try.' He pushed forward a pile of chips representing a guinea.

Clearly Mrs Lamb was not in need of assistance.

She glanced around the table, ensuring all bets were placed, then dealt the next card with a graceful turn of her wrist. She paused for a moment with a little dramatic flair that made Damian want to chuckle, then put her own card down with a tiny snap in the silence of bated breath. 'Bank pays twenty-one.'

Which meant the bank paid no one. She gathered up the chips.

'You have the most devilish luck, Mrs Lamb,' one of the fellows said.

Mrs Lamb's steady grey gaze rested on his face. 'Would you like me to call for a fresh deck?' she asked sweetly.

'Hey!' Lord James said. 'No need for that, Smythe. Mrs Lamb runs a straight-up game. Besides, that was a fresh pack.'

Smythe looked embarrassed. 'Didn't mean anything. Just saying Mrs Lamb's luck is in and mine is out.'

'Idiot,' someone in the crowd said and there was general laughter, including from Smythe.

All was well here. Better than well. It seemed Mrs Lamb had a real talent for keeping the young puppies in order. He moved on to check on the other tables.

After a while, he signalled to Albert that it was time to start the dancing. The croupiers needed a break. He needed to collect up some of the winnings and the ladies who were guests would not be happy if gambling was the only thing on offer.

He'd learned early that if he wanted to keep the men spending their money, he had to keep their lady friends suitably entertained.

Albert moved from table to table, helping each croupier wrap up her game and clear the winnings from each station. It was always a risky time, though unlike the hells where he had learned his craft, there were no ruffians ready to spot the slightest weakness and steal the proceeds.

Each of his guests was selected by him personally. They would deem it dishonourable to steal anything, or at least dishonourable to be caught stealing anything. He smiled grimly.

When Albert reached Mrs Lamb's table, some of the men complained good-naturedly about ruining their luck. Albert jollied them along and they drifted away. Mrs Lamb stood up and stretched her back, chatting with Sukey who had clearly taken her under her wing.

The footmen began moving the tables to the edges of the room, clearing a space in the centre as the two women left arm in arm for the room set aside for the staff to rest.

Leaving Pip in charge, Damian accompanied Albert back to the safe in his study. He put all the notes and coins in the safe, apart from a number of coins to act as a float when the gambling started again later, and locked the door.

'Mrs Lamb seemed to be doing very well,' he remarked mildly. 'I was surprised to see her working tonight.'

It must not have been said as mildly as he intended because Albert started and turned red. 'We were short two girls, My Lord. I hope that was all right.'

It was better than all right. Wasn't it?

'Of course. She seems very popular with the gentlemen. How is it that we were missing two girls?'

'As you know, Your Lordship, since you yourself gave her permission, Betsy went to visit her old mum. Then Meg went and took a bad turn on the way down here. I had to do something.'

He could have removed one of the tables. But that would have been less than satisfactory to his guests. Not to mention considerably reduce his profits since only a finite number of gamblers could sit at each table at one time.

'Besides,' Albert continued, 'she must have seen it was a problem because she offered.'

Now that was interesting.

He nodded. 'She seemed to take to it very well.'

'Like a duck to water,' Albert said. 'She said she had played cards with her pa. Seems to know all the rules. I watched her for a while just to be sure.'

'Very good. But please inform me of any changes to the staff in future, would you, Albert?'

'Of course, My Lord.'

The sounds of the orchestra in full swing wafted along the corridor as they made their way back. As usual, he stopped to speak to the staff where they were resting. The room had once been known as the music room, but he had filled it with comfortable sofas and chairs and there was lemonade to drink if they wished.

'Good job, everyone,' he said, giving them a broad grin. 'The night is going very well indeed. I look for the second half to be as good as the first.'

There were nods and smiles all around. They received a bonus based on the night's takings, so they were always cheered to hear things were going well.

He wandered the room, speaking to this one and that as he went until he arrived beside Mrs Lamb, seated with Sukey on a sofa. Sukey got up to let him sit down.

Mrs Lamb had removed her mask, but she still looked remarkably stunning in her old-fashioned costume. 'Thank you for coming to our aid,' he said.

'Oh, it was no trouble. I am enjoying myself.'

'Are you now?'

'I am. I must say I was glad of the mask. Although, I think…'

She hesitated.

He gave her an encouraging smile. 'You think?'

'Well…it is possible that I recognised a couple of people among the guests. I would not want them to recognise me.'

'People you have met at the houses of your other employers?' he asked, knowing full well that was not what she meant.

Her full lips tightened slightly. 'Not exactly. People I knew before I became a cook.'

For someone living a lie, she wasn't very good at concealing things.

'Do you think they will recognise you?'

She sighed and shook her head. 'If they haven't recognised me by now, I doubt they will. It was a long time since I met them.'

He rose and clapped his hands. 'Ladies.'

All heads turned in his direction.

'There are quite a number of unaccompanied gentlemen here this evening if you have a mind to dance.'

There were smiles of enthusiasm. Dancing with the guests would mean generous tips for the girls themselves. 'Please remember, dancing only. No one is to go upstairs, that area is strictly for our guests.'

If his lady croupiers started going upstairs with gentlemen guests to earn money, then his perfectly respectable card parties would become something else. A bawdy house. Something that would leave him open to criminal prosecution.

He glanced down at Mrs Lamb. 'You need not dance if you do not wish to.'

'Oh, come on, Pammy,' Sukey said. 'Half the men in that room was eying you up…they will be tripping over themselves to get a dance.'

Pammy looked a shade doubtful, then smiled. 'Why not? In for a penny, in for a pound.'

Much as he imagined his father had said when her father had seduced him into gambling away his fortune.

'That's the way,' Sukey said. And off the ladies went.

Damian followed them with every intention of keeping an eye on Mrs Lamb. He did not want her scared off by some lustful lout or, worse yet, inadvertently revealing her true identity. At least not yet.

He wanted everything to go along at his pace.

Chapter Five

When Pamela returned to the ballroom, she discovered that indeed several gentlemen were desirous of leading her on to the dance floor. Monsieur Phillippe seemed to have taken charge of keeping them in line, since he introduced her to her first partner, whom he named as Valencourt. A very young fair-haired and rather tongue-tied gentleman, whose steps had obviously been honed by a dancing master who had failed to impart any style or grace.

She recalled that he had spent a considerable amount of money at her table earlier in the evening, but had thankfully stopped when his chips ran out.

'Mr Valencourt. How kind of you to ask me to dance,' she said with a smile intended to put him at ease.

He blushed. 'Mrs Lamb. The honour is mine. Most grateful. I m-mean...' He stuttered into silence.

'The weather is very mild for this time of year,' he said, after a few minutes. He sounded as if he was following some sort of script called 'The Rules for Conversation while Dancing'.

She kept her tone light and friendly. 'Perhaps the winter will be mild also?'

He grinned and seemed to relax a little. 'You are not like the other girls,' he said, leaning close and dropping his voice. 'They always make me feel as if I have two left feet.'

'Surely not? You are an excellent dancer.'

His blush deepened. 'Thank you. It... Umm... I mean... one dances better when one has...' he swallowed '...a partner who...'

He swallowed again.

Oh, dear. Poor young man. She felt sorry for him. 'A partner with whom one feels comfortable.'

'A partner who dances beautifully,' he said in a rush.

'Why, thank you, Mr Valencourt. You are very kind.' She twirled under his arm and they promenaded down the length of the ballroom side by side.

'Not kind,' he said, sounding rather strangled.

Glancing up at his face, she saw he was once again struggling for words.

Fortunately, the music was drawing to a close and Monsieur Phillippe was trying to catch their attention.

Valencourt dutifully walked her back to him. 'Can I ask you to dance again?'

She smiled. 'Not tonight. It would not be seemly.' Actually she had no idea of the rules, but she didn't want to give the poor young man any false ideas.

The next gentleman waiting to dance with her was Lord James, the young man who had jumped to her defence when it had looked as if one of her players might accuse her of cheating after losing badly. She had been horrified by the accusation. If there had been any cheating going on, she would have refused to take part. But she had also been a little scared by the young man's outburst, though she had tried not to show it.

She smiled at Lord James as he led her out on to the floor. The music began and they danced in silence for a while, each getting used to the other as they moved through the opening steps. So far every dance had been a waltz and the patrons seemed to be enjoying themselves.

'I must thank you for your kind assistance earlier, with Mr Smythe.'

'Smythe was making a cake of himself,' he said. 'And not for the first time. Everyone knows Dart's parties are the one place one can be assured the die are not weighted and the cards are not marked. He's a gentleman, for heaven's sake.'

'Nevertheless, I appreciate your intervention.'

'I haven't seen you here before. You are not like the other girls.'

He was the second man to make this observation. 'In what way?'

He looked thoughtful as he twirled her around. 'You are more refined, and...nicer, somehow.'

'Nicer.' She chuckled. 'A milk-and-water miss, am I?'

He grinned. 'No. I didn't mean it that way. Perhaps I should have said kinder.'

'Have the other ladies been unkind to you?'

'They are not unkind. They are just not kind. For them it's all about the chips on the table. You seem to take an interest in a chap. And Betsy would have slapped Smythe down instantly, whereas you tried not to hurt his feelings.'

'Which did not work very well, until you spoke up.'

'But you see, if Betsy had been there, we might have egged him on a bit, enjoyed the argument, but tonight everyone at the table was on your side. So he left.'

'Well, I am glad for his sake he left, because he had lost a lot of money, I think.'

'And that's what makes you different. You care.'

'Now you are making me sound like some sort of saint. And I can assure you I am not.'

His laugh was infectious. 'That is the last thing I would say you are.'

Good heavens, what did he mean? Better not to ask.

On the way back to Monsieur Phillippe, Pamela was surprised to see him approached by a couple who looked—well, they looked mischievous and perhaps a little excited. Monsieur Phillip smiled at the pair and pulled something from his inside breast pocket, which he handed to the man, with what she could only describe as a knowing grin.

The pair left the ballroom at speed.

'Where are they going?' she asked Monsieur Phillippe once Lord James had delivered her safely.

'Who?'

He knew very well whom she meant. 'The couple that were with you right before I returned.'

He waved a vague arm. 'I am sure I have no idea what you mean.'

He's lying.

But there was no time to question him further, her next dance partner was already eagerly reaching for her hand. Besides, what business of hers was it when they had looked so pleased?

'Who is the new girl?'

Damian didn't have to follow the direction of Lord Hill's gaze to know he was referring to Mrs Lamb. The dancing had finished a half-hour before and the croupiers were back at their tables.

Hill, a retired army colonel, was gazing at her as if he was a wolf who had just spotted an unattended sheep.

Damian gritted his teeth and replied pleasantly, 'Mrs Lamb? She is no one in particular.' At least no one he was prepared to admit to just yet. Fortunately Lamb was a common enough last name and no one was likely to associate a croupier at his parties with the well-connected Lambs of Bexley. 'She is one of my staff who agreed to help out this evening in the absence of one of our regular croupiers.'

'If I were you, I would make *her* one of your regular croupiers. These parties of yours were getting a little mundane, old fellow. Quite dull. She has livened things up considerably.'

Mundane? Dull? What the devil was he talking about? Damian glanced around. Was the crowd thinner tonight than usual? Was the *ton* in need of more excitement?

Damn them for a bunch of spoiled wastrels.

'She's quite the beauty,' Hill went on. 'By the time I got to Monsieur Phillippe, all her dances were spoken for. All the young fellows are enchanted.'

He had noticed that much for himself. 'Why is that, I wonder?'

'I was asking myself that. She is not as intimidating as the other gals. She don't scare them. But she don't put up with any of their nonsense either. And there is an aura of mystery about her. A sense of secrets.'

Damian forced himself not to smile at the description. Mrs Lamb did indeed have secrets. And she had done well this evening. Much better than he had expected.

Perhaps he should strike while the iron was hot. Something to consider.

'I thank you for your advice. Do you have other thoughts on how we might enliven the evening for our guests?'

He had, though. Making the club exclusive would be temptation enough, along with the provision of private rooms where guests could pursue their peccadilloes, no questions asked.

'Higher stakes.'

Some men liked to live on the edge of disaster. But higher stakes meant higher risks for the house. That he would have to discuss with Pip.

Hill wandered off to join one of the other tables and Damian, as was his wont, wandered the room, checking on each of the tables in turn, except that he seemed to return to Mrs Lamb's table more often than any of the others.

What was it that drew so many of the young men into her orbit? The *ton* did indeed like novelty. It was part of the reason his club had taken off so quickly. There was nothing else like it.

But if they became bored, then that would not suit his purposes at all.

'Do you know you have the most beautiful eyes?' Mr Galt said, gazing adoringly at Mrs Lamb. 'Won't you remove your mask and let me see your face? I am sure you must be the loveliest woman here.'

Damian had to restrain himself from planting the fellow a facer. As it was he took a step closer, ready to usher the young man out.

The rules were clear. No one was to touch the lady croupiers.

Mrs Lamb smiled at him calmly. 'I take no responsibility for the eyes the Lord gave me, Mr Galt. Or the curve of my lips, Lord Raif,' she added, smiling at another of the young men. 'And, no, I will not remove my mask simply to edify your curiosity.'

There was some good-natured laughter and a fair bit of jostling of the young men who had been so bold. The sort of laughter that suggested the others also were dying to see behind her mask, but were a smidgeon glad Galt had not been successful because they wanted to be the ones who convinced her to reveal herself.

'Do you plan to make a wager, Mr Galt, or will you give your place to someone who will?'

Tonight would not be the night when she unmasked.

'Wagers, please, ladies and gentlemen,' Mrs Lamb said firmly.

Chips and sovereigns were pushed forward on the green baize. 'Blast,' said Lord James. 'I am out of cash.'

He was one of the fellows she had danced with earlier.

Lord James pulled out a notebook, clearly intending to write a vowel.

'Are you sure, you want to do that?' she said, putting her hand on the scrap of paper. 'You have lost rather a lot already.'

Damian frowned. The pile of winnings at her elbow was large, but included not one vowel? Unusual. How many more young men had she discouraged in this way?

He stepped forward. 'Your vowel is good with us, Lord James,' he said smoothly.

Mrs Lamb shot him a startled glance. 'Oh, but—'

'My dear Mrs Lamb, you have been on your feet for hours, not to mention the way these young fellows were stepping on your toes not so very long ago.' He gave her a glare when she didn't move. 'Off you go. Take a well-earned break. I will look after things here.'

A couple of the fellows gave a groan and for a moment he thought Lord James would argue, but Damien smiled at him and glanced around at the other players. 'Place your bets, please, ladies and gentlemen.'

After a brief hesitation, Mrs Lamb left the table and glided away.

A few moments later Pip arrived at his side. 'All well?' he asked *sotto voce*.

'Take over for me,' Damian said and went off in search of the blasted woman.

He found her in the retiring room pouring herself a cup of tea. They were alone.

The taste of the anger at the back of his throat was as familiar as his face in the mirror. Anger at those who had made his family flee their home. Anger at his father for playing the gentleman when he could not put food on the table. Anger at what circumstances had forced him to become.

Damn it. He had nothing to be ashamed of.

'Why the devil were you stopping him from writing his vowel? What next? Will you be letting them win?'

She glared up at him. Her eyes narrowed and her mouth thinned to a straight line.

'I beg your pardon,' she said stiffly.

'Are you deliberately trying to ruin me?'

'Are you trying to ruin that young man? He had run out of money.'

'Lord James is a wealthy young man. What he loses here tonight he will make back tomorrow on the 'Change. He would not be here if he could not afford the stakes.'

'Oh. I see. I had no idea, but—'

'Exactly. You had no idea. But you decided anyway.' He took a deep breath. 'The evening is about done. I have no further need for you. You may return to your chambers.'

'As you wish.' She put down the teacup.

She looked hurt and he felt as if he had kicked a puppy or drowned a kitten. Dammit it, she was the one at fault.

He followed her out and down the hall, making sure she made it safely to her part of the house. He didn't want some wag from his party attempting to see behind the mask, or worse. By this hour they were all half-seas over.

He and Pip always made sure the girls were not importuned by their guests, male or female. It was simply good sense and had nothing to do with feeling protective towards this woman.

Pamela was still seething about her abrupt dismissal the day before when she entered her kitchen. She halted at the sight of the man seated at her kitchen table among the dirty dishes which she had not had time to deal with the previous evening, because she had done him a favour.

How dare he? He needn't think she was going to cook him a special breakfast today.

'Good morning, My Lord,' she said stiffly. 'Breakfast will be available in the servants' hall at seven.'

'I am leaving for London in a few minutes so no need to prepare anything.'

He gave her a shamefaced glance. A rather boyishly endearing look, if she was to be honest. Her stomach gave a strange little pulse. Clearly, she needed to give that part of her a good talking to. He was definitely in her bad books.

'I came to apologise for my outburst last night.'

Well, blast the man. Here she was happily being annoyed with him and now he had completed melted her defences.

'Apology accepted.' She worked her way around him to the stove and picked up the coal scuttle.

'Allow me.'

He had moved so swiftly, so silently, she hadn't heard him come up behind her. She jumped. And he took the scuttle from her now rather nerveless hands.

'Not too much,' she said. 'Or it will smoke. Er… I mean, thank you.'

'Tell me when to stop.'

He shook the coal in a few pieces at a time. 'Yes, that is enough.'

He put the scuttle down and brushed the coal dust off his hands. 'That thing is heavy.'

'Yes.'

He looked around. 'And where do you fill it?'

'In the coal cellar. Beside your wine cellars,' she added when he looked vaguely about him.

'Oh, I see. Do I need to order more?'

'You are being very conciliatory this morning.'

He grimaced and it really was a naughty lad's expression. 'I...er...well, I was talking to Pip and he mentioned that of all the tables last night, yours was the most profitable. So I thought I would ask if you would continue on as a croupier on party nights.'

She looked at the mess. Normally she would have had this all cleaned up before she went to bed. Not that she really had anything else much to do today since there would be no one else at the house but her.

She shook her head. 'I don't think so. I am a cook. That is why you hired me. And besides,' she went on, thinking about what her taking on these additional duties would mean, 'I don't want to put Betsy or Meg out of work.'

'You don't need to worry about that.'

'Oh, but I do. You might not care about what happens to those ladies, but I do. They rely on the money you pay them.'

'I mean, you won't be putting them out of work. They will continue as before. I have had another idea. I ran it by Pip and he thinks it is a grand idea.'

'What sort of idea?' He was looking too pleased with himself.

'I would like you to become my hostess. To be in charge

of the girls while Pip and I look after the guests and security.'

'I don't think I understand.'

'You would attend the parties, dinner and, afterwards, when we play cards, move from table to table, ensuring the guests are happy, talking with them, making sure they have drinks. Generally acting as the hostess of the evening. You could also relieve each girl in turn so we never have an empty table and that way all the tables will benefit from your presence. You will, of course, be well recompensed, based on earnings for the night.'

The girls were paid according to the earnings at their table. 'Based on earnings at all the tables?'

'Yes.'

'Why?'

'I think—well, we think the house will do better, to be honest.'

Last night had been fun. At least, it had until the end. And there had been no one there who had shown any sign of recognition. The two men whose names she had recognised had visited her father only, not the family. Besides, the mask had protected her identity. But the next party might be different. What if someone she did know was one of the attendees. A relative, or a friend of Alan's. It was too much of a risk.

She shook her head. 'It is a kind offer, but I prefer to remain as your cook.'

He looked at the dishes stacked on the table. 'I suppose you did not have time to clear up last night.'

'Neither time nor inclination.'

'Yes, of course. You must have been tired. It was a long night for everyone. I will get you some help from the village, so you won't have to face a pile of dirty dishes in the morning, if that would help change your mind. Oh, I almost forgot.' He pulled a sheaf of banknotes from his pocket and handed them to her. 'This is your share of the takings from last night.'

She stared at what looked like a king's ransom. 'You cannot mean it.'

'I do.'

'So much money lost at the tables?' It seemed immoral.

'That and payment for your dances.'

'Oh. I did not realise they were paying…'

He shrugged. 'Why would the girls want to dance with the patrons for free when they could be putting their feet up in the withdrawing room?'

'Why, indeed. And what else do they do for money?'

'Now, now, Mrs Lamb, you have a very earthy turn of mind. My staff does not do anything of that sort under my roof. It is against the rules.'

'I saw couples leaving the dancing—'

'Couples who came together. Not my ladies. Now what do you say?'

He seemed very anxious for her to say yes. And if she made that amount of money each evening, she could retire to a little cottage in the country in no time at all.

It was so very tempting.

But she couldn't risk being recognised.

She shook her head. 'I am sorry. It is out of the question.'

'I see.' His voice was full of disappointment.

She felt guilty. As if she had let him down. 'You see, it is possible that I might know someone among your guests. My mother isn't pleased about my becoming a cook, but since I am always tucked away in a kitchen, no one is likely to know. On the other hand, if I was recognised acting as a hostess at what is really a gambling hell—whatever you say about it being respectable—I think it would be ruinous. Reputations other than mine would be destroyed.'

'And last night you were not concerned about this, because you knew you would leave before the unmasking?'

She nodded.

'Then continue to leave.'

'Won't people wonder why I disappear?'

'Let them wonder. The *ton* loves a bit of intrigue.'

'I really don't think—'

'Give it a try for a couple of weeks. If you don't like it, you can go back to your kitchen and I won't hold it against you.'

She looked at the wad of banknotes in her hand and back at his face—he was grinning like a schoolboy.

Her dream of her own little cottage seemed as though it could become a reality. 'Very well. I will try it for two weeks.'

'That's the ticket.' He whirled her around in a circle and took off out of the door, leaving her gasping for breath.

Oh, my word! What had she done?

Let him charm her. That was what she had done.

Chapter Six

Damian had been very careful to keep his distance from Mrs Lamb for the past two weeks. They had exchanged the odd remark relating to her new position, but for the most part he had left her in Pip's charge.

He had been shocked at how pleased he had felt when she had agreed to his proposal. It wasn't like him to feel so…giddy? He was used to being in charge of his emotions.

As a consequence, he had given himself some space. Got himself under control. After all, he wasn't the sort of man who needed anyone else to make him happy. And now it was time to put the second part of his plan in motion.

Having dressed for the outdoors, he wandered down to the servants' hall for breakfast.

Mrs Lamb was already sitting at the table, reading a newspaper.

She rose upon his entry. 'My Lord. I am sorry I did not realise you had stayed over last night or I would have prepared more of a breakfast.'

He had purposely not relayed his intention to stay the night—the first time he had done so for two weeks.

He had wanted to take her by surprise.

'No matter.'

'Were you planning on staying for dinner?'

'I was, if that won't put you out too much.' He could see her mind racing to take stock of what food she had on hand.

He browsed the offerings on the buffet. A couple of slices of cold ham, toast, marmalade, some sweet breads, and fruit.

'Did you make this marmalade?' he asked.

'I did. From the oranges you provided and the last of the little oranges from your tree.'

A sly reminder that the tree needed some care, no doubt. Well, she need not bother. He was leaving England once he had accomplished his purpose. He had decided.

He poured himself coffee and put the ham on his plate with a slice of toast and a scoop of marmalade.

He took the seat opposite her and, having eaten the ham, slathered the preserve on to his toast. He was aware of her watching him.

He took a bite of toast. 'Oh.' He had not been expecting it to taste so extraordinary.

'Is something wrong?'

'What on earth did you put in it? It isn't marmalade, its ambrosia.' It was. It had all the flavour of oranges, but more.

She chuckled, clearly pleased with his reaction. 'It is a secret.'

He wanted to smile back. Damn the woman. It seemed he had no armour against her charm. 'You had better be careful. I may end up sending you a cartload of oranges instead of a box.'

'Unfortunately, I have run out of the secret ingredient.'

'Which is?'

She smiled enigmatically.

He laughed. 'I will find out, you know.' He tasted the marmalade again. 'I think it is some sort of liquor.'

She raised an eyebrow. She definitely did not intend to reveal a thing. And he was enjoying teasing her, he realised.

She got up and poured herself another coffee and sat down again. 'How long will you be staying, My Lord? Only I may need to send to the village for supplies.'

'A day or so. I thought I might see if I could bag a duck for dinner before I started on some paperwork.'

'A duck would be a welcome addition to what I have on hand.' She looked as if she would say more.

'What?' he asked.

'I was thinking I could use a walk. I would like to see if there are any mushrooms in your woods and there is a chestnut tree I have been meaning to have a look at over near the river. Unless you prefer your own company.'

'Not at all. You would be more than welcome.' It couldn't be better. He had been thinking of broaching the matter on his mind over dinner, but he had a sense she might be more amenable to his proposal while wandering outside in the woods. As long as he didn't overplay his hand.

'Do you think it will rain?' she asked. 'It looked pretty overcast when I looked out earlier.'

'It might. I can lend you an oilskin, if you wish and some boots, too. I think there are some smaller ones, left from—' Damn it, he did not want to think about his mother.

'No need. I have my own. I am quite used to tramping around in the wet.'

Of course she was. He kept forgetting she was supposed to be a servant, because she did not talk or act like a servant.

'If you can give me some time to clear up here and get ready,' she continued, 'I will accompany you.'

'No need to hurry. I have to clean my gun and that will take a bit of time. I'll meet you outside in, say, an hour?'

'Perfect.'

And suddenly the day, although gloomy, seemed much brighter.

He must be losing his mind. He left before he did something stupid.

When she entered the courtyard, Pamela discovered Dart waiting, leant against the stable wall, his gun beside him looking like a typical English nobleman off on a hunt. Sensibly clothed in raincoat and hat, his hunting accoutrements slung on straps crossways over his chest, he looked ready for anything. Not unlike herself. In addition, he wore a pair of gaiters to protect his trousers above his walking boots.

Seeing him so dressed reminded her of when she used to go with her father on the occasional shoot. Not that Dart was anything like her father. Not in the least. Even in his heavy rain gear, he looked fit and healthy and terribly attractive.

Gah. Not something she should be thinking about her employer.

He greeted her with a wave, shouldered his gun and side by side they set off across the park.

It had rained the day before so the long grass was wet. 'This would be a beautiful lawn, if it was mowed,' she said.

'There is no one here to see it.'

True. His guests never arrived before dark and were gone long before the sun rose. At least, at this time of year. 'Still, it seems a shame. It looks more like a hayfield than a lawn.'

'Yes.'

She sensed he was not pleased with her line of conversation.

There was no pleasing the man. If she owned a house like this, she would want it to look its very best. Not only did he not seem to care, he seemed almost opposed to any sort of restoration that did not directly relate to his parties. To the making of money, in other words.

Rooks cawed somewhere ahead. 'Noisy creatures. They must have a rookery nearby.'

'Yes.'

Why had she bothered to walk with him? She would have been better company alone. She might not have bothered trekking as far as the woods either. No doubt she would have found a few field mushrooms hiding in all this long grass.

They reached the edge of the beech woods to the west of the park. Wet leaves slid underfoot, making the path treacherous.

Here and there brambles stretched long barbed tendrils to grab on to her skirts and his coat. Clearly this path was rarely used, though at one point it must have been a well-trodden route to the river.

They walked in single file and now and then he would turn to hold back a bramble or an encroaching thorn bush.

The air smelled of earth and damp. A typical autumn scent, dark yet not unpleasant. She kept her gaze peeled for any signs of fungi. They loved this sort of environment.

She spotted a blood-red ox tongue fungus clinging low on the trunk of one of the few oak trees in this woods. It was not a flavour she preferred and passed it by, remembering its location in case she did not find something more appetising.

Dart halted without warning. Looking for mushrooms off to the side, Pamela bumped into him. 'Oof,' she said. 'What is wrong?'

'Shh.' He cupped his ear, gazing off to their right.

She listened. Nothing. And then she heard it. A sort of squeaking. Some sort of rodent? She grimaced. She wasn't all that keen on mice or rats. As a cook she had to deal with them, but that didn't mean she would seek them out.

'Wait here.' He pushed off through the undergrowth.

She followed.

He gave her a dark look over his shoulder as if to say on your head be it and continued on, but she noticed he was careful not to let twigs or brambles snap back at her.

A clearing opened before them and at its edge on the other side she could see the source of what she now recognised as whimpering.

A dog. Large and black and rangy.

Its ears flattened at their approach and its lips curled back from sharp-looking teeth.

'Careful,' Dart said as she moved around him. He unshouldered his gun. 'Stay back. I may have to shoot it.'

'What? No.' As she drew closer she could see the source of the problem. Twine around the animal's paw. 'It is caught in a snare. Oh, you poor thing.'

'Don't get too close. It is liable to bite and you are now in my line of sight.'

She turned to see him loading his gun.

'You are not going to shoot it,' she said, horrified.

'I will shoot it if it attacks. Have you ever seen a case of hydrophobia? No? I have. Believe me, you won't want to take the risk.'

She knelt beside the dog warily. It whimpered and flattened itself to the ground. 'It is not attacking.'

He hunkered down beside her and reached out. The dog snarled.

'It's all right,' he said gently. 'I'm not going to hurt you.' The dog whined, then dropped his head. Its tail gave a hesitant wag.

He pulled out a knife from his belt and reached for the twine.

Pamela could see the dog was anxious by the way it tensed. She stroked its head. 'It's all right. He won't hurt you.'

The dog looked up at her and in that instant Dart reached for the snare. The dog, quick as a wink, jerked its head around and snapped.

'Damnation.' Dart sucked on one finger.

'Did it bite you?' she asked.

'No. I cut myself. Just a nick.' He dived into his pocket and pulled out a pair of gloves. 'I should have put these on in the first place.

The dog, some sort of retriever breed, though a bit of a mix of more than one something else, she thought, licked at its paw.

'Now,' Dart said firmly, 'hold still.'

The dog whined, but surprisingly held still while Dart cut the snare.

The dog rose and shook itself.

Pamela peered at its paw. 'I don't think it's been caught long. It doesn't seem to be bleeding.'

She petted the dog's head and stood up. Dart had removed his glove and was looking at his wound.

'Let me see,' she said.

'It is nothing.'

She glared at him.

He rolled his eyes and held out his hand. 'See. Nothing.'

The cut wasn't deep, but it was still welling with blood.

'Let me bind it up until we can put some salve on it at the house.' She picked up the knife he had dropped beside his gloves and, turning away from him, cut off a strip of her petticoat.

Looking rather surprised, he held out his hand for her

to bind the strip of material around his finger. 'That will keep it clean,' she said.

The dog was sitting watching them, its bright red tongue lolling and its tail wagging.

'I wonder where he came from?'

Dart regarded the animal for a moment. 'He looks a bit on the thin side. He might be a stray.'

He did look a bit scruffy.

'Off you go,' Dart said to the dog. 'Go home. And try to stay out of poachers' snares in future.'

The dog cocked its head, but didn't move.

Dart looked about him. 'It will go when its ready, I suppose. The river is this way. Not far now, as we have taken a bit of a shortcut.'

The dog followed them, occasionally leaving their trail to explore on one side or the other, but always returning after a few moments.

'It looks like you have gained a new friend,' she said with a chuckle.

Dart glared back at her. 'Someone in the village will know who owns him.'

He sounded annoyed.

An Englishman who didn't like dogs. Her father had always said you could judge a man by his dogs, how they responded to him would tell a lot about a man's character. Did his lack of liking for dogs mean something?

The trees thinned out and changed from beech to the occasional willow and the grass grew longer and the ground became wet and squelchy. And then, before them, there was the river. Not terribly large as rivers went, about ten feet across, and quite sluggish with a low muddy bank and reeds growing along its edge.

Dart checked his gun, then walked quietly towards the

bank. 'I will see if there are ducks on the water. Please remain here,' he said softly.

She nodded.

The dog disappeared off into the long grass. A moment later a duck broke cover with a whirr of wings and a quack.

'Sacre bleu,' Dart said softly, lining up. He fired. The duck came down in a flutter of feathers and landed in the river.

'Devil take it,' Dart said.

Without warning, the dog leapt from the bank into the water a little further down.

Pamela almost laughed at Dart's helpless fury at the sight of the dog about to have duck for dinner.

Dart stomped back to her. 'It is not funny. I didn't come hunting to feed a dog.'

They watched as the dog snagged his prize and swam strongly for the bank.

Once out of the water it dropped the duck and shook itself from stem to stern. Then, to Pamela's astonishment, it retrieved its prize, brought it to Damian and dropped it at his feet with a big doggy grin.

Dog and man regarded each other for a moment. 'Well, that is a surprise.' He patted the dog, picked up the duck and tied it to the lanyard at his belt.

'Good boy,' Pamela said.

The dog gave a half-hearted tail-wag, but its gaze was firmly fixed on Damian.

Damian shouldered his gun.

The dog looked puzzled.

'We only need one,' Damian said to it. 'You will get your share. Now we have to find a chestnut tree, I believe.

Damian was enjoying himself, he realised to his great surprise as they wound their way back through the woods.

He had forgotten that he had hunted in these woods with his father. The longer he had lived in France, bearing the responsibility for feeding his family, by fair means or foul, his life before Marseilles had begun to seem like a dream or one of those interminable stories his father used to tell about the good old days.

Providing for your household by hunting was somehow a great deal more satisfying than he expected. Far more satisfying than some of his nefarious activities.

He pushed the thought aside. That part of his life was behind him. Stealing scraps of food and robbing the poor box was something he would never have to do again.

He was sorry that his mother and father had not lived long enough to see how successful he had become, how he was restoring the family fortunes. And, in the process, exacting a fitting revenge.

The dog had wandered off for a few minutes, but returned as if to check on their welfare. Heaven help him, the last thing he needed was to be adopted by a dog.

'What will you do if you can't find its owner?' she asked.

Like some sort of mind reader.

'Find someone who will take him, I suppose.'

'He seems like such a good dog. Why would anyone abandon him?'

In other words, why would he not want to keep him? If she thought she could pull on his heart strings, she was in for a disappointment. He did not have a heart.

'Do you recall exactly where this chestnut tree is located?' he asked.

'Somewhere up ahead, I think.'

How did she even know one tree from another? He preferred the bustle of city streets. Trees he could do without. 'What sort of trees are these?'

'Beech.'

'How do you know?'

The look she gave him was one of astonishment, mingled with pity. 'By the shape of the leaves, the ridges on the trunk. All sorts of things.' She chuckled. 'And by all these little nuts underfoot.'

Oh. That's what those were. 'Are they edible?'

'Somewhat. Not really a delicacy.'

'The only thing I can recognise with any certainty is an oak tree.'

'That is something, I suppose, since you are an English nobleman and there are oak leaves decorating your coat of arms.'

He laughed at her wry tone.

He looked around, to see if he could spot anything that might be a chestnut tree.

'There it is,' she said.

He glanced back and she was pointing off to his right.

And then he saw it. A tree of larger girth than the others around it and with golden leaves still clinging to its branches along with clusters of green fruit.

When they reached the tree, she looked about her on the ground. 'I think it is a bit too early. There really aren't many here.' She gingerly picked up a twig with a couple of bright green whiskery-looking balls attached to it.

He reached for it.

'Stop' she said.

The dog barked at her sharp tone.

'Enough,' Damian said to him.

She laughed. 'He is protecting you. Don't touch them. They really are horribly prickly.'

'Oh, now I remember.' He remembered something else. He took the twig and dropped it on the ground. He gently captured one of the casings between his boots and split the soft shell open. Out spilled three bright glossy reddish-brown nuts. He picked them up and popped them in her basket.

'I do remember this tree. Not its location, exactly. But I remember doing this when out on a walk with my mother.'

It was a strangely painful memory he wished he had not recalled.

'It is a good thing you have sturdy leather gloves,' she said. 'Mine are far too thin for the task. Perhaps, if you wouldn't mind, you could gather up whatever we can find and I will shell them when we get back.'

He raked through the leaves and found quite a few more spiky shells. Almost enough to half fill her basket, but the majority of the harvest remained up on the tree. 'Shall I climb up?' he asked.

She glanced upwards. 'Actually, I think it is time we returned to the house, because I think it is starting to rain again. Much harder than before.'

The sky had indeed got much darker.

And, if he wasn't mistaken, the wind had picked up, too. He took the basket.

'And we still haven't found any mushrooms that you promised me for dinner,' he teased.

She pulled her hood up over her hat. 'Then we had better hurry.'

And hurry they did. They were almost to the edge of the forest when she dove off to one side. 'Yes,' she called out. 'Exactly what I was hoping for. Chanterelles.'

She foraged around, popping small, yellow, frilly fungi in the basket he held out to her as she went.

'There. That will be enough,' she said.

The rain was coming down harder, but she was grinning from ear to ear as she looked up at him. She looked positively lovely. Sweet. Happy. Full of joy at such a simple accomplishment.

And he couldn't stop himself. He bent his head and kissed her cheek. She tasted of fresh cold air and sweet, sweet smiles.

She gasped.

He stepped back, mentally shaking his head at his madness. What the devil had come over him?

She touched a gloved finger to her face as if she could still feel his touch. 'Oh.'

And he wanted to kiss her again.

Properly. On her mouth. With his hands on her, instead of clutching a basket full of prickles.

A gust of wind brought raindrops splattering down on them.

She laughed. He grinned back at her. Indescribably relieved that she didn't look the least bit offended. To his shock, she rose up on her toes and, holding on to his lapels, she kissed him back. A soft sweet brush of her warm plush lips on his mouth.

Instant arousal.

If there had been the slightest chance of a warm dry spot anywhere close, he would have pulled her close and devoured that delicious mouth. A pang seized his heart. Sweetly painful.

Another cold splat hit his cheek and brought him to his senses.

'Hurry up,' he said, his voice strangely rough. 'Before we get soaked and you catch an ague.' He took her hand and urged her forward, to the house. As they ran, the dog circled them, barking excitedly.

'Foolish animal,' she said, breathless and laughing.

He, Damian, was the foolish one. He wanted more of this. But that wasn't the plan.

They entered through the side door and discarded their outer layers and boots in the mud room while the dog remained outside, whining and yapping his disapproval at their disappearance.

Damian carried the basket through to the kitchen and set it on the table.

He opened his mouth to say something, but the vision of her glowing from exertion, windblown, and damp tendrils of hair clinging to her cheeks, robbed him of speech.

They stared at each other silently. The air tingled with unspoken longing. Not something he had ever experienced.

The dog scratched at the outside door. Dammit it.

'I better...' 'You better...' they said at the same moment and laughed.

'I will see to the dog,' he said. 'I am looking forward to our dinner.'

'Six o'clock,' she said, smiling.

His heart felt the warmth of that smile all the way to the stables. He didn't even care that the dog almost tripped him up twice.

It seemed he had reached a new understanding with Mrs Lamb and now he must use it to his advantage.

A pang of regret slid down his spine.

No. He regretted nothing. From here on, everything would go according to plan—as long as he remained in control.

Chapter Seven

Safe in her own room, Pamela unpinned her hair and set to work drying it with a towel. Inside, she was shaking. Mortified.

Alan had been right when he said there was something wrong with her. He'd been shocked at what he called her lasciviousness. He said her carnal appetites went far beyond what he would have expected from a lady. And this, after they had engaged in what she had thought was the most wonderous feelings she had ever experienced.

She recalled how in the throes of passions she had taken control of their lovemaking, rolling on top of him and...

She cut the thoughts off.

Terrified that he would not want to marry her, if he found her too unbridled, after that she had tried to restrain her unnatural passion, to be less responsive and more ladylike.

And now she had done it again. She had kissed Damian. The sensation of the brush of his warm firm lips against her skin remained like an indelible imprint.

On her lips. Humming in her body... Reminding her...

How could she feel so much when all he had done was kiss her cheek?

She went hot, then cold at the recollection of his look of shock and the way the atmosphere between them had turned awkward.

There really was something wrong with her. Some sort of aberration in her nature. Other women—other ladies, she corrected—did not rouse the way she did when kissing. Alan had assured her of this.

She had tried her best to control these sensations, to conquer her unnatural yearnings, but as demonstrated in those few moments with Damian, she had failed miserably.

Her hands trembled as she touched her lips. She had not imagined that he had returned her kiss with enthusiasm. Gently, yes. Hesitantly, yes. But there was no mistaking their mutual spark of attraction.

Clearly, she had let a handsome face get the better of good sense. Yet his male beauty wasn't the source of his allure. Not for her. It was something else. Something she had the feeling he tried to hide from the world. Kindness? Was that what she saw in him?

Certainly, he was kind in his deeds. Look at the consideration he showed for the people who worked for him. And how caring he had been with the dog, despite his denials.

She liked him. A great deal more than she should. And he seemed to like her. But if she gave in to the passions roiling inside her, he would no doubt feel the same sort of distaste Alan had felt and it would ruin everything.

She would lose his friendship. She could not bear the idea of him turning away in disgust.

And since she could not trust herself around him, from now on she really would maintain a proper distance. Keep everything strictly business and avoid any further slips.

A knock on the door brought her to her feet. 'Who is it?'

Oh, how stupid. They were the only two people in the house.

'Dart.'

'One moment.' She scooped the scattered clothing and

bundled them behind the sofa, then opened the door to see him with, one arm resting high on the doorframe, looking down at her, his dark hair tousled, his gaze intense. The man was too gorgeous for words. Breathtaking.

She clung to what little remained of her sanity. 'Yes, My Lord?' Her voice shook a little. She sounded breathless. 'Please, come in.' She stepped back to allow him to pass. 'How is the dog? Well settled?'

He paced to the window and then turned with a gesture of defeat. 'The stubborn animal refuses to remain in the stables. It is now happily ensconced beside the fire in my study.'

'Oh.' She tried not to chuckle at his chagrin.

'I will enquire for its owner in the village tomorrow, but that was not what I wanted to discuss. I came to apologise.'

She stared at him, her heart sinking oddly. 'For what?'

'For allowing myself such ungentlemanly conduct—'

'No, indeed! I turned a brotherly peck on the cheek into...' heat rushed into her face '...into something more.'

'Brotherly?' He stared at her. 'I can assure you, it wasn't in the least bit brotherly.'

She swallowed. 'I thought you might think I was far too forward for kissing you back as I did.'

A wicked smile lit his face and sent shivers down her spine. 'I liked it. I wanted you to do it again.'

Her toes curled into the carpet. Oh, goodness, she hadn't put on her slippers.

He stalked towards her and brushed her hair back from her face, peering at her expression, and what he saw seemed to take the worry from his gaze.

'I think you and I have been dancing around each other for quite some time.'

He drew close, took her hand and rubbed his thumb over her knuckles.

'I think we have. I should probably hand in my notice.'

'Why?'

'I am your employee. A servant. It is not fitting.' Not the full truth. But it would do to keep him at bay. She hoped.

'Sit,' he said and drew her down on the sofa.

She perched on the edge. If her heart had been racing before, now it seemed ready to gallop out of her chest. He did not let go of her hand. And she did not pull it away.

She could not, did not want to give up the feel of his skin on hers. Her body hummed with pleasure at his touch.

'Let me say, firstly, you have become much more than a servant,' he said. 'You have become indispensable to the success of my endeavour here. The staff is happier than they have ever been. The guests are happy. The tables are more profitable than ever. You may think I have not noticed the way you have made things run more smoothly, but I have.'

Oh. This was about the club. Not about... She shook off her feeling of disappointment. He appreciated her work. She should be pleased.

She had actually thought he might not like the changes she had wrought, making sure some of the young men did not dip too deeply, teasing them into good spirits when they lost and celebrating the occasions when they won. The very rare occasions.

'Thank you. Your words mean a great deal.'

'I wondered if you would like to become a partner, with me and Pip.'

'A partner?' She stared at him blankly. Never in her wildest dreams would she have expected such an offer. As usual, her thoughts had been focused on far more carnal matters. Shame filled her.

He must have taken her silence for doubt because he

quickly added, 'Don't answer now. Think about it. We will discuss more at dinner.'

A vision of her little cottage in the country flashed into her head. It was larger than before. A great deal larger. Was it possible that such a dream could become a reality?

He got up with a smile. 'I should leave you to dress.'

She winced. Right. She was still in her dressing gown.

He lifted a lock of hair from where it draped over her shoulder and rubbed it between his finger and thumb. 'If I may say so, your hair is quite beautiful.'

Speechless, she watched him leave.

Never in her life had she felt quite so confused. One moment he was talking business, the next he was offering compliments intended to make her blush.

She wasn't sure if she was on her head or her heels. And, truth to tell, she was feeling like a woman for the first time in a long time.

Was it possible she was losing her heart, when she had sworn she would never do so again? Or was she just missing the pleasures of the flesh?

Knowing herself, the latter was more likely.

Damien put down his knife and fork and lifted his glass. 'My compliments to the chef. That was absolutely delicious.'

Happiness made her heart feel lighter. 'Thank you. I am glad you enjoyed it. I expect you are used to a great many more dishes when Monsieur Chandon prepares your meals, but there is no one here to eat leftovers.'

He glanced down at a pair of entreating eyes. 'Except this dratted dog.'

She smiled. 'Well, yes. But I don't think he has a very discerning palate. He would be just as happy with raw meat.'

Damien grinned. 'Without a doubt. And I am just as

happy with a few plates of delicious food, than a whole table full of stuff I do not recognise covered in slimy sauces that taste nasty.'

'Oh, no. I am sure Monsieur Chandon does not make anything so unappealing.'

He grunted. 'I like food I can recognise by names I know.'

'Hmm. Then I hope you don't dislike the dessert I have made.'

'Apple pie?' he said hopefully.

'Eclair, with a chestnut purée filling.'

She got up and went to the sideboard and brought back two chocolate-topped oblongs.

'I love eclairs,' he said. He had spent many afternoons gazing longingly at a tray of them in the window of a nearby patisserie in Marseilles. Watching them disappear and never able to afford a taste—unless he managed to steal one.

He grimaced. 'I like them with custard inside, though. I don't know about chestnuts.'

'You won't know, until you try them.' She placed the plate in front of him.

He cut into the pastry with the edge of his fork. 'Mrs Lamb, or may I call you Pamela?'

'You may. But only when we are in private, My Lord,' she said primly. He liked prim. It was very sensual. At least with regard to her.

'Then you must call me Damian.' He ate a mouthful of the dessert. It was light, it was chocolate and the creamy filling was like nothing he had ever tasted. It was delicate and rich and nutty. 'Oh, good Lord.'

Her eyes widened. 'Is something wrong?'

'I have never tasted anything like it. It is absolutely amazing.' He finished the rest of it. 'Is there another.'

She laughed and got up. 'I thought you said you couldn't eat another bite.'

'That was before I tried this.'

She put another one on his plate and sat down. 'I have a feeling you were going to ask me something before we got on to the subject of dessert.'

He finished the most amazing pastry down to the last crumb. He forced himself not to ask for another.

'I am sure you guessed I was going to ask if you had considered my offer.'

'With regard to the partnership?'

He leaned his elbows on the table and leant forward. 'Yes.'

'I gave it some thought while I was cooking. I am not opposed to the idea and I certainly appreciate the honour you are doing me by asking...' She took a deep breath. How did she explain her misgivings?

'But?'

'I still do not understand why you would wish to reduce your own profits for no benefit that I can see. I am already undertaking the work you need of me. Usually a partnership requires some sort of equal financial investment. I have very little to offer in that regard.'

Of course. He certainly could not make it sound like some sort of charity. 'Naturally, you will no longer receive wages, but rather a draw from the profits the same way Pip and I do.'

'Should there not be some sort of legal undertaking? A guarantee that I would not make any less than I do under our current agreement?'

'Naturally. If you agree to this plan, I will contact my solicitor and have him draw up the agreement.'

She frowned. Was she going to turn him down? He really hoped not. 'Do you have other concerns?'

'There are things going on in this house, other than gambling. I see couples leaving the ballroom and returning throughout the course of the evening. I know they go upstairs and I have strong suspicion they pay for the privilege. There must be something amiss or it would not be done so secretively.'

'Ah, that.'

'Yes, that! Not to mention the giggles of the maids when they speak of cleaning and tidying the rooms up.'

He frowned. 'The girls are not supposed to discuss what goes on in those rooms. Indeed, it is why we all wear masks at my parties. Discretion is the watchword and one of the reasons the *ton* attend.'

'They said not one word. Just giggled and shushed each other. And I did not ask them to explain. However, I do not see how I could become a partner in a business when I am not fully informed of what the business *is*. I will not mince words. I will have nothing to do with loose women.'

Without a doubt, she was nobody's fool. 'Of course. As a partner, you would not be kept in the dark about any aspect of the business.'

'I would need full disclosure before coming to any decision.'

She was definitely intrigued, but would she be shocked? It was a gamble. She might pack her bags and leave. He thought not. Well, it was time to roll the die.

'Why don't I show you? Then you can make a decision.'

She looked surprised, as if she had expected an argument.

He rose to his feet. 'Are you ready? I just need to collect the keys from my study.'

As they walked along the corridor together, he deliberately matched his steps to hers so that she neither felt hurried nor as if he was dawdling for her sake.

In his study, the dog lay on a carpet in front of the fire. The animal opened one eye, thumped its tail in a very desultory manner as a way of greeting them and went back to sleep.

'He really is making himself comfortable,' she said.

Dart groaned. 'He has no shame.'

She laughed.

Her laughter made something inside him feel lighter. He liked it when she laughed.

Damian picked up the ring of keys from the table and a candlestick.

The dog raised its head.

'Stay,' Damien said.

The dog lowered its head with a sigh.

Damian escorted her up the main staircase.

Pamela's heart was beating a little too fast as they climbed the stairs, not the servants' stairs she had crept up the first time she had visited this floor, but the main staircase. It wasn't the climb making her breathless. She was about to discover the secrets of this house and she was both excited and worried.

Damian hesitated upon entering the corridor then, rather than choosing the first door they came to, he put a key in the lock of the second one.

She peered into the darkness. Damian plucked a candle from the wall lamp and used it to light several torchières in the corners of what proved to be a room clearly meant for bathing. A large square tub sat on a dais in the middle of the room, with a canopy of heavy red fabric which puddled on the floor at each of its four corners. Towels and bottles of perfumes and oils covered a table against the wall. There were cushions on the floor and an assortment of silk dressing gowns hanging on a stand in the corner.

She looked around in astonishment. 'You said these were withdrawing rooms, but I did not expect them to contain baths.'

He smiled gently. 'I believe I said that this is where my guests came when they needed a little privacy.'

'Couples come here to bathe together?'

He shrugged. 'Among other things.'

'Oh.' It dawned on her what these other things might be. 'In the bath? How—?' She covered her mouth with her hand before she said anything she would regret.

He clearly was trying not to laugh. 'It is challenging, but most enjoyable.'

'This is the sort of thing they do in a bawdy house. You said—'

'No. The ladies and gentlemen arrive together. Some are wives. Some are lovers. I do not question them. Whatever arrangements they make, financial or otherwise, are nothing to do with me. They simply pay for the use of the key. That ensures only one couple is in here at a time.'

'Are all the rooms like this one?'

'They all have different…themes.'

'Themes?'

He huffed out a breath. 'The themes are based around fantasies. There are some common ones and some not so common. I simply provide the venue.'

Themes? She tried to imagine what those might be.

Damian must have taken her silence as disapproval because he gave her a hard look. 'This is a way for people to indulge in their fantasies, to play sensual games, without the fear of embarrassing others in their lives, such as servants and other family members.'

Sensual games? She had never heard of such a thing. 'But surely there are other…places they can go for this sort of thing?' She swallowed. Was she really having this sort of discussion with a man and her employer?

'It is certainly possible to satisfy certain desires at a house of ill repute. Have you ever been to one?'

Her jaw dropped. She bridled. 'Of course not.'

'I didn't think so. Well, let me tell you, they tend to be none too clean and the women are likely not as healthy as they should be. Whereas here, a couple attending my party can have a nice clean room and they know each other. Some of those who avail themselves of these rooms are husbands and wives.'

Her jaw dropped.

But she knew he was right. She had seen them. Did women enjoy these games? Had Alan been wrong about her after all? 'I see.'

What did she 'see'? She certainly looked decidedly flushed and, yes, just a tiny bit shocked. Whether it was at what he was telling her, or her own reaction to it, he wasn't quite sure. He had a feeling, though, that it was the latter.

Well, she would be shocked, if she felt some sort of response. She was an innocent. And he was intent on leading her down a dark path.

Guilt rolled over him.

He could end this now. Forget the need for justice and send her back to her kitchen, her reputation and innocence intact.

The image of his mother's face flashed before his eyes. Her sadness. Her bitterness. Her lingering death.

His resolve hardened. It wasn't right that those who had

destroyed their family should live their comfortable lives on the proceeds of what his family had lost.

He had vowed to his father that no matter what, he would see justice done and visit the sins of the fathers upon the children, as was right.

Had not their parents' wicked deeds been visited upon him as a child? Had any one of them ever given a thought to the pain they had caused him?

Now was not the time to weaken. Not when everything was falling into place. This woman meant nothing to him, apart from being a means to an end.

'Would you like to see more?' The expression on her face showed intrigue, even if she remained a little nervous.

He sorted through his keys. He opened the door to the room he always thought of as the most ridiculous, though it had proved very popular. A bed, shaped like a baby's cradle but big enough for an adult, took up centre stage. There were lacy curtains at the window, rattles and a baby bottle and large-sized nappies folded neatly on a chest. Everything one might find in a nursery except on a larger scale.

'Here they play mother and baby, or nursey and baby or some such.'

'Oh.' She stifled a laugh. Clearly, she also thought it ludicrous.

He continued down the corridor. He stood in front of the door at the far end. It held the most grown-up sort of games. Something he didn't mind playing once in a while, as long as he was the one in control. It was also very popular.

He paused, key in hand.

This one might be a bit too much.

'This one is a little more risqué. Perhaps we should save it for another day.'

Wide-eyed, she stared at him.

Clearly she was tempted, but also concerned. He certainly did not want to scare her off. He waited for her decision.

'It is getting rather late,' she said breathlessly. 'Perhaps another time would be best.'

'I don't want you to think I am hiding things from you.'

'No. No. Not at all. This has been most illuminative.'

In a way, he was disappointed that she had retreated, but it really was probably just as well. 'Then it is enough for tonight?'

'Yes. I think I would like to retire now. You have given me a great deal to think about.'

'Please do not take too long to consider my offer. I should like to have this settled before I return to London tomorrow. I will need to see my solicitor and arrange to have the necessary paperwork drawn up.'

'You are leaving tomorrow?'

She sounded regretful. As if she would miss him. Good. 'For a day or so. As is usual.'

'Of course.'

He held out his arm. 'Let me escort you to your chamber.'

After a little hesitation, she took his arm and they walked back down the way they had come up.

He wished he could tell what she was thinking. Perhaps he should have waited to show her these rooms. Yet his instincts said she would have baulked at his offer if he had tried to put her off.

They arrived at her door.

She smiled up at him. 'Will you take the dog to London with you? He will miss you when you're gone.'

He gazed at her hopeful expression. 'I was thinking I would drop into the village shop and see if anyone knows who owns him.'

She nodded. 'Of course.'

'Did you want me to leave him with you? For company?'

'No. I don't think he would stay. I was just wondering what you were planning. What if no one claims him?'

'Then he will travel to London with me, I suppose.'

'I am sure he will enjoy that.' She chuckled. A low husky sound that strummed chords in his body and made his blood run hot.

'And what about you? Will you miss me?'

Her gaze dropped to the floor.

He tipped her chin up gently with one finger. 'Will you?' he murmured, his voice huskier than he expected as a sense of longing twisted deep in his chest.

She lifted her gaze to meet his. 'I prefer it when you are here.'

'Because you are lonely?' He ought to have thought about that.

'Not at all. I do not mind my own company. But I find myself wondering about what you are doing when you are in London.'

As he found himself wondering about her from time to time. Too many times.

'Did I tell you how much I enjoyed our walk today? I don't think I have enjoyed a day so much in a long time.'

Even the flickering light of the candle in the sconce by the door could not hide the way she coloured up at his words.

'I enjoyed it also,' she said softly.

Was she remembering their kiss? It seemed to hover between them. A memory filled with joy.

Her lips parted slightly on a sigh. He could not resist. He bent his head and brushed those delicate lips with his own. When she angled her head for better access, he tasted her lovely mouth with the tip of his tongue.

She made a small sound in the back of her throat and to his utter delight she wound her arms around his body, pressing close and kissed him back.

His body responded instantly. Hardening with desire. A desire long pent up and simmering beneath the surface almost from the day they met.

Not something he wanted to admit.

He moved his mouth over hers, gently encouraging, and her lips parted, welcoming him to taste and explore the delicious depths.

Even through their layers of clothing he could feel her hands moving over his back, while her soft breasts pressed against his chest. He flicked her tongue with his and heard her slight groan of approval.

Her stance widened and he pressed his knee into the space, aware of her body arching into him.

Moments passed in deep sighs and heat.

He found the doorknob behind her and turned, kicking open the door with his foot, backing her into the room.

He raised his head, looking for… Reason came flooding back. He drew back a little, staring down into her face. Dazed eyes full of sensual promise gazed back at him.

'Oh, my,' she said.

Overcome by a strong desire to kiss her again, he closed his eyes briefly. He needed to take this slowly. She was, above everything else, a lady. An unmarried one at that. If he rushed his fences now, she would run like a startled hare.

He drew in one or two deep breaths, smiling down at her. 'The perfect end to a perfect evening. Now I will bid you goodnight.'

'I… Yes. Goodnight,' she said, in barely more than a whisper.

Chapter Eight

When Pamela brought the teapot into the servants' hall the following morning, she stopped short on the threshold when she realised Dart had arrived and was already tucking into the scrambled eggs she'd prepared earlier, along with a slice of toast and some rashers of bacon. A book lay open beside his plate.

The sight of him was almost enough to make her regret her decision of the previous evening. The morning light from the high windows cast his face into chiselled relief, like that of a sculpture. His lithe elegant figure encased in forest green was a delight to the eye.

Her pulse quickened. While last night she had been determined to resist his allure, this morning, apparently, she was having trouble dredging up one reason why she should. She was no innocent miss with prospects of making a good marriage. Who would know what she did tucked away in the countryside?

Not that she should read much into that kiss. While delicious and enticing, it had been all too brief. He had withdrawn so swiftly she had the feeling he regretted it. Or perhaps—a flush of shame rose up from her chest—he thought, like Alan, that based on her responses she was unnaturally lascivious.

The memory of Alan's faint air of distaste stung her

anew. Never again would she show that side of herself and leave herself open to mockery.

She pasted a cool smile on her face and strode in.

He glanced up from his reading. 'Good morning, Pamela.'

She jumped at the sound of her given name on his lips. It sounded so warm and friendly. She should never have agreed he might use her given name when they were alone. 'Good morning, Damian.'

Strangely, she liked the way his name rolled off her tongue.

She poured tea for them both, filled her plate and sat down. It was then that she noticed the dog on his other side. It wasn't begging exactly, but it did have a hopeful look in its eye.

'We have a guest for breakfast,' she said lightly.

'This animal has not a scrap of good manners,' Damian said. 'I will be glad when I find its true owner.'

The dog was probably not going to be happy if that occurred.

They ate breakfast in silence, she sipping her tea and mentally planning menus and a list to send to the butcher as a means of blocking out thoughts about how handsome he looked freshly shaved and the way his hair gleamed beneath the candlelight, while he read his book.

Surprisingly, the silence was perfectly comfortable. Not a scrap of awkwardness.

And not a sly look in sight.

He closed his book and finished his tea. 'Do you have an answer for me?'

Right up until that moment she had not been sure what she would say to his offer of a partnership, but his calm businesslike demeanour had helped her make up her mind.

'Yes. Thank you. I would like to accept your offer of a partnership.'

'Excellent.' He rose and held out his hand. 'Welcome to the business. I will have the papers drawn up at once.'

'There is just one thing before I shake hands on it,' she said.

His gaze sharpened. 'What, pray?'

'The contract needs to include something about the dissolution of the partnership, in case one or other of us wishes to leave. It should acknowledge each person's investment. In my case, it will be my forgone wages.'

She watched him closely, wondering what he would say to her suggestion. She would never forget how angry her father had been when he had discovered that his wife had foolishly invested in a scheme that left the last ones to join paying their money to those who had set up the venture and there were no business profits to be had. Indeed, there had been no business.

Having no head for figures, her father had trusted his wife to manage the family finances and she had always done exceedingly well. That time, Mother had been completely hoodwinked.

Pamela did not understand it very well. He had not wanted to burden her with the details, but she had understood the concept of taking money from Peter to pay Paul and that in the end someone along the line would be out of pocket.

Damian looked thoughtful, as if considering the practical aspect of her proposal. At least he hadn't dismissed her suggestion out of hand. If he had, she would have immediately refused to participate.

'I will consult with my solicitor and show you what wording he suggests when I return,' he said.

Inwardly, she breathed a sigh of relief. To her surprise,

once she had made the decision to join the partnership, she realised she really wanted to be part of it. And the idea of the profits she would eventually make was dizzying.

Not only would she be a woman of substance, one who commanded respect, her future independence would be assured. She would not have to face the prospect of marriage to a man who might, like Alan, call her appetites *unnatural*.

Heat rushed to her face at the recollection. Her stomach fell away, leaving her feeling nauseous.

How she hated that feeling of shame. It made her feel small and worthless.

The new venture meant she never need endure it again. She would be financially self-sufficient and to the devil with any man who thought to denigrate her for her choice.

Three days later she had the contract in her hand.

'Well?' Damian said. 'Does it meet with your approval?'

Pamela looked up from the contract Damian had presented to her upon his arrival from London. 'It seems to cover all of the points we spoke of, though the language is rather difficult to follow.'

'If you are concerned that I am trying to pull the wool over your eyes, please feel free to have your own solicitor take a look at it.'

His voice had a chilly edge as if she had somehow impugned his honour. Which she had, she supposed. Her own solicitor. What sort of cook had her own solicitor? She could ask her stepfather's lawyer. But she had no doubt that he would be off, hot-footed, to tell her mother what she was up to and that would be the end of her foray into independence.

The thought of being forced into marriage made her shiver.

'Oh, no,' she said airily. 'I don't doubt it is all as you say.' She signed it with a flourish.

'I also took the liberty of visiting the employment agency,' he continued. 'I concluded your contract with them on your behalf. I will take the cost of the buy-out from your next draw.'

'Perfect.'

He smiled and held out his hand. 'Welcome to our partnership, Pamela. May we prosper.'

A niggle of doubt constricted her chest for a moment. What if she was making a huge mistake? What if she lost what little she had? It was too late for doubts.

She took his hand, warm, large and dry, and shook it. 'Thank you, Damian. And now I must be getting along. I have a great deal to do before our guests arrive tomorrow.'

'Since you are now a partner, I was thinking you should not need to cook for the staff and you should move to quarters more suitable for your new position.'

Oh, heavens. She surely didn't want the world to know she was a partner. What if her mother learned of it? Right now, she was unknown, like the rest of the women who worked for him, and the mask kept her identity a secret. But she knew the *ton*. They would be far more curious about her if they thought she was of importance.

'I think I would rather keep things as they are,' she said. 'There is no need for anyone to know that I have an interest in the endeavour, is there?'

For a second, she saw a shadow pass through his lovely brown gaze. Had she hurt his feelings?

Then he shrugged in that charmingly Gallic way of his. 'If that is your wish.'

'It is. However, I would like a little more help in the kitchen.'

He chuckled. 'I would say we ought to vote on it, but I know Pip would vote with you, so, yes. Hire more help in the kitchen. And while we are on the subject of duties, I would very much like you to take over the bookkeeping. It is something you can be working on when I am in town. That is if you wouldn't mind.'

'It is a fair trade.'

The study door swung open.

The dog, tongue lolling, trotted in.

'Oh.' She looked at Damian. 'You didn't find his owner?'

Damian winced. 'According to the innkeeper, he is a stray who showed up in the neighbourhood about a month ago. One of the locals in the taproom offered to shoot him. They say he's been stealing chickens.'

'And yet he brought the duck to you.'

'I know. Very odd. Anyway, it seems he's mine and he promised he would behave himself from now on since he is no longer starving.'

'It is kind of you to give him a home.'

He made a gesture of dismissal. 'It is stupid of me. I find myself needing to walk him in the morning in town, because he won't let any of the footmen put a leash on him.'

She stifled a laugh. 'Oh, dear.'

'I thought I would leave him here with you, when I go up to London.'

She looked doubtfully at the dog gazing adoringly at his new master. 'I suppose you could try. Have you given him a name?'

'The Dog.'

'Very original,' she said drily. 'I will see you at dinner. I am off to hire my kitchen maid.'

Damian watched Pamela leave his study with a vague feeling of sympathy.

The mouse had taken the cheese, now all that was required was for the trap to shut. It was too bad he liked her, when he had expected to despise her. Of his two victims, she was the one with the gumption.

He still hadn't got to the bottom of exactly why she was hiring herself out as a cook. No doubt it was some kind of rebellion against her family, which was exactly the sort of thing a spoiled brat would do. Also likely the reason she didn't want to advertise her role in their partnership.

Damian was in no hurry. Things like this needed to be accomplished with finesse and he still had one more mouse to catch. The young man was proving elusive.

But now that he had Pamela safely enmeshed, he could focus his efforts on the last of his enemies' children.

The dog thumped its tail on the carpet.

'No. I am not going to take you out,' he said. 'I have work to do.' He huffed out a breath. 'I suppose you do need some sort of name. How about Odysseus? I have a feeling you are a bit of a Trojan horse, old fellow.'

The dog whined.

'Yes, it is a bit of a mouthful. Oddy for short.'

The dog wandered over to the mat beside the hearth, curled up in a ball and closed its eyes.

'Oddy it is.'

Damian tucked the contract in his desk and opened his ledger. If he was going to pass the bookkeeping to Pamela, he ought to make sure it was current first. He sorted the bills into date order and began the tedious task of entering the amounts.

He only noticed the passage of time when he realised it was getting difficult to see properly as the light outside faded fast. He removed his spectacles and stretched.

Time to call it a day. 'Come, Oddy, we will go and check

on my horse.' He had driven himself down in his curricle earlier in the day.

Oddy sprang up, keen and eager, his nose scenting the air.

Damian collected his coat and boots from the mud room. The scent of something delicious cooking permeated the air. Oddy headed in the direction of the smell.

'Come,' Damian said. If he followed the dog, he might be tempted to kiss his cook again and then he might never get out to see to his horse. Besides, Oddy needed to learn who was master here.

He headed for the stables and, with a last regretful look in the direction of the kitchen, Oddy followed.

Outside, clouds covered the evening sky, and only the dark shape of the stables remained visible. He needed a lamp. He unhooked the one beside the back door and almost jumped out of his skin when a form appeared in front of him.

'Pamela? What are you doing?'

She held up a bunch of leaves. 'I needed some sage for the chicken.'

'You gave me quite a start.' He glared at Oddy. 'Why didn't you let me know she was here?'

Oddy wagged his tail.

'I am supposed to be here,' Pamela said calmly and bent to pat the dog. 'Dogs only warn about strangers.'

Why didn't he know that? Because he had never had a dog, or at least not since he had left England, and he barely recalled his mother's pug, who she'd had to leave behind with a friend.

'Where are you going?' she asked.

'The stables. To make sure my horse has all it needs for the night.'

She nodded. 'I meant to ask you earlier how many guests we are expecting tomorrow.'

'Forty.'

'That many?'

'Our parties are so popular I am having to turn people away. I think forty is the maximum number we can entertain comfortably. I don't want people complaining it's a squeeze.'

'Limiting the guest list will only make it all the more popular.'

'And I can pick and choose who I want for a guest.'

'The richer the better, I suppose.'

'No. That would be crass. The key is to invite the most interesting people. Fill the room with a bunch of dullards and our days are numbered.'

'You are very clever about all this.'

'I have had lots of experience. Pip and I both have.'

'While I am a mere babe in the woods. I am still not sure why you want me as a partner.'

'Because you bring an element of the tasteful to the proceedings.'

She made a choking sound of smothered laughter. 'You jest.' Clearly she did not understand her own allure.

'No.'

She shivered.

It was then that he realised she was not wearing any sort of outer garment except for her shawl.

'Why are you not wearing a coat?'

'I only slipped out for a handful of herbs.'

'And now I have kept you talking. Go inside at once.'

She drew herself upright. 'You have no right to order me about, My Lord.'

'It is for your own good.'

She folded her arms over her chest. 'I will decide what is for my own good, thank you.'

'I see. I beg your pardon. Do as you please.'

'I will.' She moved around him and headed inside.

Damian stared after her for a moment. Up to now she had seemed rather pliant. This stand-your-ground sort of attitude was an interesting development.

Interesting and possibly dangerous.

Through the slits of her mask, Pamela watched Rake Hall's guests slowly depart for home. As Damian had predicted, they were turning people away, some even arriving at the door without invitations.

Those, she left to Damian.

A couple of young men on the far side of the room raised their voices. She could see they were becoming belligerent. What was it about young men and brandy that made them argumentative?

It was Mr Long again. She'd had to intervene in an argument he had been having the previous week as well.

She sauntered over. 'Mr Long and Mr Smith,' she said, smiling. 'How are you this evening? How nice to see you both again.'

Long, a portly young fellow with an over-long forelock that flopped in his eyes, turned his angry gaze on her. 'We are having a discussion. Smith here thinks that Oxford is the better university when everyone knows that Cambridge is far superior.'

His words seemed a little slurred. 'I see. It is a friendly argument then.' She linked her arms through one each of theirs and steered them towards the nearest table while continuing to talk. 'So you are both content that you received the best of education?'

They frowned.

'I mean, I am assuming you are not intending to return to your studies?' she said.

'Lord, no,' Smith said. 'Glad to get it over and done with.'

'Me, too,' said Long. 'My tutor was an absolute beast. If I saw him again, I would plant him a facer. Make no mistake.'

'Mine sent me down for putting gin in the water jug in my second year.'

'What a good lark,' Long said, chuckling. 'I got sent down for six months. For fighting. Pater was furious…'

She left them exchanging reminiscences and moved on.

'Everything all right?' a deep voice asked from behind.

She turned and smiled at Damian. 'Yes. Just the usual disagreements about nothing. All forgotten in the blink of an eye. Mr Long seems a bit on the quarrelsome side tonight, though.'

Damian narrowed his gaze on the topic of their conversation. 'Is he giving you trouble?'

'Not really. He is easily distracted as seems to be typical of a young man feeling his oats.'

'Don't hesitate to call me if you need help.'

'I will. He is a recent addition to the guest list, I think. I don't recall seeing him before last week.'

'You are right. His family is very well connected. It would have been difficult to refuse him. Though I will, if you deem it necessary.'

'Not at all. If it happens again, I will have a quiet word with him.'

'Great men stand in dread of your quiet word,' Damian said with a twinkle in his eyes.

'No. Surely not.'

'Lord Stanley said he's terrified of one of your garden bear jaws about his drinking.'

'If he was terrified, he would stop,' she said drily. 'But I notice that he stays well within reasonable bounds since I had that talk with him.'

He put his arm through hers and they perambulated around the room. 'He's a sensible man.' They stopped at the table where Long and Smith had started to gamble. The croupier deftly handled the die.

All seemed well. She smiled at Damian and he nodded and moved on.

Without warning, Long grabbed the croupier by the wrist. 'Let me see those,' he said.

'Is there a problem?' Pamela asked brightly.

'She has been winning an awful lot,' Long said trucu-lently.

A mutter of disapproval rippled around the table.

Pamela winced at the belligerent tone. This needed to be nipped in the bud.

'Perhaps you would like me to have the die broken open?'

Long must have caught the note of anger in her voice. 'I...er...no. I was simply commenting on the bank's good luck.'

It was a dreadful thing to accuse a gentleman of cheating at games of chance. It was a slur against his honour. Indeed, any man caught cheating could expect to be ostracised from polite society. And, whether innocent or guilty, was quite likely to issue a challenge to save face.

In this case, since the profits of the tables went to Damian, he was actually the one being accused of cheating, even if the girl was the one in charge of the table.

Pamela put a hand on Long's arm, a light touch of her fingers. 'I am sure your luck will change.'

Long turned his gaze on her and his lip curled slightly. 'Well, it won't, since I won't be betting any more tonight.'

He swayed as if he was having trouble standing. He had clearly had more to drink that she had originally thought.

'The dancing will start soon,' she said. 'Have you secured a dance with the lady of your choice? Ladies always get claimed very quickly.'

His gaze sharpened somewhat. 'I choose to dance with you.'

'I am sorry,' she said, smiling at the drunken fool. 'I do not dance.'

She didn't need him tripping all over her feet. Or, worse yet, falling down. Besides, now she was a partner in the business, she never danced. Only the girls who worked at the tables danced with the gentlemen. And only if they wanted to. She doubted any of the girls would want to dance with this fellow.

'Perhaps it is time you went home. Shall I have your carriage brought round?'

'I came with Smith. He told me about the rooms upstairs. But I couldn't find anyone to bring.'

Those blasted rooms. While she knew it was a draw for some of the men and that they often spent more money trying to impress the woman they brought, sometimes they were a source of conflict.

'Perhaps you will bring a lady another time,' she said.

He peered at her from under the hank of blond hair. 'You and I could be a couple.'

'No, we could not. I need to look after the guests.'

He leaned closer. 'I am a guest. I want you to look after me.' He grabbed her wrist and started pulling her towards the door.

In all these weeks, it was the first time any of the men had challenged her and certainly none had laid a hand on her.

She glanced up to find Damian already heading her way.

She smiled at him rather shakily as he drew close. 'Mr Long, you know Lord Dart, do you not?' she said, trying to make it sound like an ordinary introduction.

Long glowered at Damian. 'Yes. It is in your pockets where my money ends up.' His voice grew louder. 'I was warned that the house always wins at Rake Hell.'

A few people close enough to hear gasped. And others began to draw closer to see what was going on. The *ton* loved a good scene as long as they weren't the ones involved.

Damian eyed the flushed young man standing before him. He was going to deserve every bit of his comeuppance.

Indeed, one more word and he was going to find himself being called out. And that would suit Damian's purpose even better than simply costing him his fortune. Not that he intended to kill the lad on the field of honour. He would simply make him look a complete and utter fool. It wasn't hard to do, with such a spoiled brat.

'Release Mrs Lamb's arm, there's a good fellow,' he said softly, but with a voice full of icy determination.

Long wobbled on his feet. He took one look at Damian's face and dropped Pamela's arm as if it were hot.

So much for Long being any sort of worthy opponent.

Damian curled his lip. 'Now, what is the problem?'

Long looked around at the staring faces. 'I was saying that the bank here always wins.'

Damian shook his head and looked around at the gathering crowd. 'Not true.' He found the person he was looking for.

'Lord Norris, did you not win one hundred guineas just last week?'

Norris grinned. 'I did. Losing it all tonight, though.'

'I did tell you last week to stop while you were ahead,' Damian said, grinning at the fellow. 'Not one to take advice, are you?'

Norris shook his head. 'It will turn about, you will see.' He headed back to the tables.

Others drifted away.

Pamela, who had looked frightened just moments before, now looked far more relaxed. She had been obviously glad to see him.

'But that wasn't what you were arguing about with Mrs Lamb, was it, Long? You were having a different kind of conversation.'

Pamela slipped away and left him to it.

Long hung his head. 'I wanted her to take me to the rooms upstairs.'

Damian's stomach tightened at the obvious insult. He wanted to throttle the fellow.

To his surprise, Pamela returned with Smith in tow. Long's friend.

'I am going home,' Smith said, clearly primed by Pamela as to his role. 'I have another party to attend.'

Long looked at him owlishly. 'You do?'

'Yes. A private party.' He winked.

'All right,' Long said. 'I will come with you.' He gave an exaggerated bow to Pamela and Damian and left.

'Young idiot,' Pamela said.

'I think he's the sort that is likely to come to a sticky end. Did he lose a lot?'

Pamela shook her head. 'I won't know until later.' The clock chimed midnight. 'Anyway, it is time to start the dancing now.'

And just like clockwork, the tables emptied and the orchestra began to tune their instruments.

Pamela hurried off to make sure everything was in order and he and Pip collected the money they had won.

'What was happening?' Pip asked, clearly referring to the contretemps from a few minutes ago.

'A bit of rudeness from one of our very important guests. I think it is almost time to call an end to the game,' Damian said.

He didn't want it getting out of hand.

When all the guests had departed, the three partners sat in Damian's study with a glass of whisky in hand, while Pip counted the money and Damian worked on the IOUs. It had become a ritual with them since Damian had done it the first time so Pamela could see exactly what was going on. It had worked so well, they had continued meeting and counting after each party.

'So many vowels,' Pamela said, looking at the pile of scraps of paper scrawled with numbers and signatures.

Damien wrote down the numbers alongside the names.

'I see Long lost a hundred pounds,' he said. 'That makes close to three hundred he owes us. I wonder if he can afford to pay?'

Damian hoped not. A man who couldn't pay his debts had to leave the country.

Pip looked up. 'He will have to borrow if not.' He wrote an amount in the ledger and pushed the bundle of notes and coins to Pamela to double-check his counting.

Damien could not help watching the businesslike way Pamela tackled the task. Businesslike and incredibly feminine.

Pamela put down a pile of twenty-pound notes. 'I don't think he should be invited again. I am guessing he drank so much because he is scared.'

Damian shrugged. 'As you wish. But my guess is he will take it very ill if he is not given the opportunity to win back some of what he lost.'

She looked concerned. 'Perhaps you should speak to someone in his family about what is going on.' She started counting the pile of guineas.

Damian gave her a hard look. 'Why do you care so much about the fellow? He came close to insulting you.'

'I believe the Longs were once friends with my family. It has been a great deal of time since I have seen any of them, of course, but I do not feel comfortable about letting him fall into a debt he might never able to repay.'

'He must repay,' Damian said. 'It is the rule.'

Either that or be forced to flee the country. What a satisfying result that would be.

Pip looked from one to the other. 'Well, my dears, I am *finis*.' He took the register from Pamela. 'It is time for my bed. I am off to Town early tomorrow. If you have finished, Madame Lamb, I will put the money in the safe and collect it in the morning to take to the bank.'

Pamela compared his total with hers and nodded. 'Please leave me twenty pounds in small denominations for purchases for the kitchen.'

He bowed. 'Very well. It shall be as you wish.'

Chapter Nine

Pamela leaned back in her chair with a sigh.

'Tired?' Damian asked his voice solicitous.

'A little,' she admitted. Bone tired, if she was to tell the truth. It might look as if she might do nothing but float around chit-chatting with the guests, but keeping some of these men civil and in order required a great deal of stamina. As well as diplomacy.

'Let me escort you to your chamber,' he said. The kindness in his voice made her feel strangely tearful. It was a long time since anyone had really cared about how she felt. Mother had been too busy establishing herself in London society to really notice much of anything.

Damian helped her to her feet and walked her along the corridor. 'You know,' he said, 'you really ought to move to one of the guest bedrooms. The bed in your current room is small and looks far from comfortable.'

'I like being near the kitchen. It makes it easier to get up and get the fire going first thing.'

'Hmmm. That is another thing. I think that you are really doing far too much. I am going to insist that we hire a new cook and relieve you of those duties.'

'Oh. But—'

'The cook would be under your supervision, of course.

But you go to bed very late after each party and then you must be up very early to make breakfast and such. Lack of sleep must, in time, wear you down.'

It was true. There were some mornings after a party when it was hard to make herself rise and get on with her day. 'Well…'

'There is a chamber in the west wing of the house you could use. It is in pretty good shape. Your scullery maid can make it up and the London staff will add it to their bedmaking duties.'

The west wing was on the other side of the house to the rooms their guests used. It was the wing where he and Monsieur Phillippe slept.

Cooking first thing and then spending the evening tending to their guests was tiring, especially since they continued their work far into the early hours after everyone left. She glanced up at him. There was only concern in his expression. Concern for her. It warmed her. She had the urge to hug him for being so thoughtful.

'You are right. It is tiring. Very well, let us hire a cook to replace me, if you think it is not too expensive.'

'Not too expensive at all since we can't have you looking haggard when our guests come, can we?'

'What will the other girls think?'

'It is not their business to think anything.' His voice was harsh. 'Besides, they are fully aware that you hold quite a different position in the household than you did when you first arrived.'

'Hiring another full-time servant to work for what is really only three days a week seems unnecessarily expensive. I can continue to look after the stocking of the pantry and so on. Why don't I hire someone from the village to come and cook on those evenings when the staff need feeding?'

He chuckled. 'Always so careful with our money. But, yes, if you think that would work, I agree.'

They had reached the door to her chamber. She turned to face him. 'Thank you for being so thoughtful.'

A faintly guilty look passed across his face. 'I don't deserve your thanks. It is more about what is good for our endeavour.'

He would never admit to being kind. He was the same when he was kind to the staff. He always brushed off any thanks.

Without thought, she rose up on her toes, put her arms around his shoulders and kissed his cheek. 'Thank you all the same.'

In a second, his arms were about her waist. He pulled her close and covered her mouth with his in a deliciously gentle kiss.

His breathing was harsh in her ears, his arms strong around her back, but tender, holding her as if she was some sort of delicate flower.

She felt womanly and feminine.

She leaned into him, kissing him back, opening her mouth as their tongues tangled in a dance of passion. Heavenly, heavenly kisses. Her heart beat far too fast and she fell into the dizzyingly lovely melding of mouths and felt the hardness of his body pressed against hers.

It was all too brief.

He broke away, gazing down at her. His gaze was hot, but also stormy, as if he were angry. His shoulders were rigid.

Had her unbridled desire caused her to ruin things between them? 'I am sorry,' she whispered breathlessly. 'I should not have...'

He gave a short sharp bow. 'You are right. It was ill done of me.'

'Oh, no. I did not... I mean...' Why on earth was she stuttering and stammering as if her tongue was too large for her mouth? Perhaps because her heart was still hammering in her chest.

'I will be driving up to London in the morning, please hire the cook as we discussed. Also have a woman from the village come and make up your new quarters while I am gone.'

'Oh.' Disappointment slowed everything to a crawl. 'When will you return?'

'In time for the next party, as usual.' His tone was frigid, almost arctic, as if he resented her questioning him. It wasn't as usual. He often stayed a few days after each party, having dinner with her each evening. It seemed that her kiss, her unwanted kiss, had ruined everything.

He reached around her and opened her door. 'I had forgotten how small this room was. Barely space enough to swing a cat.'

'I have been allocated worse,' she blurted. 'I find it cosy.' It was private, which was always a luxury when you were a servant.

His gaze hardened. 'I bid you goodnight, Pamela.'

He bowed and stalked away.

She watched him go. So tall. So manly.

What an idiot she was. The moment an attractive man came into her orbit, she could not control her desires. No wonder he had turned so cold. He must think her a wanton.

Heat washed through her at the thought of losing his good opinion as he must surely realise she was no lady.

Once more, embarrassment mixed with shame made her feel ill.

Clearly, she had done the right thing by leaving society. No doubt by now she would have made a fool of herself with some gentleman or other and caused her family a terrible scandal.

Obviously, she could not trust herself to behave in a ladylike fashion.

And now, located so close his bedroom, she was asking for trouble. The man was far too tempting for her carnal self.

And that was the problem. *She* was the problem. Something about her made a man forget he was a gentleman. And judging from the way he had withdrawn from her so abruptly, Dart also found her passion unnatural.

Unless she got herself under control, she was going to ruin everything.

No. She could not allow her proclivities to ruin her life. Would not.

No more kisses. No more passion. From now on it must be nothing but business.

Rain on the drive down to Rake Hall from London had soaked Damian to the skin.

Good.

He didn't deserve comfort.

He had almost let a sweet little kiss make him change his mind about the future, to divert him from his purpose.

A few days away from Rake Hall had helped him put things in a proper perspective.

Pamela was attracted to him, as he had intended. The fact that he found her alluring, that he liked her, had no bearing on his objectives. He could not afford to be softhearted. He had promised his father that those who benefited from the destruction of their family would be suitably punished.

He forced himself to recall the way his mother had looked those last few terrible months and how his father had sunk into despair. He had been unable to do anything for his parents while they lived, but he could certainly keep his promise to them now in death.

He finished making his horse comfortable, made sure it had food and water and strode for the house.

Stripping off his wet cloak as he entered the front hall, he made for his study and a nip of brandy to warm him up.

He stopped on the threshold.

Pamela, head bent over a ledger, was occupying his chair.

Instead of her cook's cap, her head was bare and her hair braided and twisted into ropes of gleaming chestnut.

Sensing his presence, she looked up. Her smile was hesitant, as if she was trying to judge his mood. 'Hello,' she said. 'You are a day earlier than I expected. I hoped to have this done before you arrived.'

'This?' he asked,

'Yes. I have been working on these ledgers. They are a bit of a mess and I thought to sort them out for you.' She frowned. 'There are some odd entries that I do not quite understand, but I am sure you can explain.' She turned the book towards him.

He glanced down and saw that she was talking about Long. The son of the man who, along with her father, had stolen his family's wealth. He had been keeping track of the young man's loans from the moneylender Damian had recommended. A man who acted for Damian and who was actually using Damian's money to make the loans. And because of this, Long received a better rate of interest than he could obtain elsewhere. Thus ensuring Damian held all of his debts.

How very clever of her to notice those entries as being different.

'What about them?' he said casually.

'I don't understand how he can be in this much debt. It doesn't seem to tally with his IOUs.'

Far too clever.

'I do not know anything about it. We will have to ask Pip. Do not worry about it.'

She looked inclined to argue.

'Did you manage to find a woman to do the cooking for the staff?' he asked.

'I did.'

'Is she to your liking?'

'She seems very competent. And she was very pleased to have the work. She does not mind at all that she will not live in.'

'Excellent. I hope she cooks as well as you do or the staff will be disappointed.'

She brightened at his compliment. It pleased him more than it should have to see that sweet smile.

'I actually had her make a couple of meals for me as a test before I offered her a position. She prepares good plain food. I am sure the staff will love it. And she is a very nice woman whose children are grown and who was very pleased to have a few days' work every week.'

'And have you settled into your new quarters? Are they to your liking?'

'I have. Thank you. The bed is exceedingly comfortable.' She flushed, as if embarrassed.

A buzz of excitement zinged through his veins at the thought of her in the middle of what he knew to be a large four-poster bed. He imagined all that gloriously coiffured hair of hers un-braided and free around her shoulders with that sweet smile on her face.

Too beautiful to bear thinking about.

'I see.'

She looked a little puzzled. Probably because he had sounded too gruff. Too uninterested when normally he had no trouble striking exactly the right note with the ladies.

'I am glad you find it meets your needs.' That didn't sound much better. He needed to call a halt to the awkwardness. 'I hope you will excuse me, I have some letters to go through and some bills to pay. I am sure you have things to do elsewhere. I will see you at dinner. I assume Cook will be sending our dinner to the small drawing room as you did?'

She shivered very slightly, perhaps chilled by his cool tones.

Chill was what he needed, distance, if he was going to keep his sanity. At least until he was prepared for the final act of her downfall. And that required careful orchestration.

'Yes, of course,' she said hurriedly.

'And you will join me, naturally.' There, that sounded a little more like himself.

'If you wish. Let me leave you in peace. I need to read through the menus I have prepared for Chandon. I can do that in my room.' She hesitated. 'That is, unless you would like to look at them. You know, approve them.'

'I am happy to leave the issue of menus in your capable hands. Why keep a dog and bark oneself?'

He winced. Not exactly the jolly quip he had intended.

With a cool nod, she picked up a couple of pages from the desk and bid him farewell.

Curse it. He had not intended to sound dismissive, where was his easy address? His charm? When it came to her, when he needed it most, it seemed to desert him. It was because of her. She didn't giggle or simper, the way many other ladies did. She was all business.

And yet, despite her air of competence and complete calm, he sensed a vulnerability in the depths of her gaze. Something, or someone, had hurt her in the past, though she tried very hard to hide it. Her bravery made him want to shield her from anything that might offer harm.

Though as far as he knew, the only person offering her harm was him. And he certainly had no intention of forgoing his revenge.

Absolutely not.

He had decided, had he not, that it was time to cease procrastinating and to forge ahead with his plan.

He just wished the idea didn't make him feel quite so uncomfortable.

Pamela gazed at the remains of her dinner, trying to ignore that the gentleman opposite her had barely spoken a word to her throughout the meal. She would have done anything to have been able to turn the clock back and undo their kiss. That brief moment of madness outside her chamber door had ruined everything.

Perhaps if she had not kissed him with such fervour, then they would have continued on in the easy manner they had developed in the weeks since she had arrived. A professional and friendly relationship that she had come to enjoy. No, not only enjoy. That she had come to rely on.

Now it almost seemed he was regretting offering her a partnership. She'd kissed him twice now—he probably thought she was a woman of loose morals who likely should not be trusted in his business. Perhaps he would worry that she would respond in the same way with other men and somehow put their enterprise at risk.

Was she even sure in her own mind that she would not?

The idea was like a hard cold fist squeezing the air out of her lungs.

They had eaten most of their meal in an uneasy silence, apart from the obligatory polite niceties.

'You are right, Pamela. It was ill done.'

She had gone over and over his words in her mind. He had ignored her forwardness twice now, but clearly she would not be given a third chance. Likely, if it was not for their written agreement, he would have been sending her on her way.

Well. She would make sure nothing like that ever happened again and, no matter how he behaved, she was going to continue as if nothing had happened.

'Did you find dinner to your liking?' she asked, unable to bear the heavy weight of silence any longer. 'I thought our new cook, Mrs Maize, did very well.'

She winced at the tentative tone in her voice. She sounded as if she wasn't actually sure. And she was.

'Clearly you have informed Mrs Maize of my preferences.'

She had taken great pains to do so.

He put down his knife and fork and gazed at her intently. 'The meal...' his eyes twinkled briefly '...was not a patch on the food you yourself prepare, but I am prepared to accept it, if it means your spirits are revived. Judging by your looks this evening, this is indeed the case.'

For a moment she did not quite take his meaning. As his words sank in, her face heated. Oh, my Lord, she was blushing. And there was a stupid sort of girlish giggle lodged at the base of her throat.

She swallowed. 'Thank you, My Lord.'

'Come now, Pamela, did we not agree to used our given names?'

'Yes, we did, Damian. I thank you for your compliment and for your forbearance. I agree there was a little too much salt in the soup and the chicken should have been a little more tender, but Mrs Maize is very willing to learn, so I am sure everything will soon be exactly to your liking.'

He leaned back. 'If her desserts are anywhere near as good as yours, I shall be a happy man.'

Happy.

That had been her goal, had it not, to make him happy. Or at least satisfied that he had not made the wrong decision.

She was determined to make this new venture a success. Determined to save enough to make her dream a reality.

He rose and went to the side table. 'May I help you to some trifle?'

'You may indeed.'

He set a dish before her and sat down. 'They say the proof of the pudding is in the eating,' he said with a boyish smile.

Just like that the atmosphere changed. They were easy with each other again, as if the kiss had never been.

'They do. You try it first. I will wait with bated breath.'

He chuckled. 'Are you worried I will send you back to the kitchen, if it does not pass muster?'

'I would like to see you try.'

He laughed heartily and raised his spoon to his lips.

'You will give your *honest* opinion,' she said with mock severity.

He tasted the confection. For a second, he paused, looking at her, laughter in his eyes like some sort of naughty lad bent on mischief. 'Excellent. All is as it should be.'

She let go her breath. 'As I expected. You must know I would not hire anyone who was not up to scratch.'

He reached across to where her hand rested on the table and took it in his. 'I trust you implicitly, my dear. You will pardon my teasing. You were looking just a fraction anxious.'

'Because you are so unpredictable.' She gasped. She had not intended to speak her mind right at that moment.

His eyes widened. Surprise, not anger. 'In what way?'

Heat travelled up from her chest to her face. But she had started this and it was too late to stop. 'One minute you are, well, all warm and friendly. The next you are as cold as ice. I do not know whether I am on my head or my heels.'

He leaned back and picked up his glass of red wine, looked at it reflectively and put it down again, as if he had come to some sort of decision.

'I find myself in somewhat of a quandary. I—' His voice was little more than a murmur.

She leaned forward the better to hear.

'You are a beautiful woman, Pamela. I was your employer and now we are business partners, yet against all social mores, I find myself drawn to you. I was trying...' There was a long pause.

'To protect me.' she put in.

'To protect us both, I suppose. I have a position in society to uphold.'

She frowned. Bewildered. 'As the owner of a hell?'

He chuckled. 'Of course not. I told you. This is not a hell. These are parties, to which only the noblest of families are invited. To receive an invitation to one of my parties is to be recognised as a member of *la crème de la crème*.'

She shook her head. 'I do not understand.'

'As one of the wealthiest men in England, I have no

need to win their money. Therefore, they can trust that I will not cheat them.'

How could that be when this house was decaying from neglect? And if he didn't need the money, then why do it at all? Why count every penny they won as if it was precious? 'Wealthiest?' She could not help the disbelief in her tone.

'Are you giving me the lie?' he asked mildly, but there was an edge to his voice.

'I simply do not understand why you would hold gambling parties if you do not need to make money from them. Why not simply go to White's or Boodle's or any one of a number of respectable gentlemen's clubs?'

'There. You see. You have identified exactly why.'

'I have?'

He got up from his seat, came around to her and helped her out of the chair and led her to the sofa by the fire. 'Let me pour you a brandy.'

She occasionally took a brandy with him after dinner, so his offer did not come as a surprise. 'Yes. Thank you.'

He went to the console and selected one of the decanters. 'You said,' he said as he poured, 'gentlemen's clubs'. No ladies allowed. Some friends and I were discussing this one evening at a ball and one of the ladies indicated that she thought it unfair that ladies were excluded. From there, we talked of opening places like White's to the ladies, much to the horror of the other men present.'

He handed her the glass and sat beside her with a brief lift of his glass in a toast.

She sipped at the brandy and savoured the smooth flavour.

'One lady suggested that they open a ladies' club,' he continued. 'No men allowed. Tit for tat. But where is the fun in that? I wagered that I could open a club where both sexes could mingle and enjoy together what normally they must enjoy apart.'

'But they have card parties all the time. Routs. Drums. Balls. There is always gambling.'

'Under the watchful eye of matchmaking mamas, dowdy dowagers and worried wives. Social strictures. Society's reins. Here, there is only fun in elegant surroundings and no questions asked. Anonymous fun that otherwise can only be had in sordid surroundings. The French are masters of it.'

'The rooms upstairs.'

'Indeed. Discreet rooms for couples who wish to avail themselves of the delights within them.'

'Those silly games are really such a draw?'

'Now you are a partner, I suppose you ought to be aware of *all* we have on offer.'

The dark note in his voice sent a shiver of awareness down her back. She took a quick sip of her brandy and realised she had swallowed it all in one mouthful.

It slid down her throat, warm and bracing. 'Yes. I suppose I should.'

She hoped she sounded more confident than she felt.

He finished his drink. 'Come.' He took her hand and together they walked upstairs.

Chapter Ten

Unto the breach, as his English compatriots were so fond of saying. Damian hoped he wasn't making a huge mistake by revealing this particular secret.

He had not been exactly lying when he said he was one of the wealthiest men in England. He held a great many vowels which, when added together with his own money, represented an enormous fortune. However, the chances of ever collecting on those mountains of debt were slender.

Indeed, he had no intention of attempting to collect on them. Or rather all of them. There was only one young man who would know the disgrace of ruin.

Yet it was hard to believe the recklessness of so many of his fellow peers. Did they even know how much they owed?

Unlike their debts to tailors and innkeepers and other tradesmen, the debts to him were considered debts of honour. Failure to pay a debt of honour had terrible consequences, should repayment be demanded and go unfulfilled. Dishonour was the thing most feared by any English gentleman.

Pamela's dishonour would be of a different sort.

A twinge tightened his heart. It would be hard on her, but it would not change her life so very drastically. At least, not as she lived it now. It would bring dishonour to her family name, however.

She would never be permitted a place in society.

As they passed down the corridor on the first floor on the west wing, he lit the candles in the sconces beside each door. Her hand gripped his arm tightly. Clearly, she feared what he would reveal. Yet she trod boldly onwards.

Each chamber brought a different delight to his guests, as shown on the various pictures hung beside each door. It was through the last door that she would pass this evening. For some, the height of pleasure. And usually the most difficult to obtain except in the grubbiest of surroundings.

He turned the key in the lock and threw open the door beside the picture of a whip and spurs.

He held his candle aloft to pierce the gloom inside. 'Wait there, or you might trip,' he said quietly. 'Let me light some lamps.'

'Oh, my,' she said, as light gradually filled the room and revealed all its glory. 'It's positively medieval.'

He tried to see it through her eyes. The whips and restraints hanging on the walls. The long bare marble table gleaming white. The metal bars of the triangular whipping post. The schoolroom birch twigs in varying widths and lengths neatly hanging from hooks. The velvet cushions strewn on the floor in one corner offering a place for comfort.

She turned slowly around, then walked here and there, touching the implements of pleasure-pain. There was an odd expression on her face. It was not one of shock or horror, but rather of curiosity.

She picked up one of the whips and looked at him. 'They use these whips?'

His body hardened. He turned away from her. He had no wish to scare her off.

'They?'

'The men. They whip the women. I have never seen any-one come down looking beaten. They always look…'

'Well pleasured.'

She wrinkled her nose. 'The women like to be whipped?'

'Some find it exciting, yes. And believe me, it is not al-ways the man using the whip. More often than not it is the woman who has the upper hand, so to speak.'

English school boys and their birch canes. They loved to hate them.

She swallowed audibly. 'I see.'

He spun around at the huskiness in her voice. If his body had responded before, now he was rock hard when he saw the heat in her gaze.

She wasn't just curious or slightly intrigued. She was highly aroused.

In two strides he was at her side, gazing down into her eyes, gently cupping her face between his hands, feeling the flex of her jaw. 'My dear Pamela,' he murmured. 'Have you had some thoughts of a similar nature? Daydreams, perhaps, that leave you hot and bothered?'

She blushed and looked down, as if ashamed.

'It is all perfectly natural,' he said. 'These are adult games that hurt no one.'

'Have you played such games?' she asked, peeping up at him, her eyes wide.

He chuckled. 'I have. Does that shock you?'

She shook her head. 'I had no idea such things were con-sidered so…commonplace.'

Something was troubling her. 'Then you have heard of such things before?' It seemed odd that a girl brought up in such a sheltered household would have come across such knowledge.

She glanced around the room and gave a little shiver. 'Not really.'

She was no longer aroused, rather she was uncomfortable. The shadows in her grey eyes gave him pause.

Had something about this room brought back unhappy memories?

'Come. This is a great deal for you to take in. Let me escort you to your chamber. We can discuss it again another time, if you wish.'

She seemed to relax a little.

Puzzled by her reactions, so very at odds with each other, he took her hand and led her from the room, locking it behind him.

He placed her hand on his arm and felt it tremble. He wished he could understand what was going on in her mind.

The further they walked from the chamber, the more relaxed she seemed.

Was it possible that somebody in her past had whipped her and taken pleasure in it? He tensed. Only with effort was he able to calm his rising ire.

When they reached her new suite of rooms, a few doors down from his own, she stood back as he opened the door for her and gestured her to enter. 'Would you care for a brandy?' she asked. 'I took the liberty of filling a decanter for myself, I hope you don't mind.'

Not one decanter, he noted, but three with differing contents and some glasses neatly set about them on the silver tray on the desk.

'I am glad you did. It is no more than Pip or I would do.'

She poured him a glass of brandy and indicated he should sit beside her on the sofa near the fire. 'Thank you for showing me that room, this evening.'

'Well, now you know the last of my secrets.'

She gave him a sideways glance. 'I think perhaps not.'

He stilled. 'What do you mean?'

She smiled slightly. 'I suspect there is much about you that I do not know. Just as there is much about me that you do not know.'

'What else can there be to know? You are an excellent cook. You have a fondness for animals, dogs anyway, and you are a very intelligent woman.'

She turned slightly to face him, looking doubtful. 'You think I am intelligent?'

'Indubitably. Indeed, far more so than many of my male acquaintances.'

'You are very kind. But I think if you really knew me, you would think I am foolish in the extreme.' She gazed down into her glass for a moment and then tossed back the remains of her drink and set the glass aside.

Regret filled her face.

He took her hand. 'What troubles you? If you do not like the games rooms, then we will do away with them.'

'Oh, no. It is not that.'

'Then what?'

Pink stained her cheeks. 'It was my reaction to what I saw, if I must be truthful. I felt remarkably...' She shook her head as if unable to describe what she felt. 'You must think me...naive.'

He had the feeling that was not the word she had been about to use. Intriguing, indeed. He brought her small hand to his lips and kissed it lightly. 'You do yourself an injustice. Your lack of experience is only to be expected.'

She gave a bitter-sounding laugh.

He frowned 'Has some man taken advantage of you?'

A faint sigh left her lips. 'If that were true, I would feel less stupid.' She shook her head. 'I was engaged to a very nice young man. A soldier. We planned to marry as soon as he received his promotion. Both of our families were happy about the match. Indeed, it had been planned between them since we were children. So I was not as circumspect as I should have been. We were going to be wed, after all.'

Unexpected anger surged through him. 'He did not marry you?'

Her hand convulsed in his. 'He could not. You see, there was an accident during an exercise. A gun carriage broke free. It killed him instantly.'

'Oh, my dear. I am so sorry.'

'He was such a nice boy. Very sweet. Much too good for me.'

He frowned at the sadness in her voice. 'Why would you say such a thing?'

'My father would have been so disappointed in me.'

Her father had no right to be disappointed in anyone.

'So that is why you hired yourself out as a cook.'

'When Mother married again, she decided the only way to be comfortable again was for me to make a good match. She and her new husband had already picked out a groom. How could I tell her? I felt so ashamed.'

So, Pamela Lamb, was no innocent maid after all. Her journey to ruin had started long before Damian came along. She had simply managed to keep it a secret.

Now he would bring it to its natural conclusion. A twinge of guilt twisted in his gut. A feeling of pity hollowed his gut. He could, if he wished, set her free of the trap he had wrought. Let her walk away. He would still have his revenge on the other family.

Yet it was her father who had been the ringleader of the plot to defraud his father of his fortune, he who had turned his back on his father's pleas for help. Now her mother lived at the apex of society, queening it over lesser mortals, while his mother lay in a pauper's grave.

No. Pity had no place in his heart. He had vowed at his father's grave to take revenge on those who had caused his mother's death if he ever had the chance.

He would not turn away from his sworn duty because of a pretty face, a sweet smile and delicious kisses.

Pamela could not believe she was telling Damian her innermost secret. Perhaps it was because she had been unable to tell anyone else all these years.

Despite that he did not seem particularly shocked, he must now think her the worst sort of woman. The sort of woman who had so little respect for herself that she would lay with a man to sate her desires, without any thought of the consequences, for herself or her family.

A selfish, pleasure-seeking wanton.

The trouble was, he would be right.

Her heart squeezed. Misery rose in her throat in a hot prickling sensation. Why could she not follow the rules of her upbringing and behave like a lady?

These past few weeks she had begun to feel at home. As if she had found the place she belonged, where she was respected and valued. Now he would never look at her the same way again.

She wished she hadn't spoken.

Damian gazed down at her, his expression dark, his eyes unreadable.

She swallowed. Would he now demand she leave?

'I am sure you were not the first engaged couple to anticipate their wedding vows,' he said. 'You were both young. You had no reason to expect that you would not marry.'

The kindness in his voice had emotion welling in her

throat, hot and burning. She swallowed down the lump and forced a smile. 'It is kind of you to say so.'

He tipped up her chin and fleetingly kissed her lips. 'You are quite lovely, Pamela. Any man would be tempted.'

Her heart picked up speed. It wasn't the first time he had looked at her with such intensity. Usually, right before they kissed. The attraction between them had been obvious from the start, no matter how they had tried to ignore or deny it.

Since coming to this house, she had realised how lonely she had been in her quest for independence. When Damian was at Rake Hall, she did not feel alone. She felt at home.

When he left, she did not stop thinking about him. Wondering what he was doing, who he was with. Though she tried to pretend she did not care, the thought that he might be with a woman hurt terribly.

'Are you tempted, Damian?' she asked, emboldened by the heat in his gaze and by her own rising passion.

'Constantly,' he said, his voice a little rough.

'And yet you resist.'

'It is not honourable for a gentleman to importune a servant.'

'I am no longer a servant. We are partners. Equals. Perhaps we should stop dancing around each other and enjoy each other instead.'

Oh. Had she really said what had been in her mind for so long? It seemed where he was concerned she had no control at all.

A shadow passed through his gaze. As if he found her words disturbing.

'You think I am too bold.' She shook her head. 'There I go. Making the same mistakes again, as I did with Alan.'

'Your fiancé?'

'Yes.'

'Your boldness is captivating, my dear. But for all that, you are a lady—'

She pressed a finger to his lips. 'No. I can never again make such a claim. And to be honest, I have felt so alone with my secret. And now I have burdened you, too.'

'Alone and lonely.' He spoke as if he understood the feeling. 'You miss the companionship of a friend and a lover. Someone with whom you can share your innermost thoughts.'

'You do understand. Do you have such a person in your life?'

She winced and wished she could call back the words. If he answered yes, she was not sure what she would do. Probably cry.

'I have not known such companionship. As yet, I have been too busy to think of such things.'

'You have Monsieur Philippe.'

'Yes. I have my friend, Pip. He is the very best of fellows.' He gave her a look of deep sympathy. 'But you have no such friend in your life.'

She shook her head. 'We lived very quiet lives at the vicarage, before my father died. You might say my father was my best friend. We spent a great deal of time together. He died not long before Alan. And then my life changed completely.'

'Your stepfather is an earl, I understand.'

'How did you know that?'

'I made discreet enquiries once I realised you were not the common-or-garden cook I had expected. You use your own name. It was easy to discover your true identity.'

'Will you tell my family I am here?'

He shrugged. 'Not unless you desire it.'

'No. I do not.'

'Very well.'

Relief flooded through her. She gazed up at him. 'Thank you. You are a good man.'

His laugh had a sharp edge to it. 'Hardly.'

She turned fully to face him and, in a moment of longing and gratitude, kissed him full on the lips.

For a moment, like before, he hesitated, then he returned her kiss with passion.

Her heart sang. Her body trembled with desire. Instinct said there was no going back this time. And she was glad.

His kiss deepened. His tongue danced with hers. His breathing and hers mingled loud in her ears.

This was what she had missed. The excitement of body and heart and soul. The passion. The desire.

Longing filled her.

He groaned low in his throat, drawing back a fraction, gazing down into her face. 'Are you sure you want this?'

How could he even find the mental capacity to ask?

'Yes,' she managed to whisper. 'I want you.'

Very badly.

'Then you shall have me.'

The words sent a sharp pull at her core. She moaned her pleasure at the long-forgotten sensation.

He kissed her again at length, until her bones felt liquid and her mind dizzied. She was aware of his hands wandering her body in pleasurable strokes and caresses, slowly sliding under her skirts to caress her calves and her knees.

He rose up on one knee, bending over her, gazing into her eyes.

She reached up and pulled at the knot of his cravat, pulling the ends free of his waistcoat and then unwinding it from around his lovely strong throat.

He smiled as she began undoing his waistcoat buttons. 'I think this sofa is too small for the both of us, my darling.'

My darling.

What a chord of desire those words strummed through her body.

He pulled her to her feet, swept her up in his arms with ease and carried her into the bedroom.

The strength of him made her marvel.

She felt feminine and soft and yet strong enough to conquer the world, since he was her world.

Her insides tightened and pulsed with excitement. And the deepest desire she had ever known overwhelmed her.

When he set her on her feet, her knees buckled and he held her while she gathered herself together.

'Turn around, my sweet,' he said. She leaned on the bed while he undid the laces of her gown, then stepped out of it when it fell to the floor. Such a practical garment, not a flounce or a ribbon to be seen. And her chemise was plain cotton, not lace, but he seemed not to notice when he divested her of her stays and spun her back around.

He cupped her face in his hands. 'You are so lovely.'

She relaxed. 'You also.'

'Lovely?' He laughed. 'I do not think so.' He toed off his shoes.

'I will judge.' She helped him pull his shirt over his head. His shoulders were broad, his chest wide, and she ran the tips of her fingers through the triangle of dark curls before kneeling to peel off his stockings.

His fingers busied themselves in her hair, pulling pins until her hair fell down around her shoulders. He brought her to her feet and lifted her on to the bed.

He stroked her hair, spreading it out on the pillow. 'How soft,' he said, his eyes full of appreciation.

He climbed up on the bed alongside her.

He stroked her cheek and kissed her lips, tenderly at

first, but when she slid her arms around his neck and kissed him back, hard and furiously, pressing her breasts against his chest, feeling his hardness against her thigh, he moved over her, parting her thighs and stroking her mons and the little tiny nub within its folds.

Pure bliss. Darkness and waves of pleasure overwhelmed her.

Damian watched *le petit mort* overtake her with a sense of astonished wonder. He had not realised she was so close to the edge.

Carefully he eased his shaft inside her, riding the last waves of her orgasm as her tight passage spasmed around his engorged flesh.

He had never been with a woman so incredibly quickly aroused. Even as her orgasm began to wane, he moved slowly inside her, taking one tight nipple between his lips and suckling gently.

A sound of appreciation came from low in her throat and her hips moved in counter-change to his movements, grinding her sweet soft flesh against the hard bone of his pelvis.

He played with her other nipple with the fingers of his other hand, alternating from one to the other, before moving to her throat, kissing and licking and nipping until he sensed her passion rise again.

He rose up on his hands to look down into her face, her lips full from his kisses, her eyes heavy lidded and soft.

Her hands came up to roam across his chest in small circles, her fingers gently tweaking his nipples every now and then.

She grabbed his shoulders and pulled herself up to kiss his lips.

As she fell back, he followed her down, delving into her

delicious mouth with his tongue, pressing her slender lithe body into the mattress with his weight.

Her legs came up around his waist, opening her hot slick passage to better accommodate his hard shaft, and his mind went blank, aware only of pleasure and the pain of waiting for her to be ready again. It was the purest, most delicious torture.

And then he felt her tighten around him. She made a sound of encouragement and he thrust harder and faster and finally she let go and fell apart.

Pleasured nigh unto death, he followed her into the abyss.

At some point during the night, Pamela had snuggled into Damian's arms. Awaking with the sensation of someone spooned within the curve of his body, one small pert breast filling his palm, the soft fullness of her bum against his groin, was delightfully surprising.

They fit together as if they were made for each other. Only the sound of her gentle breathing disturbed the quiet.

Damian rarely slept beside his bedmates. As a youth, his amorous adventures had been quick stolen moments with ladies of the opera while avoiding the attentions of the local gendarmerie.

More recently, he had enjoyed the company of a couple of wealthy widows who'd been only too pleased to embrace his fleeting attentions while maintaining their independence.

He had avoided any and all lures thrown out by matchmaking mamas who had seen him as fresh meat on the marriage mart upon his arrival in town.

Pamela sighed and stirred in her sleep.

Damian held perfectly still, for some reason wishing to maintain the feeling of oneness for a moment.

Even as the thought occurred to him, he shook off the odd longing and eased his arm from beneath her body and slipped out of the bed.

She stirred again.

He pulled the covers up over her bare shoulder, leaned over her and brushed her cheek with his lips. Her mouth seemed to curve in a smile.

She really was quite lovely.

And the fact that she had not been an innocent maiden made his task all the easier.

Calming maidenly fears had been one of the few things with which he had little or no experience. He had found the thought daunting.

Instead, he had discovered she was a deliciously sensual woman, who had given him one of the most pleasurable nights of his life.

He pulled his shirt on over his head and gazed down at her. With her hair burnished by the morning light spread across the pillow and her face in sweet repose she looked as sweet and innocent as an angel.

Perhaps he should forget about ruining her and her family and simply enjoy their relationship, here in the quiet of the countryside away from prying eyes.

Without doubt, if he continued the course he had chosen, their affair would end instantly and on a very sour note.

He shook his head at his foolishness. His weakness. He should know better than anyone that appearances were deceiving. Pamela was no innocent miss. And her family had played a major part in the ruination of all he had held dear.

The grand crescendo to his revenge was all arranged. The stage set and the play to open three weeks from today at his first society ball in his newly furbished London town house.

The invitations had gone out and the replies were flooding in.

No stopping things now.

Nor did he have the right. For the last ten years of his life his every waking moment had been building towards this end. To stop now not only would be a betrayal of the promise he had made to his parents, but would surely mean he had lost every last shred of his honour by being too cowardly to take action, because he feared being hurt by the consequences. Again.

The recollection of his cowardice all those years ago left a bitter taste in his mouth.

He would never forgive himself.

Damian had watched as his father opened the letter from Vicar Lamb. Watched his hope turn to despair and then rage. The letter had rejected all claims of culpability, denied any knowledge of the scheme that had brought in thousands of pounds and expressed false regret at being without the financial wherewithal to help. Sick at heart, Damian's father had tossed the letter on the fire, but Damian remembered every word.

Not long after that, his dear sweet gentle mother had become ill and when she died Damian had sworn to avenge her death. It had taken him years to reach this point.

The satisfaction of achieving his goal would make the years of struggle worthwhile.

As he had intended, he finished dressing in his room and headed for Town.

Chapter Eleven

Three days later, Pamela, seated in the study, going through the menus for the following day, could not quite believe how easily she had settled into her new life as a partner, both in business and as Damian's lover.

She enjoyed both aspects of her life. Preparing for the parties at the house, making sure they ran properly, was her first priority. Overseeing both the new cook and the rather dramatic Chandon was a challenge she also enjoyed and tested her organisational abilities to the full. Watching her nest egg grow in the ledger accounting for her part of the profits was especially satisfying.

The cottage she had imagined in her mind was no longer a vague fanciful daydream. It was now a possibility which she would soon turn into reality. If only she did not have such nagging doubts about the amount of money their guests were spending.

At least they were not getting as badly dipped as at first. After the evening when she had expressed reservations about the enormous pile of vowels they had accepted, the number had dwindled to very few.

When she enquired about it of Monsieur Phillippe, he had said that she was right to be concerned about the issue, because when they sold those vowels to a money lender, they were hugely discounted. It really was not worth their while to accept IOUs from those who likely were unable to pay their debts immediately, if ever. The fact that Damian and Monsieur Phillippe had listened to and acted on her concern had pleased her enormously.

One consequence of this new policy was that the number of people attending the parties had fallen. Not dramatically, but noticeably.

She glanced down her list of what was in the pantry and decided that the only thing she need order were peas.

The wine order, which was in Damian's purview, had arrived the day before and had been safely put away in the cellars. Fresh-cut flowers for the hall had been delivered this morning and she had arranged them in vases herself. Everything else she required was on hand.

'Good morning, my dear.' Damian's deep voice sent a zing of pleasure deep to her core. It always did.

She turned from her papers to see him standing in the doorway, hat in hand, his hair damp and slicked back, cheeks slightly reddened by the weather and his dark gaze warming when she returned his smile.

She had been expecting him and had dressed accordingly. She had purchased several new fashionable gowns now that she no longer wore her servant's garb and cook's apron.

'Good morning,' she replied, unable to contain her broad smile of welcome. 'All is well?'

'It is. Apart from the weather.' He set his hat and gloves on his desk. 'I really must get out of these wet things, it is raining cats and dogs out there.'

She realised that while his redingote must have kept his shoulders dry, his pantaloons were soaked to the knees. She began unbuttoning his coat, to help him get if off.

'Speaking of dogs,' she said, 'where is yours?'

'I left Oddy in town. He and the boot boy have made friends, thank heavens, and since I will only be away for two nights, he will be perfectly all right.'

'Only two nights.' She could not keep the disappointment out of her voice, no matter how hard she tried.

'Tomorrow will be our last party here.'

She gasped and stepped back. That she had not expected. 'The last?'

'Before Christmas, at least. Many people will be leaving London for their country estates or be busy with other holiday events. Even this week I received a number of declines to our invitation due to other social events.' He shrugged out of his coat and flung it over a chair. 'Besides, I have decided to throw a grand ball at Rake House.'

Rake House was his London town house in Grosvenor Square. That was where he lived when he wasn't here at the estate. He had told her that it was undergoing renovations and unfit for entertaining.

'I see.' Her heart felt heavy. She looked forward to the parties, particularly since it meant he would spend a few days with her. 'When will the parties here resume?' And what on earth was she to do with herself until they did?

'I am not sure they will.'

Her stomach dropped away. What on earth could he mean? The earth seemed to drop beneath her feet. She grabbed his arm. 'Why? What is wrong?'

He pulled her close, briefly kissed her cheek, smiling cheerfully, seemingly unaware of her surge of anxiety. 'We can discuss all this tomorrow night when Pip is here. Naturally I will need your assistance at the ball. Let me go and get out of these wet things.' He hurried off.

Her chest tightened. It was almost as if he was feeling

guilty. And what did he mean about her assisting with the ball?

And how typical of a man to make a dramatic announcement of what sounded like the end of their partnership and then disappear without explaining.

It really would not do.

Her mind in a whirl, she delivered her order for peas to the new cook, who would drop it off with the greengrocer on her way home, and went upstairs in search of Damian.

She entered his chamber without knocking, slamming the door behind her.

He was naked and rubbing at his hair with a towel.

He looked magnificent, broad shoulders, long limbs, dark hair everywhere.

He lowered the towel and gazed at her. His male member hardened and lengthened and rose to stand erect against his belly.

Her body stirred the way it always did when she saw him in all his glory and ready for her.

'Oh, you are pleased to see me,' she murmured, her anger dissipating, her breath quickening.

He laughed and in two strides was across the room and holding her in his arms. 'What a naughty wench you are.'

She reached down and cupped his testes, revelling in their delightfully heavy weight.

He groaned and rubbed his shaft against her hip in an explicitly suggestive thrust.

Feeling the surge of wetness between her thighs, she widened her stance in invitation.

He pulled up her skirts and entered her with one swift thrust. She leaned back against the door and held tight to his shoulders as a pleasure flooded through her body.

With him naked and her fully clothed it felt so erotic.

She reached down to squeeze his hard round bum with one hand while holding tight to his shoulder with the other. She kissed his neck, then nipped it.

With his hands flat on the door, and her pinned against it, he thrust into her hard and fast and...

Pleasure flooded through her even as he reached his own climax.

Somehow he managed to stop her from sinking to the floor and carried her to the bed. They lay side by side, panting.

'Devil take it,' he said. 'I had intended to make love to you after dinner. Long and slow.' He kissed her cheek. 'You undo all my good resolutions.'

'There is no need to forgo your plan,' she teased. 'I am sure you will be ready again by then.'

Oh, goodness, what was she doing? She had almost forgotten her purpose for coming up to see him. As always passion was her master.

But she was calmer now. And ready to listen to his explanation of his earlier remarks.

She trailed a finger through the crisp curls on his chest. 'What did you mean about never having any more parties here?'

'Oh, so that is why you came is it? Not to ravish me.'

She chuckled softly. She loved the way he accepted who she was. 'I was actually going to suggest you might want me to bring up hot water to bathe, since you got a soaking. But, yes, I did have an ulterior motive.'

He grabbed her wandering hand and brought her fingers to his lips. 'At least you are honest.'

'Would you?'

He shook his head as if to clear it. 'Would I what?'

'Like me to fetch water for a bath.'

'If anyone is going to fetch water, it will be me,' he

growled, nibbling her ear. The arousal he had satisfied a few moments before stirred again.

'Don't,' she whispered. 'You know what that does to me.'

He chuckled. 'All right. But only because it is too soon for me. Although there are all those other ways we can resolve the problem.' As he had shown her more than once.

Whereas Alan had been horrified by how easily she was aroused by the slightest touch, even suggesting there might be something wrong with her, Damian thought it wonderful.

'And you won't be entertaining here any more?' she asked tentatively, with a feeling of dread rising up to clutch at her heart.

He sighed. 'The parties are losing their cachet. It is no more than I expected. What was wicked and interesting has become pedestrian and ordinary. Soon enough the *ton* will move on to some new novelty. I would sooner leave them while they still want more than become a has-been.'

She shivered at the thought. Both at the tawdry image he invoked and at the thought of what this news meant. Their business partnership would end. But what about them? Their future. She had not looked beyond each day, until now, preferring to enjoy what she and Damian had, rather than look to what might lay ahead. Would he want her to remain here? Cook for…for whom, if there were not to be any more parties? Her heart seemed to miss a beat. 'What will we do?'

'You may do whatever you wish.'

'What do you mean?'

'You are rich now. You have choices.'

Was he saying they would no longer be together? The thought shocked her. Sent a piercing pain straight to her heart as if she had been struck by something sharp.

He had never made her any promises. Indeed, if she

thought about it, he had almost deliberately avoided talking about the future until now. As she had. Because they both knew there was no future. She was not the sort of woman a nobleman could marry. She had been mistress to two men now. And thoroughly enjoyed it, if she was to be honest.

But now, when it was clear they would likely soon go their separate ways, she could only wish things could be different. That she could be different.

Choices. He made it sound as if it was a good thing. But there was one choice she did not have. To go back and start again. She tried to sound happy, not miserable. 'So I do.'

She hoped her misery did not colour her words.

Damian hadn't thought breaking the news to Pamela would be easy, but he had not expected it to be so damnably difficult. Or that he would feel quite so guilty. Or feel a sense of loss. But then he had glimpsed all of the future.

She took a deep breath as if steadying herself. 'Let us make sure your Christmas ball is the best party any of them have ever attended. Really leave them wanting more.' The bravery in her voice caused his heart to seize as if it had been stabbed by a knife.

He wanted to hug her and tell her everything would be fine. But that would be an outright lie. He never lied when he could tell the truth. Or at least some of it.

'That's the ticket,' he said. 'You do not know what the future will bring.' He knew. Some of it.

'When is your ball to be held?'

'In three weeks' time. It will be one of the biggest social events of the season. A masquerade, of course.'

It would also be the last time anyone in London would admit to knowing him, if it all went well.

'You will act as my hostess, of course.'

She rose up on her elbow, looking down at him, her expression angry. 'Certainly not. That will not do at all. Everyone will recognise me as the woman who runs your gambling hell. Your ball will be considered beyond the pale, should you attempt to foist me off on the *ton*. No one will attend.'

He sat up with a frown and cupped her cheek in his hand. 'None of my guests has ever seen your face.' He kissed the tip of her nose.

She jerked away. 'It will take them but a moment to recognise me. It is impossible.'

He lay back down and stretched. 'Leave it with me. Nothing is impossible.'

'I mean it. I will help you from behind the scenes, but that is all I will do.' She lay down with her head on his shoulder and was quiet for a while. 'Will there be gambling, the same as here?' She wrinkled her nose, no doubt thinking there were those among the *ton* who would likely not be impressed.

'There will be a card room. It is expected. But nothing like our parties here. Just tables available for people to play cards. No croupiers.'

She chuckled. 'No special rooms upstairs, either. We don't want to shock all the old denizens.'

But that was exactly what would happen, but for a completely different reason.

She snuggled closer, her lithe body fitting along his side, her leg resting on his thigh in a most erotic manner.

His body hardened. 'We will go over the details later—right now I have other things on my mind.' He rolled towards her and kissed her cheek.

She glanced down at where his erection pressed against her thigh. 'So I see.'

Such an earthy woman. Direct. Honest. Incredibly passionate. He was going to miss her terribly when they parted. And that was not all he would miss. He would miss her companionship. A strange pang caught at his heart.

Not once in his adult life had he felt any regret about ending an affair.

For some reason Pamela was different. It was almost as if they were made for each other. He shook his head at himself for his maudlin thoughts.

She was not the woman for him. Their pasts made it impossible.

She reached for him.

'Slowly does it,' he murmured. He wanted to savour what might be some of their last moments together. 'Let us take our time. I want you out of those clothes first.'

The next evening, the three of them sat in his study counting the proceeds of the last party Damian would ever hold at this house.

'What will you do with Rake Hall, now that you won't be holding any more parties?' Pamela asked once the ledgers were closed.

He couldn't sell the house, because of the entail. 'The farm already has a tenant, so I suppose I will put in in the hands of an agent and try to rent it out also.'

'You do not want to live in it yourself? You must have so many memories of your childhood here.'

Pamela had an uncomfortable way of getting to the heart of things that troubled him.

'I was very young when I left here. Most of my youthful memories are from France.'

A stricken expression crossed her face. 'Will you return to France, then?'

'Perhaps. I am not sure when, though. I thought I might travel to the Americas.'

'America is a wonderful country,' Pip said. 'I have a cousin in Canada. He writes of its vastness. There is a lot of opportunity, I think.'

'It is so far away. It will take weeks to get there.' She sounded sad.

'Many weeks,' Pip agreed.

'Especially during the winter,' Damian added. 'I hear the Atlantic storms are quite fierce.'

A shudder shook her slight frame. 'I prefer to remain on dry land.' She looked unhappy.

As unhappy as he'd begun to feel these past few days. He half wished she hadn't been so easy to find. It would have been easier if the Vicar had left behind a son, instead of a daughter. A very beautiful daughter who... Regrets had no place in his thoughts.

There was nothing he could do, even if he wanted to, except take comfort in the fact that she would not be left destitute. What he must do was focus on his plans

'Pamela, you will travel to London with me tomorrow,' he said. 'There are a great many arrangements to be made if the ball is to be a success. In addition, you will need several new gowns.'

'Why? I told you, I do not plan to go out in public.'

'Damian tells me that you fear you will be recognised,' Pip said.

'I do not fear it, I know it. Many of your guests have met me over these past few months.'

'Not if you listen to me. Wear a dark wig. A touch of make-up, a change of accent, not even your mother will know you. Trust me in this.' He looked very pleased with himself.

She looked to Damian for his opinion.

'It will only be for a couple of weeks,' he said, with an encouraging smile. 'I will introduce you to all as a distant cousin acting as my hostess. I certainly hate to think of you shut up in the house, when we could be going about together.'

Despite being clearly tempted, Pamela still looked doubtful. 'Your distant cousin?'

'My distant widowed cousin. We will give you a new name, change your appearance, and no one will know the difference.'

'I can darken your eyelashes a touch and your brows, add a beauty spot,' Pip continued, clearly enthused. 'Indeed, you will not know yourself.'

'Do not forget,' Damian added, 'you have been masked all this time. It is quite likely you would not be recognised even without these changes.'

'You sound as if you have experience in such matters,' Pamela said to Pip, clearly intrigued by the idea.

'*Ma mère*, she was an actress,' he said. 'I spent many hours as a child watching her put on her *maquillage*. Sometimes even helping her.'

'Oh. I see.'

'I see you think I am not respectable,' Pip said with an easy chuckle.

'Not at all. For some reason I thought you were of noble birth.'

He shrugged. 'It is possible. On my father's side. But how is it one could know?'

'It doesn't matter one whit to me,' Damian said. 'You are my friend.'

'New clothes will make a difference, too. They must be the height of fashion. You will see. You will dazzle them into blindness.'

She smothered a laugh as if the idea was madness, but Damian could see she was beginning to weaken. After all, it was a chance for her to shine.

He felt slightly ill at the thought of all that brightness he saw in her eyes being snuffed out in an instant.

Dammit. He would not think like that.

She hesitated, then finally nodded.

Instead of feeling delighted, he felt…sad.

'So,' Damian said, forcing himself to sound carefree, 'it is decided. We will close the house for the season and you will travel up to town with me tomorrow.'

'The furniture should be put under holland covers,' she said. 'The pantry emptied and the remaining food donated to those in need.'

'Do not worry about it. I will put all in the hands of my agent.'

'Wonderful,' she said. 'Then all I need to do is pack.'

'Exactly,' Damian said. He pulled her close and kissed her lips. 'But not tonight. It has been a long day and I need you in your bed.'

Her gaze turned hot.

Pip threw up a hand. 'Excuse me. I will retire. I bid you goodnight.'

He closed the safe, locked it and left.

'Poor Pip,' Pamela said. 'He needs a wife.'

'I think he would be horrified by the very idea. He is too much of a butterfly to ever settle down.'

Pamela laughed.

Damien reached for her hand. 'Come here, my lovely. I have been looking forward to holding you in my arms all day.'

And that really was the absolute truth.

* * *

Pamela clung to the side of Damian's curricle as they bowled along the frosty country lanes with high hedges and tight corners at a pace she could only describe as foolhardy. His vehicle was of the high-perch sort. Exceedingly fashionable among young blades, but, in her view, exceedingly unstable.

Damian must have sensed her concern because he snaked an arm around her shoulders and pulled her closer. 'Do not fear, my dear, I am an excellent driver.'

'You cannot possibly know what is around the next corner.' she said, 'You are going too fast.'

'If there is something around the next corner, there is lots of room to pass. I have travelled this road many, many times and not once have I run into problems.'

Even so he slowed their pace.

For which she was grateful.

She was grateful for a lot of things. The improvement in her financial stability, the passion she had found in his arms, the joy she had found in his company, even though it was coloured by the sadness of loss. She could not deny she would miss him. Or that the thought of him leaving made her heart ache.

She could not imagine wanting another man, the way she wanted Damian.

What she had felt for Alan paled in comparison for the emotions twisting her heart every time she thought of Damian's departure.

Then she really must not think. It was simply too painful.

At the next junction, a finger post pointed one way to London and the other to Brighton. They had reached the main road. Twenty miles to London. By mail coach the journey always seemed interminable, but in this vehicle it would take no time at all.

The highway was wider and straighter than the country lane and she felt able to relax in her seat and enjoy the journey.

A mail coach lumbering in the other direction reminded her of the discomforts she had endured travelling from one position of employment to another. Now she was enjoying the comforts of a well-sprung vehicle that ate up the miles and provided lovely views of the countryside.

The horse settled into a trot and Damian manoeuvred around several slower vehicles with ease and skill.

'It is a long time since I was in London,' she said to fill the silence.

'Did you miss it?'

'Not at all. I prefer the country.'

He grimaced. 'I prefer the city.'

'Why is that?'

'There is too much solitude in the country. I like people. You never speak of your family. Do you not miss them?'

She froze. How to answer such a question? 'There is only my mother left and she married again. I do not particularly like her new husband.'

'Because he replaced your father?'

She sighed. 'Perhaps. It annoys me, how she fawns over him. She never did so with my father. They were always arguing.'

'About what did they argue?'

'I was not party to their discussions. I mostly heard heated voices, but I believe it was about money. Father was a hopeless spendthrift. For the most part, Mother managed the finances. Except now and then and he would spend money without discussing it with her. Then they would argue. Anyway, Mother does not approve of me and my choices, so I am better off as I am.'

'I would give anything to speak with my mother again.' He sounded terribly sad. 'She died not long after we arrived in France.'

She touched his arm in sympathy. 'How old were you?'

'Ten.'

'I am sorry.'

'It was a difficult time. My father never got over the loss.'

'Whereas my mother happily skipped on to the next man who would keep her in the style to which she had become accustomed.' She could not keep the bitterness out of her voice.

'You resent her for marrying again.'

She huffed out a breath. 'I thought at the very least, she should have waited out the mourning period. I can't even think where she might have met him, to be honest.'

'She did well to capture an earl. He doesn't seem like a bad man to me.'

Startled, she stared at him. 'Do you know my stepfather?'

'I have met him once or twice at social events.'

Why had he never said anything? 'And my mother?'

'We were not introduced, but she was pointed out to me quite recently as being the widow of the late Reverend Lamb. There is a family resemblance and I put two and two together.'

'Oh.'

'She looked to be in fine fettle, if you are wondering,' he said.

'I was not.' She tried to rein in her anger.

'So you do not think she chose well?'

He seemed to understand her concerns without her saying anything. She sighed. 'I do not know what to think. I feel as though it is a betrayal of my father. And yet she has a right to be happy. Perhaps in time I will get used to it.' While she had seen no evidence of it, she sometimes had the sense that her mother and the Earl had known each other for a long time. As if they had secrets.

She could never forget how her father had collapsed during their last argument. It was hard not to blame her mother for his untimely death.

And then there was the way Mother had tried to marry her off to a rather elderly friend of her new husband. A man in need of an heir. Her mother could at least have stood up for her against her stepfather.

There was a pause, as if he was waiting for her to tell him more. For a moment, the full story was on the tip of her tongue. She swallowed the urge to unburden herself. While her mother might have sided with her husband against Pamela, making her life with them untenable, it was none of Damian's business.

'This part of the country is very beautiful,' she said, instead 'But rather hilly.'

'It is. We will stop at Streatham to rest the horse and for us to take some refreshment.'

An extravagance. No doubt he could afford it, given how much he won from his fellow peers. It was too bad that she had joined his enterprise such a short time before he brought it to a conclusion. Still, all good things came to an end eventually and she had put away a nice little nest egg. One that would keep her comfortable for a long time into the future, if she was careful.

'Will you miss Rake Hall when you leave?'

She really could not understand anyone wanting to abandon their ancestral home. Her father had been a younger son and had never owned a home of his own. The vicarage had been theirs as long as Papa lived and it had been very dear. Being forced to leave had been a terrible sadness.

'I haven't spent enough time there to miss it,' he said.

'But you did live there as a child.'

'I think I mentioned before that I scarcely remember those days.'

'Or you do not wish to?'

His grip tightened on the reins and the horse broke stride. 'Easy,' he said softly.

The horse settled.

'I do not remember them,' he said, his voice tight, 'because they are more like a dream than reality. My life changed a great deal when we arrived in France.'

'In what way?'

'It is a long story of little interest and here we are at the Red Lion.'

They had indeed arrived at the inn. As they pulled into the courtyard of the old Tudor building with its timbered walls and red-tiled roof, an ostler ran to the horse's head.

The man touched his forelock. 'I got him, Yer Lordship,' he said, looking at Pamela with curiosity.

How stupid of her. She should have asked Monsieur Phillippe to help her with her disguise before she left for Town. Or travelled in a closed carriage. Stupid indeed.

Damian jumped down and helped Pamela to alight.

The innkeeper bustled out and his eyebrows rose to his hairline as he saw Pamela.

'Mrs Clark and I would like a private parlour,' Damian said, using the name they had decided upon for his widowed cousin. There were several branches of Clark in his family.

The innkeeper bowed. 'Certainly, My Lord.'

They followed the innkeeper inside.

Chapter Twelve

In the inn's coffee room, Damian sat at a table by the window, waiting for Pamela to join him. Until meeting Pamela, he had deliberately not thought about his childhood before going to France. What had been his had been wrenched away by unscrupulous scoundrels. From then on, he had been forced to think only about survival as his mother's health declined and his father barely eked out a living from his tutoring.

Walking with Pamela in the grounds of Rake Hall *had* reminded him of happy times with his family, but the pain of what came afterwards had tainted those memories.

For a moment, he had thought about telling her the truth about his life in Marseilles. No doubt she would think he was looking for sympathy. He didn't need anyone's pity. He needed to implement his revenge.

And if it meant losing her, at least he would have the satisfaction that he had done his duty and kept his promise. Perhaps, then, the guilt he felt over what had happened to his family would be less burdensome. How bad would a few years in prison have been, if it would have saved their lives? Every time he thought about it, he felt like such a coward.

He rose when he spotted her entrance. 'I took the liberty

of ordering a light luncheon,' he said. 'We breakfasted very early and I thought you might be hungry.'

'That is kind of you,' she said. 'Thank you.'

He seated her opposite him. 'The food here is quite good, actually. I usually stop for a bite on my way through.'

'I am glad you thought to break the journey,' she said.

'From here, we should reach London in about two hours.'

'I am looking forward to seeing your town house. Monsieur Phillippe says the renovations you have undertaken are a marvel to behold.'

'Pip is the main architect of those improvements, so I am not surprised he is pleased.' He grinned. 'But, yes. The house is much improved.'

'Will you sell it, when you go to America?' Her grey eyes held a hint of sadness.

He could not let it trouble him. 'I will. Fortunately, it is not part of the entail.'

'And what happens with the Scottish estate?'

'It isn't worth much. I would be lucky to find a buyer. There is no house, only a swathe of poor land occupied by a few crofters and a section leased to a sheep farmer. The only other property was a house in Edinburgh that was sold years ago. Rake Hall is the only property included in the entail. I purchased the house in Grosvenor Street when I first arrived in London.'

It had cost him a pretty penny, but he had needed to do it to prove he wasn't some poverty-stricken bumpkin out to make a splash.

The waiter arrived with a pot of coffee and a tray containing bread rolls, butter, slices of ham and an assortment of sweet pastries.

To her professional eye, it all looked beautifully prepared.

She poured the tea and they helped themselves from the plates set before them.

'It sounds as if your plans are set then,' she said wistfully. 'I envy you going to America, but I do not envy you the journey to get there.'

'It will be a new adventure for Pip and me.'

'Will you ever return to England?'

Much as he hated to do it, he had to make it clear that once the ball was over, he would be gone from her life. He shook his head. 'If we decide to come back to the old world, we will go to France. We both grew up there.'

The pain in her expression almost brought him to his knees.

'And the title?' she asked. 'Your responsibilities as a peer of the realm. If you have a son, he will inherit.'

Clearly she was hoping something would make him want to stay. The irony of it all was a bitter taste. Sadly, eventually she would be glad to see him go.

'By the time I leave, I will have fulfilled all the responsibilities I deem important. As for the title, it can go into abeyance for all I care.' That was how he was supposed to feel.

'You are a republican at heart, then.' She chuckled. 'A revolutionary.'

He wasn't anything so grand.

'Politics do not interest me. *You* interest me.'

She blushed. 'Not enough to keep you here in England.'

'Would you want to go to America?' He froze. Why had he asked that question, for heaven's sake? What would he say if she said yes? His heart thudded in his chest as he awaited her answer. Hope or fear. Either way it could not come about once she realised he had deliberately brought about her ruin.

'No. I have other plans.'

He breathed a sigh of relief. Or was it regret? No. Not regret. He had no room in his life for more regrets. 'What will you do?'

'A small cottage in the country. A few chickens. Perhaps I will bake pies and cakes and sell them at a local market.'

'I am sure whatever you choose to do, you will do very well.'

She gave him a smile edged with sadness. 'Thank you.'

They finished their lunch and were soon back on the road.

As they both looked to the future, neither said very much on the rest of the journey.

Sitting at her dressing table, preparing for her day, Pamela could not quite believe she was enjoying herself. The moment she had arrived in London, the whirlwind had begun and she hadn't once been near a pot or a pan or a sink full of dirty dishes.

She recalled her come out as months filled with stress. This was altogether different.

Sukey stepped back from pinning her wig and nodded in satisfaction. 'Right as a trivet, Mrs C.'

The two of them had forged a friendship during their time at Rake Hall and Sukey had been more than happy to take on the role of ladies' maid during Pamela's visit to London. Apparently, becoming a ladies' maid had been Sukey's girlhood dream.

Now Pamela was trying to train Sukey, so she could find a job working for another lady, once Pamela returned to being a cook or whatever it was she decided to do once Damian left. Trouble was, she hated thinking about his departure.

'You could say *it looks perfect*,' she suggested.

'It certainly does,' Sukey said carefully in ladylike tones.

Pamela grinned at her. 'That's the ticket, Sukey.'

They laughed. 'I was thinking,' Pamela said, 'that you should call yourself Susan, it sounds more like the sort of name a ladies' maid would use and dressers use their last names only.'

Sukey looked doubtful. 'I don't think I can learn all this in three weeks.'

'Of course you can. You are doing brilliantly. I promise.'

The young woman smiled proudly. 'We best hurry up, if you want breakfast. You have the dressmaker coming for fittings this afternoon.'

'I was hoping to visit the glover before Madame Celeste arrives. Do you think you can accompany me? I would sooner you than a footman.'

It had turned out that Sukey—no, Susan—had instinctive, impeccable taste and Pamela had taken full advantage of it.

'Of course.'

Pamela took a last peek in the mirror, happy with her reflection, though the wig was still taking some getting used to, along with the darkening of her eyebrows and eyelashes, but if she was quite honest, she would not have missed this trip to London for the world. She was having so much fun!

And her nights with Damian were heavenly. She was determined to make the most of these last few weeks with him, and it seemed as if he felt the same way.

Damian was already seated at the dining room table when she entered the breakfast room. He looked up from his paper and rose as she entered.

He took her hand and kissed it. 'You look lovely this morning.'

Her face warmed at the compliment. 'Thank you.' She filled her plate from the buffet with eggs, ham and toast.

'What do you have planned for today?' he asked when she was seated.

'First Bond Street to buy some evening gloves and then a fitting with the dressmaker. Why?'

'I thought I might take you driving this afternoon.'

They had agreed that they should be seen out and about in Town, so people would become used to seeing his widowed cousin on his arm. When she looked in the mirror and saw how different she looked, she had become sure neither the people she had met at Rake Hall nor her old acquaintances would recognise her. Pip had done an amazing job and Susan had no trouble repeating the effect each morning.

'Why not?' she said. 'My new redingote arrived yesterday and I am dying to wear it.'

'Perfect.'

'Pass me your cup, if you would care for more tea.'

He did so. 'Thank you. How is the rest of the wardrobe coming along?'

They had also agreed that she would wear nothing but clothes of the highest fashion. After all, their masked ball was to be the event of the season. They had already chosen their costumes. They would go as Antony and Cleopatra, the theme of the party being Shakespeare's plays. The *ton* was already vying for invitations.

'I have my last fitting today. Madame Celeste is not only an excellent dressmaker, she is also very quick.'

'So I should hope at her prices.'

'I have only ordered what I think I must have, nothing more.'

He reached across the table and took her hand in his, giving it a gentle squeeze. 'A man must grumble, must he not? It is expected.'

She laughed. 'You are teasing. I should know that by now.'

'I like to see you rise to the bait.'

'Were you thinking we would attend Almack's?' she asked. 'I need to make sure I have a suitable gown, if so.'

Almack's was always the fussiest of the various events the *ton* attended. There it would be easy to make a mistake and get oneself excluded from the higher echelons of society. Men were required to wear old-fashioned knee breeches, but for every young miss new on the town it was a must visit.

'I don't think so. Neither of us is on the lookout for a spouse.'

'It will not look odd, if we do not put in an appearance? You, at least, are considered a good catch.'

'It will not look odd. I have made it clear I am not on the marriage mart. Not this Season. If ever.'

She chuckled. 'Never say never.' The girl he chose to marry would be a fortunate young woman. A little sadness stole into her heart. Sadness that it could not be her.

She shook it off. She had given up on the idea of marriage a long time ago. She was quite happy as she was. And would be even happier, once she had her own little house in the country. Would she not?

And yet the thought of Damian leaving, of never seeing him again, left a very empty feeling in her chest. More like a huge hole. What if they had met under different circumstances? If she had been a proper lady, not so wanton, would there have been a chance that he might have wanted more than an affair? Had she kept him at bay, acted the prim and proper miss, would he have thought more of her?

It seemed she had squandered the one thing any lady owned: her honour.

It seemed so unfair.

A man could sow his wild oats without any consequences…indeed, he would be thought peculiar if he did not. But a woman became a pariah. Unworthy.

He said he did not want to marry, but she had no doubt he would change his mind. When he met the right woman. Some young innocent, with stars in her eyes.

Something painful twisted beneath her breastbone.

She squeezed her eyes shut. What was the point in regrets? She could not change her past.

He finished his coffee and rose. 'Enjoy your shopping, I have an appointment with my man of business, but I will be back in lots of time to take you driving.'

He bowed and left.

She rang the bell and asked the butler to notify Susan she was ready to leave, then finished her second cup of tea.

It didn't help with the empty feeling inside her heart.

She forced herself to get up and get on with her day.

Susan was waiting in the hall, dressed in a cloak and hat, and she helped Pamela into her dark blue spencer.

Albert, who in London served as the butler, opened the door. 'I don't believe it will rain, Madam,' he said, 'but I think Susan ought to carry an umbrella just in case.' He handed one over.

'I don't believe that will be necessary and besides we are going shopping. There will be a great many parcels to carry, I have no doubt. Susan won't be able manage an umbrella also. Besides, you are unfailingly correct about the weather, Albert, so I do not think we need worry.'

Albert bowed. 'As you wish, Madam.'

Outside, Susan huffed out a breath. 'Thank you. I half expected him to insist we bring John along when you said I couldn't carry the umbrella.'

John was Susan's bane, because he wanted Susan to walk out with him and Susan had developed other ambitions.

* * *

Damian drove his phaeton around from the mews and drew up at the front door.

By the time the groom had gone to his horse's head and Damian had jumped down, Pamela was already on her way down the steps.

He really liked that about her. She never shilly-shallied and was always ready on time, if not a little before.

This afternoon she looked stunning. The new redingote she had spoken of at breakfast was made of dark burgundy wool with black velvet at the collar and cuffs. She carried a black fur muff on one arm and her hat, a small affair with peacock feathers, was set at a jaunty angle. The lip rouge and blush on her cheeks were so subtly applied one could not be sure it was there at all. The light net suspended from its brim to cover her eyes made her look mysterious.

Not to mention that the coat hugged her figure in all the right places. Places he knew all too well. Desire struck him the way it did every time he looked at her and especially when she gave him back glance for heated glance as she did now.

He fought to control the urge to take her indoors and say to perdition with driving in the park.

But driving in the park was all part of his plan. To be seen by the *haute monde*.

It was beyond a doubt that any man would be proud to be seen with her, although on occasion he found himself missing her more natural self, the chestnut-haired, fresh-faced young woman he had walked with in the countryside.

But that young woman wouldn't fit with their roles of young sophisticates out on the town.

He handed her up into the carriage.

'Congratulations on your choice of costume, my dear,' he said as they started off for Hyde Park.

'Thank you. It was very costly, but Madam Celeste gave me a discount, because I promised to let everyone know where I purchase my gowns.'

'Do not bother your head about the cost.'

'Why should I not? I think you forget that the cost eats into my profit as well as yours. I prefer to consider it as an investment and I need to get the best value for my money.'

Such an independent woman. She deserved... He forced himself not to think about what she deserved. That had already been decided. 'I beg your pardon. You are right, of course. And what do you plan to do with your ill-gotten gains.'

'Ill gotten? I thought you said—'

He put up a hand. 'I speak figuratively. In jest. I mean, what will you do with your share of our profits when we part company? Invest it?'

He shouldn't be asking, shouldn't care, since he was the one forcing them apart, but he couldn't help caring.

He was going to miss her when they parted. Badly. Far more than he ever would have expected. Somehow he had allowed her to get under his skin, to steal a part of him he hadn't known existed. His heart. Too often he found himself wondering what she would think about a particular matter he was dealing with. Or how she would react to something someone said. It gave him an odd pain in his chest to think of leaving her behind.

It should not matter one whit.

Her father certainly hadn't worried about his family. And yet... The thought of her destitute and alone had recently reared its ugly head and he found it disturbing.

'I will buy a house, somewhere close to the sea. I have

always wanted to live near the coast. And if there is anything left over, perhaps invest it.'

'So you will not continue as a cook?'

'I will continue cooking for myself. I suppose it will depend on whether I will have enough to live on, as to whether I will hire out to cook for others.'

Wouldn't humiliating her family be enough of a revenge? After all, she had not been directly involved in his family's downfall. Did he really need to ruin her utterly?

Devil take it, he did not need to be having second thoughts at this stage of his plan. Everything was set. Nothing would stop it now. Nor did he want to.

Well, he might want to, but that would be letting his family down, yet again. By being selfish. By thinking about himself instead of thinking of them. The guilt from his decision not to take the risk of imprisonment, a risk that if successful would have saved his family, was a heavy weight in his chest. The only way he could make up for it in some small measure was to keep his promise.

'I see,' he said steering them through the busy streets of Mayfair and to the entrance of Hyde Park.

Carriages were lined up along the street waiting their turn to enter.

'It is busy today.'

'The dry weather has brought everyone out.'

It was dry and crisp, if somewhat smoky from all the surrounding chimneys.

They followed a barouche through the gate and made their way along Rotten Row. Several gentlemen on foot tipped their hats when they saw him. These were men who had visited Rake Hall, but he also knew them from White's, a far more respectable gentlemen's club.

He waved a hand in greeting.

When their gazes fell on Pamela, however, their expressions turned puzzled. Would they eventually realise where they had seen his *cousin* previously?

He hoped not. Not yet.

A young couple waved a greeting. Long and a young lady, with her maid trailing them at a discreet distance.

'Dart,' the young man said.

Damian leaned down to shake his offered hand.

'Have you met my fiancée, Miss Frome?'

A fiancée. This was news. 'I have not had the pleasure. Miss Frome, I am honoured.' He bowed to the lady. 'Allow me to introduce my cousin, Mrs Clark.'

Pamela inclined her head.

Long, all smiles, bowed and Miss Frome dipped a curtsy. 'Pleased to meet you, Madam,' Long said with not a glimmer of recognition. He grinned shyly. 'I received your invitation to your ball, Dart. I did not expect it.'

'Did you not?' Damian said. 'I cannot think why.'

The young man looked relieved and slightly embarrassed. 'I was wondering if you would also invite Miss Frome.'

Whereas Damian could not have been more delighted. 'Of course. If you would be good enough to furnish me with your address, Miss Frome, it will be my very great pleasure to send you and of course your parents an invitation.'

The young woman blushed and handed over her calling card. 'You will find Father in *Debrett's*,' she said primly.

Pamala was delighted that Damian had invited Long. Since their altercation in Rake Hell, he had been back only a few times and was more subdued and polite towards her, having imbibed less of his drink, clearly atoning for his awful behaviour that night, although he had not been seen there recently. Likely because of his engagement.

Perhaps he deemed that he had sown all of the wild oats and now it was time to settle down. He was one of those who initially had been getting deeper and deeper into debt. One of those on Damian's list.

They bid the young couple farewell and the carriage moved on.

Aware of many curious stares and some of outright disapproval, she kept her back straight and her smile firmly pinned on her lips. No one would possibly recognise her as Vicar Lamb's shy, awkward daughter.

Not even her mother.

She hoped. Fervently. For that theory was about to be tested. Mother and her new husband were headed straight towards them.

She resisted the urge to tell Dart to turn the carriage around and gallop out of the park.

He glanced at her, clearly sensing her concern. 'Look them straight in the eye,' he said with a pleasant smile as if he wasn't discussing her immediate ruin. In a moment the two carriages passed each other and Pamela was proud that she met her mother's haughty gaze without flinching. There certainly wasn't a hint of recognition in that frosty glare. And if her mother didn't recognise her, no one else would.

A few moments later, a gentleman on horseback drew alongside them. 'Monsieur Phillippe,' she said, beaming at his handsome face and warm expression. 'Good afternoon.'

'My dear, Mrs Clark. May I say how delightful you look?'

'You may,' she said. And blushed at her boldness. Something about this disguise made her say things she would never have dared say as herself.

'I do wish you would call me Pip, as Damian does. We are friends, are we not?'

'Very well, Pip it is.'

Pip beamed and accompanied them along the Row when Damian set his horse in motion.

Pamela did her best to ignore some of the rather pointed looks askance. Once the party was over she would never see any of these people again.

She certainly would never tell her mother or anyone else for that matter about this adventure, but she did not regret it. Meeting Damian had added something to her life that had been lacking for a long time. Affection.

She was fond of Damian.

More than fond. He seemed to be the only person who valued all the parts that made her who she was: her skill in the kitchen, her organisational abilities and, of course, their compatibility in the bedroom. His passions seemed to match hers perfectly. He had given her a sense of accomplishment. A feeling of pride in herself as a person.

When she thought about him leaving, of never seeing him again, something hot and painful rose up in her throat. She was desperately trying not to let him see how the thought of losing him was hurtful, but it was getting more and more difficult each passing day.

If she said anything, she was sure he would be astonished.

Apart from their mutual passion, she had no real sense that he felt anything deeper than a mere liking for her. For him, theirs was a primarily a business partnership, with additional benefits.

For her, it had definitely become something more. What had begun as mutual passion had gradually changed into a deep-seated need that had grown tendrils around her heart. The idea of saying goodbye was almost too painful to contemplate.

She still could not believe that in two weeks' time their association would end.

She forced herself to be practical, calm, exactly the same as him.

'Do you know anyone who could assist me with the purchase of a property?' she asked.

'You are thinking about your cottage in the country.'

'I am.'

'My man of business ought to be able to help you, if you would like me to ask him?'

'Do you have an idea of where you would like to buy this cottage?' Pip asked.

'Somewhere quiet, near the sea. Perhaps Dorset.'

'A long way from London.' He shook his head. Such a waste. 'How sad.'

She laughed at his nonsense.

An older man driving in the opposite direction doffed his hat and smiled at them. Pamela recognised him from the club. Lord Luton. Would he have acknowledged her if he had recognised her? Likely not.

They turned at the end of the Row and Pip left them to greet some others who had gathered there, while they promenaded back.

A dashing woman driving her own phaeton drew up with a flourish of her whip. Her hair was jet black and her eyes bright blue. She wore a coat the same colour as her eyes. She was stunning.

'Dart,' she said. 'Back in Town, is it?'

A faint Irish accent, Pamela thought.

'I am.'

The woman eyed Pamela up and down and seemed to dismiss her. 'Call on me tomorrow. I will be at home.'

She cracked her whip and the horses moved off.

'Who was that?' she said.

'Lady Leis.'

'She is beautiful.'

'Do you think so?'

His voice was casual. Too casual. Pamela had a strange feeling in her stomach. 'Is she—?' She did not know how to phrase it.

He glanced at her face and then back to watching the traffic ahead. 'Is she what?'

How did one ask such a question?

'Someone you know...well.'

'Well enough.'

Now what on earth did that mean? And why would it matter?

Somehow it did. She felt bruised.

Oh, now she was being stupid. They were lovers. No doubt he had other lovers in his past. As she had Alan in hers. And if he had others in his present, why would she be surprised? Had she not seen how men behaved away from their wives while working at the club? Why would she expect him to be any different? Especially since she was not even his wife.

To give it a second's thought was foolishness. Besides, from his perspective, their relationship was based purely on lust. It would be better if she thought of it that way also. Perhaps that way she could stifle the ache around her heart.

And if she had a twinge of jealousy now, it was because of the other woman's beauty, not because she had a place in Damian's life.

'A penny for your thoughts,' he said.

Not even if he offered her a hundred pounds would she tell him what she was thinking. 'I was admiring that woman's hat,' she said, nodding towards a lady wearing a high poke bonnet festooned in silk flowers.

He grimaced. 'I prefer yours.'

And from that she had to draw what little satisfaction she could.

They were almost out of the gate when a town coach cut them off.

Pamela couldn't see its occupant, because the blinds were drawn down.

She looked at Damian to see what he thought of it.

'The Duke of Camargue,' he said softly. 'I wondered if he would be here today. Excuse me for a moment.'

He handed his reins to the driver of the other coach and climbed inside.

The Duke's coachman sat with impassive expression as the two carriages remained blocking the carriageway. Other drivers began complaining loudly.

A constable strode over to see what the commotion was about.

'Move along,' he said.

The driver looked at him down his nose. 'When the Duke is ready to move on, he will do so.'

The policeman backed away.

Oh, goodness.

'Perhaps if you moved a fraction to the side...' She began to suggest.

The driver shot her a scathing look and she subsided into silence.

A good five minutes passed and Pamela felt her face getting hotter by the minute.

One passer-by even reached for the bridle of the Duke's lead horse, but the same look from the coachman that had defeated the police officer sent the fellow scurrying away.

Finally, the carriage door opened and Dart jumped down.

In a trice both carriages were moving and the traffic began to flow.

'Wasn't that a bit rude?' she said as Damian guided his horse into the street.

'When you are the Duke of Camargue, one of the wealthiest men in the world, no one ever calls you rude.'

'Well, I do,' she said.

Damian laughed. 'You would. The Duke wants to buy my land that adjoins his property. He wasn't exactly pleased when I didn't jump at his offer.'

'Why didn't you?'

'He says he will put the crofters off the land to run more sheep. I am not keen on the idea. Those people have lived on that land for centuries. In truth, the land is more theirs than mine.'

He cared. About people he had likely never met. Her heart seemed to stop beating. A painful awareness swept over her. It wasn't just that she cared for him, she had fallen in love. If they hadn't been in so public a place, she might have blurted it out without thinking.

They had both made it very clear there were no strings attached. He might think she was trying to hold on to him. Or trying to get him to admit to something he really did not feel. It would spoil the rest of their time together, when she only wanted him to have good memories.

He was leaving for the New World. She had her own plans. And he had never shown any sign of feeling anything but mere fondness. How could he? After all, she was a fallen woman.

'Besides, he isn't offering nearly enough,' Dart said.

She didn't believe him. His words were merely a front. She would not let him make her think he cared only about money.

Chapter Thirteen

The next day, when Damien entered the breakfast room after his early morning ride, he was surprised to find Pamela there ahead of him looking delicious in a morning gown of dark rose.

'Good morning, my dear.' He kissed her cheek.

She turned a beautiful shade of pink. 'Good morning, Damian.'

'You look ravishing, I must say. Good enough to eat. Where are you off to?'

She chuckled. 'I am going to Covent Garden this morning to see about the floral decoration for the ball.'

The hairs on the back of his neck rose. 'Send for the nursery man to come to you. Covent Garden is no place for a lady.'

'Really, Damian. A lady? I have already met with the nursery man. He is outrageously expensive for the particular item I am seeking. I am sure I can get it much cheaper at one of the smaller stalls.'

'There is no need to scrimp and scrape.' He browsed the buffet and helped himself to eggs and ham.

'I am not scrimping and scraping, but I refuse to be cheated.'

When he heard that tone of voice, he knew she would not be put off.

'Very well. I will accompany you.'

She looked surprised and pleased, then shook her head. 'Oh, dear, I would not put you to so much trouble. I know you are busy. I won't go alone, I promise you. I have already arranged for my maid to accompany me.'

'I will drive you,' he said firmly. 'After all, the ball is my project. And I am intrigued as to what it is you need to acquire.'

Her naughty little smile stirred his blood, as it always did. 'You will have to wait and see.'

'Because?'

'Because.'

He frowned. 'Whatever we do, it must be in the very best of taste.'

'Of course.'

He could tell from her expression he was not going to get any more out of her, likely because she thought he might try to veto her purchase.

As if he actually would. Unless he was concerned for her safety, he had discovered he could not deny her a single thing she wanted. It pleased him to make her happy, when he knew it should not. He was indulging himself in the short few weeks left to them. Perhaps hoping that they would both have some happy memories, before the sword of Damocles landed. He would feel its cut as much as she would. But he could not stop now. Could he?

Once before he had let his parent down so badly. If he had been less cowardly he would have had all the money he needed to pay for doctors and medicine. They might even have been alive today, living in comfort.

He could not now go back on his word to avenge their deaths. If he did not keep his word, what sort of son would he be?

If only he didn't like her so much.

Unlike his previous ladies, who wanted jewels or money, Pamela asked for nothing other than what was due to her. But then as his partner, she lacked for nothing in the money department. However, she could have asked for more. Most women would.

He was going to miss her very much when they parted. She was the most honest, sweetest woman he had ever met. And if he allowed himself to think about it, the thought of ruining her made him feel sick to his stomach. She would hate him when the truth came out.

A strangely hollow ache filled him.

It twisted painfully inside him. Devil take it. Sentimentality had no place in his plans.

'I will get the carriage put to.'

She gave him a puzzled look as if she sensed his disquiet. 'Very well, it seems there is no dissuading you. I will fetch my coat and hat and meet you at the front door.'

As he strode for the mews, he realised he had barely touched his breakfast. He shrugged. What did it matter that he wasn't particularly hungry?

Oddy greeted him wildly for the second time that morning.

Damian patted him. What on earth was he to do with the animal when he left for America? Perhaps Pamela would take him.

When the coachman put the horses to the barouche, Oddy immediately jumped aboard.

'I don't think I need your company today,' Damian said. 'Ladies don't like dog hair all over their clothes.'

The dog stared at him mournfully, reminding him that he always went with Damien when he took the barouche.

It was their agreement. He could not go in the phaeton, but he could go in the carriage.

Damian sighed. 'Very well. After all, it is her fault that I own you in the first place.'

'Will you be wanting the canopy raised, My Lord?' the coachman asked.

He had not bothered purchasing a town coach, since he did not plan to remain in London for more than a year and the barouche had come with the house.

The day was fair, if a little chilly. They weren't going far and he preferred not to be shut up inside unless it was pouring rain. 'Leave the front down, but put a couple of extra blankets in, please.' He could always change his mind if it was too cold.

With the carriage ready to go, Damien returned to the house to get his hat and coat.

Pamela was on her way down the stairs when he reached the front door.

Her coat today was of a bright peacock blue and the way her bonnet framed her pretty face made him want to kiss her. And perhaps forget the trip to Covent Garden.

Instead, he took her arm and walked her out of the house and across the pavement to the waiting coach. 'I hope you don't mind Oddy's company. He refused to be left behind.'

'Not at all. He can serve as our protection.'

Damian chuckled as he handed her up. 'I am all the protection you need.'

'I was not thinking about me.'

He laughed. 'I assure you, I am quite capable of defending both of us. However, Oddy has been known to show his teeth at people he doesn't like the look of upon occasion, so perhaps he will serve a purpose.'

Pamela beamed. 'Good boy.' She patted Oddy's head and the animal grinned at her.

Damian gave the coachman the go ahead and soon they were wending their way through the city traffic.

Covent Garden during daylight hours was a very different prospect than Covent Garden at night when the streets milled with the carriages of those attending the theatre and rubbing shoulders with those who hoped to take advantage of them.

During the day, the square behind the Church of St Paul was abuzz with a whole different sort of trade and person.

The predominant goods on offer were, of course, fruits, vegetables and flowers. Many of the flower girls one found selling their wares on street corners came here to buy the blooms for the posies they sold. But at this time of year there was not much on offer.

They left the carriage with the coachman and he and Oddy followed Pamela to the far end of the market.

'You have been here before,' he said, seeing that she knew exactly where she was headed.

'Only once.'

A rough-looking fellow edged closer.

Damien gave him a hard look and a grim smile. The fellow shrugged and walked off. But he wasn't the sort Damian was most worried about. It was the small lads who dodged in and around the stalls who caused him the most concern. Boys who were not unlike what he had been at that age. Boys with quick fingers and bad intentions. Though they also seemed to be giving them a wide berth.

He glanced down at Oddy whose hackles were up and whose ears were pricked. Ha! Here was the reason no one had attempted to pick his pocket or cut Pamela's purse. And he hadn't had to raise a fist or grab a collar.

While he did not relax his vigilance, he did welcome the reinforcements. At last, the dog was earning its keep.

Later, he was going to have a long talk with Pamela about coming to a place like this with only her maid for company.

A youngish woman with dark hair neatly pinned under her cap and a bit of sacking for an apron tied around her waist rose from the upturned bucket she was using for a seat to greet them.

On her stall, she had twigs of holly with berries and mistletoe sprigs tied in little bundles ready for hanging and a pile of evergreen boughs.

Relief shone in her smile. 'I hoped you would come today.'

'Good morning,' Pamela said. 'I promised I would, did I not?'

'Well, you did. But not all keeps their promise.'

'Were you able to obtain any?'

'I was. Me pa skinned both knees he did, shinning up all the trees in the woods.'

She ducked beneath a ramshackle wooden table on one side of her stall. She reappeared with a large, roughly woven carrier loosely rolled around its contents. 'Here they are.'

She set the carrier on the ground and unrolled it. Inside were a mass of tangled strands of ivy.

'Perfect,' Pamela said. 'Thank you. It is just what I was looking for.'

'Ivy?' he asked. 'What is so special about that? I am sure any nursery could supply you with that.'

The young woman looked anxious. ''Ere, it took me da hours to collect that there.'

'Well, of course we will buy it now you have obtained it, but Pamela, really? Why endanger yourself for anything so common-or-garden?'

'If the nurseryman could have supplied it,' Pamela said, 'I would have ordered it. It is not the sort of thing they grow. Not in the lengths I wanted.'

'I see.' He didn't, but if a huge bunch of ivy made her happy, then so be it. But next time she wanted to foray into the stews of London, she had better request he go with her.

'How much?' he asked the woman.

'The lady already paid, sir,' the woman said. 'Though you can pay again if you like.' She laughed.

'No. Once is enough,' Damian said. 'Thanks all the same.'

The woman rerolled the mat and tied the string. Damian carried it back to the carriage.

Quite honestly, Pamela thought Damian might have made more of a fuss when he saw what she had bought. The idea had come to her while looking at a picture of ancient Greeks at a party.

He laid the bundle on the seat opposite, leaving just enough room for the dog.

'Was there anything else you needed while we are out?' Damian asked.

'Nothing I can think of at the moment.'

'You could have sent one of the grooms to pick this up,' he said.

'When I ordered it, she wasn't sure she could supply what I needed. No one had ever asked her for ivy before.'

'And yet you paid her in advance.'

'She would have returned the money.'

'You are very trusting.'

'Too trusting, you mean?'

He seemed to freeze for a moment. As if her words had struck an unpleasant chord. A twinge of anxiety tightened her stomach. The only other person she had trusted was him.

'It seems on this occasion your trust was well founded, but I would suggest that you take a little more care about who you trust with large sums of money. Even if you do not care about the money, it is highly reckless to endanger your person in that way.'

'I thank you for the advice.' She grinned. 'I told her if she cheated me, I would send you after her and she would highly regret it.'

'You didn't?'

'No. I didn't. Actually, our housekeeper knows the family. They are from the same village and it was she who recommended I go there with my special request. She recalled a copse full of ivy nearby the village. She also told me they were well respected and honest.'

'I am sorry I called you reckless.'

'I probably should have explained.'

'Yes. You should have.'

While his words were harsh, his voice and gaze were soft as butter. The look in them melted her insides. Her heart picked up speed as he took her gloved hand and raised it briefly to his lips. 'I cannot help but be concerned about you.'

How was it that he made her feel so feminine? And cared for. 'I am well able to take care of myself.'

She didn't mean to sound defensive, but she was afraid she was beginning to rely on him, on his caring, on his protection, far more than she ought.

After all, very soon he would be departing for distant shores and she would once more be alone. She had only herself to rely on. She would never ever go back to live with her mother.

Besides, she had grown used to her independence. She liked it. Most of the time. On the other hand, she had enjoyed these few weeks of companionship.

He released her hand and she felt the loss of his touch.

'I am sorry,' she said quietly, thinking she might have hurt his feelings.

'I am sorry, too.'

'You have no reason to be sorry. I shall never forget your kindness. You and Pip. If not for you I would never have had the opportunity to—'

'Hush.' He touched a finger to her lips. 'Do not say any more. I think you may regret it if you do.'

Puzzled by the note in his voice, as if the words hurt him to say, she gazed into his eyes.

He looked away. 'Have you ever been to Vauxhall Gardens?' He gestured across the river.

'Is that where it is? I have never been there. My mother did not think it suitable. Have you been there?'

'I went there this past spring. It is quite the experience. It is too bad it is closed or I would have taken you.'

She laughed. 'Just my luck to come to London in the winter time.'

'Perhaps there are other places you would like to go that are open.'

'I would like to see the Elgin Marbles at the British Museum.'

'Ugh. Just a bunch of broken old statues. I'll take you if you wish.'

He made it sound as though she was asking him to undergo torture.

'I thought I might like to see it after I read about it in the newspaper, but I won't trouble you if it is not something you would like to do.'

'What about taking in a play? Would you like to go to the theatre?'

'That I did do when I was here and I enjoyed it immensely. I have never been to the opera.'

'Very well. The opera it is. I will see if I can borrow a box. I know a couple of people that have them.'

'Do you know what is playing?'

'I do not. I will find out.'

'Oh, dear. I am not sure I have anything suitable to wear.'

'Then you must order something right away.'

'Perhaps I should not go. An opera gown is a great extravagance and I will likely never need it again.' She sounded sad.

'All the more reason to purchase it. A memory to savour when you retire to the country. Do you think you will miss living in London?'

'I think it is the people I will miss, rather than the place.'

I will miss you.

The words hovered on her tongue, but they had always avoided speaking of feelings.

She smiled brightly. 'I am a country girl at heart. London is exciting, to be sure, but, no, I will not miss living here.'

'I'm glad.'

The fervency in his voice was genuine, and she was grateful that he cared that much.

'Will you miss England?' she asked.

He grimaced. 'I have spent so little time in England, missing it would not be logical. I may have some regrets, I suppose.' He sounded slightly wistful, then laughed. 'I think I will miss France more.'

He didn't say anything about her being one of those regrets. Hurt stabbed at her heart. But she knew he did not care for her the way she had come to care for him, so she would do well to keep such feelings at bay. What was the point of longing for something that was out of reach? Nothing could change the choices she had made in the past and she needed to accept that, enjoy what moments she had with him and when he was gone move on with life. As hard as that would be.

Oddy jumped up and scented the air.

'It seems we are almost home,' Damien said drily. 'He always knows.'

'Clever boy,' she said. 'What will you do with him when you leave?'

'I haven't decided.'

'I will take him, if you wish.' It would be something. A reminder of their time together.

'Would you? I would certainly feel better knowing he was with someone I trusted to look after him.' There was a note of longing in his voice.

And he trusted her. Even if it was only in the matter of his dog. Well, that was something, wasn't it? They would still have a connection. Perhaps he might even return to see how the dog was doing, some time in the future.

'Wonderful. Thank you. I can always rely on you, can't I?' He pulled her close and kissed her, hard, as if it was the last kiss they would ever know.

When they broke apart, she gazed up at him. And for one brief moment she was sure she saw regret in his gaze.

He looked away, as if he saw more in her face that he wanted to see. 'Now, what do you want done with this greenery?'

Jolted back to earth, she looked around. 'Perhaps the servants can find a cool place to keep it, until we decorate the ballroom. So the leaves don't drop?'

'Did you hear that, Sam?' he said to the coachman.

'Yes, My Lord. I will speak to the gardener about it.'

'Good.'

While she and Damian entered the town house through the front door, the dog seemed perfectly happy to go with the coachmen. When she said this to Damian he laughed. 'He knows he will get a bone or some other treat the moment he arrives.'

'Ah, like a man, the way to a dog's heart is through his stomach.'

'Is that why you became a cook?' He was teasing as he so often did, he knew she was not in the market for a husband.

She smiled brightly. 'How did you guess?'

He helped her out of her coat and handed it to the waiting footman.

'Well, if I am to have an opera dress made, I need to get in touch with Madame Celeste right away.'

He looked a bit disappointed.

'What? Did you have other plans?' she asked.

'They can wait until later.' The wicked gleam in his eye caused her cheeks to heat.

'That is good,' she said repressively, 'since the opera was your suggestion.'

'Oh, I thought it was your idea,' he said mildly, but his eyes were smiling.

She laughed. 'Whosever idea it was, I need to get the gown ordered right away, if we are to go.'

He tipped her chin and kissed her lips. 'Then later will be worth the wait.'

Feeling suddenly hot, she fled upstairs.

Excitement stirred Damian's blood as he waited in the drawing room for Pamela to come downstairs. He just hoped she would be pleased and not disappointed tonight.

She had been startled when he had asked her to come as herself and not as his cousin.

He had promised not a single soul would see her in the box he had rented and the hood of her opera cloak would keep her hidden from prying eyes, especially since they would enter the theatre by way of the stage door.

The doubt on her face made him wonder if she would do as he asked or ignore his request.

Footsteps on the stairs alerted him to her imminent arrival. He tossed back his drink and went to greet her.

On seeing him, she paused a few steps up.

He gazed at her in awe.

She was a vision of loveliness.

'Will I do?' The breathiness of her voice betrayed her nervousness.

'You look stunning.' He held out his hand and she continued on down.

'It is too bad it is not raining,' she said. 'It might have been easier to hide.'

'I am glad it is not raining,' he said. Glad and grateful. His plans would have been ruined. He took the white velvet-lined cape he had purchased for her from the footman. 'Have them send the carriage around, please, Jeffrey,' he said.

He held out the cape.

'Oh, my. Where did that come from?'

'It is a gift from me. You may need it this evening. It is a little chilly.'

She stroked the soft material. 'It is far too fine for a cook.'

'But tonight you are not a cook. You are my guest.'

She looked a little sceptical, but let him put it around her shoulders. She snuggled into the deep pile like a kitten seeking somewhere warm to sleep.

The cape fitted her perfectly.

'It is beautiful, thank you.' She stood on her tiptoes and brushed her lips against his in a gesture of affection.

It warmed him from his head to his toes.

Damn, he was going to miss those little kisses of hers. Not just those. All the kisses. All the loving.

So it was a good thing he was leaving soon, or he might be diverted from his purpose.

It was not long before the footman returned to say the carriage awaited them at the kerb and they stepped out into December's cold evening air and climbed aboard.

He had hired a town carriage for this evening's outing. His grooms had spent the afternoon making sure it was spotless inside and out.

'How was your day?' he asked.

'Busy. What with cooking dinner and getting ready to go out.'

'*Sacre bleu*, why did you say nothing? I could have hired someone in to help.' He should have thought of it for himself, if he was honest.

'I prefer to cook myself. What I don't prefer is last-minute invitations that require heaps of visits to the dressmaker and last-minute requests to change my appearance.'

That told him. He laughed.

He took her hand, turned it over and pressed a kiss to her pulse. Her little shiver of pleasure caused his blood to heat. He ignored his desire and said in teasing tones, 'I apologise for inviting you to spend the evening with me.'

She laughed ruefully. 'You are not the smallest bit sorry. And neither am I.'

'I want this evening to be special. I want you to enjoy every moment.' He put his arm around her and she leaned into him.

'How can I not when I am with you?'

A pang in the region of his heart made his breath catch. The knowledge that eventually she would hate him nigh brought him to his knees.

He cursed his ill luck. Why was she the one woman he had come to care for so deeply?

It wasn't until they turned on to the bridge that she noticed they were not headed for the Haymarket.

Pulling free of his arm, she leaned forward to look out of the window in the door. 'Where are we going?'

'Oh,' he said casually, 'didn't I tell you? There are no operas on offer tonight in Town, we have to go a little further afield.'

'No. You didn't mention it. Are they playing in Southwark?'

'We are not going to Southwark. This is Regent Bridge.'

She turned and stared at him. 'Regent Bridge? So we are going to...?' She tilted her head. 'We are not going to the opera, are we?'

'No. I hope you will not be too disappointed.'

'But... I can't believe you would...'

'Take you to Vauxhall Gardens? Believe it because I am.'

She shook her head. 'You said it was closed.'

'It is closed to the public, yes. But I have rented it for the evening.'

Her eyes widened. 'That must have cost a fortune.'

He shrugged. 'Since tonight will be our only opportunity to visit the gardens, I thought the price well worth it.'

'You spendthrift.' She threw her arms around his neck and kissed his cheek. 'But I love you for it.'

They both froze.

His heart pounded in his chest. Usually, with such a demonstration of affection, he would have nuzzled her neck, kissed her silly and who knew where it might have led, but right now he felt as if there was a hole in his chest where his heart ought to be.

He straightened. 'Good,' he said stiffly. 'I am glad you are pleased.' God, that sounded so stilted. He forced himself to smile, but even that felt stiff and awkward. He cleared his throat. 'Wait until you see what else is in store.'

She took a deep breath as if to steady herself. 'Who else will join us? People who know me from the club? Do you think they will put two and two together when they see me in all this finery? Oh. I should have brought a mask. They only ever see me with a mask.'

'Do not worry. We are the only guests.'

The coach drew to a halt and the door opened to reveal a man in red livery. 'Welcome to Vauxhall Gardens.'

They stepped down and went through the entrance. Thousands of multi-coloured lanterns swinging in the branches of trees and on lamp posts lit the buildings and the Grand South Walks ahead of them.

Damian glanced at her face, trying to judge her reaction. Why the hell had he turned into a block of wood when she had said those words? It wasn't as if they actually meant anything more than she was happy with his surprise.

They were lovers, yes, but love, true love, didn't enter into it. How could it, given what he had planned? His throat dried.

She would hate him once the truth came out.

He felt as a huge hole had been carved in his chest. And he deserved it. He certainly didn't deserve love. He had proved that when he had decided to save himself rather than save his family.

An emptiness hung between them. There was nothing he could think of to say.

'They lit all these lights for us?' she said, finally breaking the silence.

'Yes.'

'How pretty it is. Magical.'

His shoulders loosened. 'It is quite the sight.'

She cocked her head on one side. 'Do I hear music?'

'You do.'

'Come, let us see.' She quickened her pace.

They entered the grove, and gazed at the Gothic Orchestra pavilion where a quintet was playing a waltz. He had given the order that they play nothing but waltzes.

She spun around, looking at the supper boxes and the lights in the trees strategically placed on the dance floor. 'I can just imagine it full of people.'

It should be full of people. He would take pride in showing her off.

Devil take it, where had that thought come from?

His stomach fell away. He would be showing her off at the ball. But he knew without question that there would be no pleasure in keeping his promise to his father. There would only be pain.

He pushed thoughts of the future away, caught her in his arms and they effortlessly came together into the dance, twirling and gliding among the trees, her face glowing in myriad coloured lanterns.

It was as if they had been partners all their lives. Of course, he was holding her closer than he ought, but there was no one here to see or care.

When the dance ended he led her away from the orchestra to one of the overlooking supper boxes.

Chapter Fourteen

Pamela had heard about the famously shaved ham at Vauxhall, but now here she was, eating it in a private box in the Gardens.

She could scarcely believe that Damian had gone to so much trouble on her behalf. The moment she realised where they were, what he had done, she had entirely lost her heart.

She knew she had fallen for him, but now she knew he was the only man she would ever love. Not that she could ever tell him so.

His reaction to her words earlier had made it perfectly clear he did not feel the same.

It hurt. Terribly. But she wasn't going to let her sadness spoil the evening. It was not his fault she was the only one in love.

He was her friend and her lover. And neither of them had wanted more. She was going to treasure the memory of this evening for the rest of her life.

She glanced around the box. It was delightfully decorated with paintings of scenes from the tempest.

A waiter brought them champagne.

'To my beautiful partner,' Damian said, raising his glass.

For a moment her heart seemed to stop beating. Business partner, he meant. She blinked back the hot moisture that had welled in her eyes and sipped at the wine while the waiters delivered a salad and roast chicken among other dishes.

'Thank you so much for doing this. How on earth did you manage to get them to open for just two people?'

He looked a little guilty. 'The owner is indebted to me.'

'Oh. Don't tell me. You forgave his debt.'

'I did. Not very businesslike of me, but worth every penny. Besides, who knew when he would be able to pay me back, if at all. I am pleased you like my surprise.'

'It is wonderful.'

While they ate, a soprano joined the orchestra and sang a selection of songs from various operas.

'Will you dance with me again?' he asked when she finished her dessert, a delicious cheesecake.

'I would love to.' She would dance with him as many times as he wished, because after tonight she would likely never dance with him again. After the ball, she would find and leave for her seaside cottage and he would be travelling to the other side of the world.

This evening was like a fond farewell.

Her heart ached.

But how could she be sad when he had gone to so much trouble to give her such a wonderfully special gift? She gave him her brightest smile as he led her on to the dance floor.

They did not talk as they danced. The music and the movement of their bodies seemed to be the perfect conversation. A harmony of spirits.

She closed her eyes and sank into the pleasure of being held in his arms as if the world no longer existed.

Reality would return tomorrow, but tonight she would enjoy the dream.

A bell rang in the distance and it seemed to be some sort of signal because the orchestra ceased playing.

'There are some sights you should see while you are here,' he said, tucking her arm under his and matching her steps perfectly. He led her away from the pavilion and down one of the lantern-lit walks.

They strolled along the Grand Walk and when they turned into a narrower walk they discovered a beautiful waterfall in a bucolic country setting and lit by strategically placed lights. This was the famous cascade.

'It really does look like water,' she said in amazement, knowing full well it was a mechanical display. 'And sounds like it, too. Oh, and the water wheel actually turns. How wonderful. How very clever.'

For a full ten minutes they watched as the water cascaded down into a pool and mechanical people, carriages and wagons crossed over a bridge.

She was so wrapped up in the spectacle that it was a while before she glanced up at Damian to see his reaction. He was looking at her with an odd expression on his face.

'It is quite marvellous, isn't it?' she said.

He smiled. 'Yes. Marvellous.'

Why did she have the feeling he wasn't talking about the mechanical wonder before them?

The performance came to an end and curtains painted with a country scene closed over the tableau.

'That was lovely,' she said. 'Thank you.'

'There is more.'

They crossed to the South Walk to admire the triumphal arches. As they walked, the sound of music once more floated across the gardens.

They wandered in the opposite direction admiring the statues, groves and piazzas as they went.

At the end of the South Walk the lanterns ended, though the walk continued to the right and left.

'The infamous dark walk,' Damian said.

'Infamous?'

He chuckled, led her a short way along the walk where the trees seemed to close over them and she could barely see a hand in front of her face. He pulled her close and kissed her.

Deeply, sweetly and somehow full of longing.

Carried away on his passion, she put her arms around his neck and kissed him back.

Finally, he drew back, his breathing heavy, his voice husky. 'You see? Infamous.'

She laughed at his nonsense. 'I think it is you who is infamous. The walk is quite innocent.'

He tipped her chin with a fingertip. 'I wish you were wrong.'

She frowned and peered at his expression, but already he was leading her back to the lit path.

When they returned to the grove, a waiter handed them glasses of champagne and the singer performed for them once more.

'One last dance, my darling girl, and then we must go.'

'One more,' she agreed.

One turned into two and then three. And then it really was time to leave.

They strolled hand in hand back to their waiting carriage.

'I think that is the best evening of my life,' Pamela said, when they climbed aboard and she was wrapped in his arms.

'I am glad,' Damian murmured against her hair. 'You deserve it. I—'

She waited for him to finish.

'I wish I could do more,' he said finally.

'You have done a great deal for me,' she said. 'I cannot believe I made enough money to actually buy a house so close to the shore. It is a dream come true. And it is all thanks to you. I shall never forget your kindness.'

'You may not think that way, once we part,' he said. 'But I hope, in time, you will remember this evening with some sort of pleasure.'

His voice was full of regret.

'I don't understand.'

'You will.'

Back at the town house, he escorted her upstairs and they made love, slowly and with great tenderness.

She realised as he got up and left her room that this had been his way of saying goodbye.

She tried not to cry.

But eventually, she had to turn her pillow over, it was so damp.

As the next few days passed, and the ball drew ever closer, Damian found himself in his study, supposedly working on his wine inventory, but pondering how Pamela was going to react to the upcoming unmasking.

He had seen her expression of anxiety when her mother had approached them in Hyde Park. And he could not help but admire the way she had straightened her shoulders and met the other woman's gaze head on.

Pamela had backbone. And the thought of what he was about to do to her was niggling at his conscience day and night.

Especially at night, when she lay sweetly in his arms. She trusted him. And he was about to destroy that and more.

He kept telling himself that his plan would not affect her as badly as how her father's actions had affected his family. She had no interest in remaining in society. It was her mother and stepfather who stood to lose the most.

Her mother would feel the sting of the *ton*'s wagging tongues and would certainly not be welcome in society for a very long time, if at all.

And nor would Damian, of course.

It wasn't that society would care that he had a mistress—what they cared about was that they had been duped by him and by her and her family.

Pamela would, of course never speak to him again. And nor did he deserve that she should.

Next Thursday would be the end of the Earl of Dart's rule of London. The end of Rake Hell.

And he would walk away whistling.

The only fly in the ointment was Camargue's sudden appearance in the park.

Camargue had apparently been surprised to discover someone using a title that had been thought to have gone into abeyance and had hotfooted it to London to meet the new Earl—something Damian had not been expecting, since the old fellow hadn't left his castle for ten years or more.

Camargue been strangely pleased to think the title had found a successor and had begun talking in earnest of plans for the future for their adjacent lands.

Damian hadn't had the heart to inform the old man he had no intention of actually going to Parliament to substantiate his claim to his father's title and that instead he and Pip would be off to the Americas.

The butler knocked on the door and announced, 'The Right Honourable Mr Long.'

Surprised, Damian leaned back in his chair. 'Long,' he said, ignoring the young man's outstretched hand, except to notice it was trembling. 'I was not expecting you, was I?'

'Perhaps you should have been,' Long said with more force than Damian would have expected.

'How can I be of assistance?' Damian drawled, gesturing to the seat in front of the desk.

Long sat. 'It is about the vowels of mine you hold.'

Damian frowned. 'Yes.'

'I heard from one of my friends that you let him pay his debts off at a heavy discount.' He smiled shyly. 'I would like to do the same. I admit I got in way over my head, but I have stopped gaming now that...' he blushed '...now that I am about to be married. I would like to pay off my debts at the same discount you offered my friend. I believe I can do it over the next three months, if you will allow me the time.'

This was exactly what Damian had been planning. He leaned back and shook his head slowly. 'You clearly do not recall the terms of our agreement. The club manager refused to accept any more vowels from you and I personally loaned you the money with which to play. Are you now saying you will go back on your word to pay me back in full?'

'Oh, but, surely the club and you are the same thing?' His voice had risen a notch. A note of panic.

'Not at all. You borrowed from me personally, not the Rake Hell. It is a debt of honour. I have your vowels.'

'I have to pay the full amount?' He sounded completely shocked.

'Of course.'

'I—oh. I see.' His voice shook, but he straightened his shoulders. 'I assume you will give me time?'

'One is expected to redeem one's vowels in short order,' Damian said. 'But I can wait a day or two. After all, we are friends, are we not?' He smiled benignly. 'Naturally, since it is a debt between gentleman, I won't be charging you any interest on the delay.'

The young man's face blanched. 'Thank you. A day or two?' He sounded breathless. 'Yes. Yes of course.'

'The day of my ball will do. You are coming, of course.'

He looked frozen, but managed to speak. 'Yes. Miss Frome is looking forward to it immensely.

'Wonderful. I shall look forward to meeting her again.'

Long hurried off.

No doubt he would be scurrying around town, trying to find someone to loan him the money to pay Damian off.

A gentleman's debts of honour must be paid before any others. If they were not, a man could not hold up his head. He would become *persona non grata*.

The way his father had.

But there wasn't a money lender in London who would give Long the amount of money he needed. Damian had seen to it personally.

Damian, frowned. Why didn't seeing the culmination of all his plans gradually unfold make him feel good?

Nonsense. He was delighted. This was exactly what he wanted.

On her way downstairs, Pamela was surprised to see Mr Long in the hall by the front door putting on his coat.

'Good day,' she said. 'What brings you here so early?'

'Mrs Clark.' He bowed. 'I am here about some business with His Lordship,' he choked out. His expression was distraught, almost tearful.

'Is something wrong?'

'I owe His Lordship a great deal of money and I do not know how I am going to pay.'

Puzzled, she frowned. She had thought Damian had resolved all of those issues at the club. 'Oh, I see.'

He squeezed his eyes shut for a second. 'I was a fool

to allow myself to fall into debt. I have very little time to come up with the money. Excuse me.' He grabbed his hat, bowed and left.

Determined to get to the bottom of his obvious upset, Pamela made her way to Dart's study and entered without knocking.

The dog lying beside the hearth wagged its tail in greeting.

Damian withdrew his gaze from the view from the window into the street and it settled on her face. 'Good morning.'

'Good morning. I just met Mr Long on his way out. Apparently he owes a great deal of money.'

'Indeed he does.' He seemed completely unperturbed. 'He was absolutely sure his luck would change, despite my assurance it would not.'

'He is little more than a boy.'

Damian's face hardened. 'I doubt he would thank you for that descriptor.'

'Can you not come to some sort of arrangement? As the club did with some of the others?'

'My dealings with Mr Long are really none of your business.'

She recoiled, shocked at his harsh tone of voice.

'As a part-owner in the club—'

'You have no say in the matter. The club refused to accept any more of his vowels. As you yourself requested, I might add. He borrowed my money. Begged me to lend it to him. It is a debt of honour.'

The words struck like blows. She had never heard him speak so harshly.

'Do not look at me like that, Pamela. I cannot afford to let it go. Am I to be ruined to save him?'

How had she been looking at him? 'How can him not paying his debt land you in ruin?'

'How do you think I came up with such a large sum of money?'

'From the club?'

'Please. Do you think I would go behind my partners' backs and lend money that had already been refused?'

She frowned. 'You borrowed it?'

'Exactly.'

She sat down. 'Oh, my good Lord. Is it a really large sum of money?'

'Some might call it a king's ransom. Forgiving would leave me horrendously in debt.'

Her stomach fell away. 'Why would you do such a thing?'

'He asked me.'

She frowned. 'There is no possible way he asked you for such an enormous amount of money.'

'He was in debt already. He owed money all over town. He thought it would be better to consolidate his debt. He begged me to help him. The young fool needs to learn a lesson.'

The vengeful note in his voice sent a spike of fear down her spine. 'I think he has learned his lesson. And surely you knew when he borrowed the money that it was far more than he could ever repay.'

Eyes cold as ice, he shrugged. 'He said he could. I took him at his word.'

For the first time in a long time, he was shutting her out. Hiding something. And she did not like this version of Damian one bit.

'You want to hurt him.' The words shot out of her mouth before she could think about them. They were instinctive. A sense that he was doing this on purpose.

She waited for his scathing outburst at her accusation.

And waited.

He merely looked bored. 'What do you think gives you the right to take me to task about a matter of honour?'

The remark cut deep as she realised that he was implying she had no honour so therefore how could she judge.

She glared at him. 'I know the difference between right and wrong.'

'Do you? I wonder. I hope you will excuse me, I have a meeting at my club.'

He got up and walked out of the room with the dog trailing behind him.

She paced across the room and stared out of the window, down into the street. She heard the front door close. Watched him saunter down the street without a care in the world. Her head hurt. But worse than that, her heart hurt.

Damian, who she knew as kind and generous, was showing not a scrap of mercy to poor young Mr Long.

Why on earth would Damian have let himself get into debt for the sake of someone else? There must be some reason he had loaned such vast sums of money.

On the other hand, Damian had given him time to pay when he could have asked for it back immediately. But apparently now he would wait no longer. Men were strange creatures with regard to their honour and vowels and all that nonsense.

Perhaps Mr Long could borrow it elsewhere and pay Damian back.

She thought she'd been helping Mr Long when she told Pip to stop accepting his vowels. Instead he had gone to Damian for a personal loan.

What a disaster.

And it was partly her fault.

There had to be something she could do to help. She

could give him her share of the money she had earned. Her stomach fell away. It would be the end of her dream of a cottage by the sea.

But would it be enough?

And would his honour allow him to accept her offer? She had to at least try.

The first thing she needed to do was find out where Mr Long lived. She couldn't actually call on him, but she could send him a note asking him to meet her somewhere.

As long as she had her maid with her and it looked like a chance meeting, there shouldn't be any problem.

It took longer than she expected to arrange a meeting with Mr Long. But finally he had replied that, yes, he would meet her at the British Museum in the room devoted to the Elgin Marbles. She had always wanted to see them, so she had decided she might as well accomplish two things at once.

And as she sat on a seat amid the statues and friezes, she was very glad she had. It was awe inspiring to know that these stones had been carved so long ago. How sad that they had suffered so much damage. Surrounded by them, she could almost imagine herself cast back to ancient times.

'Mrs Clark.'

Mr Long looked as if he hadn't slept or eaten since she saw him last. He seated himself beside her. There were a few other people walking around the room inspecting the statues, but no one within earshot.

'Mr Long. Good day. Thank you for agreeing to meet me.'

'I am sorry I did not get your note right away. I went out of Town. To Newmarket.'

Her stomach gave a little flip of dismay. 'Newmarket?'

'There was a horse. A sure thing, I was told.'

'And?'

She waited for the worst.

'It won.'

'You mean you are solvent again? You can repay your debt?'

'Some of it.'

'Although I cannot entirely feel comfortable about you taking such a risk, I suppose it is good news.'

He shook his head. 'His Lordship seemed determined I should pay the full amount. Perhaps with a partial payment I can convince him to wait. If not... Do you think you can put a good word in with him for me?'

Damian had told her to mind her own business. 'I can try. I am not sure he will listen. Can you not ask your father for help?'

'My father is experiencing some financial difficulties of his own.' His shoulders slumped. 'I will have to leave the country if it becomes known I reneged on a debt of honour.'

'I don't understand.'

He groaned. 'I will be beyond the pale. Blackballed. Even my family will turn their backs on me. And no doubt they will also be affected by the scandal.'

'Oh, dear. How much can you pay back?'

'A little over half.'

'Very well. I will speak to Lord Dart on your behalf.'

He took her hand and kissed it. 'Will you indeed? I am in your debt for ever.'

'I think it best that from now on you do not owe anything to anyone.'

He groaned. 'I won't. I still don't understand how I could have been so foolish.'

Chapter Fifteen

Finally, the evening of the ball had arrived. Damian knew Pamela had been trying to speak to him and he had no doubt it was about young Long, so he had taken an unplanned trip to Rake Hall and stayed overnight, and now, arriving in a downpour in the dark and soaked through to the skin, he had arrived barely in time to change into his clothes for the evening.

While at Rake Hall he'd spent his time wandering the rooms, trying to think of a way of accomplishing his goal without involving Pamela.

No matter which path he began on, it always led to the same place. He could not destroy the Lamb family name, the way his family's name had been ruined, without Pamela also being dragged down.

The Lambs were not as important to his revenge as the ringleader of the fraud, Long, but when confronted all those years ago, Vicar Lamb had refused to even acknowledge his guilt.

A groom dashed out of the stables to take charge of the horse. Wearily, cold to the bone, he climbed down to discover Pip awaiting him.

'*Mon ami,*' Pip said, his face grave. 'I am glad to see you.'

Damian's heart skipped a beat. His thoughts went to Pamela. 'What has happened?'

'There is this Duke. Camargue. He has been asking for you.'

Damian let go a sigh of relief. 'Camargue. You don't need to worry about him. He is pressing me to sell him land.'

'He is in haste, apparently. He demands that you attend him. I told him you are out of town. He demanded I get you back. *"It is urgent,"* he said. But he will not say what he wants. So I cannot help him. So now he sends a fellow to camp out in the hall. Awaiting your return. Naturally, he goes to tell his master you have arrived, the moment you pull up. Therefore, if you are hiding from this Duke, you had better hide now.'

'What the devil? I'm not hiding from him. I will go and see him in good time. Right now, I need to get out of these wet clothes.'

Pip looked at him. 'Why did you go in an open carriage in December?'

'I needed some fresh air.'

'And is Pamela in need of fresh air also? Is that why she looks so pale?'

He frowned. 'Are you telling me she is ill?'

'She does not say so. She wanted to know where you were, also with some urgency.'

A cold fist seemed to clutch at Damian's heart. A sense of something about to go wrong. Nothing would go wrong. He had planned every last detail.

'Leave me to worry about Pamela.'

Pip nodded. 'Then all is in train.'

'It is.' They walked together into the house. 'First and foremost, I need a hot bath.'

Damian gave instructions to the butler for water to be brought up and went to his chamber.

He had removed all but his breeches when Pamela strode in. 'There you are.'

'Indeed. I am here.'

And there she was, obviously annoyed and very beautiful. He had not seen her so angry before. Her grey eyes were no longer clear calm pools a man could drown in, but dark with storms swirling in their depths.

'Please. Do not sound so innocent. I have needed to speak with you these past three days and you have deliberately been avoiding me.'

'Why would I do that?' he drawled. 'But if you do not mind, I am about to bathe. I am soaked through from the rain.'

As if to prove his point, a footman entered with the tub followed by a couple more with buckets of hot water.

They ignored Pamela.

'I don't mind at all,' she said, placing herself in a chair and crossing her arms. 'We can talk while you bathe.'

He waited for the tub to be full and the servants to be gone before he stripped himself off and climbed into the steaming water.

Under other circumstances, he might have invited her to join him, but somehow he didn't think such an offer would be appreciated.

As the door closed behind his valet, she jumped up and prowled towards him.

He held out the soap. 'Would you?'

She gave him a blank look. 'Would I what?'

'Wash my back.'

'I need to speak to you about Long.'

He sighed. No back wash then. 'Again?'

'Yes. It seems he can repay half the money he owes you and…'

'He needs to repay all of it.'

'I am sure he will. But he needs more time.'

'When he asked me for the money, I did not ask for more time. I gave it to him when he needed it. Now I need it to repay my debt. If I don't, I will be paying a great deal in interest.'

Or he would be, if he had in fact borrowed it.

She threw up her hands, picked up a washcloth and the soap. Damien leaned forward to give her better access.

She worked up a lather and began vigorously scrubbing his back.

It felt wonderful.

'There must be something you could do,' she said. Her tone was matter of fact, not wheedling or whiney.

She was asking him to help because she was a kind and generous woman.

And he had planned her ruination. He felt ill.

He snatched the washcloth from her hand. 'What is this young fellow to you? Why are you taking such an interest in him?' The words tasted sour in his mouth, but he could no longer bear to have her this close and not give in to her demands and forgo the revenge he had worked so hard for these many years.

She recoiled. 'What are you talking about?'

'It seems to me that you are taking more interest in his problem than in mine. There must be some reason for it. I know you met him in secret at the British Museum.'

Her face turned fiery red. 'What? How do you know?'

'I asked a footman to keep an eye on you.'

'How dare you?'

'How dare I? You were the one who went wandering off to Covent Garden without a moment's thought. You don't think I would let that happen again, do you?'

'You have no business telling me what I can and cannot do. And to answer your question, no, I am not having an affair. Mr Long is engaged. You know that. He is about to be married. But if he cannot repay the debt, he will be forced to leave the country and the marriage will be called off. I simply want to find a way to help him.'

'At my expense.'

'You must think I am a complete fool,' she snapped. 'I know you could easily afford to forgive part of the debt, if you wished. I am not sure why you are doing this, but I get the feeling you are doing it on purpose. I had no idea you were so cruel and unfeeling.'

Astounded, he stared at her. She wasn't angry, she was furious. As if it really mattered to her what happened to young Long.

Long's father hadn't given a damn about what would happen to Damian's family all those years ago.

If she knew the truth, she wouldn't ask. Would she? But then if she knew the truth, she would learn of her own father's complicity in the scheme.

He hesitated.

'Well?' she snapped.

'This is business. The man owes me hundreds of pounds. You are not being logical.'

'Logical?' She handed him the washcloth. 'I know you could find a way to get your blood without a pound of flesh.' She stalked out. Left him feeling…bereft. Alone.

Well, he had been alone for years. It was nothing new. She should be grateful that he had decided that only Long would bear the weight of his retribution, not treat him like some sort of ogre.

But then he would never tell her that, would he, or she

would guess at his original intentions. Intentions he would not be able to carry through.

Damn. He should have guessed that whereas most women would have given up upon realising he was serious, Pamela would stand by her guns.

And his accusation of unfaithfulness had been a low blow indeed.

Damn it all.

A tap on the door made him look up. Hope leaped in his chest. Had Pamela changed her mind?

His valet entered.

Hope dissipated. 'Pass me a towel, please. I'm done here.'

His valet obliged. 'Apparently His Grace, the Duke of Camargue, awaits you in the drawing room.'

Good Lord. What now? Dukes did not normally show up on one's doorstep like common men. They summoned lesser mortals. Clearly the matter of what the Duke had described a worthless tract of land had become a matter of urgency.

'Then I must hurry.'

Pamela entered the drawing room and stopped in surprise at the sight of an elderly gentleman rising to his feet. 'I beg your pardon. I was unaware that Dart was entertaining.'

And she wasn't prepared for visitors. She'd been coming for her reticule containing her calling cards. She needed to send a message to Mr Long.

She could see it on the table containing her needlework bag.

'I am Camargue,' the elderly man said, peering vaguely at her over the top of his spectacles.

Camargue. The Duke. She dipped a curtsy. 'Mrs Clark.'

'Delighted to make your acquaintance.'

The Duke spoke with a heavy Scottish burr and leaned heavily on a cane.

'Please, be seated. I am sure His Lordship will not be long.'

She eyed her reticule. Should she grab it and leave? Come back later or—?

'Good afternoon, Your Grace,' Damian said from behind her.

'Dart,' the Duke said. 'Good of you to see me so soon after your journey.'

'I didn't realise the Duke had come to call and came to fetch my needlework,' Pamela said, scooping up both bag and reticule. 'I will leave you to your conversation.'

'You are Dart's hostess,' Camargue said. 'I have heard about you.'

She gave Damian a panicked glance.

'Mrs Clark is a distant cousin,' Damian said. 'She serves as my hostess while I am a bachelor.'

Camargue looked from one to the other with a knowing expression. 'Cousin, eh? Dear me. Is that what they are calling it now?' He put up a hand when Damian opened his mouth to speak. ''Tis no matter. Perhaps Mrs Clark can convince your butler to provide a cup of tea for an old man who is fair drookit after walking here in the rain.'

'You walked?' Damien sounded astonished.

'No sense in spending an hour putting the carriage to for the sake of a ten-minute walk.'

'Perhaps you would prefer something stronger,' Damian said. 'I have whisky if you prefer.'

'No, no. Tea will be perfect.'

'Of course.'

Pamela rang the bell and ordered tea. No doubt the Duke

would expect her to pour it also. She looked at Damian whose expression was one of resignation.

She sat down and waited for the tea to arrive.

Damian seated himself on the sofa near Camargue's chair.

'To what do I owe the pleasure of your call, Your Grace?' Damian said.

'My man of business said you returned our offer unsigned. I came to find out why. You won't get more elsewhere. It is more than generous for such a scabby bit of land.'

Damian smiled briefly. 'Possibly.'

'If you think you will wring more out of me, my boy, you are off by a mile,' the old man growled.

'I have no intention of selling the lands at the moment.'

'Is that right?' The old man chuckled. 'Then you are a fool. There is no access to that land except by way of mine.'

Damian's shoulders stiffened very slightly.

If she had not known him so well, Pamela might not have noticed.

Damian expression remained mild and polite. 'Not fool enough to believe you are going to so much trouble for a half a dozen sheep.'

'A half-dozen, is it? More like a hundred dozen. There's money in wool.'

The butler entered with a tray followed by a footman with a plate of petit fours.

The Duke rubbed his paper hands together. 'Tea. Just what I need.'

Pamela poured him a cup. Damian waved his off and she poured one for herself.

'No, lad, I will not be put off. You will sell me the land and the longer you wait the lower the price will be.'

Damian's eyes twinkled. 'Your Grace, I believe you are neglecting one salient fact.'

The Duke looked up sharply, the vague, decrepit old man seeming to disappear in an instant. 'And what would that be, pray? Oh, is it the future of a few miserable crofters now occupying the land? My man tells me most of them haven't paid their rent in years. I have a plan to solve that problem.'

'And that would be?'

He grinned triumphantly, revealing a mouth full of broken teeth. 'Send them to America.'

Damian's face revealed nothing of his thoughts. 'I see.'

'Well? Will it serve?'

'What about the coal?' The calm in Damian's voice was so cold it made Pamela shiver.

The Duke waved a dismissive hand. 'Coal? Who said anything about coal?'

'I sent a man north to take a look at the land after you approached me in Hyde Park. He says the locals believe there is a seam of coal that runs from your pit right under my land.'

'Not such a fool after all,' the Duke muttered and took another swig of his tea.

'The price you offered for the land is a pittance and I will not sell.'

'It won't do you any good. Your access to the sea is blocked. If you mine it, I'll not give you permission to cross my land.'

'Then I suppose I will have to go around it.' While Damian sounded calm enough, Pamela had the sense he was furious with the old fellow for trying to dupe him.

The Duke gave a nasty chuckle. 'Then you will lose more than ye gain. That land is not worth a penny more than I offered. I bid you good day, young fellow. When you are ready to talk business, you may send word to my man of affairs.'

The Duke snatched up his walking stick and rose to his feet.

Pamela got up to ring the bell.

'No need, Mrs Clark,' Damian said with a grim smile. 'I will show the Duke out myself.'

Pamela watched the two men leave. All that animosity over a little bit of coal. She had not been able to help feeling pleased that Damian had not wanted to dispossess the people who lived on his land. But now it seemed that he was holding out for a better offer, since, as far as she could tell, Damian cared for no one but himself, given the way he was behaving towards Mr Long.

'There,' Susan said, putting the finishing touches on the glossy black wig Pamela had chosen for the evening. This one fell long and straight down her back. 'Is it to your satisfaction?'

'It looks lovely. Thank you.' If only she felt more confident that no one would see through her disguise. To her eyes it looked patently false.

Still everyone would be wearing wigs and masks and other forms of disguises this evening so she would not stand out.

'It is I who should be thanking you,' Susan said. 'Without your help, I would never have even dreamed of becoming a ladies' maid. I am very grateful for everything.'

Pamela had written her an outstanding reference letter and Susan had already landed another position, starting after Pamela and Damian's planned departure.

'It is nothing that you do not deserve,' Pamela said.

'I just wish I could continue working for you. I will miss you.'

They had become friends long before Susan had become her maid.

'Once I am settled you must come to visit me when you have some time off. Promise me.'

'Oh, I will. You will send me your address the moment you know it.'

Pamela's stomach sank a little. She had no idea where she might end up next. 'Of course I will, but give me yours now so I can reach you.'

Susan wrote out her address on a piece of paper and tucked it into Pamela's jewellery box.

'Time for us to get you into your dress,' Susan said. She picked up the gown laid over the bed and stroked the silky gold material. 'Queen of Egypt. You will make a fine queen.'

They both laughed.

She couldn't wait to see Damian as Antony. Though she was still angry with him, she had come up with an idea to solve the problem, if Damian wouldn't change his mind.

This was the last evening she would appear as Mrs Clark, the Earl of Dart's cousin. After today she would simply continue her life as herself.

Strangely, she had the feeling she would miss it. She had already begun to miss Damian. These last few days she had hardly seen him and when she did they had argued.

She stepped into the tunic-like dress and held still while Susan fastened it down the back.

She still didn't know how she would fare living alone in the depths of the countryside. Nonsense. She would manage as she had for years, only this time she would be pleasing only herself.

'Where does this go?' Susan said, holding up a belt fashioned to look like a snake.

'It ties around the hips, quite low. Look, here is the picture of what it is supposed to look like.' The dressmaker had drawn up the design for her and Damian's approval.

'Oh, yes. I see now.' Susan fastened the belt around her hips.

'Now for the jewellery.' Susan fastened bangles around her arms and a golden headband across her forehead, then stood back to admire the effect. 'This is so much fun. I don't think I would recognise you if I didn't know you.'

Pamela laughed. No one actually knew her. Not any more. Except perhaps Damian and he really didn't seem interested any longer.

'Now for the make-up.'

Susan looked at the picture. 'I can do it like this, if you wish.'

Kohl-rimmed eyes, ruby lips and darkened eyebrows. 'Perfect.' If only her eyes weren't such a distinctive shade. They were the only thing about her that she could not change.

When Pamela went downstairs an hour later, she felt certain she would not have recognised herself, but still she was glad of the mask she held in her hand. She would put it on before their guests arrived.

Tonight there would be several people here that she knew well, including her mother. Quite possibly, they would be a lot closer than they had been when they passed each other in the carriage.

Damian was in the drawing room, looking like a god in his Roman robes and the crown of olive leaves on his brow. It was the first time he had ever appeared in costume. Clearly, he was set on making this event a success.

He also had not yet donned his mask.

He gazed at her for a long moment and nodded his approval. 'You look like every man's dream of Cleopatra.'

She wasn't quite sure if it was a compliment or not, he sounded so grim. 'Thank you.'

He handed her a glass of sherry. 'Fortifications before the hordes arrive.'

She smiled and swallowed a mouthful. 'I need it. I just hope I haven't forgotten anything important.'

'Everything is just as it should be. And I have to say that the ivy-clad columns are a very nice touch.'

'I am glad you like them.'

He tossed back his brandy and held out his hand for her glass. She finished it and handed it over.

How distant they were with each other, how restrained. No doubt he did not want her losing her temper the way she had the other evening.

Together they climbed the stairs to the ballroom.

They stood at the double doors waiting to greet the guests as they arrived and she gazed at him. Soon they would part and would never see each other again. 'I am sorry if I have been a bit of a trial to you recently,' she said.

He closed his eyes briefly. 'I am sorry, too. Very sorry. I hope you will remember that.'

He turned away to speak to one of the footmen at the drinks table.

What on earth did he mean?

But there was no time to enquire. The butler was announcing the first of their guests.

And if an evening's success was to be judged by how many people could fit in a ballroom and the various antechambers, the ball was definitely the event of the Season.

There was just enough space left for people to dance

and that was only by dint of footmen judiciously moving people back from encroaching on the dance floor from time to time.

All evening she had tried to find Mr Long to let him know about her lack of success with Damian, but so far she hadn't seen him or his fiancée. Either that or she hadn't recognised them.

She should have asked him about his costume. There were a great many Romeos and Juliets, a quantity of Macbeths, not to mention Titanias and Oberons, with the odd donkey-headed Bottom thrown in.

There were even two other couples dressed as Antony and Cleopatra, but neither of the men looked anywhere near as gorgeous as Damian, who stood head and shoulders above the crowd.

She had danced a good few dances, too, none with Damian though, sadly. He had been busy charming their guests.

As he should, of course.

'He is magnificent, is he not?' Pip said, handing her the glass of champagne he had offered to fetch.

He must have seen her staring at Damian like some sort of lovesick fool. 'As always.' She hoped she sounded lighthearted, not miserable.

'And yet you are not as happy as I have seen you.'

Clearly she was not much of an actress. She took a deep breath. 'I suppose I am a little sorry we will soon go our separate ways.'

Pip glanced across at where Damian was in the middle of a group of ladies and gentlemen, regaling them with some story or other. They seemed to hang on his every word.

'I do not think he is so glad about it either.'

'Really? He seems perfectly happy to me.'

'Yes. He wears his mask well.' He gave her a look. 'A quiet cottage by the sea will be welcome after all this excitement?' He sounded doubtful.

'Indeed.' Strangely the cottage was a good deal less appealing than it had been as an impossible dream. Perhaps she had become too accustomed to all the excitement around Damian. Or perhaps it was the thought of living there without the man himself.

She tried to shake off her sadness. 'I am looking forward to it immensely.'

'It is a bargain *incroyable*, according to my agent. You must finalise the purchase before another snaps it up.'

'First thing tomorrow.' she said, realising that he had noticed she had been procrastinating.

She sipped calmly at her champagne. He was right, it was an incredible bargain. To keep the agent waiting was unfair.

She smiled at him. 'I think you better dance with Lady Simpson, she has been staring at you for the past five minutes.'

He grinned. 'Ah, yes. We have an assignation later. She does not like me to speak with other ladies.'

'You are going to miss your lady friends when you depart.'

'There are always new friends to be made,' he said with a wink and headed for the lady in question.

She took a deep breath. It was time to go back into the fray. Once last round of being charming and then she would leave, she did not want to be around for the unmasking. There was really no point—with or without her mask she was not herself.

Finally, there was Mr Long. Alone. His fiancée must be elsewhere.

She eased her way through the crowd to Romeo's side. 'Have you made your arrangements with Lord Dart?' she asked.

'Mrs Clark, I scarce knew it was you,' he said.

'Good. But did you?'

'I haven't been able to see him, but I sent a message saying I could come up with half of it...'

A gentleman dressed in Tudor robes, muttered something to his companion wearing a tricorn and powdered wig. 'It is Long,' his companion replied. 'The effrontery of the fellow.'

They made a show of turning their backs.

A gap opened up around her and Mr Long. A circle of disdain.

Long turned fiery red. 'Someone must have learned about me not meeting my obligation. Did he not agree to receiving a partial payment?'

Pamela's stomach fell away. 'No, but I have thought of a plan. I did not expect people to know... '

'Everyone knew tonight was the deadline.' Long looked mortified. 'I would not have come if I had known he refused to wait. You should have let me know.'

'I had no idea the deadline was tonight. You did not tell me.' Her mind raced. She had to do something. 'I will speak to him.'

'It is too late.' Long strode away, his head held high, but the view of the *ton* was made perfectly clear as they moved aside as if his touch could cause contamination.

She felt slightly ill. Only one person could have let fall that Long had failed to discharge his debt of honour by the appointed time. Damian. She scanned the room, looking for his imposing presence. There. Near the orchestra.

She started towards him.

The clock struck midnight.

Oh. No. She did not want to be here for the unmasking. She would have to speak with him after the ball. She was not going to allow this to happen to poor Mr Long.

It would be even more of a disaster if she was recognised.

She turned to make her way out of the room.

A hand caught her arm. Pip.

'Where are you going?' he asked.

She tugged to free her arm. 'Pip. You know I always leave before the unmasking.'

'Not this time, I think.'

'What?'

She glanced down the room to where Damian was already making his way up on to the dais with the orchestra. About to announce the unmasking.

'Pip. Let me go. What are you doing?'

But he wasn't looking at her. His grasp remained firm and he was watching Damian.

Chapter Sixteen

$\sim\!\!\sim\!\!\sim\!\!\sim$

As arranged, the orchestra was finishing up a waltz a few minutes before midnight. Damian glanced around for Pamela.

This was the moment he had chosen to reveal her identity. To ruin her in the eyes of society.

He gave a sigh of relief as he saw her making her way to the ballroom doors. His plan had been to ask her to dance with him. One last dance, right before the unmasking, and then—

But of course he had not. Could not do so.

The thought of hurting her, of causing her any sort of pain, made him feel physically ill.

Call him a coward, dishonourable, whatever it was his father would have thought of him, he wasn't going to ruin an innocent woman because her mother and father had behaved badly to his parents.

At least Long had not escaped his net. He had arranged for his man of business to drop a word or two in several gossips' ears and they had done the rest. He just wished he didn't feel sorry for Long. Or regret that Pamela would never forgive him.

Dammit all.

He smiled at a lady dressed as a shepherdess, leaving

the floor with a gentleman dressed as Pan. 'Ready for the unmasking?' he asked.

She giggled.

Pleased that no harm would come to Pamela, Damian felt suddenly lighter and happier as he strode for the dais.

Everyone was chattering and laughing excitedly as they waited to remove their masks.

Something made him glance over towards the double door. A sort of stir among the crowd. To his horror he saw that Pamela had not left.

She was standing alongside Pip. It took a moment to realise that the reason she had not departed was because Pip had hold of her arm.

The clock struck twelve.

Pip looked over at him, expectantly.

Devil take it, he had not told his friend he had changed his mind. Had not thought to. He shook his head.

He saw comprehension dawn on his friend's face and his grip on Pamela's arm relax.

She looked from Pip to him and back. Her eyes widened.

He made a shooing motion with his hand and saw her move toward the door.

He breathed a sigh of relief. 'Let reason prevail. Let all our revellers be revealed,' he called out as expected. He removed his mask.

Around the room people untied the strings of their disguises, laughing and exclaiming as the people around them were revealed.

Footmen moved among the guests with trays and drinks.

'A toast, ladies and gentlemen. To King and Country.'

'The King,' everyone said.

'To our host,' someone called out.

'Dart,' chorused around the room.

A commotion beside the doors caught his attention. He stared in shock. Pamela was standing in the entrance, her mask gone, held in the hand of a drunken reveller dressed as Henry the VIII, if he wasn't mistaken. The man was trying to snatch a kiss. As he pulled her close, her wig came off and her chestnut hair cascaded around her shoulders.

'Unhand me,' Pamela said.

'Oh, my goodness,' a woman said in the sudden silence. 'Pamela Lamb, is that really you? But I thought you were...' Everyone looked from Pamela to Damian.

Damian's heart went cold like ice and his stomach fell away.

A buzz of shock rippled through the room. He could see her mother collapsed against her stepfather with shock.

By the time he made it across the room, Pamela was gone.

Dear God. What had he done?

Exactly what he had set out to do.

Although the *ton* had been thoroughly titillated by the scandal at his ball, two days later, Damian was still dealing with the aftermath of what in his mind he could only think of as a debacle.

After long and hard reflection during his sojourn at Rake Hall, he had returned to London having decided that punishing the Longs would be revenge enough, since it was Long's father who had been the chief instigator of the fraud. That he was still alive to see his only son ruined made it doubly sweet. Pamela's father, on the other hand, was long gone, so would not know the sting of shame.

He had felt as guilty as hell, coming to such a conclusion, but had been able to rationalise it as justice, a fair punishment for a guilty man, rather than revenge on an innocent woman.

But, despite his best efforts, he had failed to save Pamela from his own machinations, because some drunken lout had taken a fancy to seeing her unmasked. If only he had let Pip in on his decision, all might have been well, but truth to tell he'd been somewhat ashamed of his weakness when it came to Pamela. He'd thought she would simply slip away as she had planned and that would be an end to it.

To Damian's astonishment, the following morning, Long had come up with the money he owed and demanded that Damian let everyone know he had not reneged on his debt of honour.

Although Long was one day late, no one among the upper one thousand would fault him for that and so Damian had been forced to spend the last two days making sure the damage was undone.

The fact that Pamela had been unmasked and that the Longs had got off scot-free after all had been a bitter pill.

Knowing Pamela would have been pleased Long was not ostracised, did not make it any easier to swallow. To make it worse, she and everyone associated with her had been turned into pariahs.

And he'd thought he'd had it all under control.

He hadn't felt like such a failure since the day his mother died.

He'd been too much of a coward to save his mother and now he'd all but destroyed the woman—he had to face it— the woman he loved. This time, no matter what it took, he was going to set things right.

The moment he could break free of the Long nonsense, Damian had set off for the cottage she had purchased. Only to discover she had not purchased it at all. Another family had moved in.

Where the devil had she gone?

He had tried her mother's house, but she had been shocked when he asked about her 'wayward daughter' as she called her and denied any knowledge of Pamela's whereabouts and never wanted to see her again.

Clearly all she could think about was salvaging her own reputation by distancing herself from her child.

And so, here he was back at his town house, trying to guess where Pamela might have gone while Pip regarded him with sympathy. 'Have you tried the agency where you found her before?'

'I did. No luck there.'

Pip pursed his lips. 'Let me see what I can discover.'

'If I have failed to find her, I don't know why you think you would succeed,' Damian flung at him. 'Why the devil did she not buy that cottage? She was so taken with it. I suppose she must have bought something else.'

'I have the answer for that, *mon ami*. After a few discreet enquiries, I have discovered that it was Pamela who gave Long the money to pay his debt.'

Damian groaned. 'I should have known she would do something like that.'

'Indeed.'

The pain in his chest felt as though a knife had pierced his heart.

And now she was out there somewhere without a penny to her name and no doubt hating him.

The pain grew worse at the thought of where she might be with no friends and no money.

Pip frowned. 'You know, she is very friendly with her maid, Susan, who left when she did. She said she had no reason to stay, now her mistress was gone. Perhaps they are together. Or her family might know something.'

A tiny seed of hope germinated in his heart.

'Why did you not say so before?'

'I did not think of it before.'

'Do you have an address?'

'As luck would have it, I do.'

Seated on Susan's bed in the tiny attic chamber in a tenement in the Seven Dials, Pamela stared blindly at the newspaper she had in her hand. A week had passed since the ball and she still felt numb from the realisation that Damian had intended to reveal her true identity. He and Pip had planned it all along.

She had seen the guilty looks on their faces. They had known exactly what they were doing.

Her heart squeezed painfully. Why on earth would he do that? What had she ever done to him? Surely not because he had discovered she intended to help Long.

How cruel. Even the enveloping numbness could not dull the pain.

But she could not remain here sobbing her heart out because of Damian. She was imposing on Susan and her family and that she must not do for any longer than necessary.

She made herself read the notices for cooks wanted. Naturally, all of them required references. And where was she supposed to get those?

Certainly not Damian.

She had her references from earlier positions but a gap would always be seen as a red flag to a potential employer.

'You should open a pie shop,' Susan said from her chair by the window, where she was mending her stockings. 'Your pies are delicious. I would eat it every night, if you did. You would make a fortune.'

She had been cooking for the family over the fire as a way of paying her rent.

'It costs a great deal to set up a shop,' Pamela said. 'Money for rent and pots and pans and food to cook.' She had not a penny to her name. She had given everything to Mr Long. And she was glad she had stopped Damian from his cruelty.

A commotion in the street brought Susan to her feet and peering down from the tiny dormer window.

'Oh-ho! Who is this a-parking a carriage outside?'

Pamela ran to look. 'Oh, no. Dart. Why on earth did he think of coming here? Don't let him in.'

Susan ran downstairs to the front door. Pamela could hear the sound of arguing voices, but not what they said.

Heavy footsteps on the stairs told her that Susan had not been successful in keeping Dart out. She froze.

Should she hide?

Why? She had no reason to hide. She had no reason to be ashamed. How dare he come chasing after her!

He knocked on the door.

'Who is it?' she called out.

'You know very well who it is.'

Her heart was racing so hard she could scarcely utter another word. 'Go away.'

'No.'

Typical Dart.

'What do you want?'

'I want to explain.'

She frowned. That she had not expected. Rather she might have expected him to demand an explanation for her sudden disappearance. 'Explain what?'

'Pamela, may I come in?'

'And if I say no?'

'Then I will wait out here until you say yes.'

She sighed. 'Very well, come in if you must.' She folded her arms over her chest.

The door opened to reveal Dart with an anxious-looking Susan peering around him.

'It is all right, Susan. I will speak to His Lordship. Please give us a few minutes.'

The girl nodded. 'I'll be downstairs. Give a shout if you need me.' She gave Dart a pointed glare and left muttering something about people barging into other people's homes.

Damian winced. 'I couldn't do anything else. She was determined to keep me out.'

'You should have taken no for an answer.'

'I needed to speak with you.'

'I don't think we have anything to say to each other. Not only did you try to ruin poor Mr Long, you intended my ruin also.'

'About that—'

'I do not care to hear your excuses.'

The thought of it somehow seemed to penetrate the cold. It hurt. Badly. All over again. She turned away. Pretended to look out of the window, but could see nothing because her vision was blurred.

'You don't understand,' he said.

'No. I don't. And I do not care to either. Please leave.' Somehow she managed not to start sobbing.

'Please. Give me a few minutes. To explain.'

'Very well. Five minutes. I have a great deal to do today.' Five minutes was about all she thought she could bear of the pain of seeing him here.

'I made a promise to my father, when he was dying,' he said softly, with a note of pleading in his voice. 'I promised I wouldn't let the people who ruined my family get away with it. My mother might have been alive now if they hadn't cheated my father.'

She turned back slowly. 'Long cheated your father? He couldn't have.'

'Not him. His father. He offered my father a chance to invest in a scheme he said would make him rich. Another man, a man my father thought was a good friend, encouraged him to borrow the money to invest. He couldn't pay it back when the scheme collapsed. The scheme was a fraud.'

'That is why you were brought up in France?'

'Father was ruined. Left with nothing. We had to flee to France to avoid our creditors. To avoid prison. My mother was delicate. She could never have survived in prison.' He gave a bitter laugh. 'She didn't survive the awful conditions in Marseilles either. Nor did my father for very long. I was fourteen when he died.'

'How did you survive?'

'I lived on the streets. Doing what I had to do. That is where I met Pip. But I swore to my father as he lay dying that I would avenge Mother's death. That I would have justice for the way my father was cheated. It took me years to reach the point where I could return to England and keep my promise.'

The pain in his voice was tangible.

She sat down on the bed and gestured for him to do the same. 'So you are punishing Long's son? That hardly seems fair.'

'It hardly seems fair that his son got to live a life of ease while I was forced to steal to eat.'

'I see.'

'My father said the sins of the father's should be visited upon the children, as they were visited upon me.'

She frowned. 'Are you saying my father was involved? Is that why…?'

Damian grimaced. 'He was the one who talked my father in to borrowing the money to invest in the scheme. While he profited, my father lost everything.'

She shook her head. 'I don't believe you. He wasn't the sort to— What sort of investment was it?'

'Each person who brought a new person into the group got that person's money less a percentage that was paid to Long and to the person who brought them in. My father was supposed to get someone else to join to get his money back. But shortly after he paid his money, he was told the group collapsed.'

'That sounds like robbing Peter to pay Paul.' And it also sounded very familiar.

'Exactly. It was a scam. Only the people who invested early profited. The ones who came later lost their money. It was your father, a supposed friend, no less, who convinced my father to join.'

'So I was another of the children of a sinner, to be punished. I will have you know that my father would never cheat anyone. Not knowingly. He wasn't that sort of person.'

'I couldn't do it. I—I care for you too much. I—'

Hearing him say he cared for her would have made her heart sing only a couple of weeks ago, but now she didn't know how she felt.

'Well, you accomplished your goal. I am well and truly beyond the pale now. So I hope you are happy.'

'I am not in the least happy.'

'And you continued with your plan to ruin Mr Long despite telling me you would think about it.'

'To keep my promise to my father. You must see that I had to avenge my mother's death. I swore I would.'

'And now you have. I hope you are happy.'

He looked miserable. 'Long paid his debt. So I achieved nothing.'

'You achieved my ruin.'

'In the end, it was not what I wanted. I had decided justice would be served if only Long fell. Please. You have to believe me.'

'Believe you or not, it is done.'

He took a deep breath. 'Not necessarily. If we marry—'

She stared at him, incredulously. 'Marry? Why would I marry you?'

The pain those words caused in Damian's chest robbed him of speech.

Why indeed?

He couldn't actually think of a good reason, except that it would salvage her reputation in the eyes of society. He was losing her and he had to somehow find a way not to.

'When it came to it, I realised I could not do anything that would hurt you. I did not intend for your identity to be revealed. If Pip—'

'Pip knew what you were about? He was in on the plot? I trusted you both.' She could not keep the bitterness out of her voice. They had lured her in with the promise of money. 'What a fool you must think me.'

'No! I do not think you a fool. I think you are the most wonderful woman I ever met.'

Her expression was incredulous.

'I don't blame you for being angry, but please do not blame Pip. It was all my doing. Please. Let me make amends.'

She shook her head. 'It doesn't matter to me. I care nothing for what society thinks of me. It doesn't make the slightest difference in my life as a cook. The only thing I need from you is a letter of reference.'

'I—I love you,' he blurted out. The only thing he could do now was to be absolutely honest. Anything less would be an insult to her intelligence. And if she did not feel the same way about him, then so be it.

And the pain at that thought seemed ten times worse.

'I love you,' he said again, this time with more confidence. More conviction. 'And so I will tell you every day until you believe me. And I will never stop trying to win you, unless you marry someone else. I mean it. I will be on your doorstep every day.'

She stifled a rueful chuckle. 'I can just imagine my next employer putting up with so determined a follower.' She turned her face away. 'How can I know you mean it? How can I trust you? As far as I can see, you are driven by guilt, not love.'

He cupped her cheek in his hand and turned her face towards him. He gazed into her eyes, the soft dove grey that held so much pain. Pain he had put there.

'Never in my adult life have I ever told anyone I loved them. I have been too busy planning how I would accomplish my goals. With you it is different. I need you. Unless you are near, I am not happy. You make me want to be better than I am.'

Her expression remained doubtful. He truly had lost her trust. Until now he had not realised how important that trust had been.

His case was hopeless.

How could he even consider forcing her to do anything she did not want to do? 'I'm sorry. I am being selfish. If you do not return my feelings, if marriage to me is not what you want, then I will accept your decision. Leave you in peace even though it will break my heart.'

She sighed. 'You would truly leave me in peace?'

A pain squeezed in his chest. He closed his eyes briefly. 'It will not be easy, but I will do it, if that is what you want. It is as simple as this: my happiness is yours to command, but your happiness means more.'

She stared at him for long moments as if trying to read what was in his heart.

'I love you, Pamela,' he said softly. 'I want only what is best for you. If you want that cottage of by the sea, it is yours. If you want to be a cook, I will arrange for a position with a friend. If there is some other dream you wish to fulfil, I will do my best to bring it about.'

'What about your promise to your father?'

His heart ached at the doubt he heard in her voice. 'Long's father should have been punished. He should not have been allowed to hide what he did behind the skirts of respectability. But… I let my quest for revenge take over my life and it has cost me the best thing that ever happened to me.'

She sat silent for a while, staring into space, her hands clasped tightly in her lap. He did not know what he was going to do when she told him to leave.

'I need to know the truth, Damian. I don't believe my father would have had anything to do with a scheme to defraud others of their money.'

'That is what you want?' How the hell was he to find the answer to that?

'My father was judged guilty by your father, by you. If he did what you said he did, then will it not always stand between us?'

A smidgeon of hope filled his chest. 'I would not allow it.'

She pursed her lips. 'The past would always be there whenever you think of your mother, when you visit your childhood home. It would be there, lying in wait, like some dark vengeful beast, waiting for a moment of weakness.'

'You paint a grim picture of me.'

'You loved your mother. You lost her when you were still a child. You still carry the pain of her loss. Can you forgive those who caused her death?'

He closed his eyes and for the first time in a long time remembered the days before she died. The slow wasting away of a beautiful soul. The anger rose inside him. He hung his head. 'I cannot forgive.'

'Then I need to know the truth.'

'There is only one person who might know the truth of it.'

'My mother.'

'Are you willing to ask her?'

She let out a breath. 'I am.'

Damian tamped down his hope. After his earlier conversation with Lady Malcom, he feared she would not be helpful.

Chapter Seventeen

'**H**er Ladyship is not at home,' Mother's butler pronounced when Pamela and Damian showed up on the doorstep.

'Not at home to me or actually out of the house?' Pamela asked.

The butler looked down his nose and started to close the door.

Damian stuck his booted foot out. 'We will wait in the hall while you ascertain the truth of the matter.' He shouldered past the man and Pamela followed him in.

Damian was not a man to be stopped by a mere butler. Pamela tried not to smile at the thought. Their errand was serious.

Much depended on what Mother had to say, because she did not believe that Damian could truly put the past behind him. And if she married him with this cloud hanging over their heads, she had no doubt that it would come back to haunt them.

And she could not live with the doubt.

To her astonishment, Damian followed the butler up the stairs. He glanced over his shoulder and she hurried after him.

The butler looked back at them full of indignation, but one glance at Damian's face had him hurrying onwards.

And still Damian reached the drawing room before him.

He walked in.

'My Lady!' the butler said from behind him. 'He would not take no for an answer.'

Her mother, seated on the *chaise longue* with an embroidery hoop in her hands, glared. 'What do you—?'

Her mouth snapped shut at the sight of Pamela squeezing around the butler to stand beside Damian.

'How dare you bring that—?'

Damian stepped towards her.

Mother pressed her lips together with a little shake of her head.

She swung her feet down and sat up. 'That will be all, Willers,' she said to the butler.

The man left.

Damian closed the door.

'Well,' said Mother. 'To what do I owe this…this intrusion?'

There was no sense in beating about the bush. 'Did you know that Father defrauded Lord Dart's father?'

Her mother's eyes widened. She made a face. 'I—' She shook her head. 'I know nothing about it.'

Her expression said she was not telling the truth.

'Mother, please. You must tell us.'

'I think you owe me that much,' Dart said.

Mother stiffened. 'I owe neither of you anything. Do you know how furious Lord Malcom is with me after your behaviour at the ball? He is most displeased with the pair of you. Several people have already rescinded our invitations.'

Damian gave her a hard look. 'Do you not owe it to your daughter to let her know the truth about her father?'

He still believed her father guilty, no matter that Pamela

was sure he was not. She was right to see the matter as an insurmountable difficulty.

'The truth, Madam.'

Her mother looked from one to the other as if trying to work out what it was they wanted to hear. She let go a breath. 'Dash it all. If you must know, Pamela, your dearest papa was an idiot with money. We were badly dipped for most of our marriage, living from one disaster to another. He was always giving money to anyone who begged for his aid. I do not know how we managed to stay out of debtors' prison.'

Pamela's stomach sank. 'I knew my father was kind to all he met. I did not realise his kindness was a problem.'

'Of course not. Do you think we would have let you worry about such things? That was why I was so upset when you refused to entertain any of the suitors I suggested after Alan died. I did not want you to go through what I went through with your father. You were a very stubborn and foolish girl.'

Shocked, Pamela stared. She had never suspected her mother of wanting to protect her.

'When Long explained his investment proposition, your papa refused to have anything to do with it. He told me all about it later. It seemed to me like a wonderful opportunity.'

Pamela shot Damian an 'I told you so' look. Her mother seemed not to notice. 'As I said, your father never did have a head for finances.' A guilty expression crossed her face.

Pamela's heart stilled. 'Mother. What did you do?'

'What was I supposed to do? Half the time we didn't have enough money to pay the butcher. I wrote to Long, explained that after some thought Lamb had changed his mind and sent him a sum of money to invest.'

'Where did you get the money without Father's knowledge?'

'I sold some jewellery. It was mine. Inherited from my mother. I received a good return on our money, too.' She grimaced. 'Of course, your father was too busy looking after his flock and reading all those dusty books of his to notice our situation had improved.'

'What about my father?' Damian asked. 'It was Lamb who got him drawn into the scheme.'

She shook her head. 'No. I wrote to him. Without my husband's knowledge.'

'What?' Pamela said. 'How could you?'

'Long was threatening to remove us from the plan if we did not come up with more investors. I didn't want that. I wrote to several of my husband's old friends. I was doing them a favour, I thought.'

'Why on earth would they listen to you, Mother?' Pamela said.

Her mother waved a dismissive hand. 'I was quite adept at writing as your father. I had to. To stave off tradesmen when necessary.'

'You mean you committed forgery?' Damian said in chilly tones.

She glanced at Damian. 'Lord Dart's father was the only one who responded. He had been falling into debt and saw it as a way to repair his fortunes.' She wrung her hands. 'I thought I was helping, Pamela. Then the money dried up and no one could get their investment back.'

'So that is why Lamb denied any responsibility for the scheme,' Damian said. 'Because he truly hadn't been involved.'

Mother winced. 'If he had known, he would have wanted to pay the money back. We would have been paupers. We were barely making ends meet once the investment failed. It was a disaster.'

Sick to her stomach, Pamela stared at her mother. 'But he did find out, eventually, didn't he? I heard you and him arguing the day before he died.'

'He found the ledger I had been hiding in my sewing room.' Mother looked sad. 'His heart gave out...' her lips pursed '...leaving us to fend for ourselves. I was lucky Malcom came to our rescue, but you, you ungrateful hussy, had to ruin everything.'

'Mother!' Pamela looked at Damian, who was staring at her mother. 'I am so sorry for what happened to your family. It seems it is our fault, after all.'

His gaze left her mother's face and came to rest on hers. 'Your father did not betray mine.'

'My mother did.'

He shook his head. 'What hurt my father most was the way your father cast him to the wolves, when they had been such close friends in their youth. It was the one thing that made him so angry. So vengeful. I think he would be happy to know your father was an innocent in all of this.'

'Well, he has had his vengeance now,' Mother said. 'Our family name is ruined. We will have to leave town for several years. Malcom is very angry, might I say.'

The truth was not quite what Pamela had expected, but she was happy to know her father was not responsible for the downfall of Damian's family. 'It serves you right.' She got up. She could no longer bear the sight of her mother.

She glanced at Damian. 'It seems that justice has been served after all.'

And since there was no more to be said, she walked out of the room and down the stairs.

She was aware of Damian following.

At the front door, she turned around. 'I really am sorry.'

He took her hand and brought it to his lips. 'It was not

your fault. And it seems my father and your mother were equally fooled by an unscrupulous fellow.'

'Who has, because of me, not been punished. But I am glad the young Mr Long was not made to pay for his father's crimes.'

'You are the sweetest, nicest person a man could ever wish to meet. I had spent so long being angry, I could not see what I was missing from my life. I meant what I said, earlier. I love you and would be honoured if you would become my wife.'

The sincerity in his gaze held her entranced. She shook her head. 'I am beyond the pale.'

'I put you there. So it is only right I join you. Besides, I care nothing for London and its society. And after what happened at my ball, I doubt they care much for me. I am off to the New World. Please. Won't you come with me? I love you beyond anything.'

She had never cared about society. Not for a moment. A sense of a new beginning welled up inside her. And looking into his eyes she knew he was telling the truth. 'Yes.' She smiled. 'Yes, I will.'

He swept her into his arms. 'I love you so very much.'

She pressed her hand to his cheek gazing up at him. 'I love you too.'

His mouth came down on hers in a long hard kiss.

A cough behind them broke them apart. The butler was holding the door open. 'Good day, My Lord. Madam.'

They laughed and stepped out into the street.

Epilogue

Susan pinned the pale pink silk rose in Pamela's hair and stepped back to admire her handiwork. 'You look beautiful.'

Pamela smiled at her friend and erstwhile maid. 'I am so glad you agreed to come with me.' She had also agreed to stand as a witness to her marriage.

Susan touched her arm. 'Me, too. It will be quite an adventure.'

Pamela took a deep shaky breath. Butterflies seemed to dance in her stomach. Was she right to trust Damian? Was it love, or a sense of duty that had made him offer marriage? He said it was love, but… It was too late for second thoughts now.

She straightened her shoulders. 'Let us go.'

Damian was waiting downstairs with the Vicar who had agreed to wed them at short notice once Damian obtained a special licence.

When she descended, Damian and Pip were waiting at the bottom of the stairs. Damian looked up and smiled. As usual he looked so darkly handsome in his impeccably fitted coat. The pink rose in his lapel matched the rose in her hair. But it was the sweetness in his smile that tugged at Pamela's heart and it slowed to a steady beat. Together they would face anything.

He ran up to meet her and put his arm through hers.

'You look lovely,' he murmured, kissing her cheek. Feeling as if she was floating, she walked the rest of the way down the stairs.

At the bottom, Pip offered his arm to Susan and, to Pamela's surprise, she saw a secret little smile pass between them. Oh, dear. Perhaps she would be wise to warn Susan about Pip's butterfly ways. But not today.

As they entered the drawing room a sliver of pale winter sunshine chose that moment to find its way into the room and illuminate the spot before the Vicar.

Her heart lifted.

She glanced at Damian to find him looking down at her, the love in his eyes clear for anyone to see. Her heart welled with joy and confidence. 'I love you,' she whispered.

He gave her hand a squeeze. 'Always and for ever, my darling,' he murmured.

* * * * *

HISTORICAL

Your romantic escape to the past.

Available Next Month

A Scandalous Match For The Marquess Christine Merri|
How The Wallflower Wins A Duke Lucy Morris

....

Uncovering The Governess's Secrets Marguerite Kaye
Rescuing The Runaway Heiress Sadie King

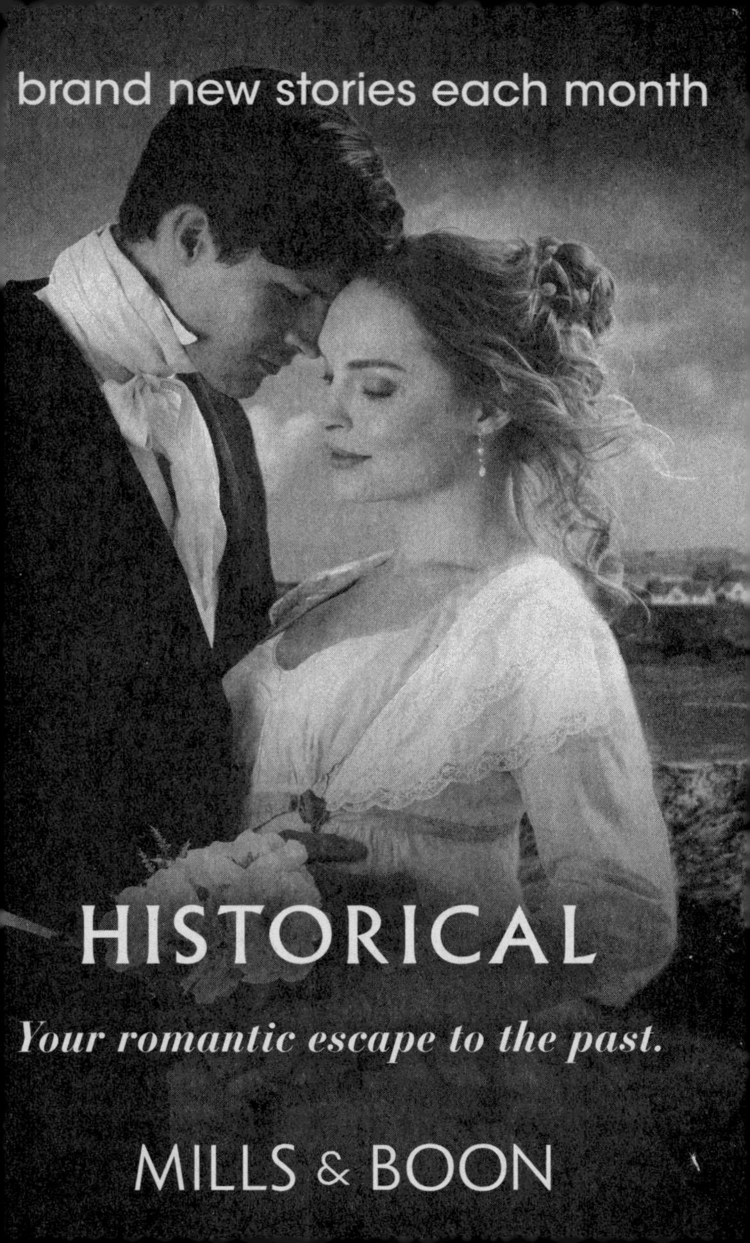
brand new stories each month
HISTORICAL
Your romantic escape to the past.
MILLS & BOON

Keep reading for an excerpt of a new title
from the Historical series,
A DEAL WITH THE REBELLIOUS MARQUESS
by Bronwyn Scott

Prologue

Holmfirth—
February 5th, 1852

Fleur Griffiths loved her friends more than she hated whist, which explained why she was up an hour past midnight, playing poorly at cards in Mrs Parnaby's lace-curtained parlour and being positively trounced by Emma Luce, who was on her way to navigating a grand slam. Normally, by one in the morning, she would be asleep beside her husband. They all would. Except *this* evening they'd sent their men home without them. Fleur sighed and tossed out a useless card—Emma was unstoppable tonight—and reassessed her reasoning for the late night. It wasn't all due to her affections for her friends. It was about the quarrel, too. She was here because she didn't want to be *there*, in their temporary lodgings with Adam, not yet. Her temper was still too hot.

She and Adam had fought—hard—tonight right before all three couples had left their lodgings on Water Street in the nearby village of Hinchliffe Mill for supper at Mrs Parnaby's in Holmfirth proper. Beneath the table she pressed a hand to the flat of her stomach. They'd fought about the baby, or rather the potential of a baby. Nothing was certain yet. She wanted children, Adam did not.

Neither had made a secret of their preferences when they'd married eight years ago. She'd always assumed the issue would work itself out, that Adam would come around in time. But he remained adamant in his stance that a man should not start a family in his late fifties. Now, though, it seemed possible that nature disagreed with him. Her courses were late and with each passing day, her hopes rose that there would be a son who would grow up and take over Adam's news syndicate, a collection of newspapers that stretched from London to York in the north and all the way to Bristol in the west.

Surely, with such a legacy on the line, Adam would see the merit of having a son, someone to carry it all on. What was the point of all this work and sacrifice to build the newspaper empire if there was no one to leave it to when she and Adam were gone? But Adam had been grim tonight when she'd floated the idea. 'Let's hope it's just stress causing the lateness,' he'd said. She should have left it alone. After all, nothing was decided. But she'd pushed the issue. She'd gone to him, helping him with his neckcloth, pressing up against him, flirting as she fussed with his clothes. 'Would it really be so bad?' she'd cajoled, hoping for a smile. She did not get one.

'Yes, yes, it would,' was the terse response she'd got instead and, because there was a real possibility the child was no longer the hypothetical subject of an old argument, she'd not let the discussion go. Hot words had been exchanged along with blunt opinions that had sustained hurt on both sides.

She tossed another card. Would this hand ever end? It wasn't she and Adam's first fight. They were a rather volatile couple in private, something that would surprise Emma and Antonia with their perfect marriages and doting husbands. *They* didn't have disagreements. They had discussions. Not so with her and Adam. Fleur prided herself on having a 'real' marriage where there were quarrels and hard truths and imperfections but where there were also apologies, commitment from them both to do better and sex—the glorious, heated sex that reminded her that, beneath it all, Adam loved her and she loved him, desperately, completely. Together they could conquer anything.

Tonight had felt different, as if here at last was something they'd not get past. When Emma had suggested an impromptu round robin of whist after supper, Fleur had let Adam go without a kiss or whispered, 'I love you.' She'd stood apart from him in the hall while the others had said goodnight to their husbands and the three men had headed back to the Water Street lodgings. No doubt, the men would stay up a while, have a drink together and discuss the business of the mill that had brought them all to Holmfirth. Then they'd retire.

She knew Adam would retire first. He didn't like late nights. In London, he preferred to rise early and get into the office while it was still quiet. She knew his routine, his preferences, intimately. She'd spent eight years adapting her schedule to fit his. If not, she might never have seen him. Adam loved his work as much as he loved his wife. On nights like tonight, nights where they fought, she wondered if he didn't love it more. Or perhaps she was just selfish in wanting all of his attention.

Emma was just about to claim the last trick when Fleur heard it—a sound in the street: running feet, a shout. She froze and looked up from her hand. She could not hear the words, but she knew what panic sounded like. The shout came again, closer now. 'The embankment's breached, the river's in Water Street!'

Oh, God, the men! Adam, asleep in his bed. Would he even have a chance? Similar thoughts were mirrored on the faces of Emma and Antonia. Fear galvanised them. The four women raced to the lace curtains to peer out into the night. They could see nothing but darkness, but they could *hear*. Even at their safe distance, they could hear the river ravaging, hear its heavy churning as it rushed through Holmfirth, hungry to devour the next village in its path.

'We'll be safe here,' Mrs Parnaby tried to assure them, but Emma was inconsolable in her panic. She raced for the door.

Fleur grabbed for her. 'Help me, Antonia! Help me hold her!' The silly fool meant to go out after them. With Antonia's help, she wrestled Emma from the door. 'What do you think it will accomplish, you running out there? You can't see a thing,' Fleur scolded her friend too harshly in her own panic. 'It's too late to warn them.' She forced Emma to sit.

Antonia took Emma's hand and knelt beside her. 'They're strong men, they can take care of themselves.' That was Antonia, always the optimist. Fleur could do with a little of that optimism herself right now.

Mrs Parnaby was all bustling practicality, ordering a

tea tray. 'We'll go help when the water has settled and there's less chance of us being another set of people in need of rescue ourselves.' Fleur knew what that meant. It meant there was nothing to be done until daylight. Fleur noted the grimness around the woman's mouth. Despite her hopeful words, Mrs Parnaby already feared the worst and, in truth, Fleur did, too.

It was the longest night Fleur could remember, especially given that their vigil hadn't started until half-past one, the night already well advanced. But the five hours until there was enough light to be abroad dragged at a snail's pace, the hall clock seemingly frozen in time. None of them could sleep. They spent the night wide awake in the parlour, ears craning for the sound of footsteps, for a knock on the door. None came.

The moment it was light, they donned cloaks and followed Mrs Parnaby to the Rose and Crown Inn, but morning did not bring relief, only reality, and what a grim reality it was to see the result of what they'd heard last night. Fleur noted it all with a reporter's eye as they picked their way through mud and debris: the dead cow mired in the muck, the various parts of metal machinery deposited willy-nilly wherever the river tired of carrying them, the heavy oak furniture reduced to sharp, dangerous splinters, the timbers and stones that had once been houses, torn asunder, the sheer amount of ruined home goods, and the oddness of the things that had survived intact.

They passed a credenza still whole and a set of uncracked blue dishes. Fleur wondered if their owner would find them. How many miles had that credenza travelled down the river? There was hope in that. Some things in the river's wake had survived the night. Perhaps that meant their husbands had, too.

Others were at the Rose and Crown. It was fast becoming a gathering point, a place where families could find each other, where people could exchange news and where those in need could get help, medical care, a blanket and a hot meal.

Fleur tied on an apron and went to work immediately. There were children who'd come in alone, bedraggled and looking for parents, armed with horrifying stories of having spent the night clinging to the roof timbers of their homes and praying the water wouldn't reach them. Those were the *least* horrifying tales. Others told terrible stories of watching their families being swept away in the raging current.

She spent the morning washing faces, spooning broth, the journalist in her avidly listening to stories and asking questions. She offered reassurance where she could. Across the room, she saw Antonia do the same, quite often with a small child on her hip. Antonia had always been good with children. Fleur tried to keep her eyes from the door, to keep her attentions on those she could help. She tried not to think of Adam. He would come. If he was with Antonia's husband, Keir, he'd be out there helping those in need first before helping himself. He would come when he could.

There *was* good news. James Mettrick, one of the men they'd come to do business with who also lived on Water Street and had been in his residence at the time of the flood, straggled in mid-morning, bruised but alive.

This was tempered with the reality that his family had not survived. Fleur clung to the knowledge that survival was possible. If James Mettrick had survived, perhaps Adam had, too. Perhaps Adam was still out helping others. Perhaps he'd been pushed downstream and needed transport back, or perhaps, heaven forbid, he was hurt and even now some kind stranger was caring for him as she was caring for others. It gave her own hope a much-needed second wind.

That second wind was short-lived. At ten o'clock, George Dyson, the town coroner, arrived. Fleur tracked him with her eyes as he sought out Emma. Fleur watched Emma nod before Emma turned her direction with a gesture that indicated the three of them should adjourn to the Rose and Crown's private parlour.

In the parlour, Antonia stood between her and Emma, gripping their hands as Mr Dyson cleared his throat and addressed them, using Emma's title, Lady Luce. The formality lent an ominous quality to his tone and Fleur braced herself against words that never prefaced the positive. 'I wish I had better news.' Oh, God. Fleur felt her stomach sink. 'I will be blunt; Water Street didn't stand a chance. The river hit it from the front and the side, absolutely obliterating the buildings.' He paused and swallowed hard.

How many times today had he needed to deliver bad news? Fleur wondered. But the wondering didn't make his next words any easier to hear. 'James Mettrick's family and the Earnshaws, with whom you had business dealings, are all gone. Their homes are entirely destroyed.' Homes that had been next to the ones Fleur and her friends had rented.

The world became muffled to Fleur. She was vaguely aware of Emma arguing something about James Mettrick, the son, surviving. Dyson was shaking his head, delivering the death blow as gently as possible. 'Lady Luce, the bodies of your husband and his friends have been recovered.' There was more. Fleur didn't care. She'd get the details later. For now, all that mattered was knowing they were gone. Garret was dead. Keir was dead. *Adam* was dead.

No, it had to be a mistake. Adam couldn't be dead. Not when there was unresolved anger between them. Not when there might be a child to raise. Her world reeled. She staggered forward, catching herself on the fireplace mantel lined with blue ware pieces like the set they'd seen in the mud, unbroken and whole. Rage surged. Damn it all! Why should the universe choose to save dishes over the life of one good man, *her* man? It wasn't right. But she could make it right. She picked up the blue ware piece nearest her and threw it hard against the wall, watching it shatter into a thousand pieces. Like her heart. Her life. Her very soul.

Anger began to burn, a source of fuel against her grief. This was what Adam had feared—that the dam was insufficient to its task. It was the reason Garrett had asked him to come, to bring his investigative journalistic talents to bear on determining the quality of not only the mill, but the river that mill depended on. Now the very worst had happened. Naturally? Or as the result of human error? If it were the latter, she could make sure someone paid for all they'd taken from her.

* * *

Apparently, one could live on anger, at least for four days. While Emma and Antonia had stayed in with their grief at Mrs Parnaby's, Fleur had gone out, channelling her rage into walking the muddy, ruined streets of Holmfirth. She helped with the recovery effort from daybreak to sunset. She helped rehome those who'd lost everything. She sat on the committee charged with collecting funds to distribute to those in need—of which there were many when the realisation set in that the river had destroyed homes *and* jobs. There was no work to go back to, no income to earn. In the evenings, she wrote copious articles to the newspapers Adam owned, sharing first-hand testimonies of survivors and reports of the developing situation. She instructed the editors to send artists to draw pictures. She wanted lithographs printed, she wanted word spread far and wide about the depth of tragedy in Holmfirth.

Anger could only go so far, though. It kept her fuelled and busy. But it could not change the fact that Adam was gone. 'We're widows now. Widows before the age of thirty,' Fleur ground out, pacing before Mrs Parnaby's fireplace. The woman had been a generous hostess, taking in three women who were only supposed to have been dinner guests.

Emma spoke up as if reading her thoughts from across the room. 'I think it's time to go. There's nothing more we can do here.'

Fleur raised an eyebrow in challenge. Nothing more to do here? There was plenty to do here. She couldn't possibly leave now. But of course, Emma would be thinking about concerns with Garrett's estate and his investments. She would need to be in London. Antonia nodded agreement, citing the need to take over the reins of Keir's department store project. That was a bold move on Antonia's part. Fleur was aware of Antonia's gaze on her as her friend asked, 'Shall we all travel together as far as London?'

Fleur shook her head, not daring to look at her two closest friends. They would argue with her. They'd not been out in the streets and seen what she had seen. 'No. I think I'll stay and finish Adam's investigation. There are people to help and justice to serve.' She would take rooms at an inn if Mrs Parnaby needed her privacy back.

Emma's face showed disagreement. 'Do you think that's wise, Fleur? If this disaster was man-made, there will be people who won't appreciate the prying, particularly if there's a woman doing it. You should think twice about putting yourself in danger.'

'I don't care,' Fleur snapped. She loved Emma, but they often butted heads, both of them stubborn. 'If Adam died because of carelessness or greed, someone will pay for that. I will see to it and I will see to it that such recklessness doesn't happen again.'

Emma's gaze dropped to her waist and Fleur snatched her hand away from her stomach. She'd been unaware she'd put it there. But it was too late for Emma's sharp eyes. 'And Adam's babe? Would you be reckless with his child?'

Fleur reined in her anger, softening her voice. 'I do not know if there is a child. It is too soon.'

Emma relented with a nod. 'Just be careful, dear friend. I do not want anything to happen to you.' Emma rose and came to her, Antonia joining them. They encircled each other with their arms, their heads bent together. This would be their private farewell. 'We're widows now,' Emma echoed her words.

'We have lost much,' Fleur murmured, 'but we are still friends. Whatever else changes, that will not, no matter where we go, no matter what happens.' She looked at the pale faces of her friends, her resolve doubling. For Garrett, for Keir, for Adam, for Antonia, for Emma, and for herself, there would be justice for them all.